Honoré de Balzac (1799–1850) worked for three years in a lawyer's office, preparing to practice law, but in 1819, he devoted himself to writing. His early stories were hackwork published under various pseudonyms. In 1829, he published *Le Dernier Chouan*, the first story to bear his name and his first success. Over the next twenty years, Balzac's literary output was prodigious: three or four novels a year, sometimes more. All became part of *La Comédie Humaine*, a panorama of the whole of French society, some of the most important works of this series being *Eugénie Grandet* (1833) and *Père Goriot* (1834). He also wrote plays and the popular *Droll Stories* (1833).

Henry Reed (1914–86) was a noted poet, translator, and writer of radio plays. In addition to *Père Goriot*, his translations include *Eugénie Grandet*. His poems were published in two volumes, *A Map of Verona* and *Lessons of the War*.

Peter Brooks is the author of a number of books, including *Reading for the Plot*, *The Melodramatic Imagination*, and *Henry James Goes to Paris*. He was a longtime professor of comparative literature and French at Yale University and University Professor at the University of Virginia.

Honoré de Balzac

PÈRE GORIOT

"All is true."
—SHAKESPEARE

TRANSLATED AND WITH AN AFTERWORD BY
HENRY REED
AND WITH AN INTRODUCTION BY
PETER BROOKS

SIGNET CLASSICS

SIGNET CLASSICS
Published by the Penguin Group
Penguin Group (USA) Inc., 375 Hudson Street,
New York, New York 10014, USA

USA | Canada | UK | Ireland | Australia | New Zealand | India | South Africa | China

Penguin Books Ltd., Registered Offices: 80 Strand, London WC2R 0RL, England
For more information about the Penguin Group visit penguin.com.

Published by Signet Classics, an imprint of New American Library,
a division of Penguin Group (USA) Inc.

First Signet Classics Printing, August 1962
First Signet Classics Printing (Brooks Introduction), December 2004

ISBN 978-0-451-52959-6

Printed in the United States of America
10 9 8 7 6

ALWAYS LEARNING

PEARSON

*To the great and illustrious
Geoffroy Saint-Hilaire
as a tribute of admiration for
his labors and his genius.*

—Balzac

CONTENTS

INTRODUCTION

I envy anyone opening *Père Goriot* for a first reading. A world of excitement awaits, an impassioned drama, an adventure in finding out and making sense of. Balzac was fond of James Fenimore Cooper's tales of dangerous forays into the trackless forests of the New World. His young heroes newly arrived in Paris face another sort of wilderness, requiring another kind of pathfinding amid the potential ambushes of the city, another kind of struggle with dangerous urban savages. The young hero of *Père Goriot,* Eugène de Rastignac, has been sent to Paris by his aristocratic but impoverished family to study law. But law is nearly beside the point of his true initiation into the lure of love, wealth, and power—and the ways to gain access to them all. His name has become proverbial. If you call someone "a Rastignac" in France, everyone knows you mean a young man whose ambition will admit no obstacles. The drama in which he plays such a central role—though note it's not named for him—brings onstage just about all that's important in life.

Père Goriot begins with a long traveling shot over the "valley of ever-peeling plaster" (p. 5) on the Left Bank of Paris where we discover the Maison Vauquer, a boardinghouse for those on their way up, like Rastignac, or on their way down, like Goriot, or those like Vautrin (alias Jacques Collin, alias "Cheat-Death"), who have reasons to seek anonymity in the less than fashionable parts of Paris. The description of Madame Vauquer, mistress of the somewhat greasy premises, is a classic of

realism: it demonstrates with panache how the person
and the place fit together, how the person has been produced by her environment, and in turn how she creates
the particular atmosphere of the place. It's an example
of Balzac's belief in what you might call the Bronx Zoo
principle: the animals must all be seen in their habitats.
He in fact liked to compare his work to that of a zoolo-
gist. He wrote early in a century that would see science
make extraordinary progress and gain great prestige, and
he was perhaps the first novelist to see his own work as
that of a kind of social naturalist.

But the lodgers of the Maison Vauquer are not simply
social types. They raise questions that neither Rastignac
nor the narrator is prepared to answer at this point. Mademoiselle Michonneau, Monsieur Poiret, Victorine Taillefer, Old Goriot—they all have past histories that are
going to be brought to bear on Rastignac's drama. His
own adventure gets under way in darkness and mystery.
He has just returned from the ball given by his relative
the Vicomtesse de Beauséant—who stands at the summit
of Parisian society—and has fallen into a reverie over
his neglected law textbooks. He has already begun to
dream of making it in high society, and of conquering a
desirable woman, and he realizes that both dreams depend on money. He hears a groan from the next room
and tiptoes out to peek through the keyhole. He sees
Goriot twisting an ornate silver bowl into an ingot and
hears him pronounce the phrase "poor child" (p. 39).
Then he hears the front door of the boardinghouse—
which he's sure the servant has bolted from within—
mysteriously open, and Vautrin pads in with an unknown henchman. There are things here that need
investigating.

Then there are those two beautiful young women who
come from time to time to visit Goriot, suggesting to
some of the lodgers that he must be an old voluptuary
keeping mistresses. His claim that they are his daughters
initially arouses disbelief. When Rastignac meets one of
them at the famous ball, then sees her again early the
next morning outside the moneylender's, it is Vautrin

who tells him who she is and where she lives. And then he draws the lesson: "Last night at the top of the wheel, at a duchess's. . . . This morning at the bottom of the ladder, at a moneylender's. That's the women of Paris for you. If their husbands can't keep them in insane luxury, they sell themselves" (pp. 48–49). To which Rastignac replies: "You make me desperate to know the truth" (p. 50). We're off, on a high adventure to find out about this and all the other truths that lie hidden under the facades of Paris.

All that Rastignac learns is subject to critical commentary by Vautrin, who knows his Paris from the bottom up, so to speak. He is one of Balzac's most remarkable creations, a figure who has stepped out of Gothic romance into Parisian reality, who prefigures Superman in Metropolis—though his mastery of the destinies of others comes less from physical prowess than from force of intellect and knowledge of the ways of the world. He makes clear—lucidly, cynically, irrefutably—what the stakes of Rastignac's ambitions are. He is one of the most terrifying, though perhaps also endearing, father figures ever provided by a novelist to his young protagonist. He is counterbalanced by the titular father of the novel, Goriot, whose paternity is spiritual and creative— he tells Rastignac, "when I became a father, I understood God" (p. 135)—but also, to his daughters, overwhelmingly financial. Paternity can make you sentimental; it can also leave you horribly exploited.

The *"père"* attached to Goriot's name is both a belittling epithet, referring to an old fellow who's over the hill, and an indication that the novel turns in crucial ways on the question of paternity. Shakespeare's *King Lear* was somewhere in the back of Balzac's mind when he began this story of father and daughters and betrayal. But beyond that, the title evokes a larger issue of paternity, of orderly transmission of social knowledge and moral norms from one generation to another. "The country will perish if fathers are trodden underfoot. Of course it will. Society, the whole world, turns on fatherhood" (p. 269). Goriot in his rantings speaks truth, and the society Balzac portrays is, in the novelist's view, dangerously close to coming undone. A self-proclaimed monarchist and Catholic, Balzac saw the society of the nineteenth century as headed toward disintegration. The Revolution of 1830, which overthrew the Bourbon monarchy restored after the fall of Napoleon, brought to the throne a so-called "citizen-king," whom Balzac saw as a mere stepping-stone toward the chaos of democracy.

The regime change of 1830 arrived just as Balzac was emerging as a novelist, and it gave him the opportunity to put into historical perspective the world he was writing about—principally, French society of the Restoration period, extending from the end of the Napoleonic epic at the Battle of Waterloo, in 1815, to the end of the restored Ancien Régime monarchy in 1830. Looking back across the divide of 1830, Balzac sees the world of the Restoration as a whole, and this knowledge helps him to see what that world is heading toward. It's one of his great claims to being the first true realist: he sees society as a totality. Oscar Wilde came close to the heart of the matter when he declared: "The Nineteenth Century, as we know it, is largely an invention of Balzac's." Balzac "invents" the new century by being the first writer to give form to its emerging urban agglomerations, its nascent capitalist dynamics, its rampant cult of the individual personality. By conceptualizing, theorizing, and dramatizing changes that he mainly deplored, he initiated his readers into understanding the shape of the century.

The destinies of the new century would be played out predominantly in cities—and in France there is only one city that matters. Balzac himself made his way to Paris in 1814, in order—like Rastignac—to study law, which he never practiced, preferring to write novels in a garret while he pursued various ill-fated get-rich-quick schemes, including a printing and publishing business that swiftly went bankrupt. Paris doubled in size during the first half of the century, mainly through immigration from the French provinces. If some of the new arrivals were ambitious young men like Rastignac and Balzac—drawn to the sphere where talent could prosper and gain recognition—many more contributed to the creation of a new sense of a dangerous urban underclass. Paris was becoming a jungle. It required survival skills. It required especially that you learned to read the signs that would alert you to lurking enemies, let you avoid mantraps, and lead you to your quarry.

For Rastignac, learning Paris is partly a matter of avoiding its mud holes—the literal ones that get your boots muddy when you are too poor to cross Paris in a cab, and the moral mud holes that the Vicomtesse de Beauséant and her friend the Duchesse de Langeais explicate for him (an explication confirmed by Vautrin in a different idiom). And it is partly a matter of climbing up to the social summits. Mesdames de Beauséant and de Langeais are at the very top: leaders of the Faubourg Saint-Germain, as it was known—the sector of Paris where the old aristocracy had its dwellings, the world of hereditary privilege. There are many shades and gradations below this highest peak. Anastasie Goriot is married to the Comte de Restaud, a cut below the top echelon (and strapped for money, which explains his marriage to someone of plebeian origin), while Delphine Goriot is the wife of the Baron Nucingen, an immensely wealthy Alsatian banker, a parvenu (his title is recently minted) who is both ridiculed for his unpolished manners and sought after for his financial clout.

No novelist before Balzac made the city such a looming and living presence, and he offered a model for Dickens' London and Dostoevsky's Saint Petersburg: cities as labyrinths, as total environments. Return to provincial life is unthinkable once you have experienced the heightening of all sensations that Paris provides. Vautrin harbors a pastoral dream, of living as a plantation owner in Virginia—but it's clear that never can be. He can't escape the city. In the final scene of the novel, Rastignac stands on the heights of Père-Lachaise cemetery, looking down at the wealthy districts of Paris stretched before his possessive gaze. Paris viewed from above becomes readable; its streets and quarters and monuments take on meaning and social significance. Balzac returns again and again to the "semiotics" of the city, how to decipher its meanings: its shop signs, its topography, the physiognomy of its different quarters, the costumes of its inhabitants.

To succeed in Paris—as Rastignac's principal mentors, Madame de Beauséant and Vautrin, both tell him—is at once to learn its codes and to unlearn more elementary moral catechisms. The structure of society is a scandal, and success in this structure will necessarily entail moral compromise or worse. As Vautrin tells him, "[T]hat's the crossroads of life, young man: choose." Vautrin at once adds: "But you have chosen" (p. 111). Yes, in the sense that Rastignac already knows he will never be content with a life of mediocrity. He's got to do something big— the question is simply one of means, not ends. His drama will entail stark choices that have to be made—choices that he might wish to mask from himself, if only Vautrin would let him. Ultimately, Balzac always returns us to the moral stakes of life—not in any naive or moralistic sense, but in a demonstration that life is about ethical commitments.

It is not despite but because of Balzac's flamboyantly reactionary stance (there was a bit of grandstanding in it, as in the pseudo-aristocratic "de" he added to his name) that he perceived so clearly the trends of his time: the decline of the landed gentry, the rise of the commercial bourgeoisie, the end of what he nostalgically saw as an ordered, organic society with each person in an assigned role, and—above all—the coming of the cash nexus. As Goriot cries out, "Money buys you everything, even daughters" (p. 267). All human relations seem to have a sordid economic component. Balzac has always been a favorite of Marxist critics, starting with Karl Marx and Friedrich Engels themselves, since he grasped so acutely the "contradictions" of this society—saw that it was destroying its declared moral bases, saw that it was headed for another social upheaval. Marx wrote:

Constant revolutionising of production, uninterrupted disturbance of all social conditions, everlasting uncer-

tainty and agitation distinguish the bourgeois epoch
from all earlier ones. All fixed, fast-frozen relations,
with their train of ancient and venerable prejudices
and opinions, are swept away, all new-formed ones
become antiquated before they can ossify. All that is
solid melts into air.

Père Goriot is the work of a thirty-five-year-old who
up to then had to his credit the Gothic "potboilers"
written during the 1820s (and published under pseudonyms), then the succès de scandale of the anonymous
Physiology of Marriage (a cynical anatomy of marriage),
then the real success of the flamboyant and allegorical
The Fatal Skin [*La Peau de Chagrin*] and the first brief
narratives that he labeled "scenes of private life." He
was not yet considered a "serious" writer, but an enter-
tainer. Written with great speed, in sessions that, sus-
tained by strong coffee, could go nearly round the clock,
during the fall of 1834, *Père Goriot* began serial publication in the *Revue de Paris* in mid-December, then was
published as a book in 1835.

In the course of writing the novel—at the moment
when he was describing his hero's first call upon Madame de Beauséant—Balzac drew a line through the first
name he had given to this protagonist, Massiac, and
wrote instead Rastignac. Now Rastignac already existed—in Balzac's fiction. He had made an appearance
in *The Fatal Skin* as a secondary character, a somewhat
world-weary and older young man who initiates that
novel's hero into a life of gambling and dissipation. In
choosing to make the hero of *Père Goriot* a character
whom readers had already met at a later stage of his
life, Balzac stumbled upon the technique of "returning
characters" who link his various novels together into the
larger whole he would eventually call—with proud refer-
ence to Dante—*The Human Comedy*. The more we read
of his novels, the more we discover various aspects and
characteristics and life stages of literally hundreds of
characters. Some forty-eight of the characters in *Père
Goriot* reappear in other novels. Many of them are for-

ever bit players; others become principal figures in other novels. Some, like the doctor Bianchon, the lawyer Derville and the moneylender Gobseck, serve as vital linking figures throughout many novels, creating the sense of a complete peopled social world.

The returning characters enable Balzac to create an ensemble that is more than simply the accumulation of its parts. We have multiple perspectives on one person and different angles of vision on a given situation. The novella *Gobseck*, for instance, will give us quite a different picture of the struggles between the Comte and the Comtesse de Restaud; another novella, *La Maison Nucingen*, will fill us in on how Rastignac later rose to fame and fortune. It's like a film that can unfold on several screens simultaneously. And in the library you can find a "dictionary" of Balzacian characters, a set of biographies of the hundreds of men and women (and a few animals) who appear and reappear in the ninety-odd novels and tales that make up *The Human Comedy*. At the same time, each novel is complete in itself, intended to stand alone.

Balzac lived from his pen, at the dawn of an era of what the contemporary critic Sainte-Beuve would stigmatize as "industrial literature." Balzac was the first French novelist to serialize his fiction in installments in the daily newspaper, though he couldn't adapt easily to the requirements of the genre: he wrote over length, he was late with copy. He was a popular success, but usually in debt nonetheless. He rewrote his novels in printer's proofs, over and over, and the cost of making changes—then as now—was borne by the author. But he understood that literature was becoming a commodity and that the Romantic ideal of "the poet" was giving way to the marketplace. Printing, distribution, advertising—these were the realities that an author could try to control (as in the abortive enterprise of the print shop), but that ultimately controlled him. The new century would be dominated by the industrialist, the financier, the speculator.

It took several generations for Balzac to be considered "a classic" in France. He was accused, by the official guardians of French style, of writing badly. His plots are melodramatic, leading to theatrical showdowns; his prose can be hyperbolic, reaching toward the sublime sentiment and the audacious metaphor. If he lacks purity of form and elegance of diction, his qualities may nonetheless seem to us postmoderns part of our own sensibility. Like Balzac's generation, we can appreciate excess, ornamentation that may be somewhat baroque, bitter tears, and thunderous climaxes.

Balzac is once again, I think, a novelist who matters to us. Two masters of our modernity who have only grown in stature over the years, Marcel Proust and Henry James, both found in Balzac their principal inspiration. Proust was above all impressed by Balzac's subtly muted but persistent attention to unavowed forms of sexual desire, visible in Vautrin's devoted attentions to Rastignac—and in Rastignac's rejection of them. James repeatedly holds Balzac up to aspiring novelists as the master to study if the novel is to recover what he calls its "wasted heritage." Whatever Balzac's faults, James finds him at the end of the day simply more serious than any other novelist—more serious in the attempt to represent society, people, life itself. All novelists imagine, pretend—and "Balzac's great glory is that he pretended hardest."

—PETER BROOKS

PÈRE GORIOT

PART ONE

PRIVATE LODGINGS

1

Madame Vauquer, formerly Mademoiselle de Conflans, is now an old woman. For the past forty years she has kept a private lodging house in a Paris street running between the Latin Quarter and the Faubourg Saint-Marceau. The street is called the Rue Neuve-Sainte-Geneviève, and the house is called the Maison Vauquer. It is a respectable establishment, and though it accepts with equal readiness the young and old of both sexes, no adverse comment has ever been made about its morals. True, for a period of thirty years no young woman was ever seen there; and young men lodged there only when meager family allowances compelled them to. But at the point when our drama begins, in 1819, there was one poor young girl staying there. We have used the word "drama"; and however discredited the word has become from wanton misuse and distortion in the gloomy literature of our age, we still must use it here. Not that our story is dramatic in the strict sense of the word; but the telling of it may well provoke a few private tears, if not public ones.

Will it be understood outside Paris? It is doubtful. Its setting, its atmosphere, its local color and detail, can be appreciated only between the hill of Montmartre and the heights of Montrouge, in that famous valley of ever-peeling plaster and muddy black gutters; that valley where suffering is always real and joy very often false, and the everyday turmoil so grim that it is difficult to imagine any catastrophe producing more than a momen-

5

tary sensation there. Nevertheless, affliction is sometimes so densely attended by vice and virtue that it takes on an aspect of grandeur and solemnity; ordinary selfishness and self-absorption are suspended for a moment in pity. But the impression is like a pleasant fruit, and just as quickly gulped down. The chariot of civilization, like the car of Juggernaut, barely pausing because some spirit hardier than the rest stands in its path, quickly crushes the upstart, and drives gloriously on. You will do the same. You will hold this book in your white hand, and settle deeper into your soft armchair, murmuring: "I think I may enjoy this." And after you have read about the obscure sufferings of a father named Goriot, you will dine with a good appetite, blaming your own insensitiveness on the author and accusing him of poetic exaggeration. No! Realize this: this drama is not an invention; it is not a novel. "All is true." It is so true that you can all see hints of it in your own homes, in your own hearts perhaps.

The house which Madame Vauquer lets out as lodgings is her own property. It stands in the lower part of the Rue Neuve-Sainte-Geneviève, at the point where the ground drops down to the Rue de l'Arbalète. Carriages rarely attempt this steep rough slope, so that comparative silence reigns in all the streets huddled between the Military Hospital and the Panthéon. The somber colors reflected from the cupolas of these two buildings darken the entire atmosphere of the place and impart a yellow tinge to the air. Here the pavements are dry, there is neither mud nor water in the gutters, grass grows along the walls. The spirits of the most carefree visitor droop with those of the passersby; the sound of a carriage is an event; the houses are sunk in gloom, the garden walls look like prisons. A Parisian losing his way here would see nothing but lodging houses and institutions, penury or boredom, old age declining into death, bright youth pressed into drudgery. In the whole of Paris there is no district more hideous; and none, we must add, more unknown. The Rue Neuve-Sainte-Geneviève in particular is like a bronze picture frame. It is the only frame suited to our story, for which the reader's mind must be prepared by dark colors and solemn thoughts: he must be made to feel like the traveler going down into the catacombs, the daylight fading step by step, the drone of the guide becoming steadily hollower. A true comparison! Who is to decide which is the grimmer sight: withered hearts, or empty skulls?

The front of the Maison Vauquer is set at right angles to the street and faces a small garden plot. From the Rue Neuve-Sainte-Geneviève you see the house in profile. Along the house front runs a cobbled sunken alley some six feet wide; between this and the garden there is a gravel path bordered with large blue and white earthenware pots planted with geraniums, oleanders, and pomegranates. You are admitted to the path by a gateway in the wall, surmounted by a signboard inscribed with the words: MAISON VAUQUER, and underneath: *Private lodgings for both sexes and others.* In the daytime, through a latticed gate with a jangling bell, you may distinguish at the far end of the little path, on the wall facing the street, an imitation arch, painted to look like green marble, the work of a local artist; in front of this artificial embrasure stands a plaster Cupid, whose flaking surface may encourage those with a taste for the symbolic to see in it an allegory of those Cupids of Paris who come to be cured at the nearby Hospital for Venereal Diseases. On its base a half-obliterated inscription indicates the epoch when the ornament was erected, by its evident enthusiasm for Voltaire, who had returned to Paris in triumph some forty years earlier:

> Whoe'er you be, your master see:
> He is, or was, or soon shall be.

At nightfall, the latticed gate is replaced by a solid door. The garden is the same width as the front of the house, and is enclosed between the street wall and the party wall of the house next door; the whole of this house is invisible under a mantle of ivy, a picturesque effect that strikes passersby as unusual for Paris. Both walls have vines and fruit trees trained up them: their dusty, emaciated fruit are the subject of an annual bout of anxiety on the part of Madame Vauquer, and of much conversation thereon with her boarders. The centerpiece of the garden is a large bed of artichokes, a word that Madame Vauquer, in spite of being formerly Mademoiselle de Conflans, and in defiance of pedantic comment from her guests, persists in calling "artlechokes." Alongside them grow patches of sorrel, lettuce, and parsley; and they are flanked by fruit trees trained in the shape of obelisks. Two narrow side alleys lead to a clump of linden trees at the bottom of the garden. Under these is a painted green table surrounded by seats; and, in the dog days, those guests who are rich enough to permit themselves coffee sit out here and enjoy it in weather hot enough to hatch an egg.

The house, four stories high not counting the attic, is built of rough stone and daubed with the yellow wash that gives the same squalid appearance to almost every house in Paris. The five windows on each floor have small square panes and are fitted with blinds, no two of which are adjusted to the same level or angle, a confusing effect. The side of the house has two windows on each floor; the two on the ground floor are enlivened with heavy iron grilles. Behind the building is a yard about twenty feet wide, inhabited by a happy family of pigs, hens, and rabbits; at the bottom of the yard is a woodshed. Between the shed and the kitchen window an icebox is slung; the greasy water from the kitchen sink flows just underneath it. A narrow yard door, opening on the Rue Neuve-Sainte-Geneviève, allows the household refuse to float out into the street whenever the cook washes out the back yard with water, which she does from time to time as a precaution against plague.

The two rooms on the ground floor seem to have been reserved by Nature for the use of paying guests. The first room, which you enter by a French window, is lit by the two windows on the street. This is the sitting room. It communicates with the dining room, which is itself separated from the kitchen by the well of a staircase whose wooden steps are inset with colored polished tiles.

It would be difficult to find a more depressing sight than the sitting room: the horsehair sofas and chairs with their alternating dull and glossy stripes; in the exact center of the room, the table with its gray Flemish marble top; and in the exact center of the table, the white china tea set with its faded gold pattern, popular everywhere these days. The flooring of the room is far from even; the walls are paneled halfway up, the upper half of each wall being covered with glazed wallpaper illustrating the main episodes in the story of Telemachus. The classical characters are done in color. The panel between the barred windows offers the boarders a view of Calypso's banquet to the son of Ulysses. For forty years this picture has been the subject of ribaldry on the part of younger guests, who believe that they rise above adversity by laughing at the meals their poverty condemns them to. The stone fireplace, whose well-swept hearth makes it quite plain that only on very special occasions is a fire ever lit in it, is surmounted by two vases filled with ancient artificial flowers under glass; between them stands a particularly unsavory pale blue marble clock. The room exhales a smell for which the language has no expression, unless we call it *odeur de pension.* A chilly commingling of the stuffy, the moldy, and the fusty, it is damp to the nostrils, and it penetrates the clothes; it evokes the staleness of rooms where people have just finished eating; it is the stink of sculleries, pantries, sickbeds. Possibly it might be described, if some system could be invented for estimating the basic quantities of catarrhal and similar sickening exhalations contributed to it by each separate boarder, young and old.

And yet . . . ! In spite of these blank horrors, this room, compared with the dining room next door, is as fresh and sweet as a lady's boudoir. The paneling in this room reaches right to the ceiling; it was once painted, but the color, now unidentifiable, serves merely as a background for the curious patterns traced on it by successive layers of grime. Against the walls stand greasy sideboards, laden with piles of thick, blue-bordered Tournai plates, round tin dish mats and chipped, cloudy decanters. In one corner there is a box with numbered pigeonholes for the grubby, wine-stained table napkins of boarders. Indestructible pieces of furniture, elsewhere disowned, have landed here like the wrecks of civilization at the Home for Incurables. Here you would observe a barometer, with a monk who comes out when it rains; disastrous, appetite-removing engravings, in varnished wooden frames with gilt beading; a tortoise-shell wall clock inlaid with copper, and Argand lamps inlaid with oil and dust; a green tiled stove; a long table covered with oilcloth so greasy that a playful diner can autograph it with his finger; broken-backed chairs; pathetic little esparto mats, continually fraying but never completely disintegrating; pitiful foot warmers, the hinges loose, the woodwork charred, the foot-holes broken. But any adequate description of how old, cracked, rotten, rickety, worm-eaten, one-handed, one-eyed, decrepit, and moribund is the furniture in the place, would only delay our narrative, and this the busy reader would never forgive. The red-brick flooring is full of valleys hollowed out by years of rubbing and ruddling. To put it briefly, unpoetic poverty reigns here: pinched, concentrated, threadbare poverty. If it is not yet deep in the mire, it is already bespattered; if it is not in rags and tatters, it is about to collapse from rottenness.

The room is to be seen in its full glory at seven in the morning, when Madame Vauquer's cat comes in, leaps onto one of the sideboards and directs a loud morning purr at the milk in a number of bowls covered with plates. The widow herself traipses in shortly behind him in her battered slippers. A loop of imperfectly adjusted false hair dangles from under the net cap that adorns her head. The fat old face beneath it, with the nose jutting from the middle of it like a parrot's beak; the podgy little hands; the body, plump as a churchgoer's; the flabby, uncontrollable bust—they are all of a piece with the reeking misery of the room, where all hope and eagerness have been extinguished and whose stifling, fetid air she alone can breathe without being sickened. Her face, with the bite of the first autumn frost in it; the wrinkles round her eyes; the expression in them that can quickly change from the set smile of a ballet dancer to the embittered scowl of a bill discounter—her whole person, in fact, explains the house, as the house implies her person. The prison cannot be run without a jailer; you can't imagine one without the other. The unwholesome corpulence of this little woman is the product of this life, as typhus is the product of the exhalations of a hospital. The knitted wool petticoat, showing below her top skirt (itself made out of an old dress, through the holes of which bits of cotton-wool padding protrude) sums up the sitting room, the dining room, and the garden; it announces the kitchen and heralds the boarders. When she is there, the exhibition is complete.

At the age of fifty-four, Madame Vauquer was like all women who have *had their share of trouble*. She had the glassy eye, the innocent air of a procuress about to raise hell for a higher price; and she was prepared for any act of meanness or betrayal that might improve her own condition. Nevertheless, she was *a good woman at bottom,* according to the boarders, who took it as a sign of poverty that she whined and coughed like themselves. What had the late Monsieur Vauquer been? She never talked much about him. How had he lost his money? "During the troubles," she would reply. He had treated her very badly, leaving her only "these poor eyes to weep with," this house to live in, and a dispensation from ever showing the slightest sympathy for anyone else: she had been, she said, through quite enough herself.

Hearing her mistress pottering about, Sylvie, the buxom cook, hurried in to lay the breakfast table. As a rule the day boarders came in only for dinner, at thirty francs a month. At the time our story begins, the full boarders numbered seven.

The two best apartments in the house were on the first floor. Madame Vauquer lived in the more modest of these, and the other was let to Madame Couture, the widow of a paymaster of the French Republic. She had with her a very young girl named Victorine Taillefer, toward whom she acted as guardian. These two ladies paid the sum of eighteen hundred francs a year. Of the two apartments on the floor above, one was occupied by an old man named Poiret, the other by a man of about forty who wore a black wig, dyed his mustache, described himself as a retired merchant, and gave his name as Monsieur Vautrin. There were four rooms on the third floor. Two of these were permanently let: one to an old maid named Mademoiselle Michonneau, the other to a retired manufacturer of vermicelli, Italian *pasta*, and starch, who was always referred to as old Goriot. The two remaining rooms were reserved for birds of passage, such as the impecunious students who could, like Goriot and Mademoiselle Michonneau, afford only forty-five francs a month to cover board and lodging. Not that Madame Vauquer was at all keen on such guests, and she accepted them only when no one better was forthcoming: they ate too much bread.

At present, one of these two rooms was occupied by a young man from near Angoulême who had come to Paris to study law, and whose numerous family submitted to the sharpest privations in order to send him twelve hundred francs a year. Eugène de Rastignac was one of those young men whom misfortune compels to earn a living; from their earliest years they know the hopes their family set on them, and therefore map out a fine career for themselves by calculating from the start the range of their studies in the hope of adapting them in advance to possible social changes that they intend to be among the first to exploit. If it had not been for his lively curiosity, and his success at introducing himself into the drawing rooms of Paris, this story could not have been painted in the true colors it will unquestionably owe to his shrewd intelligence and his desire to unravel the mystery of a frightful situation that had been concealed with great care by its creators and its victim alike.

Over the third floor were a loft for drying clothes, and two attic rooms occupied by Sylvie and Christophe, the man-of-all-work. Apart from the seven full boarders, Madame Vauquer could also count on an average of eight students of law or medicine each year, and two or three regular customers who lived nearby. These came in only for dinner. The dining table could seat eighteen, and, at a pinch, twenty; but in the morning only the seven permanent residents appeared, and breakfast always had the air of a family meal. Everyone came down in slippers, and exchanged comments on the dress or behavior of the day guests or on the events of the night before. They expressed themselves with the freedom of intimacy. These seven lodgers were Madame Vauquer's spoiled children, and the care and attention she allotted to each of them were regulated with an astronomer's precision according to the amount they paid.

These creatures, brought together by chance, were all beset with the same problem. The two tenants on the second floor paid only seventy-two francs a month. Madame Couture was the only guest who paid more than this. Such low terms are to be had only in the Faubourg Saint-Marceau, between the Maternity Hospital and the Salpêtrière, and are in themselves sufficient sign that the boarders were weighed down by more or less evident difficulties. And the depressing interior of the house itself was reflected in the equally dilapidated clothing of its inmates. The men's clothes had been worn almost to pieces, their linen was frayed, the original color of their coats could only be guessed at, and their boots would in smarter districts have been thrown on the rubbish heap. The women's dresses were faded, dyed, re-faded; their old lace was darned, their gloves were shiny with long use, their collars ragged and discolored. But whatever their clothes, almost all of these people had sturdy frames, constitutions that had withstood the storms of life, cold hard features, half-obliterated like the worn faces on coins withdrawn from circulation. Their withered mouths were armed with avid teeth. There was in all of them a suggestion of drama, either already over or still being enacted: not the drama of footlights and painted backdrops, but living, wordless drama, icy drama that tore hotly at the heart, drama long drawn out.

The elderly spinster Mademoiselle Michonneau wore over her tired eyes a filthy green taffeta shade rimmed with brass wire: it would have made the Angel of Pity himself recoil. Her shawl, with its thin drooping fringe, seemed to be draped over a skeleton, so angular was the shape it hid. Once this woman must have been pretty and shapely. What acid had eaten away her pretty shape? Was it vice, grief, cupidity, excessive love? Had she been a poor shopkeeper, a dealer in secondhand clothes perhaps? Or simply a harlot? Was she paying for the triumphs of a flamboyant girlhood, when everyone had rushed forward to please her, by an old age at sight of which everyone fled? Her shrunken face was forbidding, her blank look chilled you. Her voice was like the sound of a grasshopper in its thicket at the onset of winter. She said that she had formerly looked after an old gentleman afflicted with catarrh of the bladder; his children, thinking him penniless, had abandoned him. The old man had left her a life annuity of a thousand francs, periodically disputed by his heirs, who made her the object of slanderous accusations. Though the play of passions had ravaged her features, faint traces of fairness and delicacy still visible in her complexion allowed one to suppose that her body also preserved some remnants of beauty.

Monsieur Poiret was a kind of automaton. He was to be seen regularly in the walks of the Jardin des Plantes, a limp old cloth cap on his head, his yellow ivory-knobbed cane in his hand, the loose shabby folds of his coat floating behind him and barely concealing an almost empty trouser and blue-stockinged legs that tottered like a drunken man's. Under his grubby white waistcoat, a coarse, tattered, muslin shirt front was uneasily attached to the necktie knotted round his scraggy neck.

Seeing this gray shadow drifting along, there were many who doubted if he really belonged to the bold race of the sons of Japheth who flaunt about the Boulevard des Italiens. What work could have shriveled the man up like this? What passion had darkened his bulbous face, which even as a caricature would have been unconvincing? What had he been? Well, perhaps he had been a clerk at the Ministry of Justice, in the office that deals with the expenses claimed by the public executioner for the black veils for his parricides, the sawdust for his guillotine baskets, the cord for his knives. Perhaps he had been a supervisor at the gates of a slaughterhouse, or an assistant sanitary inspector. At all events, he seemed to have been one of those donkeys who help to grind our great social mill, one of the underlings who never see their masters, some cogwheel on which public misfortune or disgrace depends—one of those men, in short, of whom we say when we see them: "Yes, but we couldn't manage without them." Their faces, ashen with moral and physical suffering, are not seen in fashionable Paris. But Paris is indeed an ocean. Sound it: you will never touch bottom. Survey it, report on it! However scrupulous your surveys and reports, however numerous and persistent the explorers of this sea may be, there will always remain virgin places, undiscovered caverns, flowers, pearls, monsters—there will always be something extraordinary, missed by the literary diver. The Maison Vauquer is one of these curious monstrosities.

Two of the faces there formed a striking contrast with the rest of the boarders and diners. Although Mademoiselle Victorine Taillefer had the sickly pallor of a girl in the grip of consumption, and although her habitual sadness, her troubled air, and her fragile and impoverished appearance were in keeping with the general misery that formed the background of this picture, nevertheless her face was not old, and her voice and movements were full of life. This young unfortunate seemed like a shrub, with yellowing leaves, newly transplanted into the wrong soil. Her complexion, her tawny fair hair, her excessively slim figure suggested the grace that modern poets were just beginning to discover in the statuettes of the Middle Ages. Her eyes, gray flecked with brown, expressed Christian gentleness and resignation. Her plain, inexpensive clothes showed off her youthful figure. She was pretty by juxtaposition. Happy, she could have been enchanting; happiness is the poetry of womanhood, as clothes are its disguise. If the gaiety of a ball could have thrown its rosy light on that wan face; if the graces of a civilized life could have filled out and brightened those already faintly hollowed cheeks; if love could have put life into those sad eyes, Victorine could have held her own with the prettiest of girls. She lacked the things that give a woman a second life: the pretty clothes, the love letters.

Her story itself could have furnished the subject for a book. Her father considered that he had reasons for disowning her and refused to have her near him. He allowed her only six hundred francs a year, and had completely disinherited her in order to leave his entire fortune to his son. Victorine's mother had died heartbroken in the arms of Madame Couture, a distant relation who now looked after the orphaned Victorine as though she were her own child. Unfortunately Madame Couture had nothing in the world but her own marriage settlement and her pension; she might one day leave this unhappy girl, inexperienced and resourceless, at the mercy of the world. The good woman took Victorine to mass every Sunday and to confession once every two weeks, so that she might at least grow up devout. And she was right. Religious feelings offered a possible future to this disowned child.

Victorine still loved her father and once every year went to his house, taking with her her mother's last written plea for forgiveness. And every year the door was inexorably shut against her. Her brother, her only possible means of communication with her father, had not been to see her once in the last four years, and had sent her no assistance. She still prayed God to unseal her father's eyes and to soften her brother's heart. And she prayed without reproaching them. Madame Couture and Madame Vauquer could not find enough words in the whole dictionary of abuse to describe the infamous millionaire's conduct; but hearing their insults, Victorine would interpose her own gentle words, like the moan of a wounded ringdove, whose cry of pain is still a song of love.

Eugène de Rastignac had an unmistakably southern face, pale, with black hair and blue eyes. His appearance, manners, and general bearing proclaimed the son of a noble family whose early upbringing had been in the best traditions. Although he had to be sparing of new clothes, and the best suit of one year had to be the everyday suit of the next, he could on occasion appear dressed like a fashionable young man-about-town. But on ordinary days he wore an old shabby coat and waistcoat, with trousers to match, mended boots, and the eternal student's frayed, black, ill-knotted necktie.

Between these two young people and the others, Vautrin, the man of forty with the dyed whiskers, stood halfway. He was one of those whom the vulgar describe as "a bright spark." He was very muscular, with broad shoulders, a well-developed chest, and thick square hands with prominent tufts of fiery red hair on the fingers. His face was prematurely lined, and the occasional hardness of it was offset by his easy, engaging manners. His deep resonant voice, in keeping with his boisterous gaiety, was in no way displeasing. He was cheerful and obliging. If one of the locks stuck, he would in no time take it to pieces, mend it, oil it, file it, and replace it, with the comment: "I know their little ways."

He knew the ways of a lot of other things too: ships, the sea, France, foreign countries, men, business, the law, current events, mansions, and prisons. If anyone was heard grumbling rather more than usual he was instantly ready to help. He had often lent money to Madame Vauquer and to some of the boarders; but his debtors would sooner have died than not pay him back, for in spite of his friendly manner there was something in his bold searching look that inspired fear. There was an unshakable composure even in the way he spat; he gave you the feeling that to get out of a difficult position he would not stop short of crime. His stern judicial eye seemed to penetrate to the depths of every problem, every moral scruple, every feeling.

His habits were regular: he always went out after breakfast, returned for dinner, disappeared for the whole evening, and let himself in about midnight with a pass-key given him by Madame Vauquer. He alone was accorded this privilege. But he was, after all, very much her favorite. He would often call her "Mamma," and throw his arms round her waist. She did not quite realize the exceptional talent involved in this piece of flattery: for simple as the gesture seemed to her, he was, in fact, the only man in the place with arms long enough to go round her waist. It was characteristic of Vautrin that he extravagantly paid fifteen francs a month for the coffee and brandy he took after dinner.

Anyone more observant than his fellow boarders—the young men caught up in the whirl of Parisian life, the older ones indifferent to everything that did not touch them directly—might have wondered a little at the ambiguous impression this man produced. He knew, or had guessed, the secrets of everyone in the place; his own thoughts and activities no one could fathom. Although his patent good nature, his invariable pleasantness and gaiety, had been erected as a barrier between himself and the others, flashes of the sinister undercurrents in his character were often seen. There were frequent satirical outbursts, some of them worthy of Juvenal, against the absurdities of the law, against high society and its self-contradictions. He evidently bore some deep-rooted grudge against the social order; and somewhere in his life there was a carefully shrouded mystery.

Attracted, perhaps unconsciously, by Vautrin's strength and Eugène's looks, Victorine divided her surreptitious glances and secret thoughts between them; but neither appeared to devote much thought to her, though her position might be changed overnight and make her a very desirable match. In any case, no one in this group ever bothered to discover whether the misfortunes asserted by the others were genuine or invented. In their

various predicaments, they had come to feel only mutual
indifference and distrust. They all knew they were powerless to help one another; their capacity for sympathy
had become exhausted, so often had everyone's woes
been recited. Like old married couples, they had nothing
left to talk about. Nothing remained but the contacts of
an automatic life, the creaking of unoiled machinery.
They could walk unheeding past a blind man in the
street; they could listen unfeelingly to a tale of hardship;
they were unmoved by the most terrible death agony:
death seemed to them merely the solution to the problem of poverty.

The happiest among these desolate creatures was Madame Vauquer, who reigned over this private asylum.
To her boarders, silence and cold, drought and damp
made the little garden seem like an unbroken steppe,
but to her it was a smiling glade. For her alone this sad
yellow house, with its counting-house smell of verdigris,
was a place of charm. These prison cells belonged to
her. The convicts had been sentenced to penal servitude
for life; she fed them, and they respected her authority.
Where else in Paris could the poor creatures find, at the
prices she charged, wholesome and sufficient food, and
rooms that they were at complete liberty to make, if not
elegant or comfortable, at least clean and tidy? She
might easily have committed the most disgraceful injustice against them: her victims would still have borne it
unprotesting.

Such a gathering was likely to show in miniature the
elements of a whole social order. It did so. Among the
eighteen guests, as in every school, as in society, one
sorry outcast had been picked out by the others as a
butt and laughingstock. And this wretched figure became
for Eugène de Rastignac, now about to begin his second
year in Paris, the most striking of all the people among
whom he was condemned to pass the two coming years.
It was the long-suffering flour merchant, old Goriot; it
was on Goriot's head that the painter or historian would
have made the highlight fall. How was it that this almost
malevolent scorn, this mingled persecution and pity, this

disrespect for suffering, had come to fall on the oldest boarder in the place? Had he given cause for it by some folly or eccentricity of the kind that people condone less readily than they condone vice? There is something of this quality in most social injustice. Perhaps it is fundamental to human nature to load everything on to the back of anyone prepared, whether from real humility or from weakness or indifference, to endure it. Do we not all like to demonstrate our power at the expense of someone or something else? The feeblest of creatures, the street Arab, will still ring every doorbell in freezing winter, or clamber up some new monument in order to scribble his name on it.

2

Goriot had come to live at Madame Vauquer's six years before, in 1813. He was then about sixty-two and had just retired from business. He had first taken the rooms now occupied by Madame Couture, and had paid twelve hundred francs a year, as a man to whom a hundred francs one way or the other meant nothing. Madame Vauquer had refurbished the three rooms of the apartment "in consideration of a sum payable in advance," providing them with yellow calico curtains, varnished wooden armchairs covered in imitation velvet, a few cheap paintings, and wallpaper that a suburban tavern would have rejected. The easygoing way in which he had allowed himself to be cheated had made Madame Vauquer assume at once that old Goriot—though at this period he was still respectfully called Monsieur Goriot—was a fool who knew nothing about business.

He had come with a well-stocked wardrobe, the splendid outfit of a man who at his retirement denies himself nothing. Madame Vauquer had noted with pleasure eighteen cambric shirts, whose exquisite frilled fronts were further embellished by the two large diamond-headed pins, linked by a small chain, that Goriot always sported with them. He usually wore a clear blue coat with a white linen waistcoat, changed daily; below this hung a heavy gold chain and seals, moving in rhythm with the fluctuations of the well-defined pear-shaped belly beneath them. His snuffbox was gold, too, and had a locket of hair set into it; this was taken to indicate a

number of past conquests. When his landlady accused
him of being a lady-killer, a faint gay smile crossed his
lips, the smile of a respectable man who enjoys being
teased about some little private naughtiness.

His silver chests (he used the working-class pronunciation *chesses*) were crammed with handsome, heavy
pieces of household silver. The widow's eyes gleamed as
she obligingly helped him to unpack and arrange the
forks, spoons, ladles, cruets, tureens, plates, and silver
breakfast sets. They were objects he had not wished to
get rid of, for they were mementos of the anniversaries
of his married life. "This," he said to Madame Vauquer,
as he put away a saucer and porringer embossed with a
pair of billing turtledoves, "was the first present my wife
ever gave me. It was our first wedding anniversary. Poor
dear, it cost her every penny she'd saved before we were
married. I'd rather scratch for food on the ground than
part with that. Thank God I shall be able to have my
breakfast out of this bowl every day for the rest of my
life. . . . I've nothing to worry about, I can keep the
wolf away for a long time yet." And indeed, Madame
Vauquer's magpie eye had already examined certain en-
tries in the Register of the National Debt which, she
roughly computed, must assure the excellent Goriot an
income of eight to ten thousand francs a year. From that
moment on, Madame Vauquer, the former Mademoiselle de Conflans, began to dream.

Although some affliction of the eye made Goriot's
eyelids permanently inflamed, swollen, and drooping, so
that he was continually having to wipe them, Madame
Vauquer found his appearance pleasant and dignified.
Also, something about his prominent fleshy calves and
his long square nose hinted at spiritual qualities to which
the widow appeared to attach great significance. The
good man's simple, guileless, moonlike face confirmed
this. Here, surely, was a good, sturdy, dumb animal, with
his heart where his brains ought to be. A barber came
every morning from the École Polytechnique to powder
his hair, which was arranged in five points over his low
forehead and seemed to go well with his face. Although

a trifle uncouth, Goriot was always so smartly turned out, so lavish in his use of snuff—he took it with the air of a man who knew the box would always be full of the best Macouba—that on the evening of the day he first moved in, Madame Vauquer retired to her bed, roasting like a basted partridge over the fire of a sudden longing to throw off the winding sheet of the late Monsieur Vauquer and emerge reborn as the second Madame Goriot.

To be married, to sell the boardinghouse, to walk on the arm of this fine flower of respectability, to become a lady of importance in the neighborhood, to do good works for the poor, to go on little Sunday outings to Choisy or Soissy or Gentilly; to have her own private box at the theater instead of depending on the complimentary tickets the boarders occasionally gave her in July—that was her dream, the Eldorado of many a little Paris household. She had never told anyone that she had, penny by penny, saved up forty thousand francs. Certainly, as far as money went, she regarded herself as a very acceptable match. "As for the other things, I bet I'm as good as he is," she thought, turning carefully over in bed as though to reassure herself of the existence of those charms whose deep impress was discovered every morning by Sylvie as she made the bed.

And so she too began to employ Monsieur Goriot's hairdresser, and to spend a little money on new clothes. She excused this as needful in giving the house a tone appropriate to the distinguished persons who frequented it. She took considerable trouble to try to elevate the class of boarders she took in, and announced that henceforth only ladies and gentlemen of exemplary refinement would be accepted. Whenever a newcomer appeared, she would boast of the fact that Monsieur Goriot, one of the most prominent and distinguished businessmen in Paris, had specially selected her house for his retirement. She distributed a prospectus with the letterhead MAISON VAUQUER, in which she said that the house was "one of the oldest and most highly recommended private apartment houses in the Latin Quarter. From it could be had a most charming view over the valley of the

Gobelins" (this was true, if you climbed up to the top floor) "and a *lovely* garden, at the far end of which *stretched* an AVENUE of linden trees." She touched also upon the bracing air and the quietness of the spot.

This prospectus attracted Madame la Comtesse de l'Ambermesnil, a woman of thirty-six who was awaiting the settlement of her late husband's affairs and the award of the pension due her as the widow of a general who had, she said, "died in *actions*." Madame Vauquer now began to pay great attention to the meals; fires were kept going in the sitting rooms for close on six months, and the promises in the prospectus were so well fulfilled that she was even a little out of pocket. Furthermore, the countess told Madame Vauquer, whom she had begun to address as "dear friend," that she would introduce two new boarders to her: the Baronne de Vaumerland, and the Comtesse Picquoiseau, a colonel's widow. These were friends of hers who were just on the point of relinquishing their lodgings in the Marais district, where the terms were much higher than at the Maison Vauquer. Both ladies would shortly be very well off: they had only to wait till the War Office had completed its labors. "Which of course it never does," she added.

Every evening after dinner the two widows went up to Madame Vauquer's room; there, over currant wine and a plate of the landlady's own special private cakes, they had little heart-to-heart talks. Madame de l'Ambermesnil warmly approved of her hostess's ideas about Goriot; they were excellent ideas, and she had guessed them from the start; and she thought him a most suitable man.

"He is, my dear," Madame Vauquer would agree; "he's as sound as a bell. And so well preserved! He could still give a woman quite a nice time."

The countess made a number of kindly suggestions to Madame Vauquer on the subject of her appearance: it was not, she thought, quite up to the level of Madame Vauquer's ambitions. "We must put you on a war footing," she remarked. After prolonged cogitation, the two ladies went shopping in the Wooden Market near the

Palais-Royal. There they bought a bonnet and a feathered hat. The countess next took her friend to a shop called "La Petite Jeannette," where they chose a dress and a scarf. Fully accoutered and ready for the fray, Madame Vauquer bore an undeniable resemblance to a well-known advertisement for boiled beef. No matter: she felt such a sense of personal improvement that in an unwonted access of generosity she gratefully pressed on the countess the gift of a hat costing twenty francs. The truth of the matter is that she was hoping to enlist her friend's services in sounding Goriot and putting in a good word for her. Madame de l'Ambermesnil lent herself very amicably to this maneuver and after a brief siege contrived a parley with the old man. Alas, he recoiled with such bashful obstinacy from her advances—they were, in fact, solely prompted by her private intention of appropriating him for herself—that she retreated from the interview, outraged by the man's rudeness.

"Angel," she said to her friend, "you're never going to get any change out of *that* man. He's suspicious and he's mean and he's horrid and he's silly. And he'll only cause you trouble."

So embarrassing was the situation between Monsieur Goriot and Madame de l'Ambermesnil that she could no longer bear to be under the same roof with him, and the following day she departed, neglecting to pay her last six months' board, and leaving personal effects behind her to the value of about five francs. The most searching inquiries on Madame Vauquer's part failed to elicit from anyone in Paris the slightest information about the Comtesse de l'Ambermesnil. Madame Vauquer often dwelt on this shameful episode, reproaching herself for her excessive trust, though a cat could scarcely have been more suspicious; but she was like many people who distrust their own family and yet will confide in the first stranger they meet. This is an odd but true fact of life; its roots may be easily traced in the human heart. Perhaps such people have no more to gain from the people they live with; they have exposed the emptiness of their souls to them, they feel secretly criticized by them, and feel the severity of the criticism to be just. But they still retain an invincible need for reassurance, or are consumed by the wish to appear possessed of qualities they lack; and so they hope to compel respect or affection from strangers, even at the risk of forfeiting them later. There are also some individuals, born ungenerous, who cannot be kind to their friends or relatives because they would be fulfilling a duty thereby; whereas if they are kind to a stranger, they feel an increase of self-respect. The nearer people are to them, the less they like them; the farther away they are, the more willing they are to help them. In Madame Vauquer both of these essentially shabby, false, and despicable natures were combined.

"If I'd been here," Vautrin used to say to her, "you'd never have had this trouble! I could have told you straight away what that old strumpet was up to. I can tell them a mile off."

Like all unimaginative people, Madame Vauquer was in the habit of never looking beyond the small circle of events to discover their causes. She preferred to palm her own faults off onto other people. After this disaster, she always believed that the honest flour merchant was the real cause of her misfortunes; she had begun, she said, to see him as he really was. As soon as she realized the futility of her advances, to say nothing of their heavy production costs, she was not slow to discover a reason. And thus she began to notice that her lodger had, as she put it, always had rather odd ways. It had been proved to her that her tenderly cherished hopes were based on a dream, and that, as the countess had so forcibly expressed it, she was never going to get any change out of *that* man. And the countess appeared to know about such things.

Inevitably, she went farther in hostility than she had ever gone in friendship. It had been her expectations, not her love, that had been disappointed. If the human heart sometimes finds moments of pause as it ascends the slopes of affection, it rarely halts on the way down. But after all, Monsieur Goriot was one of her boarders, and she was obliged to suppress her wounded vanity, to stifle the sighs her disappointment caused her, and, like a monk infuriated by his superior, to swallow her craving for revenge. Petty minds gratify their feelings, good or bad, by unceasing petty acts. The widow devoted all her feminine malice to devising covert persecutions against her victim. Her first move was to cut off the "extras" recently introduced at table.

"Stop the gherkins, stop the anchovies! We're just throwing money away," she instructed Sylvie the morning she reverted to the former bill of fare.

Goriot was a frugal man, and the thriftiness necessary to a self-made man had degenerated into habit with him. Soup, boiled beef, and a plate of vegetables had always been, and always would be, his favorite meal. It was therefore very difficult for Madame Vauquer to torment her lodger; and she could discover no way of offending him. Outraged at finding that he could not be attacked directly, she fell back on disparaging him to his fellow boarders, persuading them to share her dislike for him; and for their amusement they served her lust for revenge. By the end of the first year, her suspicions had reached such a pitch that she began to wonder how it was that a former merchant, with seven or eight thousand francs a year, and silver and jewelry fine enough for a kept woman, should be living in her house and paying out so small a proportion of his wealth for his board and keep.

During the greater part of his first year Goriot had usually dined out once or twice a week; then, gradually, he had begun to eat in town only once or twice a month. Goriot's little outings had suited Madame Vauquer's interests too well for her not to be displeased at the progressive regularity with which her boarder was now taking his meals at home. The change was attributed less to a steady decline in his fortunes than to a wish to annoy his landlady. It is one of the meanest habits of pygmy minds to attribute their own meannesses to other people. Unfortunately, at the end of his second year, Monsieur Goriot did much to justify the gossip about him by asking Madame Vauquer to let him move up to the second floor and to reduce his board to nine hundred francs. His need to economize was so pressing that he did without a fire throughout that winter. Madame Vauquer requested payment in advance; Monsieur Goriot agreed to this. And from that day on she always referred to him as "old Goriot."

What was the cause of this decline? It was hard to discover. As the false countess had observed, Goriot was a hypocrite, "one of those quiet ones." It is always assumed by the empty-headed, who chatter about themselves for want of something better, that people who do not discuss their affairs openly must have something to hide. And so the hitherto respected merchant gradually became a scoundrel, the elderly beau was now an old rogue. It was sometimes asserted that he was one of those men who haunted the Stock Exchange, and, having already ruined himself in speculation, was, in the eloquent language of finance, "selling short" in stocks and bonds. This was the opinion of Vautrin, who came to live at the Maison Vauquer around about this time.

Sometimes it was said that he was one of those minor gamblers who count on winning ten francs every night of the year. Sometimes it was decided he was a police spy; but Vautrin insisted he was not "sharp enough for that sort." It was also suggested that he was a miser who dealt in small-term loans; and that he played double or quits on lottery tickets. The most obscure vices, shames, and weaknesses were attributed to him. Only, however ignoble his behavior or vices might be, the aversion he inspired never led to his dismissal: he paid his rent. And after all, he had his uses; he was always there to be the target for everyone's wit or contempt, whichever their mood inspired.

The theory that seemed most likely, and the one most widely accepted, was that of Madame Vauquer. According to her, this man, "so well preserved, as sound as a bell, who could still give a woman quite a nice time," was an old rake. And, what was more, one with peculiar tastes. The facts on which she based her slanders were as follows.

Some months after the departure of the disastrous countess, who had lived for six months at her landlady's expense, Madame Vauquer had heard, one morning before she got up, the rustle of a silk dress on the stair, and the light footsteps of a young woman tiptoeing up to Goriot's room; the door had opened expectantly. Sylvie immediately came up, and announced to her mistress that a young girl, "got up like a goddess, in laced prunella boots, and not a speck on them, and much too pretty to be respectable," had slipped "like an eel" from the street into the kitchen, and had asked which was Monsieur Goriot's room. Madame Vauquer and her cook had listened intently; they had overheard many affectionate words during the visit, which had lasted for some considerable time. When Monsieur Goriot showed his lady out, the buxom Sylvie had promptly seized her shopping basket as though to go to market, and had followed the loving pair.

"Would you believe it, madame?" she said on her return. "There was a great big splendid carriage waiting at the corner of the Estrapade, and I saw him help her in! Why, he must still be lousy with money if he can keep *that* up!"

At dinner that day, Madame Vauquer rose and closed one of the curtains; the sun had been shining into Goriot's eyes.

"All the pretty ladies are after you, Monsieur Goriot," she said, alluding to the morning's visitor. "Even the sun is chasing you."

"That was my daughter," he said with a touch of pride that the boarders promptly interpreted as the fatuousness of an old man trying to preserve the decencies.

A month after this visit, Monsieur Goriot received another. His daughter had on the first occasion come in day clothes. This time she came after dinner, dressed to go out. The boarders, chatting in the drawing room, caught a glimpse of a pretty, slim, graceful, golden-haired girl, much too refined to be a daughter of anyone like Goriot.

"Two of them!" exclaimed Sylvie, who had not recognized her.

Some days later, another girl, a tall shapely brunette with dark brown eyes, asked to see Monsieur Goriot.

"Three of them!" said Sylvie.

This second young lady, whose first visit to her father had also been in the morning, reappeared several days later, in the evening, in her carriage, dressed for a ball.

"Four of them!" said Madame Vauquer and Sylvie together. They saw in this fine lady no trace of the simply dressed girl of the earlier visit.

At that time Goriot was still paying Madame Vauquer twelve hundred francs a year. She found it quite natural that a wealthy man should have four or five mistresses; she even rather admired him for pretending they were his daughters. Nor did she raise any objection to his making assignations with them at the Maison Vauquer. Only, since these young women seemed to account for Goriot's indifference to herself, she went so far, at the beginning of the second year, to refer to him as "an old goat." But after her boarder had declined to the nine-hundred-franc class, she insolently demanded, the next time one of the ladies called, what he thought he was turning the place into. Goriot replied that the lady was his elder daughter.

"How many daughters have you got?" she acidly demanded. "Three dozen?"

"Only two," he answered, with the meekness of a man reduced to complete submissiveness by poverty and ruin.

Toward the end of his third year here, Goriot cut down his expenditure still further, and moved up to a room on the third floor, for which he agreed to pay forty-five francs a month. He gave up his snuff, dismissed the barber, and stopped powdering his hair. The first time his landlady saw the real color of his hair, a dirty greenish gray, she let out a shriek of astonishment. His face, which had insensibly become sadder and sadder under the pressure of private grief, seemed the most melancholy of all those round the table. There was no longer room for doubt. Goriot was an old rake. Only the skill of his doctor had preserved his eyesight from the malignant effects of all the medicines he was forced to take for his diseases. The disgusting color of his hair was the result of his dissipations, and the drugs he took in order to continue in them. The physical and mental state of the old man gave confirmation to these absurd rumors.

His fine linen, long ago worn out, had been replaced by calico at half a franc the yard. His diamond pins, his gold snuffbox, his watch chain and other pieces of jewelry had vanished one after another. In place of his blue coat and his other nice clothes, he now wore, whatever the time of year, an overcoat of coarse brown cloth, a mohair waistcoat, and thick gray worsted trousers; he grew steadily thinner; his calves shrank; his face, once plump with a prosperous tradesman's contentment, grew deeply lined; his brow was creased; the angle of his jaw grew sharper. By the end of his fourth year in the Rue Neuve-Sainte-Geneviève, he was barely recognizable. The good flour merchant who at sixty-two had looked like forty, the hale and hearty citizen whose lively carriage had delighted all who saw him, whose smile had kept something of his youth, now looked like a pale, feebleminded dodderer of seventy. His piercing blue eyes had turned a dull leaden gray. They had faded; they no longer watered, but their inflamed lids seemed to be weeping blood.

Some were horrified at him, others felt pity. Young medical students, noticing the droop of his lower lip and the significant sharpness of his facial angle, pummeled him about for some time without effect, and declared that he was sinking into a state of cretinism. After dinner one evening, Madame Vauquer said to him jokingly: "So those daughters of yours have stopped coming to see you?" It was his relationship to them she meant to cast doubt on; but Goriot started as if she had pricked him with a knife.

"They do come sometimes," he said in a troubled voice.

"Aha! You still see them!" shouted the students. "Good for old Goriot!"

But Goriot heard nothing of the jests his reply had provoked. He had withdrawn once more into a brooding state. Superficial observers took it to be the senile torpor of failing intelligence. Perhaps had they known him better, they might have been keenly interested in the problem of his physical and mental condition. It would have been very easy to find out whether Goriot really had been a flour merchant; and how much he had made. But the old people who felt any curiosity in the matter never left the neighborhood, clinging to the boardinghouse like oysters on a rock. As for the others, the delights of Paris itself engulfed them the minute they left the Rue Neuve-Sainte-Geneviève, and the poor old man they had just been laughing at slipped from their minds.

For all of them, the pinched old people and the careless young ones alike, Goriot's arid poverty and his air of stupefaction were incompatible with any sort of wealth or ability at all. As for the women he called his daughters, everyone was of the same mind as Madame Vauquer. With the remorseless logic that a habit of always thinking the worst develops in old women who pass every evening in gossip, she had said: "If old Goriot had daughters as well off as all those ladies who've been here to see him seem to be, he wouldn't be living here, on the third floor, at forty-five francs a month, and going about dressed like a beggar." This conclusion was incontrovertible. And so, at the end of November, 1819, when our story begins, everyone in the boardinghouse had his own fixed opinion about the unfortunate old man. He had never had either wife or daughters. Debauchery had reduced him to the condition of a snail—"an anthropomorphous mollusc, classifiable like Poiret with the *cloth-cappifera*," in the words of a clerk from the Museum who was one of the day boarders. But Poiret was an eagle, a man of the world, compared with Goriot. Poiret did, after all, speak and argue and answer. True, he never actually said anything when he spoke and argued and answered; he merely repeated in slightly different words the remarks of the previous speaker. But at least he joined in the conversation, he was alive, he appeared to have feelings; while old Goriot, added the museum clerk, was permanently stuck at freezing point.

3

Eugène de Rastignac had just returned from the country; he was in a frame of mind known to most highly gifted young men, or men who have been momentarily forced, in a testing situation, to rise above the common level. During his first year, the small amount of work necessary for the first examinations had left him time to savor the visible, material delights of the town. And a student can never have enough time if he intends to learn the repertory of every theater, familiarize himself with the windings of the Parisian maze, study its customs, its language, its special pleasures, and prowl about all its haunts, good and bad. He will also attend such lectures as seem amusing enough, and pore over the treasures in the museums. At this period he will be filled with enthusiasm for frivolities that seem momentous. He hero-worships a professor at the Collège de France, paid to adapt himself to the level of his listeners. He straightens his tie and strikes attitudes for the benefit of the women in the boxes at the Opéra Comique.

These successive initiation ceremonies bring him out of his shell; his horizons widen, and he begins to distinguish the strata that compose human society. On some sunny day he may have stood in wonder, dazzled by the procession of carriages on the Champs Elysées. It is not long before he wants one himself.

Eugène had gone through this apprenticeship without realizing it; and after passing his first law examinations, he had gone back home for the holidays. His boyhood illusions gone, his provincial outlook also, he was back in the bosom of his family with a broadened mind and an excited ambition; and he saw distinctly how things really stood in the ancestral home. His father, mother, two sisters, two brothers, and an aunt whose income consisted of annuities, lived on the little estate of Rastignac. The property produced about three thousand francs a year, and was subject to the uncertainties of all wine-growing country; nevertheless twelve hundred francs had to be extracted from it every year for Eugène. The constant privation that everyone nobly tried to conceal from him; the inevitable contrast between his sisters, who had seemed so beautiful when he was a child, and the women in Paris who had personified for him the sort of beauty he had before seen only in dreams; his large family's insecure future, which depended on himself; the thriftiness with which they hoarded the most insignificant products; the wine at table, made from the lees of the wine press—the sight of all this, and of a crowd of other things it would be pointless to record, increased tenfold his craving for success and his longing to distinguish himself.

Like all men of character, he wanted to make his way by his own unaided efforts. But his temperament was distinctly that of the south; and, when it came to the point, his resolves were regularly beset by the hesitations that invade young men when they are at last on the open sea and do not know which way to direct their energies, nor from which corner the wind is likeliest to fill their sails. At first he had decided to throw himself blindly into work; but he had been immediately diverted by the need of acquiring connections. He had observed how strong the influence of women was in social life, and suddenly he decided to strike out into society and find himself patronesses. Surely they would be forthcoming for a young man whose native wit and enthusiasm were reinforced by a smart appearance and just that degree of virile handsomeness that women so easily find attractive? These ideas assailed him during the walks in the fields he had formerly so much enjoyed with his sisters, who now found him greatly changed.

His aunt, Madame de Marcillac, in her younger days had been presented at court, and had been acquainted with the high aristocracy there. Suddenly the ambitious young man realized that the reminiscences with which his aunt had so often lulled him to sleep might contain the seeds of great social conquest, at least as important as the successes he was aiming at in law school. He questioned her about family ties that might be reestablished. After shaking the branches of the family tree, the old lady decided that out of all the people who could help her nephew in the self-centered tribe of rich relatives, the least reluctant would be Madame la Vicomtesse de Beauséant. She wrote a formal old-fashioned letter to this young woman and gave it to Eugène: if he was successful with the viscountess, then she would introduce him to his other relations.

A few days after his return to Paris, Eugène sent his aunt's letter to Madame de Beauséant. She replied with an invitation to a ball the following evening. Such was the general situation in the boardinghouse at the end of November, 1819.

It was two o'clock in the morning when Eugène returned home from Madame de Beauséant's ball. As he danced, the high-minded young student had vowed to himself that in order to make up for the time he was wasting, he would work till morning; for he was still under the spell of an artificial energy aroused in him by the splendors of society. It would be the very first time he had worked throughout the night in the silent quarter. He had not dined at Madame Vauquer's. His fellow boarders could think he had not returned from the ball till daybreak, just as he had sometimes returned, his silk stockings splashed with mud and his dancing shoes ruined, from festivities at the Prado or balls at the Odéon.

Before bolting the door for the night, Christophe had opened it for a moment and looked up and down the street. Eugène appeared at this moment and was able to go up to his room without making a noise, followed by

Christophe, who was making a great deal. Eugène un-
dressed, put on his slippers and an old coat, and lit his
peat fire; he did all this so rapidly that his almost noise-
less preparations were drowned in the clatter of Christophe's heavy boots. He sat thinking for a few moments
before plunging into his law books. He had discovered
only that night that the Vicomtesse de Beauséant was
one of the social queens of Paris, and that her house
was considered the pleasantest in the whole of the Faubourg Saint-Germain. Moreover she was, both by title
and by fortune, one of the leaders of the aristocratic
world. Thanks to Aunt Marcillac, the penniless student
had been kindly welcomed in this house, quite unaware
of the extent of the favor. Admission to these gilded
halls was like being awarded a patent of nobility. His
appearance in such society, the most exclusive in all
Paris, conferred on him the right to go anywhere. Dazzled by the brilliance of the gathering, and exchanging
barely a word with the viscountess herself, he had con-
tented himself with singling out from the crush of Parisian goddesses that thronged the rout one of those young
women whom all young men worship at sight. The Comtesse Anastasie de Restaud, tall and well-proportioned,
was reputed to have one of the prettiest figures in Paris.
Imagine a pair of large dark eyes, marvelous hands, a
shapely foot, fire in her movements, a woman the
Marquis de Ronquerolles had described as a thoroughbred. This quickness of temper was not a defect; her
contours were full and round, though no one could have
accused her of being plump. A *thoroughbred,* a *woman
of mettle*—such locutions were beginning to displace the
heavenly angels, the Ossianic shapes of the old mythol-
ogy of love. The contemporary dandies had rejected
them. But to Rastignac, Madame de Restaud was simply
"the desirable woman." He had succeeded in writing his
name twice in the list of partners on her fan, and had
been able to talk with her during the first quadrille.

"Where may I see you again, madame?" he had asked
abruptly, with the impulsive warmth that women find
so pleasing.

"Oh," she had said, "in the Bois, at the Bouffons, at my home, anywhere. . . ."

And the adventurous young southerner had done all it is humanly possible to do in the space of one quadrille and one waltz to become friends with this delightful countess. He had told her he was a cousin of Madame de Beauséant's; and the woman—whom he took to be a great lady—had invited him to call on her whenever he wished. Her farewell smile had made the visit seem an obligation.

He had been lucky enough to be introduced to a man who was not contemptuous of his ignorance—a mortal sin among the illustrious fops of the time, the Maulincourts, the Ronquerolles, the Marsays, the Ajuda-Pintos, the Vandernesses and so on, all there tonight in their shining vanity, their elegant women crowding round them. Happily for the innocent student, it was the Marquis de Montriveau that he fell in with. A lover of the Duchesse de Langeais, the man was a general, as simple as a child; and from him Eugène learned that the Comtesse de Restaud lived in the Rue du Helder.

To be young, to be athirst for society and women, and then suddenly to have two houses open their doors to you! To have your foot in the Faubourg Saint-Germain at the Vicomtesse de Beauséant's, and your knee in the Chaussée d'Antin at the Comtesse de Restaud's! To see before you a vista of all the drawing rooms of Paris, confident that your good looks will win you help and protection in some woman's heart! To walk the tightrope and feel so certain of your acrobatic skill that you can give the rope a superb kick, with such a charming woman as your balancing pole! Such were his thoughts. The woman rose sublimely before him, in front of his peat fire, amid his law books and his poverty. Small wonder that as he pondered the future he saw it brimming with success. So intensely did his future joys crowd into his wayward thoughts that it was as if Madame de Restaud was there beside him—when a sigh like the groan of a laboring St. Joseph troubled the silence of the night and struck so vividly into the young man's heart that he took it for the last gasp of a dying man.

He opened his door quietly; across the corridor he could see a line of light under old Goriot's door. Fearing his neighbor might be unwell, he bent down and peered through the keyhole into the room. There he saw the old man engaged in such criminal-looking work that he felt it was no more than his public duty to find out exactly what the so-called flour merchant was up to so late at night. To the crossbar of his upturned table, Goriot appeared to have tied, with the aid of a thick cord, a richly decorated silver plate and bowl; with great strength, he was now squeezing and twisting them, apparently with the aim of converting them into ingots.

"God! What a man!" thought Eugène at the sight of the old man's muscular arms. With the aid of the rope he was silently kneading the silver mass as though it were dough. "Is he a thief? Or a fence?" he wondered. Were his stupidity and helplessness merely a pretense? Did he live like a beggar in order to carry on his trade more safely? Eugène straightened himself, and then looked again through the keyhole.

Goriot, who had unwound the rope, now took the mass of silver, placed it on a blanket on the table, and began to roll it into a bar, an operation he achieved with remarkable ease.

"He must have the strength of Augustus King of Poland," thought Eugène, when the rounded bar was almost complete.

Goriot gazed sadly at his handiwork, and tears stood in his eyes. He blew out the taper by whose light he had been twisting the metal, and Eugène heard him sigh as he got into bed.

"He must be mad," he thought.

"Poor child," said Goriot aloud.

These words made Eugène think it might be wiser to keep silent about what he had seen and not condemn his neighbor too readily. He was about to go back to his room when suddenly he heard a mysterious noise, that must have come from men in cloth slippers mounting the stairs. Eugène listened, and was in fact able to distinguish the alternate breathing of two men. He had heard neither the sound of the door nor the steps of the men, but all at once he saw a faint light coming from Monsieur Vautrin's room on the floor below.

"Strange goings-on in a respectable boardinghouse," he thought. Going down a few steps, he listened again, and caught the chink of money. The light went out, the double breathing was heard once again, still without any sound of a door. Then, as the two men went downstairs, the sound grew fainter.

"Who's that?" cried Madame Vauquer, throwing open her bedroom window.

"It's only me! I've just come in, Mamma Vauquer!" came Vautrin's deep bass voice.

"That's odd! Christophe bolted the door," thought Eugène, going back to his room. "You obviously have to stay up all night to find out all the goings-on in Paris."

His ambitious thoughts of love had been interrupted by these small events, and he turned to his books. But, disturbed by the suspicions aroused in him by Goriot, and further disturbed by the image of Madame de Restaud who kept flitting before him like the harbinger of a brilliant future, he eventually went to bed, and slept like a top. Out of every ten nights young men vow to study, they give seven to sleep. You have to be over twenty to stay up all night.

4

The next morning Paris was cloaked in one of those thick fogs that envelop and darken it so completely that the most punctual folks are deceived by the weather. Business appointments are missed. Everyone thinks it's eight o'clock just as midday strikes. At half past nine, Madame Vauquer had still not stirred from her bed. Christophe and Sylvie, also behind schedule, were placidly drinking their coffee, which Sylvie had made with the cream from the boarders' milk. The rest of the milk she had boiled for a very long time so that Madame Vauquer would not observe this illegal tithe-gathering.

"Sylvie," said Christophe, as he dipped his first bit of toast into his coffee, "two more people came to see Monsieur Vautrin last night. If the old girl asks anything, just keep quiet about it, will you? Vautrin's all right."

"Did he give you anything?"

"He gave me his monthly twenty francs, same as usual; it's his way of saying keep your mouth shut."

"They're as mean as they make them in this place, apart from him and Madame Couture," observed Sylvie. "They give you a New Year tip with one hand and take it back with the other. Or they'd like to."

"Yes, and what is it they give when they give it?" demanded Christophe. "A stinking five-franc piece. And for the last two years old Goriot's been cleaning his own shoes. And that old miser Poiret, he never cleans his at all. He'd rather drink the blacking than put it anywhere near them rotten old slippers of his. And there's that

41

undersized law student, too: he has the nerve to give me eight francs. Eight francs! It don't even pay for my brushes. 'Sides which, he takes all his old clothes to the second-hand. What a lousy dump this is!''

"Oh, I don't know," said Sylvie, drinking her coffee in little gulps. "We've got better jobs than most round here. The living's good. But anyway, what about Pa Vautrin? Has anybody said anything to you?"

"Yes, a gentleman came up to me in the street the other day and asked me, 'Isn't it your place there's a big tall gentleman as dyes his whiskers?' So I said: 'No, sir, he don't dye them. A busy man like him don't have the time.' So I told Vautrin about it, and he said: 'Quite right, lad! That's the way to answer people back. It's annoying when people get to know your little weaknesses. Good marriages have been spoiled that way.' "

"Yes, and they were trying to get at me about him, down at the market. Asked me if I'd ever seen him put his shirt on. The idea . . . Listen!" she said, breaking off. "There's the Val-de-Grâce striking quarter to ten and nobody up."

"Don't be daft, they've all gone out. Madame Couture and the young lady went to mass at Saint-Etienne at eight. And old Goriot went off somewhere with a parcel. The student won't be back till after his lecture, at ten. I saw them all go while I was doing my stairs. Old Pa Goriot bumped up against me with whatever it was he'd got: hard as a piece of iron it was. What does the old man *do*, I wonder? The others whizz him about the whole time like an old top. He's a decent old stick in his way. He's better than any of *them* are. He don't give you much himself, but them ladies he sends me with a message to sometimes, they hand out all right. And got up very smart they are, too."

"Them he calls his daughters, d'you mean? There's a dozen of them."

"I've never been to but the two of them—the two as comes here."

"I can hear the missus moving. She'll be creating. I

must go on up. Stay and keep an eye on that milk, Christophe. And mind the cat."

Sylvie went up to Madame Vauquer's room.

"What's this, Sylvie? It's a quarter to ten! You've let me sleep on like a top. I've never done such a thing in my life!"

"It's the fog. You could cut it with a knife."

"But what about the breakfasts?"

"There was no holding the lodgers this morning. They was out as soon as up."

"I've told you not to call them lodgers, Sylvie," complained Madame Vauquer. "They are guests."

"They're whatever you say they are, ma'am. Anyway, you can put an early lunch on. Michonneau and Poiret haven't stirred. They're the only ones in the house, and they're sleeping like a pair of logs."

"Don't talk like that, Sylvie, you sound as if they . . ."

"As if they what?" demanded Sylvie with a loud guffaw. "One and one makes a pair—after all!"

"I was wondering, Sylvie: how did Monsieur Vautrin get in last night after Christophe had put the bolts on?"

"Oh, but he hadn't, ma'am. He heard Monsieur Vautrin down below, and went down and let him in. That must have been what you . . ."

"Pass me my dressing gown, and go and see to the lunch, as quick as you can. Prepare what's left of the mutton with a few potatoes; and give them some stewed pears; the cheaper ones."

A few moments later Madame Vauquer came down. Her cat had just knocked the plate off one of the bowls of milk, with its paw, and was greedily lapping.

"Mistigris!" she shouted. The cat leaped back, and then came sidling up to rub against her legs. "Yes, I know you, you old hypocrite! Sylvie! Sylvie!"

"What is it, ma'am?"

"Look what the cat's been up to!"

"It's that silly Christophe's fault. I told him to lay the table. Where's he got to? Never mind: I'll make old Goriot's coffee with it. I'll fill it up with water, he won't notice. He never notices anything, not even what he's eating."

"Where's the old fool gone to?" asked Madame Vauquer, as she began to lay the table.

"I don't know. He's up to all kinds of tricks."

"I've overslept," sighed Madame Vauquer.

"But you look as fresh as a daisy, ma'am."

At this moment the gate bell rang, and Vautrin's deep voice was heard singing in the sitting room:

> *"I've traveled the whole world over,*
> *They know me everywhere . . .*

"Ah! Good morning, Mamma Vauquer!" he cried, coming in and seeing his landlady, and taking her gallantly in his arms.

"Get along with you!"

"Say 'you bad boy!' Go on, say it! Do you really mean it? I'll help you set the table. That's nice of me, isn't it?

> *"And I'm ready to be the lover*
> *Of dark . . .*

"I've just seen something very odd.

> *. . . Or red, or fair."*

"What?" asked Madame Vauquer.

"Old Goriot. At half past eight this morning in the Rue Dauphine—at the goldsmith's, where they buy people's old forks and gold trimmings. He got a good price for some piece of silver plate or other. And for somebody who doesn't know the job, he'd twisted it about pretty well too."

"Go on! You don't say?"

"Yes. I'd just come from seeing a friend off on the Royal Mail. I was on my way back, and I thought I'd follow old Goriot—just for the fun of it. He came back up here, to the Rue des Grès, where I saw him go into Gobseck's place. Gobseck's a well-known moneylender, a real stinker: he'd make dominoes out of his father's bones, if he thought he could. He's a Jew and an Arab and a Greek and a gypsy, all in one. And no one's ever managed to lift a penny from him; he puts it all in the bank."

"But whatever's old Goriot doing?"

"He isn't doing anything," said Vautrin. "He's *undo*-ing. He's been fool enough to ruin himself chasing after girls, and . . ."

"There he is!" cried Sylvie.

"Christophe!" Goriot was heard calling. "Come up-stairs with me." Christophe followed him upstairs. A few moments later he came down again.

"Where are you going?" Madame Vauquer asked him.

"On an errand for Monsieur Goriot."

"What's that you've got there?" asked Vautrin, snatching a letter from Christophe, and reading the ad-dress. "*To Madame la Comtesse Anastasie de Restaud.* Where are you taking it?"

"To the Rue du Helder. I've got orders not to give it to anybody except the countess."

"What's inside it?" asked Vautrin, holding the letter up to the light. "A banknote? No." He half opened the envelope. "A receipted bill!" he cried. "Well, the gallant old stick! Go on, Christophe, you scavenger," he said, placing a hand on the man's head and spinning him round like a top. "You'll get a good tip for that."

The table was set. Sylvie was boiling the milk. Ma-dame Vauquer was lighting the stove, assisted by Vau-trin, who was still quietly murmuring:

> *"I've traveled the whole world over,*
> *They know me everywhere . . ."*

Just as the meal was ready, Madame Couture and Ma-demoiselle Taillefer came in.

"Where have you been so early, fair lady?" Madame Vauquer asked Madame Couture.

"We've been to mass at Saint-Etienne. Don't you re-member, we have to go and try to see Monsieur Taillefer today? Poor Victorine, she's trembling like a leaf," said Madame Couture. She sat down, took off her shoes and held them up to the fire, where they began to steam.

"Come and get warm, Victorine," said Madame Vauquer.

"It's all very well praying to God to soften your father's heart," said Vautrin, bringing up a chair for the girl. "But it'll take more than that. You need a friend to tell the ugly old savage a few home truths. They say he's worth three million; and he won't give you a dowry. And a pretty girl needs a dowry these days."

"Poor child," said Madame Vauquer. "Never mind, dear, your father's only saving up trouble for himself, the old—" She broke off at a sign from Madame Couture; tears had come into Victorine's eyes.

"If he would only let us see him," said Madame Couture. "If I could only speak to him and give him his wife's last letter. I've never dared trust it to the post; he knows my writing. . . ."

"Oh, injured women, hapless and innocent," chanted Vautrin. "Is that the state you're in? Never mind, in a few days' time I will look into the matter myself; and all will be well."

"Oh, sir," said Victorine, with a burning, tearful look at Vautrin, who remained unmoved, "if you ever do manage to see my father, please tell him that my mother's honor and his affection mean more to me than all the money in the world. If you could persuade him to be even a little less harsh with me, I'd never forget it as long as I—"

"I've traveled the whole world over," sang Vautrin, ironically.

At this point Goriot, Mademoiselle Michonneau, and Poiret came downstairs, lured perhaps by the smell of the gravy with which Sylvie was disguising the remains of the mutton. As the seven were greeting one another and seating themselves at the table, ten o'clock struck, and Eugène's footsteps were heard.

"Well, Monsieur Eugène," said Sylvie, "so you're eating with the rest of them today, then?"

The student greeted his fellow boarders and sat down next to Goriot.

"I've just had an extraordinary adventure," he said, helping himself liberally to the mutton and cutting himself a slice of bread, under the intent stare of Madame Vauquer.

"An adventure . . . !" said Poiret.

"Well, what are you surprised at, old cloth-cap?" Vautrin asked. "Monsieur Eugène is made for adventures."

Mademoiselle Taillefer stole a timid glance at Eugène.

"Well, what *was* your adventure?" asked Madame Vauquer.

"Last night I went to a ball at Madame la Vicomtesse de Beauséant's. (She's a cousin of mine.) She has a magnificent house, with all the rooms hung with silk, and—oh, well, anyway, she gave us the most marvelous party, and I was as happy as a king—"

"Fisher," added Vautrin, interrupting him.

"What do you mean, sir?" asked Eugène sharply.

"I said 'fisher,' because kingfishers have so much more fun than kings."

"It's true," murmured the echoing Poiret. "I'd much sooner be a carefree little bird like that, bec—"

"Anyway," said Eugène, cutting him short, "I danced with one of the most beautiful women at the ball, a ravishing countess, the most enchanting woman I've ever seen. She had peach blossoms in her hair, and some other flowers at her waist—real ones, they scented the air—but oh, well, anyway, you'd have had to see her to know what I mean. It's impossible to describe how *alive* a woman looks when she's dancing. Well, this morning I actually *saw* this divine creature, about nine o'clock, on foot, near *here*, in the Rue des Grès! I can't tell you how my heart thumped, I imagined . . ."

"That she was coming here," said Vautrin with a searching look at Eugène. "She was quite certainly going to see Papa Gobseck, the moneylender. Go deep enough into any woman's heart in Paris and you'll always find the moneylender's even more important than the lover.

Your countess's name is Anastasie de Restaud. She lives in the Rue du Helder."

At the name, Eugène stared hard at Vautrin. Goriot looked up sharply and fixed the two speakers with a piercing, anxious stare that took the other boarders aback.

"Christophe will be too late! She'll have gone there already!" he moaned.

"I guessed it," whispered Vautrin, leaning over to Madame Vauquer.

Goriot continued to chew automatically, without knowing what he was eating. Never had he looked more vacant and lost than at this moment.

"Who the devil can have told you her name, Monsieur Vautrin?" asked Eugène.

"Aha! Never you mind!" replied Vautrin. "Old Goriot knew it! Why shouldn't I?"

"Monsieur Goriot!" exclaimed Eugène.

"Well?" said the old man. "So she looked very lovely last night?"

"Who?"

"Madame de Restaud."

"Look at the old miser," said Madame Vauquer, "look at his eyes glinting."

"He really does keep her then?" whispered Mademoiselle Michonneau to the student.

"Why yes! She was wildly beautiful," said Eugène. Goriot was staring avidly at him. "If Madame de Beauséant hadn't been there, my divine countess would have been the queen of the ball. The young men wouldn't look at anyone else. I was the twelfth on her list; she danced every single quadrille. The other women were furious. If there was ever a happy woman last night, it was Madame de Restaud. It's quite right what they say: the three most beautiful sights in the world are a ship in full sail, a galloping horse, and a woman dancing."

"Last night at the top of the wheel, at a duchess's," commented Vautrin. "This morning at the bottom of the ladder, at a moneylender's. That's the women of Paris for you. If their husbands can't keep them in insane luxury, they sell themselves. If they can't sell themselves, they tear their mothers' wombs out to find something to dazzle the world with. There's nothing they won't do. I know them!"

Goriot's face had beamed like the sun on a fine day as he listened to Eugène. It now darkened at Vautrin's cynical observations.

"Well," said Madame Vauquer, "what about this adventure you said? Did you speak to her? Did you ask her if she'd like to study law?"

"She didn't see me," said Eugène. "But fancy seeing one of the prettiest women in Paris, in the Rue des Grès, at nine in the morning, a woman who can't have got home from a ball before two! Don't you call that strange? It could certainly never happen outside Paris."

"Bah! Stranger things than that happen here," said Vautrin.

Mademoiselle Taillefer had scarcely listened, so preoccupied was she with the ordeal that lay before her. Madame Couture motioned to her to go up and dress. When the two ladies left, Goriot left also.

"Well, did you see him?" said Madame Vauquer to Vautrin and the others. "Those women of his have obviously been his ruin."

"No one will ever make me believe," cried Eugène, "that the lovely Comtesse de Restaud belongs to old Goriot!"

"We don't really mind whether you believe it or not," said Vautrin. "You're still too young to understand Paris; you'll find out later that there are a great number of what are called men of special tastes there. . . ."

At these words Mademoiselle Michonneau looked at Vautrin with an air of understanding. It was not unlike that of a battle horse at the sound of the bugle. "Aha!" Vautrin broke off, and gave her a meaningful look. "*We've* had *our* little passions too, haven't we?" At this the old maid dropped her eyes, like a nun confronted by a nude statue.

"Well," he resumed, "these people get one idea fixed

in their minds, and they never let go of it. They thirst only for a particular water from a particular well—often a tainted one. For a drink from it, they'd sell their wives and children; they'd sell their souls to the devil. For some of them the well means gambling, or the Stock Exchange, or a collection of pictures or insects, or music; for others it means a woman who knows how to make pastry for them. And you could offer men like that all the women in the world instead, and they'd only laugh; they want only the one who'll satisfy their special passion. Quite often the woman doesn't even like them, or treats them with contempt, and charges very high prices for their scraps of satisfaction; but our jokers never have enough, they'll pawn their last blanket to give the woman their last penny. Old Goriot is one of them. The countess exploits him because he keeps quiet; and that's high society for you! The poor old thing thinks of nothing but her. Except for his passion, as you saw, he's a dumb animal. But once mention the subject and his eyes sparkle like diamonds. It wasn't difficult to guess the secret. He took some silver along to the smelter's this morning, and later I saw him going into Gobseck's in the Rue des Grès. Now listen to this: when he came back, he sent that ass Christophe round to the countess's—Christophe showed us the address on the letter; and the letter contained a receipted bill of exchange. It's obvious if the countess went to Gobseck's too, it must have been a matter of some urgency. Old Goriot's been gallantly forking out for her. It doesn't need much piecing together, does it? And it proves, my dear young student, that while your countess was laughing and dancing and smirking, and twitching her dress, and waving her peach blossoms about, she was actually shaking in her shoes, as they say, thinking about her dishonored bills—or her lover's."

"You make me desperate to know the truth!" cried Eugène. "I shall call on Madame de Restaud tomorrow."

"Oh, yes," Poiret echoed. "You must call on Madame de Restaud tomorrow."

"And perhaps you'll find friend Goriot there too, come to get the reward for his gallant action."

"This Paris of yours," said Eugène in disgust, "is nothing but a cesspool."

"And a very strange one, too," said Vautrin. "If it dirties your carriage as you pass, you're respectable. If it dirties your feet, you're a rogue. Hook a mere trifle up out of it, and you're put on show in the law courts. Steal a million and you're pointed out in every drawing room as a model of integrity. And to keep this system of morality going, you pay thirty million francs a year to the police and the law. Charming!"

"What!" exclaimed Madame Vauquer. "Has old Goriot had his silver breakfast set melted down?"

"Did it have two doves on the lid?" asked Eugène.

"That's the one, yes."

"He must have been very attached to it, he was crying as he twisted it up. I accidentally saw him."

"He thought the world of it," said Madame Vauquer.

"You can see, then," said Vautrin, "the old man really is in a state. That woman knows how to tickle the soul out of him."

Eugène went up to his room. Vautrin left the house. A few moments later, Madame Couture and Victorine got into a cab summoned for them by Sylvie. Poiret offered his arm to Mademoiselle Michonneau, and the two of them went off to pass the two fine hours of the day walking in the Jardin des Plantes.

"There you are, you see," said Sylvie. "They're as good as married. They're walking out together today for the first time. They're both so dried up, if they knock against each other they'll burst into flame."

"You'd better keep away from Mademoiselle Michonneau's shawl, then," laughed Madame Vauquer. "It'll go up like tinder."

When Goriot came in at four o'clock, he saw Victorine sitting under the smoky lamplight. Her eyes were red, and Madame Couture was describing to Madame Vauquer their fruitless call that afternoon on Monsieur

Taillefer. Taillefer, exasperated by their annual visits, had this time received them in order to have things out with them.

"Do you know, my dear," Madame Couture was saying, "he didn't even ask Victorine to sit down? She stood up the whole time we were there. He told me—he didn't lose his temper, he was just very cold—to spare ourselves the trouble of calling on him. He said the young lady—he didn't call her his daughter—was only damaging herself in his eyes by pestering him (*once a year*: the monster!) He said Victorine's mother had married him without a dowry, so Victorine had no claim on him. He said such cruel things the poor child burst into tears. She threw herself at his feet and boldly said it was only for her mother's sake she persevered like this; she'd obey his wishes without a murmur, she said, but she begged him to read her poor mother's last words. Then she took out the letter and handed it to him. She said such beautiful, touching things to him—I can't think where she can have learned them, God himself must have put the words in her head; I cried like a child when I heard her. And do you know what that old horror did while she was talking to him? Cut his nails! Then he took the letter that her poor mother had cried such tears over when she was writing it, and threw it on the mantelpiece, and said: 'Very well!' He was going to help his daughter to her feet, but she tried to kiss his hands and he pulled them away. Isn't it wicked? And his great lump of a son came in and never even spoke to her—his own sister!"

"They must be monsters!" said Goriot.

"And then," said Madame Couture, ignoring the old man's exclamation, "they both went away. They bowed and asked me to excuse them: they were very busy, they said. That was our visit. But at least he did *see* his daughter this time. I don't know how he can say she isn't his, they are as alike as two drops of water."

The permanent residents and the day boarders began to arrive, greeting one another with the flippant banter that in certain circles in Paris passes for wit. Some popular new joke is always the beginning of this; and its effect always lies in some special gesture, or way of pronunciation, or some new and ephemeral piece of slang that will be dead within a month. A political event, a trial in the courts, a popular song, an actor's gag, anything will do to start the game off: a game of battledore and shuttlecock with words and ideas. As a consequence of the recent invention of the optical illusion called the Diorama, which had quite surpassed the earlier Panoramas, artists and their friends had taken to ending every word they thought fit with "rama." A young painter, who regularly dined at the Maison Vauquer, had infected his fellow guests with the habit.

"Well, *Monsieurre* Poiret!" said the museum clerk. "And how's our little healthorama this evening?" Then, without waiting for a reply, he turned to Madame Couture and Victorine, and said: "Ladies, you're upset about something."

"Are we going in to dinnaire?" asked Horace Bianchon, a medical student and a friend of Eugène's. "My little stomach's just about *usque ad talones.*"

"It's perishing coldorama!" said Vautrin. "Move along a bit, Goriot! Dammit, your foot's taking up the whole stove."

"Illustrous Monsieur Vautrin," said Bianchon, "why do you call it coldorama? There's just a healthy little nipporama in the air. That's all it is."

"No, it isn't," said the museum clerk, "it's as cold as hellorama."

"Yes, yes, yes!"

"Here's his Excellency the Marquis de Rastignac, Doctor in Uncivil Law," cried Bianchon, throwing his arm round Eugène's neck and almost throttling him. "Come on, the rest of you!"

Mademoiselle Michonneau came softly in, bowed to the company without speaking, and went over to join the three other women.

"That old vampire always gives me the creeps," Bianchon murmured to Vautrin. "I'm studying Gall's phrenology. I can tell at once the Michonneau woman has the bumps of Judas."

"Ah, you've met Judas, have you?" inquired Vautrin.

"Who hasn't?" said Bianchon. "I swear that pasty-faced old maid reminds me of one of those long white worms that gnaw through pieces of wood."

"But that's life for you, young man," said Vautrin, combing his mustache.

> *"A rose, her life has been a rose's life,*
> *a morning, and no more."*

"Aha! Here comes a mighty brothorama," said Poiret, as he saw Christophe reverently bearing in a tureen.

"Pardon me, Monsieur Poiret," said Madame Vauquer. "That isn't broth, that's soup."

The young men burst out laughing.

"Got you, Poiret!"

"Got you in the eye!"

"Chalk up two points for Mother V.," said Vautrin.

"Did anyone happen to notice the fog this morning?" asked the museum clerk.

"The fog," pronounced Bianchon, "was a frantic and unparalleled fog; it was a doleful fog; it was a melancholy pea-green wheezing old fog. In fact, it was a Goriot fog!"

"A Goriorama," said the painter, "you couldn't see through it."

"Hey, m'lord Goriotte! They d'be talkèn about *yü!*"

Goriot was sitting at the lower end of the table, near the service door. He looked up: he had just been sniffing at a piece of bread under his table napkin, an old professional habit that asserted itself now and then.

"Well," Madame Vauquer called sharply to him, in a voice that drowned the noise of the cutlery, "what's the matter with the bread? Isn't it good enough for you?"

"On the contrary," he replied, "it's made with first-class Etampes flour."

"How can you tell?" asked Eugène.

"The whiteness and the taste."

"The smell, you mean," said Madame Vauquer. "You were sniffing at it. You're becoming so economical these days you'll be living on the smell from the kitchen before long."

"In that case you must take out a patent," cried the museum clerk. "You'll make a fortune."

"Go on with you," said the painter, "he only does that to try and convince us he really used to be a flour merchant."

"Is your nose really a corn-taster then?" asked the clerk.

"Corn-what?" asked Bianchon.

"Corn-crake!"

"Corn-cob!"

"Corn-icle!"

"Corn-elian!"

"Corn-ea!"

"Corn-ucopia!"

"Corn-erstone!"

"Corn-orama!"

The eight replies came like rapid gunfire from all parts of the room, and caused all the more amusement because poor Goriot looked at the diners with the puzzled expression of a man trying to understand a foreign language.

"Corn . . . ?" he asked of Vautrin, who was seated next to him.

"Corn plasters, old boy!" said Vautrin, cramming Goriot's cap down on his head with a smack, so that it covered his eyes.

The poor man, bewildered by this sudden onslaught, sat for a moment without moving. Christophe, thinking he had finished his soup, removed his plate, so that when Goriot, pushing back his hat, took up his spoon he merely hit the table with it. Everyone burst out laughing.

"Sir," said Goriot, "your jokes are extremely ill-mannered. If you take any further liberties with me—"

"Yes?" said Vautrin quickly. "You'll what?"

"Well, one day you'll be sorry for it."

"In hell, do you mean?" asked the painter. "In that dark little corner where they put naughty boys?"

"Mademoiselle," said Vautrin to Victorine, "you're not eating anything. Was daddy very stubborn again?"

"It was horrible," said Madame Couture.

Eugène, who was sitting next to Bianchon, said: "The young lady could take out a summons for maintenance against him, he's preventing her from eating. Do look at the way old Goriot is staring at her."

The old man had forgotten his meal and was contemplating the unhappy young girl. There was genuine sorrow imprinted on her face, the misery of the cast-off child who still loves her father.

"You know, Bianchon," whispered Eugène, "we've been wrong about old Goriot. He isn't a fool or a weakling. You say you study phrenology: try your system on him and tell me what you think about him. I saw him last night twist up a piece of silver as though it were wax; and the look on his face as he did it it was quite extraordinary. There's a big mystery in his life somewhere, and I'm sure we ought to investigate it. It'd be worth doing. No, you needn't laugh, Bianchon. I'm not joking."

"That man's a case for a specialist," said Bianchon. "Very well, if he agrees, I'll dissect him."

"No, just feel his bumps."

"I don't know that . . . Stupidity can be catching, sometimes. We might all get it!"

PART TWO

AFTERNOON CALLS

1

At three o'clock the next afternoon, Eugène, in his smartest clothes, set out to call on Madame de Restaud. On the way he surrendered himself to the wild, capacious dreams that fill young men's lives with such charming emotions. Obstacles and dangers cease to exist at such times; success lies all about them; the mere play of fancy fills life with glamour; and despondency and sadness rise up instantly at the collapse of schemes that have no existence outside their own fevered cravings. If they were not ignorant and timid as well, social life would be quite impossible.

Eugène picked his way along the streets with infinite precaution; he did not wish to get his clothes splashed. But his mind was full of the witty remarks and brilliant conversation with which he was about to entertain Madame de Restaud. Busily he prepared the fine words, the Talleyrand epigrams; minutely he invented circumstances that would favor the declaration upon which he was basing his future. And, alas, poor youth, his clothes did get splashed, and he was obliged to pause at the Palais-Royal to have his shoes polished and his trousers brushed. "If I were rich," he thought, as he changed a two-franc piece he had brought in case of emergency, "I could have taken a cab, and thought in comfort."

At length he arrived at the Rue du Helder and asked to see the Comtesse de Restaud. The cold rage of a man who knows that he will one day succeed had gripped him as he caught the contemptuous glances of the servants who had seen him cross the courtyard on foot, and had heard no sound of a carriage at the outer gate. This was all the more wounding, since Eugène had already felt a stab of inferiority as he entered the courtyard and saw there a fine horse pawing the ground, richly harnessed to one of those dashing gigs that instantly proclaim a life of indolent luxury and an easy familiarity with all the blessings that Paris can provide. At once he felt angry with himself. The witty, well-stocked drawers of his mind snapped shut, and he lapsed into blankness. His name was taken up to the countess by a footman and he waited for a reply in an anteroom, standing on one foot at one of the windows, resting an elbow on the window latch and gazing absently down into the courtyard. He grew bored with waiting and would have taken his leave, had he not been endowed with that southern tenacity that can, when the way ahead is clear, accomplish miracles.

"Sir," said the footman, "madame is in her room, and is very busy. She didn't give me an answer, but if you would care to go in the drawing room, there is someone waiting there already."

Rather admiring the frightful authority with which such people can in one word criticize and condemn their betters, Eugène resolutely opened the door by which the footman had gone to speak to the countess. His intention was to make these insolent lackeys realize that he knew his way about the house; but instead he carelessly blundered into a room containing lamps, sideboards, and an arrangement for warming bath towels; beyond it were a long dark passage and a back staircase. The stifled mirth he heard in the anteroom put the crowning touch to his embarrassment.

"The drawing room is this way, sir," said the footman, with that false respect that always seems like an extra mockery. Eugène stepped back so hastily that he collided with a bathtub; luckily he clutched at his hat in time to prevent it from falling in. At the end of the long passage a door opened, and Eugène heard the voices of Madame de Restaud and Goriot, and the sound of a kiss. He returned to the anteroom, crossed it, and followed the footman into a small sitting room. Noticing that the windows looked onto the courtyard, he went over and looked out. He was eager to see if this Goriot was his Goriot. His heart was beating strangely. He was remembering Vautrin's appalling observations. The footman stood waiting for him at the door leading to the drawing room. Suddenly an elegant young man strode through it, saying impatiently: "I'm going, Maurice. You will tell Madame la Comtesse I waited over half an hour." The young man doubtless had reason for his rudeness; humming an Italian air, he walked over to the window where Eugène was looking out. His purpose in doing so was apparently to inspect Eugène rather than to see into the courtyard.

"But Monsieur le Comte would do better to wait just a moment longer: madame is free now," said Maurice, returning to the anteroom.

At this moment Goriot came out of the little back door by the carriage entrance. He had just held up his umbrella and was about to open it before he noticed that the great gate had swung back to allow passage to a tilbury driven by a young man wearing a ceremonial ribbon. Goriot had just time to leap back in order to avoid being crushed. The rustle of his umbrella had startled the horse; it shied a little and plunged toward the steps. The young man looked round angrily, saw Goriot going out, and nodded to him. It was the strained politeness a man in difficulties shows to moneylenders, or the token of respect insisted on by a disreputable person, which one later blushes for. Goriot replied with a friendly, good-natured wave. The whole scene was over in a flash. Too absorbed to see that he was not alone, Eugène suddenly heard the countess's voice.

"Ah, Maxime, you were going away," she said, with reproach and a touch of resentment in her voice.

She had not been aware of the arrival of the tilbury. Eugène turned quickly round and saw her, coquettishly dressed in a white cashmere wrap. Her hair was loosely piled up on her head in the daytime fashion of Parisian

women. A perfume seemed to emanate from her; she
had doubtless just come from her bath, and her beauty,
thus softened as it were, seemed more voluptuous. Her
eyes were moist. A young man's gaze misses nothing: it
takes in a woman's glamour as a plant takes in its
needed sustenance from the air. Eugène could feel the
freshness of her hands without even touching them. Her
neck was a call to love, and he saw, through the cashmere, the rosy curve of her breast, which the loose folds
of her wrap left partly uncovered. His eyes lingered
there. The countess had no need of a corset, and only a
belt emphasized the slimness of her waist. Her slippered
feet were very pretty. The young man she had addressed as
Maxime bent over her hand to kiss it. Eugène noticed
him for the first time, and the countess noticed Eugène.

"Ah! It's you, Monsieur de Rastignac," she said; and
no man of intelligence could have mistaken the meaning
in her tone.

What the countess conveyed in her voice, Maxime
conveyed by a stare. He looked at the countess and at
Eugène in a way sufficiently pointed to invite the intruder to withdraw. "I say, my dear, I do hope you're
going to send this little ass away." This was clearly and
intelligibly written on the young man's insolent, proud
face. The countess was studying Maxime with that expression of complete submissiveness that unwittingly be-
trays all a woman's secrets. Eugène felt a violent dislike
for the young man. In the first place, his beautiful curled
fair hair showed him how awful his own must look.
Then, too, Maxime's boots were exquisite and clean,
while his own, despite the care he had taken while walking here, had again attracted a little mud. Finally, Maxime had on a coat that showed off his figure smartly and
made him look like a pretty woman; while Eugène, at
half past three, was wearing evening clothes. The bright
child of the Charente felt the superiority given to the
slim, tall, clear-eyed, pale young dandy by his costume.
He was obviously one of those men capable of ruining
fatherless children.

Without waiting for Maxime to speak, Madame de

Restaud passed quickly into the next room, the skirts of her wrap floating behind her, folding and unfolding like the wings of a butterfly; and Maxime followed her. Eugène, furious, followed Maxime and the countess. Thus the three found themselves together before the fire in the great drawing room. The student was well aware that he was annoying the hateful Maxime; but he wished to annoy him, even if he offended Madame de Restaud thereby. Suddenly, as he remembered that he had seen the young man at Madame de Beauséant's ball, the nature of their relationship dawned on him; and with that youthful boldness that leads either to great folly or to great success, he said to himself: "This is my rival, and I intend to beat him." Rash youth! He was unaware of Comte Maxime de Trailles' habit of provoking an insult, drawing first, and killing his man. Eugène too was an able marksman, but never yet had he brought down twenty out of twenty-two clay pigeons, one after another. The young count threw himself into an armchair by the fire, picked up the tongs and began poking the coals so violently, so sulkily, that Anastasie's pretty face at once clouded with anxiety. She turned on Eugène one of those coldly interrogative looks that ask so clearly, "Why don't you go?" that well-bred people automatically rise to deliver what might be called their "exit lines."

Eugène smiled amiably and said: "Madame, I was anxious to see you, in order to—"

He broke off. A door had opened, and the gentleman who had been driving the tilbury came in. He ignored the countess, looked suspiciously at Eugène, and held out his hand to Maxime: "How d'you do," he said in so fraternal a manner that Eugène was greatly surprised. Young men fresh from the country know nothing of the charms of triangular domesticity.

"Monsieur de Restaud," said the countess to Eugène, with a gesture in the direction of her husband.

Eugène bowed very low.

"This gentleman," she continued, presenting Eugène to the count, "is Monsieur de Rastignac. He's related to

Madame la Vicomtesse de Beauséant through the Marcillacs. I had the pleasure of meeting him at her ball the other night."

Related to Madame la Vicomtesse de Beauséant through the Marcillacs! These words, which the countess uttered in a slightly emphatic way, with the pride that a hostess feels in proving that only people of distinction are allowed in her house, had a magical effect. The count's coldly formal manner vanished, and he returned Eugène's bow. "I am glad to make your acquaintance, sir," he said.

Maxime de Trailles also cast an uneasy glance at Eugène and at once dropped his insolent attitude. The powerful mediation of a name had, like a magic wand, unlocked thirty pigeonholes in the southerner's brain and restored to him all his witty prepared speeches. A sudden light broke through the hitherto murky atmosphere of Parisian high society. Goriot and the Maison Vauquer were far from his thoughts at this moment.

"I thought the Marcillacs were extinct?" Monsieur de Restaud said to Eugène.

"Yes, sir," replied Eugène. "They are. My great-uncle, who was the Chevalier de Rastignac, married the Marcillac heiress. They had only one daughter, and she married the Maréchal de Clarimbault, who was the father of Madame de Beauséant's mother. We are the junior branch of the family, and we're all the poorer because my great-uncle, the vice admiral, lost all he had serving the king. The republican government refused to admit our claims when it liquidated the East India Company."

"Wasn't your great-uncle in command of the *Vengeur* before 1789?"

"He was, yes."

"Then he must have known my grandfather, who commanded the *Warwick*."

Maxime shrugged his shoulders slightly, and looked at Madame de Restaud as if to say: "If he's going to talk ships with this young man, we are lost." Anastasie understood. With a woman's admirable resourcefulness, she smiled and said: "Come with me, Maxime. I've something I want to ask you about. Gentlemen, we'll leave you sailing together on the *Warwick* and the *Vengeur*." She rose, and beckoned with satirical perfidy to Maxime, and the two of them moved toward the boudoir. But the two young morganatics (a pretty German expression for which we have no equivalent) had barely reached the door when the count broke off his conversation with Eugène and called crossly:

"Anastasie! Do stay here, my dear, you know I—"

"Don't worry, I'm coming back," she interrupted. "I only want to tell Maxime what I want him to get for me."

She returned almost immediately. All women who are compelled to humor their husbands in order to enjoy complete liberty themselves, know just how far they may go without losing this precious trust, and never offend them in the smaller things of life; and the countess had realized from her husband's tone that it would not be safe to remain in the boudoir. Eugène was the cause of the trouble. And the countess indicated this to Maxime by a cross glance and gesture in Eugène's direction. Maxime responded by saying succinctly to the count, his wife, and Eugène: "Look: you're all busy. I don't want to be in the way. Good-bye." And he made for the door.

"No, do stay, Maxime!" the count called after him.

"Come and dine tonight," said the countess; and once more leaving the count and Eugène, she followed Maxime into the first drawing room, where they remained together until it seemed reasonable to suppose that the count would have got rid of Eugène.

Rastignac could hear them in the next room, their laughter, their talk, their silences. And he maliciously sat on, joking with the count, flattering him and leading him on to new subjects. He was determined to see the countess again and discover the exact relationship between her and Goriot. Clearly in love with Maxime, at the same time managing to rule her husband, and secretly connected in some way with the old merchant, the woman seemed to him a complete mystery. He wished to solve the mystery; it might give him some sovereign power over this eminently Parisian woman.

"Anastasie!" called the count again.

"Come on, my poor Maxime," she said. "There's no help for it. Till this evening . . ."

"I hope, Nasie," he whispered in her ear, "that you're going to drop this little fellow. His eyes glittered like coals when your wrap fell open. He'd be certain to tell you he was in love with you, and compromise you, and I should be obliged to kill him."

"Are you mad, Maxime?" she said. "These little students are just excellent lightning rods, that's all. I certainly intend to make Restaud jealous of him."

Maxime laughed and went off. The countess followed him out and stood at the window in order to watch him get into his carriage, crack his whip, and set his horse stamping. She waited till the great gate had closed after him before returning.

"Did you know, my dear," the count greeted her, "that this gentleman's family estate isn't far from Verteuil, on the Charente? His great-uncle and my grandfather used to know each other."

"Ah, I'm glad we have friends in common," the countess remarked absently.

"We've more than you think," murmured Eugène.

"What?" she asked quickly.

"Well," he replied, "I've just seen a gentleman leaving here, who lives in the next room to me at my lodgings: old Goriot."

At the name, embellished as it was with the word "old," the count, who was poking the fire, threw down the irons as though they had burnt his hands, and rose to his feet.

"Sir, you might at least have said *Monsieur* Goriot!" he exclaimed.

The countess went pale at her husband's show of temper; then she reddened in obvious embarrassment. She replied with forced casualness, in a voice she strove to make natural: "You could not know anyone we're fonder of. . . ." She broke off, and looked at her piano as if it woke an idea in her. "Do you like music?" she asked.

"Very much," said Eugène, who had blushed at the stupefying thought that he had just committed a serious blunder.

"Do you sing?" she asked, going over to the piano and running her hands rapidly over the keyboard.

"No, madame."

The Comte de Restaud was pacing up and down the room.

"What a pity. You're missing a great way to success: *Ca-a-aro, ca-a-aro, ca-a-a-ro, non dubitar*," she sang.

With Goriot's name, Eugène had clearly waved another magic wand, but it had had quite the opposite effect of the words: "related to Madame de Beauséant." He was in the position of a man who has been specially privileged to visit a great collector's house, only to bump clumsily against a showcase filled with statuettes and knock off three or four badly stuck-on heads. He stood there, wishing he could sink through the floor. Madame de Restaud's face had become hard and cold, and her expressionless gaze avoided meeting that of the unfortunate student.

"Madame," he said, "you wish to talk to Monsieur de Restaud, so may I wish you good-bye, and—"

"Any time you care to call," said the countess hastily, interrupting him with a gesture, "Monsieur de Restaud and myself will be delighted to see you."

Eugène bowed deeply to both of them, and went out. Monsieur de Restaud followed him and insisted on accompanying him as far as the anteroom. Once the door had closed behind Eugène, the count turned to Maurice and said: "Whenever that gentleman calls again, neither madame nor myself will be at home."

As soon as Eugène set foot outside, he saw that it was raining. "Well," he thought, "I made a blunder there: why, or how serious, I don't know. And now I'm going to ruin my coat and hat into the bargain. I ought to have stayed in my corner, pegging away at law and concen-

trating only on becoming a common magistrate. What's
the use of my thinking of going into society? To move
about there in any sort of comfort, you need hundreds
of cabs, and polished boots, and gold watch chains, and
white doeskin gloves at six francs a pair for the afternoon, and yellow gloves at night. Damn you, Goriot, you
old fool!"

He had reached the street gates. The driver of a hack-
ney coach, obviously on his way back from taking home
a newly married couple and delighted at the thought of
making a little extra money in his employer's time,
raised an inquiring finger as he saw Eugène standing
there, in his black suit, white waistcoat, yellow gloves,
polished boots, and no umbrella. Eugène was in one of
those blind rages that drive a young man deeper and
deeper into the abyss he has entered, as if it were the
one hope of finding a happy way out. With a nod, he
accepted the coachman's suggestion. He had less than a
couple of francs in his pocket.

He climbed into the cab. A few orange petals and
threads of tinsel attested the passage of the bridal pair.

"Where to, sir?" asked the coachman. He had already
taken off his white gloves.

"Damn it!" Eugène thought, "I've let myself in for it,
I may as well do something useful with it. Drive to the
Hôtel de Beauséant," he said.

"Which one?" asked the driver.

Sublime question! Eugène was dumbfounded by it.
The apprentice dandy did not know there were two
houses of that name, or that his indifferent kinsmen were
so numerous.

"The Vicomte de Beauséant's in the Rue de—"

"Grenelle," the driver interrupted with a nod. "You
see, there's the other one as well, in the Rue Saint-
Dominique, where the count and the marquis live," he
went on, as he put up the steps.

"Of course," said Eugène coldly. "Everyone's making
fun of me today!" he brooded as he threw his hat on
the cushions before him. "This little escapade's going to
cost me a king's ransom. But at least I shall be visiting

my so-called cousin in solidly aristocratic style. . . . Old
Goriot's already let me in for at least ten francs, the old
villain! . . . I'll tell Madame de Beauséant about my
adventure. It ought to make her laugh. . . . I expect
she'll know all about the criminal relations between that
old bobtailed rat and the lovely countess. . . . Anyway,
it's more important to make my cousin like me than to
waste time running after an immoral woman like
that. . . . In any case, she looks far too expensive. . . .
If the fair viscountess's name is so powerful, her influence must surely be mightier still? Let's aim high. If you
want to storm the heavens, you must aim at God!"

These words are but a brief summary of the thousand
and one thoughts that buffeted him about. The sight of
the falling rain restored a little of his calm and confidence. If he was going to squander two of the precious
five-franc pieces that he still possessed, they would be
usefully employed in preserving his suit, his shoes, and
his hat. It was not without a spasm of glee that he heard
his cabman calling: "Gate, please!" A red and gold
Switzer pushed back the groaning house gate, and it was
a sweet satisfaction to Eugène to have his coach pass
under the gateway, swing round in the courtyard, and
pull up under the awning over the steps. The coachman
in his red-bordered, blue greatcoat got down and pulled
out the steps.

As he got out of the cab, Eugène heard a sound of
stifled mirth from under the peristyle. Three or four
footmen had been laughing at the sight of this plebeian
wedding coach. The student understood their laughter
as soon as he saw another coach already there: one of
the most elegant broughams in Paris, harnessed to two
fine, restive horses with roses in their ears; a powdered
coachman, with a smart cravat, held on to the reins as
if the horses were trying to escape. At Madame de Restaud's in the Chaussée d'Antin, Eugène had seen the
smart gig of an ordinary man of twenty-six. In the Faubourg Saint-Germain the resplendent carriage of a man
of rank stood waiting; and thirty thousand francs could
not have bought it.

"Who's here?" wondered Eugène, realizing rather belatedly that there must be very few unbusy ladies in Paris, and that the capture of one of these queens would demand more than kinship. "Damnation! My cousin probably has her Maxime too."

He went up the steps, profoundly depressed. As he approached, the glass door opened; the footmen were now as solemn as judges. The ball he had been to had been given in the great reception rooms on the ground floor of the mansion. He had had no time to call on his cousin between the invitation and the ball itself. This would be the first time he had entered Madame de Beauséant's own apartments. He was thus about to see for the first time in all its glory the individual elegance that reflects the soul and character of a woman of distinction. It would be all the more interesting since he now had Madame de Restaud's drawing room as a standard of comparison.

He followed a footman between the banks of flowers that lined the great, red-carpeted, white-and-gold staircase, up to Madame de Beauséant's room. It was half past four, and the viscountess was at home. Five minutes earlier, and she would not have received her cousin. But Eugène as yet knew nothing of the minutiae of etiquette in Parisian society, and he was still ignorant of her history: one of those spoken biographies whose latest installments are whispered nightly through every drawing room in the town.

Her name had for the past three years been linked with that of one of the wealthiest and most distinguished Portuguese nobles, the Marquis d'Ajuda-Pinto. It was one of those innocent relationships so enchanting to the pair concerned that no intruder can be tolerated. The Vicomte de Beauséant himself had set the town an example, by his respect, grudging or otherwise, for this "morganatic" union. Anyone who, in the early days of this friendship, called on the viscountess at two in the afternoon would always find the Marquis d'Ajuda-Pinto there. She could not shut her doors against visitors; it would have been indecorous. But she would receive them so coldly, and study the cornice with such earnest interest, that they would quickly realize they were in the way. As soon as it became known in Paris that Madame de Beauséant found callers in the afternoon a nuisance, she was granted perfect solitude during that period. She would appear at the Bouffons or the Opéra in the company of her husband and the Marquis; but the viscount, in his well-bred way, would always leave his wife and the Portuguese as soon as he had seen them to their seats.

It was now Monsieur d'Ajuda's duty to marry. He was going to marry a Mademoiselle de Rochefide. In the entire world of fashion only one person was unaware of this, and that was Madame de Beauséant. A few of her friends had certainly made vague references to the fact. She had laughed at them: they were envious of her happiness and wished to disturb it. Nevertheless the banns were now about to be published. And although the handsome Portuguese had come that afternoon with the intention of announcing the wedding, he had so far not dared to utter a single word about it. Why? There is probably no harder task than to present a woman with such a *fait accompli*. There are men who would face an enemy in a duel, a sword pointed at their chest, rather than a woman who, after a steady two-hour flow of lamentation, will pretend to faint and ask for her smelling salts. And so at this moment the marquis was on thorns, and longing to get away. He had been telling himself that Madame de Beauséant would hear the news anyway, that it would be kinder to write to her, it would be easier to deal with this gallant assassination by correspondence than by word of mouth.

It was therefore with a start of joy that he heard the footman announce: "Monsieur Eugène de Rastignac." But alas, a woman in love is even more resourceful in forming suspicions than she is in varying her love making. When she is at the point of being abandoned, she interprets the meaning of a gesture more quickly than Virgil's courser who could divine from a distant stirring in the air the approach of love. And so it must be recorded that Madame de Beauséant had observed her lover's involuntary movement—slight, but so simple as to be frightening.

Eugène did not yet know that you must never call on anyone in Paris without previously extracting from friends of the family a detailed history of the husband, the wife, and the children; only thus may you avoid those momentous indiscretions of which they say so picturesquely in Poland: "Yoke five bullocks to your cart!"—presumably meaning that you will need at least that to get you out of the mud. (If these conversational disasters have no name in French so far, one can only suppose that the wide publicity given to the slightest scandal renders them impossible.) Eugène, fresh from his catastrophe with Madame de Restaud, who had not even given him time to yoke five bullocks to his cart, was probably the only person in the whole of Paris who could have rounded up his team so quickly and driven them straight on to Madame de Beauséant's. Still, even if he had been terribly in the way with Madame de Restaud and Monsieur de Trailles, he was now at least helping Monsieur d'Ajuda out of an awkward situation.

"Good-bye," said the Portuguese, making for the door as soon as Eugène appeared. It was a pretty little drawing room in pink and gray, and its luxury seemed content to be simple refinement.

"But only till this evening, surely?" said Madame de Beauséant, turning her head to look after the marquis. "Aren't we going to the Bouffons?"

"I can't," he said, his hand on the doorknob.

Madame de Beauséant rose and summoned him back. She had taken no notice at all of Eugène, who remained standing on one side. He had been dazzled by the marvelous, rich glitter of the house; it was like being in the *Arabian Nights*. But his hostess had apparently not noticed him, and he couldn't think how to efface himself. The viscountess had raised the forefinger of her right hand and made a pretty gesture toward a stool at her feet. There was such intense tyrannical passion in the gesture that the marquis relinquished the doorknob and came back.

Eugène watched him, not without envy. "It's the man with the brougham," he thought. "But do you really have to have prancing horses and liveried coachman and piles of money before you can get a woman in Paris to look at you?" The demon of luxury gnawed at his heart, a fever for gain seized him, a thirst for money dried his throat. He had a hundred and thirty francs left of his quarter's allowance. His father, mother, two brothers and two sisters, and his aunt, did not, among the lot of them, spend two hundred francs a month. This rapid comparison between his present condition and his distant goal merely added to his bewilderment.

"Why?" asked the viscountess, smiling. "Why *can't* you come to the Italiens?"

"Business! I have to dine at the English ambassador's."

"Get your business over quickly!"

Once a man starts to deceive, he is, ineluctably, compelled to pile lie on lie. And so Ajuda laughed and said: "You insist?"

"Of course I do."

"That's what I wanted to make you say," he replied, with one of those subtle looks that would have reassured any other woman. He took the viscountess's hand, kissed it, and left.

Eugène ran his hand over his hair and was about to wriggle into a bow, thinking that Madame de Beauséant would now look at him; but she immediately jumped up, darted into the gallery, and ran to the window, from which she could see Monsieur d'Ajuda get into his carriage. Listening intently to catch his order, she heard the page repeat to the coachman: "To Monsieur de Rochefide's." These words, and the way in which Ajuda leaped into his carriage, had the effect of a thunderbolt on the poor woman; she came back, a prey to deadly fears. Of all possible disasters in the world of fashion this is the most terrible. The countess went into her bedroom, sat down at a table, took out a pretty sheet of notepaper, and wrote:

> Since you are dining at the Rochefides', and not at the English Embassy, you owe me an explanation. I shall wait for you.

She corrected a few letters which her convulsively trembling hand had distorted, signed it with a *C* that stood for Claire de Bourgogne, and rang the bell.

"Jacques," she said to her footman, who appeared immediately, "I want you to go at half past seven to Monsieur de Rochefide's. Ask for the Marquis d'Ajuda. If Monsieur d'Ajuda is there, you will leave this note for him without waiting for an answer. If he is not there, bring the letter straight back to me."

"Madame has a visitor in the drawing room."

"Ah, yes, of course," she said, opening the door.

Eugène was beginning to feel highly uncomfortable, when the viscountess reappeared, and said to him in a voice whose agitation tugged at his heartstrings: "Do forgive me, I had to write a note. I am all yours, now." She scarcely knew what she was saying, for what she was thinking was: "So he wants to marry Mademoiselle de Rochefide! But does he think he's free? If that marriage is not broken off before tonight's out, I shall . . . But no, it will all have blown over by tomorrow morning."

"Cousin . . ." Eugène began.

"What!" said the viscountess, with a freezing stare.

Eugène understood at once. In the last few hours he had learned so much that he was now on the alert.

"Madame," he corrected himself, blushing. He hesitated, then went on: "Please forgive me. I'm so desperately in need of shelter that a scrap of kinship would have done me a lot of good."

Madame de Beauséant smiled, but still sadly; she could already feel disaster drumming in the air.

"If you knew the situation my family is in," he went on, "you'd enjoy being one of those fairy godmothers who used to like sweeping away obstacles for their godsons."

"Very well . . . cousin!" She laughed. "What can I do to help you?"

"I don't even know. I'm already very fortunate in being even so remotely related to you. But now I'm confused. . . . I can't remember what it was I wanted to ask you. You're the only person I know in Paris. . . . Ah, yes, why I wanted to see you was to ask you if you would accept me as a poor child who wants to tie himself to your apron strings, and would be willing to die for you."

"Would you kill a man for my sake?"

"I'd kill two," said Eugène.

"You child! Yes, you're still a child," she said, struggling with her tears. "*You* could love someone faithfully!"

"Oh!" he said with a toss of the head.

His boastful answer had intrigued the viscountess. The young boy from the south was scheming for the first time in his life. Between Madame de Restaud's blue room and Madame de Beauséant's pink one, he had worked his way through a whole three-year course in Parisian Law: a code never actually mentioned, though it constitutes a system of high social jurisprudence which, properly learned and applied, can accomplish anything.

"Ah, yes, I remember. . . ." said Eugène. "I met Madame de Restaud at your ball, and I called on her this afternoon."

"You must have been rather in the way," said Madame de Beauséant with a smile.

"Oh, yes, I'm an ignoramus. I shall set everyone against me, if you refuse to help me. I'm sure it must be extremely difficult in Paris to meet a young, pretty, rich, smart, unattached woman, and I need one to teach me what you women are so good at expounding: life. I shall always find a Monsieur de Trailles, wherever I go. . . . But I came to ask you to solve a puzzle for me, and to tell me exactly what blunder it is I've committed. I mentioned an old—"

"Madame la Duchesse de Langeais," announced Jacques, interrupting Eugène, who could not repress a movement of intense irritation.

"If you wish to succeed," whispered the viscountess, "you must first learn not to be so demonstrative. . . . Ah, my dear, how are you?" she said, rising to greet the duchess, whose hands she pressed with the affectionate warmth she might have shown a sister. The duchess responded with the most charming caresses.

"Here are two close friends," thought Eugène. "I shall have two protectresses now. These two women must surely both like the same sort of people; this one will also take an interest in me."

"What happy thought brings you here to see me, dear Antoinette?" asked Madame de Beauséant.

"Well, I saw Monsieur d'Ajuda-Pinto calling at Monsieur de Rochefide's, so I felt sure you'd be alone."

Madame de Beauséant neither blushed nor bit her lip; her expression did not change, and her brow indeed seemed to become if anything smoother, as the duchess uttered her deadly words.

"If I'd known you were engaged . . ." the duchess went on, turning toward Eugène.

"This gentleman is Monsieur Eugène de Rastignac, a cousin of mine," said the viscountess. "Have you any news of General Montriveau?" she asked. "Sérisy told me yesterday they never see him nowadays. Has he been to see you today?"

It was generally thought that the duchess had been deserted by Monsieur de Montriveau, with whom she was desperately in love. Her friend's question went right to her heart, and she reddened as she answered: "He was at the Elysée yesterday."

"On duty with the guard," said Madame de Beauséant.

"Clara, I suppose you know," said the duchess, with a look of intense spitefulness, "that the banns are being put up tomorrow for Monsieur d'Ajuda-Pinto and Mademoiselle de Rochefide?"

This was too violent a blow, and the viscountess went pale; but she replied with a laugh:

"That's one of the rumors silly people enjoy putting about. Why ever should Monsieur d'Ajuda confer one of the greatest names in Portugal on the Rochefides? The Rochefides never even had a title till the day before yesterday."

"But they say Berthe will bring two hundred thousand francs a year with her."

"Monsieur d'Ajuda is too wealthy to have to think of things like that."

"But, my dear, Mademoiselle de Rochefide is charming!"

"Indeed?"

"Anyway, he's dining there tonight; everything's settled. I'm terribly surprised to find you know so little about it."

"And what was this blunder you were speaking about?" said Madame de Beauséant, turning back to Eugène. "This poor child has come out into society so very recently, dear Antoinette, that he doesn't understand a thing we're talking about. Be kind to him, and let's leave all that till tomorrow. Tomorrow I'm sure everything will be official, and you'll be able to make any announcements you choose with complete authority."

The duchess turned on Eugène one of those insolent stares that envelop a man from head to foot, flatten him out, and leave him at zero.

"Madame," he said, "quite unintentionally, I seem to have plunged a dagger into the heart of Madame de Restaud. Unintentionally: that's my crime." He had had enough acuteness to sense the biting sarcasm under the women's affectionate interchange. "People go on being received, even feared perhaps, provided they realize exactly when they're causing pain. But a person who wounds without realizing the extent of the wound is looked on as a fool, a blunderer who doesn't know how to use his opportunities; and everyone despises him."

Madame de Beauséant cast one of those melting looks

at Eugène in which the truly great of soul are able to concentrate both gratitude and dignity. Her glance was balm to the wound made in the student's feelings a moment before by the auctioneer's glance with which the duchess had assessed him.

"And, would you believe it?" Eugène went on. "I was getting on quite well with Monsieur de Restaud. You must know, of course," he said, turning to the duchess in a way at once humble and malicious, "that I'm only a poor wretched student as yet, utterly alone, almost penniless, and—"

"Hush, Monsieur de Rastignac. We women never want things other people don't want."

"Oh, well!" said Eugène, "I'm only twenty-one. One has to learn to put up with the disadvantages of one's age. Besides, I'm here in the confessional . . . and I can't imagine a prettier one to kneel in. One commits the sins here that one begs forgiveness for in the other."

A distant look of extreme disapproval came into the duchess's face at the irreverent coarseness of this remark. She turned to the viscountess and said: "The gentleman has just arrived—?"

Madame de Beauséant suddenly laughed frankly at both of them.

"He's just arrived, yes, my dear, and he's looking for a lady to give him lessons in taste!"

"Madame," said Eugène, turning to the duchess, "isn't it natural to want to learn the secrets of the things that fascinate us? Damn," he added to himself, "I'm talking to them like a hairdresser."

"But Madame de Restaud, I believe, is a pupil of Monsieur de Trailles," said the duchess.

"I didn't know anything about that," said Eugène; "that was why I flung myself so blindly between them. But at all events, I was getting on very well with the husband, and I saw the wife would put up with me at least for a little while, when it occurred to me to tell them I happened to know a man I'd just seen leaving the house by a back staircase. I'd heard him giving the countess a kiss."

"Who was it?" the two women asked.

"An old man who lives for forty francs a month in the Faubourg Saint-Marceau, just like me. A real unfortunate, whom everyone laughs at. We call him old Goriot."

"Why, you poor simple child!" exclaimed the viscountess. "Madame de Restaud was a Mademoiselle Goriot."

"Yes, the daughter of a flour merchant," said the duchess; "a little woman who was presented at court on the same day as a pastrycook's daughter. Don't you remember, Clara? The king burst out laughing and made a joke in Latin about flour. He said they were people of—what was it?—people—"

"*Ejusdem farinae*," said Eugène.

"That was it," said the duchess.

"Then he's her father!" said Eugène, with a grimace of disgust.

"Of course; the old man had two daughters he was half crazy about, though the pair of them have more or less disowned him by now."

"Isn't the younger one married to a banker?" said the viscountess, turning to Madame de Langeais. "A banker with a German name, a Baron de Nucingen? And isn't she called Delphine? A fair-haired woman, who has one of the side boxes at the Opéra? She comes to the Bouffons and laughs very loudly to make people look at her—isn't that the one?"

The duchess smiled and said: "My dear, I wonder at your taking any notice of such people. Only somebody as madly in love as Restaud could have let himself get covered all over with flour for the sake of Mademoiselle Anastasie. And he can't have made a very good bargain either! She's in Monsieur de Trailles' hands; he'll ruin her."

"They've cast off their own father," said Eugène.

"Yes, indeed, their father; the father; a father," the viscountess joined in. "A good father, who they say gave them five or six hundred thousand francs each, to make sure they'd be happy and marry well, and only kept eight or ten thousand a year for himself. He believed his daughters would always remain his daughters, and that he'd made two new lives for himself in their homes, two houses where he'd be worshiped and cherished. Within a couple of years his sons-in-law had turned their backs on him as if he were the lowest of the low. . . ."

Tears came to Eugène's eyes. The pure, sacred emotions of family life had recently refreshed his spirits; he still clung to the charming convictions of youth; and this was only his first day on the battlefield of Parisian civilization. Deep feeling is so communicative that for a moment the three looked at each other in silence.

"Yes," said Madame de Langeais. "God knows it all seems strange and horrible. Yet we see it every day. Is there no reason for it? Tell me, Clara, have you ever thought exactly what a son-in-law is? A son-in-law is a man for whose sake we bring up, you or I, a dear little creature we feel bound to by a thousand ties, and who for seventeen years will be the joy of her family—she'll be what Lamartine calls its 'soul unsullied'—and who after that time, will be its plague. Once a husband has taken her from us, he will begin to use his love as an ax to cut out, root and branch, all the feelings that attached her to her family. Yesterday, our daughter was everything in the world to us, and we to her. Tomorrow she becomes our enemy. Isn't this a tragedy we see happening every day? In one place you find a daughter-in-law being outrageously insolent to a father-in-law who has sacrificed everything for his son. In another, a son-in-law turns his mother-in-law out of doors. I hear people complain that there's nothing dramatic about society nowadays; but the son-in-law drama is terrifying—to say nothing of all the marriages we know of that have turned into farces. I know all about what happened to that old flour merchant. I seem to recall that Foriot—"

"Goriot, madame."

"Yes, this Moriot was chairman of his district during the Revolution. He was in on the secret of the great famine, and he began piling up a fortune by selling flour at ten times the price he paid for it. He could get all the

flour he wanted. My grandmother's steward used to sell
it to him for enormous sums. Like all those people, this
Moriot was certainly in with the Committee for Public
Safety. I remember my grandmother's steward telling
her that she could feel quite safe at Grandvilliers because her corn was such an excellent civic passport. Well,
this Loriot, who sold corn to the cutthroats, had only
one passion. He adores his daughters, they say. He
roosted the elder with the Restauds, and grafted the
other on to the Baron de Nucingen, a rich banker who
claims to be a royalist. As you can imagine, under the
Empire, the sons-in-law weren't too high and mighty to
have the old '93 man about the place. That would go
down very well under Bonaparte. But as soon as the
Bourbons came back, the old man began to get on Restaud's nerves and even more on the banker's. The
daughters, who were possibly still fond of their father,
hoped to be able to run with the hare and hunt with the
hounds, and keep both father and husband; they used to
receive Goriot when there was no one else there. They'd
make up little affectionate excuses. 'Papa dear, come
and see us at *such and such* a time, it'll be nicer, we can
be alone.' And so on. . . . My dear, I believe that real
feeling always has eyes and brains: poor old Ninety-
three's heart must have bled when all this happened. He
saw his daughters were ashamed of him; he knew that
if they loved their husbands, then he must be embarrassing his sons-in-law.

"Someone had to make a sacrifice. And he was the
one—because he was a father. He went into voluntary
exile. . . . And when he saw his daughters were happy,
he realized he'd done the right thing. The father and the
daughters were all accomplices in this little crime. And
we see the same thing everywhere. Old Doriot would
have been nothing more than a grease spot in his daughters' drawing rooms. He'd have felt in the way there,
he'd have been distressed. And what's happened to this
father can happen to the prettiest woman in the world.
If she begins to bore the man she loves, he goes away,
he resorts to subterfuges to escape her. It can happen

to any of our feelings. The human heart is like a treasure-house: empty it at one go, and you're ruined. We are as hard on a feeling for showing itself too completely as we are on a man for not having any money. This father had given everything. For twenty years he'd given his life-blood, his love; he'd given his whole fortune away in one day. And once they'd squeezed the lemon dry, his daughters threw the peel in the gutter."

"Society is monstrous," said the viscountess, plucking at the threads of her shawl and not looking up, for she was touched to the quick by the words Madame de Langeais had aimed at her in telling this story.

"Monstrous? No," said the duchess. "That's its way, that's all. If I talk like this it's simply to show that I'm not taken in by society. I think as you do," she said, pressing the viscountess's hand. "Society is a quagmire. We must try and keep safely on higher ground." She rose, kissed Madame de Beauséant on the forehead, with the words: "You are very beautiful at this moment, my dear. I have never seen such pretty roses in your cheeks." Then, with a slight bow to Eugène, she went out.

"Old Goriot is sublime!" said Eugène, remembering how he had seen him twisting the silver in the night.

Madame de Beauséant did not hear; she was lost in thought. Some moments went by in silence, and the poor student, in a kind of ashamed stupor, felt he could neither go, nor stay, nor speak.

"Society is monstrous and wicked," the viscountess said at last. "The moment misfortune comes to one, there's always a friend ready to come and tell one, ready to come and stick a dagger into one's heart and ask one to admire the hilt. Sarcasm and mockery, already! Ah! But I shall not give in!" She raised her head like the great lady she was, and her proud eyes were bright.

"Ah!" she said, seeing Eugène, "you are still there!"

"Still," he said pathetically.

"Well, Monsieur de Rastignac; treat society as it deserves to be treated! You want to be a success: I will help you. You shall really find out how corrupt the women are here, and how despicably vain the men. I've read very extensively in the book of society, but there were apparently still a few pages I didn't know. Now I know them all. The more coldly you calculate, the further you'll go. Strike without pity; and you'll be feared. Look on men and women simply as post-horses, and leave them behind as soon as they're exhausted. In that way you'll reach your goal. And another thing: you will never get on here without a woman to look after you. She must be young, and rich, and fashionable. And if you have any real feeling, hide it like treasure. Never let anyone suspect it, or you'll be lost. You won't be the executioner any longer, you'll be the victim. If you ever fall in love, don't show it! Don't ever divulge it till you are absolutely certain you know whom you're opening your heart to. If you want to make plans to preserve your love—I know it doesn't exist yet—then learn to distrust everyone round you.

"Listen, Miguel . . ." (the name slipped out innocently, and she did not notice the error) "there is something even more horrible than a father being deserted by two daughters who wish he were dead: it's the rivalry between two sisters. Restaud comes from a good family, they've accepted his wife, she's been presented at court. But her sister, her rich sister, the beautiful Madame Delphine de Nucingen, married to a man of enormous wealth, is half dead with vexation and envy. There's an immense gulf between her and her sister; they're not sisters any more. They've disowned each other. Just as they've disowned their father.

"Now, Madame de Nucingen would lick the dirt all the way from the Rue Saint-Lazare to the Rue de Grenelle, to be allowed into my drawing room. She thought Monsieur de Marsay would help her achieve that, so she became Marsay's slave. And she bores him to death. He doesn't care two straws for her. If you introduce her to me, you'll be her little favorite, she'll worship you. Love her afterward, if you can; if not, just make use of her. I'll receive her a couple of times, at some large reception, say, when there are hundreds of other people here.

But I won't have her here in the daytime. I'll bow when
we meet, that will be enough. You've shut the countess's
doors against yourself by mentioning Goriot. Oh, yes,
my dear, you may call there twenty times from now on,
and twenty times you'll find her not at home. They'll
have forbidden you the house. Very well, then, get Goriot to introduce you to Madame de Nucingen. You shall
be the beautiful Madame de Nucingen's standard-bearer.
If she favors you, other women will adore you. Her rivals, her friends, her very closest friends, will all want
to take you away from her. There are some women who
love the men already chosen by other women, just as
there are poor tradesmen's wives who think if they wear
our hats, they acquire our manners. You will have your
successes. And in Paris, success is everything, it's the key
to power. If women think you're clever and talented, the
men will think the same, if you don't undeceive them.
You can go for anything you choose then, you'll have a
foothold everywhere. Then you'll see what the world is,
a collection of fools and knaves. You must try to be
neither. I offer you my name as your Ariadne's thread
to guide you through the labyrinth. Don't discredit it,"
she said, throwing back her head with a regal glance at
the student. "Give it back to me untarnished. And now,
leave me to myself: we women also have our battles
to fight."

"If you should ever need a volunteer to light a trail
of gunpowder for you . . . ?" said Eugène.

"Well?" she asked.

He struck his chest, smiled in answer to his cousin's
smile, and left.

2

It was five o'clock. Eugène was hungry, and afraid he might be late for dinner. This increased the delight he felt in being driven rapidly across Paris. The purely mechanical pleasure left him free to struggle with the thoughts that assailed him. When a young man of his age is treated with contempt, he flies into a violent rage, shakes his fist at the whole world, and vows vengeance; at the same time his self-confidence wavers. Just now Eugène was overwhelmed by the words: "You've shut the countess's doors against yourself."

"I'll call!" he said to himself. "And if Madame de Beauséant is right, and I'm forbidden the house . . . I . . . Madame de Restaud shall find me in every drawing room she enters. I'll learn to fence and shoot. I'll kill her Maxime for her."

"And where will you get the money from?" inquired an inner voice. At once the wealth displayed at the Comtesse de Restaud's shone before his eyes. He had seen there the kind of luxury a Mademoiselle Goriot would naturally hanker after: the gilt, the expensive objects all on show, the insensitive luxury of the newly rich, the wanton extravagance of the kept woman. This fascinating picture was immediately wiped out by the stately mansion of the Beauséants. His fancy, transported into the upper regions of Parisian society, stirred a hundred dark thoughts in his heart; his imagination was liberated and so was his conscience. He saw the world as it is: laws and morality powerless against wealth, and success the *ultima ratio mundi*. "Vautrin is right," he murmured. "Success is virtue!"

Back at the Rue Neuve-Sainte-Geneviève, he ran up to his room and came down again with ten francs for the cabman. He went into the nauseating dining room, where he saw the two rows of diners busily feeding, like animals at a trough. He found the sight of their poverty, the sight of the room, horrifying; the transition was too abrupt, the contrast too complete. He felt his ambition whipped to greater intensity. On one side, fresh, charming images of social life at its most elegant, young vivid faces surrounded by the wonders of art and luxury, passionate minds full of poetry; on the other, gruesome pictures rimmed with grime, and countenances where only the strings and machinery of passion remained. The admonishments, the alluring offers of help wrung, in the first anger of desertion, from Madame de Beauséant, came back to him. The poverty round him underlined them. Eugène resolved to dig two parallel trenches to lead him to success. He would concentrate simultaneously on learning and on love; he would become both a clever lawyer and a man of fashion. He was still a child, and did not know that these two lines are asymptotes, and can never meet.

"You look gloomy, my lord," said Vautrin, with one of those looks of his that always seemed to go straight to the most secret corners of the heart.

"I'm not in the mood to put up with jokes from people who call me 'my lord,'" Eugène answered. "If you're going to be a lord in Paris you need a hundred thousand francs a year; living in the Maison Vauquer isn't exactly a sign of being in fortune's favor."

Vautrin looked at Eugène with fatherly superiority as though to say: "Poor lad, I could eat you at one mouthful." He remarked: "I expect you're in a bad temper because you were unsuccessful with the beautiful Madame de Restaud."

"She has forbidden me the house, because I told her her father took his meals at the same table as we do!" said Eugène loudly.

The diners all looked at one another. Goriot dropped his eyes, and turned aside to wipe them: "A bit of your snuff went in my eye," he said to the man next to him.

"Anyone who annoys Monsieur Goriot in the future will have me to deal with," said Eugène, looking at the old man's neighbor. "He's worth all of us put together. I'm not referring to the ladies," he said, turning to Mademoiselle Taillefer.

Eugène's remark had caused a sensation. And Eugène had uttered it in such a way as to reduce the rest of the table to silence; all except Vautrin, who observed satirically: "If you're going to take old Goriot under your wing and be his exclusive protector you'll have to learn to use a sword and pistols."

"So I will," said Eugène.

"And you've opened your campaign today?"

"Possibly," replied Eugène. "But I don't have to account for my actions to anyone; especially as I don't try to guess what other people are up to at night."

Vautrin shot a sidelong glance at him. "My lad," he said, "if you don't want to be taken in by puppet shows, you must go right behind the scenes, and not be satisfied with peeping through holes in the tent. That'll do," he added, seeing Eugène about to flare up. "We'll have a little talk together whenever you're ready."

The meal grew oppressive and chilly. Goriot, plunged into deep misery by the student's remark, did not realize that the general attitude to him had undergone a change, and that a young man powerful enough to silence his tormentors had offered to protect him.

"Do you mean," whispered Madame Vauquer, "that Monsieur Goriot is actually the father of a countess, then?"

"And a baroness," replied Eugène.

"Fatherhood's the only thing he's capable of," Bianchon whispered to Eugène. "I felt his bumps; he's only got one, the paternity bump. He must be the Eternal Father."

Eugène was too preoccupied to be amused at Bianchon's flippancy. He was determined to make good use of Madame de Beauséant's advice, and was wondering where and how he was to find money. It was depressing that the savannahs of society now unfolding before him should be fruitful and barren at the same time. When dinner was over, he was left alone in the dining room with Goriot.

"So you saw my daughter?" said the old man, in a trembling voice.

Wakened from his meditation, Eugène took Goriot's hand and looked at him with something like compassion: "You are a brave, noble man," he said. "We'll talk about your daughters later on." He rose, without waiting for further comment from Goriot, and went up to his room and wrote the following letter to his mother:

Dearest Mother:

  Can you, I wonder, help your babe-in-arms even more than you've done already? I am in a position where I may be able to make my fortune very quickly. I need 1200 francs, and I must have them whatever happens. Don't tell father I have asked you, he would perhaps be against it, and if I don't get the money I shall be so desperate I shall feel like blowing my brains out. I'll explain the reasons as soon as I see you: it would take me volumes to describe the situation I'm in. I've not been gambling, dear Mother, and I'm not in debt; but if you really want to preserve the life you gave me, you must find this sum for me.

  You see, I have begun to call on the Vicomtesse de Beauséant, who has taken me under her wing. So I have to go into society, and I haven't even the money to get myself a decent pair of gloves. I'm quite able to live on bread and water, I can go hungry if necessary; but I can't manage without the tools they use to work the vines in these parts. I must either make my way, or stay in the gutter forever. I know all the hopes you've put in me, and I hope I shall quickly fulfill them. Dear kind Mother, couldn't you sell some of your old jewelry? I'll soon replace it. I know the family position well enough to be able to appreciate such sacrifices, and you will know I don't ask you to make them just for nothing. I'd be a monster if I did. It is only overriding necessity that makes me beg like this. Our whole future depends on this *subsidy,* without which I can't begin my campaign; and life in Paris is a perpetual battle. If, to make up the full sum, there is no other way than to sell Aunt's old lace, tell her I'll send her some more, much better, later on. . . . *Et cetera.*

Next he wrote to his two sisters and asked them for their savings. He knew they would make the sacrifice for him gladly and unhesitatingly, but he appealed to their delicacy not to mention it to the rest of the family. He played on the strings of honor, so well tuned and so resonant in the hearts of the young. All the same, once the letters were written he could not repress a feeling of apprehension. His heart was pounding, and he was trembling. The young adventurer knew the spotless nobility of those two souls, buried away down there in their solitude. He knew what distress he would cause his sisters—but he also knew what joy they would have in their secret conversations at the bottom of the orchard, about him, their beloved brother.

His spirits rose steeply, and he imagined them secretly counting over their tiny treasures. He saw them gleefully using all their girlish ingenuity to send him the money *incognito*—a sublime gesture, and their first attempt at deception. "A sister's heart is a diamond of purity, a well of love!" he exclaimed. He was ashamed of having written. How intense their prayers for him would be, how pure their souls, soaring heavenward! And how distressed his mother would be if she were unable to send him the whole sum! And these noble feelings, these ghastly sacrifices were to provide him with a ladder to get to Delphine de Nucingen. . . . A few tears ran down his cheeks: they were the last grains of incense thrown on the sacred altar of Family. He walked up and down in despairing agitation. Goriot, catching sight of him through the half-open door, came in, and asked: "What is the matter, sir?"

"Ah, my dear neighbor, it's simply that I am still a son and a brother . . . just as you are a father. You're right to be concerned about the Countess Anastasie: she's at the mercy of a Monsieur Maxime de Trailles, who will certainly be her ruin."

Goriot withdrew, stammering a few words whose sense Eugène did not catch.

The next day he went to mail his letters. He hesitated till the last moment, but finally dropped them in the box, saying, "I shall win!"—the cry of the gambler, the cry of the great general, the compulsive cry that has ruined more men than it has ever saved.

A few days later Eugène called on Madame de Restaud, and was not received. Three times he returned, and three times was refused admission, although he always went at times when Maxime would not be there. The viscountess had been right.

And the student studied no more. He went to his lectures, answered the roll call and, having proved he was there, disappeared. He reasoned as most students do: he would postpone his studies till the final examinations came round. He had decided to run his second and third years' courses into one; he would study law seriously and in one stretch, at the last moment. And so he would have fifteen clear months in which to navigate at leisure the seas of Paris, learn how to manage women, and perhaps land a fortune.

He saw Madame de Beauséant twice during this week, taking care only to call just as the Marquis d'Ajuda's carriage was leaving. For some days further this famous woman, the most poetic figure in the whole Faubourg Saint-Germain, clung to her victory and managed to delay the marriage between the marquis and Mademoiselle de Rochefide. But these final days, which the fear of losing her happiness made the most ardent of all, could only hasten the catastrophe. The Marquis d'Ajuda, in agreement with the Rochefides, had regarded the quarrel and the reconciliation as a fortunate circumstance. They were hoping that Madame de Beauséant would become used to the idea of the marriage and would eventually agree to sacrifice her afternoons in the inevitable interest of a man's career.

So that in spite of the most solemn promises, repeated daily, Monsieur d'Ajuda was only acting a part; and the viscountess acquiesced in the deception. "Instead of jumping honorably out of the window, she's letting herself be rolled down the stairs," said Madame de Langeais, her best friend. Nevertheless, these final gleams lasted long enough to keep the viscountess in Paris; and her young cousin profited from the fact. She felt a certain superstitious affection for him. He had shown himself full of devotion and understanding in a situation where women find no genuine sympathy or pity in anyone. If a man speaks gentle words to them at such a time, he does so only as an investment.

To be perfectly sure of the terrain before attempting his advance on the house of Nucingen, Eugène needed to know all about Goriot's earlier life. Such reliable information as he managed to collect may be briefly summarized.

Before the Revolution Jean-Joachim Goriot had been a common workingman employed by a flour merchant. He was able and thrifty, and when his employer was accidentally killed in the first uprising in 1789, Goriot was enterprising enough to buy up his stock and set up in business himself in the Rue de la Jussienne, near the Corn Exchange. He had had the great good sense to accept the chairmanship of his district so that his business might be protected by the most influential people in this dangerous period. His wisdom in this had laid the foundation of his fortune, whose beginnings dated back to the days of the famine, real or artificial, that had sent the price of grain in Paris soaring to such prodigious heights. The common people were almost killing each other outside the bakers' shops; meanwhile certain others quietly went and bought Italian *pasta* from the grocers. It was in this year that Citizen Goriot amassed the capital that later enabled him to carry on his business with all the advantages a large reserve of money confers on its owner. What happened to him was what happens to all men of merely average ability: he was saved by his mediocrity. Moreover, his success remained unobserved until the time when it was no longer dangerous to be rich; and therefore he aroused no one's envy.

The corn trade seemed to have absorbed his whole intelligence. In anything to do with corn, or flour, or tailings, whether it involved recognizing quality, or source, or means of storage, anticipating market prices, prophesying the abundance or poverty of a harvest, finding cheap cereals, or laying in stores from Sicily or the Ukraine, there was no one like Goriot. Anyone who saw Goriot conducting his business, or explaining the export and import laws, studying their principles, seizing on their weak points, would have thought that here was a man who could well have become a minister of state. Patient, active, energetic, reliable, and efficient, he had an eagle's eye; he foresaw everything, knew everything, concealed everything. He combined a diplomat's understanding with a soldier's staying power. Outside his own province, a dim, humble shop on whose steps he spent every hour of his leisure leaning against the doorpost, he became once again a stupid, uncouth workman, a man unable to follow an argument, and insensitive to any pleasure of the mind; a man who always fell asleep at the theater.

Such characters are nearly all alike. In almost all of them, you would find a noble passion in the heart. Two exclusive feelings had filled Goriot's heart, had absorbed its moisture, as the grain business had consumed his intelligence. His wife, the only daughter of a rich farmer from the Brie district, was the object of his devoted adoration, his boundless love. Goriot had adored in her a delicate but firm nature, sensitive and gentle, which contrasted sharply with his own. If there is one feeling innate in a man's heart, is it not pride in perpetually protecting someone weaker? If to this you add love, the lively gratitude that all honest men feel toward the source of their pleasures, then you will understand a host of moral oddities.

After seven years of unclouded happiness, Goriot, to his everlasting misfortune, lost his wife. She was beginning to exercise a certain sway over him beyond the sphere of the affections. Perhaps she might have educated that sluggish nature, perhaps have taught it to care for the things of the world and of life. In his new condition, the instinct of fatherhood developed in Goriot to the point of madness. The affection that death had frustrated he transferred to his daughters, who at first gave his feelings complete satisfaction. However bright the proposals made to him by merchants and farmers anxious to bestow their daughters on him, he refused to marry again. His father-in-law, the only man he had ever had any liking for, claimed to know definitely that Goriot had vowed fidelity to his wife even after her death. The people of the Corn Exchange, unable to comprehend this sublime folly, joked about it, and bestowed on Goriot a certain grotesque nickname. The first of them who, in a moment of drunkenness on market day, was rash enough to utter it in his presence received from Goriot's fist a blow on the shoulder that landed him headfirst against one of the pillars in the Rue Oblin. The unreflecting devotion, the suspicious, delicate love Goriot felt for his daughters, was so widely known that one day one of his rivals, who wished to get him out of the market in order to get control of the bidding, told him that Delphine had just been knocked over by a carriage. Goriot, ashen pale, rushed immediately out of the Exchange. For some days he was ill as a result of the painful condition the false alarm had induced. And though he did not lay his murderous fist across the man's back, he drove him from the Exchange by forcing him, at a period of crisis, into bankruptcy.

The upbringing he gave his daughters was of course preposterous. Goriot's income was over sixty thousand francs, and he spent no more than twelve hundred a year on himself. His sole joy lay in gratifying the caprices of his daughters. The very best instructors were engaged to teach them the accomplishments that are considered part of a good education. They had a "companion"; fortunately for them, she was a woman of intelligence and taste. They went riding, they had a carriage, they lived as the mistresses of a wealthy old lord might have lived; they had only to express even the most extravagant wish, and their father would rush to execute it; he demanded no more than a caress in return. Goriot put his daughters on a level with the angels, and naturally, poor man! far above himself. He loved even their acts of unkindness.

When his daughters became of an age to marry, they were allowed to follow their own tastes in choosing their husbands; each of them was to have for dowry one half of her father's fortune. Courted for her beauty by the Comte de Restaud, Anastasie developed aristocratic leanings that took her from under the paternal roof to launch out into high social spheres. Delphine loved money: she married Nucingen, a banker of German origin who had been made a baron of the Holy Roman Empire. Goriot remained among the flour bags. His daughters and sons-in-law were soon horrified to see him continue in his trade, although it was his whole life. After resisting their pressure for five years, he agreed to retire on the proceeds of his business and the profits of the last few years: a capital that Madame Vauquer, when he came to live with her, had estimated as bringing in eight to ten thousand francs a year. He flung himself into the lodginghouse as a consequence of the despair that had seized him as he saw his daughters forced by their husbands to refuse not only to have him live with them, but even to receive him openly.

This was all the information that could be obtained from Monsieur Muret, the man who had bought Goriot's business. The conjectures that Eugène had heard from the Duchesse de Langeais were thus confirmed. So ends the prologue to this obscure but dreadful Parisian tragedy.

PART THREE

ENTRY
INTO SOCIETY

1

At the end of the first week in December, two letters arrived for Eugène, one from his mother, the other from his elder sister. The glad relief that thrilled him at the sight of the familiar handwriting was not unmixed with dread. These two flimsy envelopes would bring life or death to his hopes. It was the thought of his family's poverty that caused him dread; but he had tested their love for him so often before that he had no doubt they would give him the last drop of their blood. His mother wrote:

My dearest boy:

I am sending what you asked for. Make good use of this money, I could never again, even to save your life, find such a sum for you without letting your father know, and that would make trouble here at home. To obtain it would mean mortgaging the property. I cannot, of course, criticize plans I know nothing about; but what are they, that you should be frightened of confiding in me about them? They can't have required "volumes" to explain, one word is enough to a mother, and that word would have spared me agonies of uncertainty. I can't hide from you the dreadful effect your letter had on me. My dear son, what can possibly have led you to frighten me in this way? You must have been suffering when you wrote, I can tell from the way I suffered on reading it.

What *is* this career you are embarking on now? Are

97

you going to throw away your life and happiness, pretending to be something you are not, and going about with people you can't possibly mix with without spending money you can't afford, and wasting valuable time from your studies? My good Eugène, believe your mother's love when I say twisted ways never lead to good. Patience and resignation ought to be the virtues of young men in your position.

I'm not reproaching you, and I wouldn't like this gift we send you to bring any bitterness with it. I am only speaking like a mother, who is trusting, but cautious too. I know you know what your duties are, and I know too that your heart is pure and your intentions excellent. So I can say without fear: Press on, my darling. I am worried simply because I'm your mother. But everywhere you go, our loving prayers and blessings will go with you. My dear boy: you must be sensible and grown-up. The future of so many people you love depends on you; and your success will be ours too. All our hopes are for you, and we all pray God to help you in whatever you undertake. Your Aunt Marcillac has been indescribably kind and understanding about all this. She knew what you meant about the gloves. But she gaily said she "had a weakness for elder sons."

Dear Eugène: love your aunt, I won't tell you all she's done for you, till after you've succeeded. If I did, her money would burn your fingers. You children can't understand what it costs to part with one's little reminders of the past. . . . But what wouldn't we part with, for you? She asks me to send you a kiss on the brow from her, and hopes that kiss will bring you the strength to be happy. The kind good woman would have written herself if it were not for the rheumatism in her fingers. Your father is well. The 1819 harvest is better than we had dared hope.

Good-bye, dear boy. I won't say anything about the girls, because Laure is writing to you. I'll leave her the pleasure of letting you know all the news from home. Heaven bring you success! Ah, yes, do succeed, my dear

Eugène, you've taught me a suffering I could not endure a second time. I know now at last what it means to be poor, and to long for wealth to give to my son. But I mustn't go on. . . . Good-bye. Don't leave us without news. Your mother sends you a loving kiss.

By the time he had read to the end, Eugène was in tears. He thought of Goriot destroying his silver and selling it to pay his daughter's debts. "Your mother has destroyed her jewels!" he told himself. "Your aunt must have wept over the relics she sold for you. What right have you to condemn Anastasie? You're only doing for your own selfish future what she did for her lover! Who is worse, she or you?" His insides felt gnawed by a feeling of intolerable heat. He wanted to turn his back on society; he wanted not to accept the money. He felt that fine, noble, secret remorse whose quality is rarely taken into account by men as they judge their fellows, but which persuades the angels in heaven to pardon men whom their earthly judges have condemned.

He opened the letter from his sister; and its innocent and charming phrases brought comfort to his heart:

Your letter came just at the right moment, dear brother. Agathe and I wanted to spend our money in so many different ways that in the end we didn't know what to decide to buy. You were like the King of Spain's servant when he stopped all his master's watches; you have restored harmony. It's quite true! We'd been continually squabbling about what, out of all the things we wanted, we ought to settle on, and we'd never once thought, dear good Eugène, of something that would satisfy all our requirements. Agathe simply jumped for joy. We were like two madwomen all day, "so much so" (as Aunt says) that Mother put on her strict expression and said: "Young ladies, whatever is the matter with you?" If she'd really scolded us, I believe we'd have liked it even more. Ah! What pleasure it must be to a woman to suffer for the one she loves! I was the only one who felt worried in the midst of all our joy. I'm sure I'll make a bad wife, I'm so extravagant. I'd bought myself two belts, and a nice bodkin to pierce the eyeholes in my stays, the silliest waste of money, so I didn't have as much left as that fat Agathe, who's careful and hoards up money like a magpie. She had 200 francs! And I, poor friend, have only 150. I'm punished for it, I could have thrown my belts down the well, it'll be sheer torture wearing them now. I've robbed you.

Agathe was sweet about it. She said: "Let's send the 350 francs and say it's from both of us." But I haven't been telling you exactly how everything happened. Do you know what we did to carry out your instructions? We took our glorious money and went out for a walk, and as soon as we were on the high-road we ran all the way to Ruffec and handed the money right over to Monsieur Grimbert, the head of the Royal Mail Office. We flew back home like swallows. "Is it happiness that makes us so light?" Agathe asked. We said, oh, so many things I shan't repeat to you (Monsieur Parisien) too many of them were about yourself. Oh, dear brother, we do love you, that's all. As to keeping it secret, Aunt says little *masks* like us are capable of anything, even of keeping quiet.

Mother and Aunt have been on a mysterious visit to Angoulême and have both preserved silence on the political reason for the journey. They decided to go only after long meetings from which we and Monsieur le Baron were excluded. Great rumors are flying about in the State of Rastignac.

The openwork sprig muslin robe which the Infantas are embroidering for Her Majesty the Queen is progressing in the utmost secrecy, we have only two more widths to do. It's been decided that the wall they were going to build down at Verteuil is to be a hedge instead. The lower orders will lose fruits and vines thereby, but visitors will enjoy a fine view.

If the Heir Presumptive is in need of handkerchiefs, he is advised that the dowager Princess of Marcillac, excavating her treasuries and trunks (known as Pompeia and Herculanum) has unearthed a piece of cambric she didn't know she had, and that the Princesses Agathe and Laure are ready to place their thread, their needles, and four rather red hands at his disposal. The two young princes, Don Henri and Don Gabriel, continue in their deadly habits of stuffing themselves with jam, annoying their sisters, refusing to learn anything, bird's-nesting, making a row, and cutting osiers, in defiance of state regulations, to make switches with. The papal nuncio, vulgarly known as Monsieur le Curé, threatens them with excommunication if they persist in neglecting the holy canons of grammar for the ones they use when playing soldiers. Good-bye, dear brother: never did a letter bear so many prayers nor so much gratified affection. The things you will have to tell us, when next you come home! And you can tell me *all*, I'm the elder. Aunt has hinted you are having a great success in society:

"A lady's name is said: the rest is silence." (I mean, of course, when *we're* there!)

One other thing, Eugène, if you'd like us to, we can do without handkerchiefs and could make you some shirts. Let me know at once about this. If you need fine, well-made shirts straightaway we'll have to start at once. And if there are any fashions in Paris we don't know about, could you send us a pattern, especially for the cuffs? Good-bye, good-bye! I send a kiss for the left side of your forehead, the temple exclusively dedicated to myself. I leave the other leaf of this for Agathe, who promises not to read anything I've said. Though, to be on the safe side, I shall stay with her while she writes.

Your loving sister,
Laure de Rastignac

"Ah, yes!" said Eugène, "yes, success, whatever the cost! No wealth on earth could repay such devotion. I'd like to lay every imaginable happiness at their feet, all at the same time. Fifteen hundred and fifty francs!" he thought, after a pause. "Every penny must be made to tell! Laure is right—trust a woman!—my shirts are all thick linen ones. A girl's as knowing as a thief when she wants to make someone else happy. Undemanding for herself, thoughtful for me, she's like the angel who forgives the faults of mortals without understanding them."

The world was his! Already his tailor had been sent for, sounded, and won over. After seeing Maxime de Trailles, Eugène had begun to realize the influence a tailor can exercise over a young man's life. He is either a mortal enemy or a friend, and alas, there is no middle term between the two extremes. Eugène's tailor was one who understood the paternal aspect of his trade and regarded himself as a hyphen between a young man's past and future. The grateful Eugène was eventually to make the man's fortune by one of those remarks at which he was in later years to excel: "I know two pairs of his trousers that have each made matches worth twenty thousand francs a year."

Fifteen hundred and fifty francs, and all the clothes he cared to have! At this point the poor southerner felt all doubts vanish. He went down to breakfast with that indefinable air about him which the possession of even the smallest sum of money gives a young man. The moment money slips into a student's pocket, an imaginary pillar rises inside him for him to lounge against. His movements are freer, his deportment improves, he looks people frankly in the face, he has space to move about in. Yesterday shy and humble, expecting blows; today he could strike a prime minister. Remarkable things go on inside him. He wants the world, and can have the world. He is wayward, gay, generous, expansive; the fledgling of yesterday has learned to stretch his wings. When he is penniless, a young man will snatch his crumb of pleasure like a dog that faces a thousand dangers to sneak a bone, crunches it, sucks the marrow from it, and scurries off again. But a young man who can jingle a few fleeting gold pieces in his pocket lingers over his pleasures, savors every detail of them, luxuriates in them, floats on clouds, and forgets even the meaning of the word "poverty." All Paris is his. Oh, age when ev-

erything shines and flames and glitters! Age of joyful
strength that no one makes the most of, neither man nor
woman! Age of debts and mortal fears, all of them ten
times enhancing every delight! No man unfamiliar with
the left bank of the Seine, between the Rue Saint-
Jacques and the Rue des Saints-Pères, knows a thing
about human life! "Ah! If the women of Paris did but
know!" thought Eugène, gulping down Madame Vauquer's stewed pears at a farthing apiece, "they'd all
come here in search of love!"

The gate bell rang, and a postman from the Royal
Mail appeared in the dining room. He asked which was
Monsieur Eugène de Rastignac, and handed him two
moneybags and a receipt to sign. Eugène felt a look
from Vautrin dart at him like the stroke of a whip.

"Now you'll be able to pay for your fencing and shooting lessons," he remarked.

"Your ships have come home," said Madame Vauquer, eying the bags.

Mademoiselle Michonneau did not dare to look at the
money, for fear of showing her covetousness.

"You have a good mother," said Madame Couture.

"Monsieur Eugène has a good mother," echoed Poiret.

"Yes, mummy has bled herself," said Vautrin. "Now
you'll be able to have your fling in society, and fish for
dowries, and dance with the peach-blossom countesses.
But take my tip, young man, learn to shoot." He
sketched the movement of a man taking aim at an
enemy.

Eugène wished to give the postman a tip, but found
nothing in his pocket. Vautrin fumbled in his, and threw
the man a one-franc piece. "Your credit's good," he
told Eugène.

Eugène was obliged to thank him, though ever since
their sharp exchange on the day he had come back from
seeing Madame de Beauséant, he had found the man
unbearable. During the whole eight days, they had been
silent in each other's company. Eugène could not discover why. Intellectual ideas project themselves according to the forcefulness of their conception, and land

where the brain directs them, by a mathematical law comparable to that which governs the firing of a shell from a mortar. Various are the effects thereof. There are impressionable minds in which new ideas lodge and wreak havoc. And there are heavily fortified minds, skulls with ramparts of brass, against which the will of another person flattens out and drops like a bullet against a wall. Again, there are woolly, flabby minds, where other people's ideas are deadened like gunshot in the soft earth of a redoubt.

Eugène had one of those heads full of gunpowder, which blow up at the lightest shock. He was too young and eager not to be susceptible to the contagion of ideas and feelings that cause us to be unconsciously affected by so many strange phenomena. His mental vision had the same far, clear range as his lynxlike eyes. Indeed, all of his inner senses had the same mysterious reach, the flexibility in attack and recoil that always surprises us in men of character, who, like expert fencers, can find the weak spot in any armor.

Moreover, in the last month Eugène's qualities had developed no less remarkably than his faults. His faults were demanded of him by society and the achievement of his growing ambitions. Among his qualities was that southern vivacity that makes its owner drive straight at any problem to be solved, and never allows a man from south of the Loire to tolerate the slightest uncertainty. This quality is considered by men from the north as a fault: they point out that even if it was the source of Murat's success, it was also the cause of his death. It follows naturally from this that when a southerner is able to combine the cunning of the north with the boldness of beyond the Loire, he is a full man: he may even win the crown of Sweden. Eugène could therefore not bear to remain long under fire from Vautrin's batteries without attempting to find out if the man were his friend or his enemy. At every turn it seemed to him that this singular character probed into his feelings and read his heart, while remaining himself impenetrable. Vautrin had the motionless profundity of a sphinx who knows and sees everything and says nothing. But now that Eugène's pockets were full of money, he rebelled.

"Do you mind waiting a moment?" he said, as Vautrin got up to go out, after lingering over the last mouthful of his coffee.

"What for?" asked Vautrin, as he put on his wide-brimmed hat and took up his swordstick. He had a habit of twirling this in the air from time to time as though challenging a gang of footpads.

"I want to pay my debt," said Eugène, untying one of the bags and counting out a hundred and forty francs for Madame Vauquer. " 'Short reckonings make long friends,' " he said to her. "Now I'm paid up till New Year's Day. Can you change me this five-franc piece?"

"Long friends make short reckonings," Poiret echoed, with a glance at Vautrin.

"Here's your franc," said Eugène, handing the coin to the black-wigged sphinx.

"Anyone would think you were afraid to be in my debt," said Vautrin, with a searching look at Eugène and one of the cynical smiles that had exasperated the young man so often before.

"Of course," he replied. He had risen, with his two bags in his hand, to go up to his room. Vautrin was going out by the door into the sitting room, while Eugène was about to leave by the door into the little hall by the staircase.

"Do you realize that what you just said to me, Monsieur le Marquis de Rastignacorama, wasn't exactly polite?" said Vautrin, shutting the drawing-room door sharply and coming over to the young man. Eugène looked at him coldly, and then, closing the dining-room door behind them, drew Vautrin into the little hall. Here there was a door leading to the garden, with an iron-barred window above it. Sylvie, emerging from the kitchen at this moment, heard Eugène say: "*Monsieur* Vautrin, I am not a marquis and my name isn't Rastignacorama!"

"They're going to fight," said Mademoiselle Michonneau indifferently.

"Fight!" echoed Poiret.

"Surely not," murmured Madame Vauquer, fondling her pile of francs.

"But they're going down there under the linden trees!" exclaimed Victorine, looking out through the window into the garden. "Oh, the poor young man! And he was in the right, too!"

"Let us go upstairs, my dear," said Madame Couture. "It's none of our business."

They got up to go, but the large figure of Sylvie was blocking the doorway. "What's going on now?" she asked. "I just heard Monsieur Vautrin say to Monsieur Eugène: 'We've got to get this straight,' he said, and there they are trampling all over our artichokes."

At this moment Vautrin reappeared. "Mamma Vauquer," he said with a smile, "don't be frightened, I'm just going to try out my pistols down there under the lindens."

"Oh, sir!" said Victorine, clasping her hands, "why do you want to kill Monsieur Eugène?"

Vautrin stepped back and contemplated Victorine for a moment. Then, in a teasing voice that made the poor girl turn scarlet, he said: "More romances, eh? He's very nice, isn't he, that young man? Good: you've given me an idea. I'll see you're both very happy, my pretty child."

Madame Couture took her young charge by the arm and drew her away, whispering: "Really, Victorine, you're quite impossible this morning."

"I don't want anybody letting off pistols in my garden," said Madame Vauquer. "Don't you go frightening all the neighbors and fetching the police in at this time of day."

"Now keep cool, Mamma Vauquer," said Vautrin. "Never mind, we'll go to the shooting gallery instead." He rejoined Eugène, and took him familiarly by the arm. "I suppose even if I showed you I could hit an ace of spades five times running, from thirty-five paces away, it still wouldn't damp your courage? You seem to me in rather a bad mood; you'd be fool enough to let yourself get killed."

"You're backing out," said Eugène.

"Now don't make me lose my temper," retorted Vautrin. "It's not cold today; let's go and sit down there. I want to talk to you. You're a good little lad and I wish you no harm. I like you. And you can take Trompe—(damnation!) Vautrin's word for it. And I'll tell you why I like you. Incidentally, I know you as if you were my own son, and I'm going to prove it. Put your bags down there." He pointed to the table.

Eugène placed his money on the table, and sat down. He was intensely intrigued by Vautrin's change of manner. A moment ago he'd talked of killing Eugène and now seemed to be posing as his protector.

"You'd very much like to know who I am, and what I've done, or what I do now, wouldn't you?" said Vautrin. "You're too inquisitive, little man. No, no, don't get upset. I shall say far worse things than that! I've had misfortunes. Hear me first, and you can talk after. I can tell you my previous history in a couple of words. Who am I? I'm Vautrin. What do I do? Whatever I like. So let's get on. You want to know about my character? I'm good to people who are good to me, or whose hearts speak to mine. I'll let them do anything to me; they can kick me on the shins, and I don't even say, 'Look out!' But, by God, I'm like Satan with a man who crosses me, or doesn't suit me. And I may as well warn you that I think about as much of killing a man as I do of *that*!" And he spat forcefully on the ground.

"The only thing is, I force myself to kill a man decently, if I do have to kill him. I'm what you'd call an artist. I've read the Memoirs of Benvenuto Cellini. Yes, me, and in Italian, what's more! He was a proper man, Cellini. I learned two things from him: to imitate Providence, who kills us at random; and to love beauty wherever I find it. And don't you agree it's a fine part to play: to be alone against the whole world, and lucky with it?

"I've given a great deal of thought to the nature of your present predicament. . . . My boy, dueling is a game for children, and quite pointless. When there's a couple of living men, and one of them's got to disappear, only an imbecile would leave such things to chance. Dueling? It's a matter of heads or tails, that's all. I can put five bullets through the ace of spades one after another from thirty-five paces away. And when you have a little talent of that kind, you feel pretty sure you can cope with anybody. Well! I once aimed at a man at twenty paces, and missed him. And the fool had never touched a pistol in his life before.

"Look," said this extraordinary man, undoing his waistcoat and exposing his chest. It was as shaggy as the back of a bear and the tawny pelt filled Eugène with a slightly horrified disgust. "The young cub singed my fur," he said, taking Eugène's finger and placing it over a hole in his breast. "But I was a child at the time, I was your age, twenty-one. I still believed in things: I believed in woman's love and all the rest of the nonsense *you'll* soon be getting mixed up in. You wanted to fight me, didn't you? Suppose you'd killed me? Suppose I was in my grave? Where would you be? You'd have to clear out to Switzerland and live on papa's money; and he hasn't got very much. I want to show you exactly the position you're in; to show you exactly how it looks to a man of experience who's examined the problems of the world and sees that there are only two courses open to a man: stupid obedience, or revolt. I take orders from no one: is that clear? Do you know what *you're* going to need, to carry out your ideas? A million; and straight-away. Without that you might as well go and drown yourself, as others have done before you, to try and find out if there's a Supreme Being.

"That million francs . . . I'm going to give it to you." He paused, and looked at Eugène. "Aha! You looked a bit kinder at Grandpa Vautrin, when I said that. (You looked like a girl putting on her best frock and smacking her lips like a cat with a saucer of milk because a man says: 'Till this evening' to her.) All right. I'm ready for you. And this is your present balance sheet, young man. Back at home, there's papa, mamma, aunt, two sisters of eighteen and seventeen, two brothers, fifteen and ten.

That's the crew list. Aunt brings up the girls. Priest comes and teaches the boys their Latin. The family gets chestnut soup for dinner oftener than it gets white bread. Papa has to be very careful with his trousers; mamma can barely rise to one dress for winter and one for summer; the girls manage as best they can. We've a cook and manservant, to keep up appearances, papa being a baron. I know all about it, I've been in the south. That's the way things are there, if they're sending you twelve hundred francs a year, and your little patch of ground only brings in three thousand.

"As for ourself, we're ambitious. We're related to the Beauséants, and we have to walk everywhere to go. We want to be rich, and we haven't a farthing. We eat Mamma Vauquer's stews, and we like the fine dinners of the Faubourg Saint-Germain. We sleep on a truckle bed, and pine for a mansion. I don't blame you for wanting things. Not everyone, my boy, is capable of ambition. Ask women what sort of men they look for, they'll say ambitious ones. Ambitious men have stronger backs, and richer blood, and warmer hearts than other men. And women like to be strong themselves, it makes 'em feel happy and beautiful; so naturally they like men to be even stronger, prodigiously strong, even at the risk of being destroyed by them. I've inventoried your desires like this, in order to ask you a question. The question is this. We're as hungry as a wolf, and we've got sharp little teeth: how are we to fill the pot?

"To start off with, we have our lawbooks to get through: they're not very amusing and they don't teach us anything. But it has to be done. So be it. We become a lawyer, so that we can later be made chairman at an assize court, and send poor devils far better than we are to hard labor, just to prove to the rich they can sleep in peace. It isn't amusing, and it takes a long time. First, a couple of years slouching about Paris, pressing our nose against shopwindows. And it's very tiring to keep hankering after things you never get. If you were just a bloodless slug, there'd be nothing to worry about: but you have the wild blood of lions in your veins, and an

itch to do twenty crazy things a day. You will submit to
this torture, the ghastliest ever known in God's hell.

"And suppose you're a sensible boy, and live on milk
and poetry: noble as you are, you'll have to start your
career—after enough suffering and privation to madden
a dog—by becoming assistant to some idiot in a village
hovel where the government will chuck you a thousand
francs a year, like scraps to a butcher's mongrel. Bark
at thieves, plead for the rich, send anyone with a spark
of life to the guillotine. Thanks very much! If you
haven't any influential friends, you'll stay rotting in your
county court. Round about thirty, you'll be a magistrate at
twelve hundred francs a year, if you haven't thrown in your
hand before then. At forty, you'll marry a miller's
daughter, worth about six thousand a year. Thanks
again!

"On the other hand, if you have a little influence,
you'll be a public prosecutor at thirty, with a salary of
three thousand francs. In that case it'll be the mayor's
daughter you marry. If you play a few dirty little political
tricks, such as making a slip over a name on some docu-
ment or other, at forty you'll be an attorney general,
and may even get into parliament. Observe, dear child,
that we shall have collected a few little stains on our
conscience, have had twenty years' worry and hidden
poverty, and our sisters will be resigned old maids.
Allow me further to point out that there are only twenty
attorney generals in the whole of France, and that there
are twenty thousand of you after the jobs, including a
number of jokers who'd sell their own families to get a
step further up.

"If all this disgusts you, let's see what else there is.
Does the Baron de Rastignac want to become a barris-
ter? Good! Then he must drudge for ten years, spend a
thousand francs a month, have a library, and chambers,
go out into society, kiss solicitors' gowns for briefs, and
lick the High Court floors. If all this led to anything
worthwhile, I wouldn't say don't. But can you show me
five barristers in the whole of Paris who at fifty earn
more than fifty thousand francs a year? Pah! Sooner

than lower myself to that I'd be a pirate. Besides, where would you find the cash to start with? That's not much fun either. There's one possible resource: a wife's dowry. D'you want to get married? That would be a millstone round your neck; and if you marry for money, what about our feelings of honor, our noble name? Better to begin your revolt against human conventions this very day. It wouldn't matter crawling like a snake before a wife, and licking her mother's shoes, and doing things so low they'd sicken a pig, if it was even a way to happiness. But you'd be as miserable as the stones in a sewer, with a woman you'd married on those terms. Better to war with men than grapple with a wife.

"And that's the crossroads of life, young man: choose. But you have chosen. You've called on our cousin Madame de Beauséant, and caught the whiff of luxury. You've called on Madame de Restaud and caught the whiff of a woman of Paris. You came back here that day with a word written across your forehead. I recognized it: *Succeed!* it said: succeed at all costs. 'Fine!' I thought, 'that's the kind of fellow I like.' You needed money. Where to get it? You bled your sisters. All brothers pick their sisters' pockets more or less. Your fifteen hundred francs, scraped together God knows how, in a place where there are more chestnuts than five-franc pieces, will slip away as fast as soldiers out looting. And what will you do then? Work?

"Work, as you understand it at the moment, lands you in your old age at Mamma Vauquer's in a room fit for old boys like Poiret. The problem of quick success is the problem that fifty thousand young men in your position are trying to solve, at this very moment. You are a single one in that battle. Imagine the efforts you have to make; imagine the slaughter! You'll have to eat each other like spiders in a teapot; for we all know there aren't fifty thousand places. Do you know how people get on here? Either by dazzling genius or by skillful corruption. You must either cut through this mass of men like a cannon ball, or creep into it like a plague. Honesty is no use at all. Men bow before the power of genius. They hate it, they try to throw mud at it, because what it takes it never shares; but they bow to it, if it perseveres. In a word, men go down on their knees to it, if they haven't managed to trample it in the mud.

"Corruption flourishes, talent is rare. I mean that corruption is the weapon of countless nonentities, and you will feel it jabbing you everywhere. You will see women with husbands earning no more than six thousand francs a year all told, spending more than ten thousand a year on clothes. You will see clerks earning twelve hundred francs a year able to buy land. You will see women prostituting themselves in order to ride in the carriage of a peer's son on the reserved highroad to Longchamp. You've seen that poor old simpleton Goriot compelled to discharge a bill of exchange endorsed by his daughter, whose husband has fifty thousand francs a year. I defy you to take a simple stroll anywhere in Paris without coming on some infernal piece of graft. I'd wager my head against one of those lettuces there that you'll stir up a wasps' nest in the home of the first woman you fall for, provided she's rich, young, and pretty. They're all of them dodging the law, all of them completely at odds with their husbands. I'd never finish if I started describing all the trade that goes on, on behalf of lovers, or clothes, or children, or housekeeping, or vanity—rarely for any good motive, I assure you. And so any honest man is the common enemy.

"But what do you think an honest man is? In Paris, an honest man is one who keeps his mouth shut, and takes and doesn't share. I'm not referring to the poor drones who do the hard work everywhere without ever getting the slightest reward for their labors, the ones I call the Brotherhood of God's Down-at-Heels. To be sure, that's virtue at the height of its stupidity; but it's poverty too. I can just see the faces those fine people will pull if God plays us the dirty trick of not being there on Judgment Day. So if you want quick success, you must either be rich to start with, or look as if you were. To get rich, what you have to do here is play high. Play low, and you're sunk! In any one of the hundred professions you might enter, if there are a dozen men who get on rapidly, the public calls them thieves. Draw your own conclusions. That's life as it is. It's no prettier than cooking, it smells as nasty, and you can't make a stew without getting your hands dirty. What you have to know is how to wash them properly after—those are the ethics of our age.

"If I talk to you about society in this way, it's because I have the right to, I know it. Do you think I'm complaining? Not at all. It's always been like that. Moralists will never alter it. Man is imperfect. He is sometimes more hypocritical, sometimes less; in which cases, the simple will say he hasn't, or has, principles. In every million of this higher livestock, there are perhaps a dozen daredevils who stand above everything, even the law. I am one of them. If you are above the ruck, go straight forward, and keep your head high. But you will have to fight against envy, slander, and mediocrity, against a whole world. Napoleon was once called up before a war minister named Aubry, who nearly sent him to the colonies. Take your pulse! See if you think you can get up every morning with more determination than you had the night before. If you can, I'm going to make you an offer no one would refuse. Listen carefully. You see, I have an idea.

"My idea is to go and live a patriarchal life on a huge estate, a hundred thousand acres, say, in the southern United States. I want to be a planter there, and have slaves, and make a few nice little millions out of selling my cattle and my tobacco and my timber. I shall live like a king, and do exactly everything I want: a life unthinkable in the plaster foxhole we all huddle in here. I'm a great poet. I don't put my poems on paper: they consist of actions and feelings. I have at this moment fifty thousand francs. That will buy me only about forty Negroes. I need two hundred thousand francs because I shall want two hundred Negroes if I'm really going to satisfy my taste for the patriarchal life. You see, Negroes are just grown-up children; you can do as you like with them with no inquisitive public prosecutor coming to investigate. With this black capital, in two years I shall have three or four millions. If I succeed, no one is going to ask me: 'Who are you?' I shall be Mr. Four-Million, American citizen. I shall be fifty, I shan't be worn out, I shall enjoy myself exactly as I choose.

"Now, briefly: if I can arrange a dowry for you of a million francs, would you give me two hundred thousand? Twenty percent commission—that's not excessive, is it? You will teach your little wife to love you. Once you're married, you'll start to look uneasy, guilty; you'll go about looking very sad for a couple of weeks or so. Then one night after a little fun and games, you'll confess, between kisses, that you're two hundred thousand francs in debt, taking care to murmur 'Darling!' at the same time. This little comedy act goes on every night among the most distinguished young couples. A young woman doesn't shut her purse against the man she's in love with. Do you think you'll lose? No. You'll find a way to recoup your two hundred thousand francs on some business deal. With your money and your brains you'll build up a fortune as large as you can possibly wish for. Ergo, you'll have made, in six months, your fortune, your charming wife's, and good Papa Vautrin's, not to mention that of your family, blowing on its fingers all through the winter for lack of firewood. Don't be astonished, either at what I suggest, or at what I ask! Out of every sixty good marriages in Paris, forty-seven end in arrangements like that."

"But what do I have to do?" Eugène broke in eagerly.

"Practically nothing," said Vautrin, with a gleam of pleasure in his eyes like the mute expression of the angler who feels a fish at the end of his line. "Listen carefully! A poor unhappy wretched girl's heart is like a sponge: it longs for love to soak it through, it expands the minute a drop of tenderness falls on it. To court a young girl living in solitude, despair, and poverty, who never suspects she'll one day come into a fortune! Why, by God, it's like holding a fistful of trumps, or knowing the winning numbers in a lottery, or gambling on the Stock Exchange and knowing the share movements beforehand. You build an indestructible marriage on deep foundations. When the girl's millions come rolling in, she'll throw them like pebbles at your feet. 'Take them, my love! Take them, Adolphe! Alfred! Take them, Eugène!' she'll say, if Adolphe or Alfred or Eugène have had the common sense to make sacrifices for her. And all I mean by sacrifices is selling an old coat to take her out and give her mushrooms-on-toast at the Cadran Bleu, and take her to a theater after; or pawning your watch to buy her a shawl. I don't have to tell you about the scribbles and twaddles so dear to women in love— such as splashing water on the paper when you write from a long way away, to look like tears. You look as if you were well up in that lingo already.

"Paris, you see, is like a forest in the New World, where twenty species of wild tribes swarm, the Illinois, the Hurons, all living by hunting different things. You are hunting for millions. To trap them you use the snare, the blowpipe, the quail call. There are other kinds of hunters too. Some go after dowries; some lie in wait for bankruptcies; some people fish in other people's consciences; some trade newspaper proprietorships, subscribers and all; and any man who comes home with his gamebag well filled is greeted and feasted and received in good society. Let us do justice to the hospitable soil of Paris! You're dealing with the most accommodating city in the world. The proud aristocracies of every capital city in Europe may refuse to admit some crooked millionaire to their ranks; but Paris will welcome him with open arms, flock to his parties, eat his dinners, and drink toasts to his crimes."

"But where am I to find the girl?" asked Eugène.

"She's here, right in front of your eyes!"

"Mademoiselle Victorine?"

"Exactly!"

"What do you mean?"

"She's already in love with you, your little Baronne de Rastignac."

"She hasn't a penny," said the astonished Eugène.

"That's the point. A couple of words more," said Vautrin, "and you'll see what I mean. Papa Taillefer is an old scoundrel who's reputed to have murdered one of his friends during the Revolution. He's one of my bright sparks who have an individual viewpoint. He's a banker, the head partner in the house of Frédéric Taillefer and Company. He has an only son, to whom he means to leave everything he has, in order to spite Victorine. I don't like that sort of unfairness. I'm like Don Quixote, I like to take the side of the weak against the strong. If the will of God were to deprive him of his son, Taillefer would take his daughter back. He must have an heir of some sort—a stupid convention inherent in human nature; and I know he can't have any more children himself. Victorine is sweet and gentle; she'll soon win him round. He'll be humming with sentimentality like a German top. She'll be too grateful for your love to forget you; you'll marry her.

"I myself will take on the part of Providence; I'll make up God's mind for Him. I have a friend I'm devoted to: a colonel from the Army of the Loire, who's just joined the Royal Guard. He always takes my advice; and he's become an ultraroyalist. He isn't one of those fools whose opinions never change. And if I dare give you one more word of advice, my angel, it's precisely that: stick to your opinions as little as you stick to your words. When they're asked for, sell them. When a man boasts that he never changes his mind, he's taking it on himself always to go along one straight line, an ass who believes in infallibility. Principles don't exist, only events. Laws don't exist, only circumstances. The intelligent man weds himself to them in order to control them. If fixed principles and laws really existed, nations wouldn't keep changing them like shirts all the time. A man can't be expected to be better behaved than a whole nation. The man who did the greatest imaginable damage to France is now a venerated idol, because he has always seen everything in red—when the very best he deserves is to be put into the Museum of Ancient Machinery and labeled 'La Fayette.' While Talleyrand, whom everyone casts his stone at, and who has enough contempt for humanity to spit all the curses at it that it deserves, was the man who prevented the partition of France at the Congress of Vienna. We owe him crowns and we give him mud. Oh yes, I know what goes on! I know a lot of men's secrets! Enough. I shall hold an unshakable opinion on the day I find three minds in agreement about the application of a principle, and not before; and it'll be a long wait. In the courts you cannot find three judges with identical views on any single article of the law.

"To return to this man I mentioned. He'd re-crucify Christ if I asked him to. One word from his papa Vautrin, and he'll pick a quarrel with this young lout who never sends his sister a single five-franc piece, and . . ." Here Vautrin stood up, and went through the motions of a fencing master guarding and lunging. ". . . And out with him!" he added.

"But that's horrible!" said Eugène. "Is this meant for a joke, Monsieur Vautrin?"

"There, there, there, keep calm!" Vautrin rejoined. "Don't be a baby. Though if it amuses you, get angry, fly into a temper! Say I'm a monster, a criminal, a knave, a bandit, but don't call me a cheat or a spy! Go on, fire your broadside! I'll forgive you, it's so natural at your age! I was once the same myself. Only, think for a moment. You will do worse some day. You will go and flirt with some pretty woman, and accept money from her. You've thought of it already!" said Vautrin. "Because how are you to succeed if you don't market your love-making? Virtue, dear student, is not divisible. It either is, or isn't. We are told to do penance for our sins. A pretty system, isn't it, that quits you of a crime by an act of contrition? Seduce a woman so that you can get on to a higher rung on the social ladder; sow dissension among the children in a family; practice any of the infamies that are done daily in the home, in the pursuit of pleasure or self-interest—do you consider those to be acts of faith, hope, and charity? Why do we give only two months in prison to a philanderer who in one night robs a child of half its fortune—and hard labor for life to a poor devil who steals a thousand-franc note with aggravating circumstances? Those are the laws for you! There's not a single article in them that doesn't touch absurdity. The gentleman with yellow gloves and yellow words has committed murders where no blood has been spilt; the blood has been *given*. The other man has opened a door with a crowbar—and both are deeds of darkness! Between what I propose and what you'll do one day, there's no difference, apart from the bloodshed. You think there are absolutes in that world! Then disregard your fellow men, and just see how many loopholes there are that you can get through in the Code. At the bottom of every great fortune without apparent source, there's always some crime—a crime overlooked because it's been carried out respectably."

"Don't say any more, sir, I don't want to hear it. It would only make me distrust myself. At present, feeling is the only thing I understand."

"As you please, sweet child. I thought you were tougher," said Vautrin. "I'll say no more. One last word, however." He looked fixedly at the young man. "I have told you my secret," he said.

"A young man who refuses you will certainly be able to forget it."

"Good! I like to hear you say that. I shall find someone less squeamish, you'll see. Remember what I want to do for you. I give you two weeks. You may take it or leave it."

"The man must have a brain of iron!" thought Eugène as Vautrin strode calmly away, his cane under his arm. "He told me bluntly exactly what Madame de Beauséant told me in polite phrases. . . . It was like claws of steel tearing at my heart. . . . Why do I want to get to know Madame de Nucingen? He guessed my motives as soon as the idea occurred to me. . . . This brigand here has told me in a couple of words more about virtue than ever I've learned from men or books. . . . And if there's no compromise in virtue, does that mean I've robbed my sisters?" He threw the bag on the table and sat plunged in numbing meditation. ". . . To be faithful to virtue, a heroic martyr . . . ! Pah! Everyone believes in virtue; but who's virtuous? Nations worship freedom: where is there a free nation on earth? . . . My youth so far is like a blue unclouded sky: to want greatness and wealth . . . doesn't that mean being ready to lie and bow and crawl and stand up again and flatter and deceive? And agreeing to be the lackey of men who've also lied and bowed and crawled in their day? Before you can be their accomplice, you have to be their servant. . . . No! No! I want to work honorably, devotedly. I want to work night and day, and owe my success to nothing but my own hard work. It'll be the slowest possible way to success, but at least when I lay my head on the pillow at night, there'll be no troubling thoughts in it. . . . What can be more lovely than to look at one's life and find it spotless as a lily . . . ? My life and I are like a young man and his betrothed. . . . Vautrin showed me what can happen after ten years of married life. . . . Damnation! My head's going around. I don't want to think about anything; the heart's the best guide. . . ."

Eugène was roused from his reflections by the voice of Sylvie, who announced that his tailor had called. He went to meet him, his two moneybags in his hands, and he was not displeased at the fact. After he had tried on his silk evening suits, he put on his new day clothes, which completely transformed him.

"I'm as good as Monsieur de Trailles now," he thought. "At last I look like a gentleman."

"Sir," said Goriot, coming into Eugène's room. "You were asking me if I knew which houses Madame de Nucingen visits."

"Yes!"

"Well, she's going to a ball at Marshal Carigliano's on Monday. If you can be there, you'll be able to tell me if my daughters enjoyed themselves, and what they'll have been wearing, and everything."

"How did you find that out, dear Monsieur Goriot?" asked Eugène, offering him a seat by the fire.

"Her maid told me. I hear about everything they do from Thérèse and Constance," said Goriot gleefully. He was like a lover still young enough to take pleasure in a stratagem that brings him near his mistress without her knowing it. "*You* will see them!" he said, without trying to disguise his painful envy.

"I don't know yet," said Eugène. "I shall go and see Madame de Beauséant, and ask her if she'll introduce me to the Marshal's wife."

He was thinking with a kind of inward joy of how he would present himself to the viscountess, dressed as he always would be from now on. What moralists describe as the mysteries of the human heart are solely the deceiving thoughts, the spontaneous impulses of self-regard. The sudden changes in character, about which so much has been said, are instinctive calculations for the furtherance of our own pleasures. Seeing himself now in his fine clothes, his new gloves and shoes, Eugène de Rastignac forgot his noble resolve. Youth, when it swerves toward wrong, dares not look in the mirror of conscience; maturity has already seen itself there. That is the whole difference between the two phases of life.

In the last few days, the two neighbors, Eugène and Goriot, had become firm friends. There were psychological reasons for their secret friendship, just as there were for the feelings of antipathy between Vautrin and Eugène. The bold philosopher who wishes to observe the physical effects of our emotions will find more than one proof of their effective materialization in the relations they create between ourselves and animals. No physiognomist is quicker at divining character than a dog is at recognizing whether or not a stranger likes him. *Linked atoms*—a proverbial expression we all use—are one of those facts that linger on in languages. We *feel* loved. The feeling imprints itself on everything in and out of sight. A letter is a soul, so faithful an echo of the speaking voice that to the sensitive it is among the richest treasures of love. Goriot, whose unreflecting passions had raised him to the sublimity of canine nature, had sniffed the pity, the admiring kindliness, the youthful sympathy for him in the student's heart.

Not that this nascent bond had so far led to any great intimacy. If Eugène had expressed a wish to meet Madame de Nucingen, it was not with the expectation of being introduced to her by Goriot himself. He merely hoped for a little useful information. And Goriot had hitherto done no more than comment on Eugène's remarks at the dinner table on the day of his two afternoon calls.

"My dear sir," he had said the next day, "whatever made you think Madame de Restaud was angry with you for mentioning my name? My two daughters are very fond of me. I'm a happy father. It's only that my two sons-in-law have behaved badly toward me. I don't want those two dear creatures to suffer because I don't get on with their husbands, so I prefer to see them in secret. And this little intrigue gives me countless pleasures that a father who can see his daughters whenever he wishes can have no idea of. *I*—you realize—can't see *mine* like that. So whenever it's a fine day, I find out from their maids if my daughters are going out, and I go to the Champs-Elysées and wait for them to pass. My heart leaps up when I see their carriages coming. I admire the way they're dressed, they throw me a little smile as they go past, and it lights up the whole day for me like a burst of sunshine. And I stay there; they have to come back the same way. I see them again! The fresh air has done them good and put color in their cheeks. I hear someone close by say: 'There's a beautiful woman!' and it rejoices my heart. Aren't they my own flesh and blood? I love the horses that draw them, I wish I were the little dog on their laps. I live in their pleasures. We all have different ways of loving: mine does no one any harm, so why should anyone bother about me? I'm happy in my own way. Am I breaking the law if I go and watch my daughters leaving for the ball in the evening? It's terrible for me when I get there too late, and they tell me: 'Madame has just left.' One night I waited till three in the morning to see Nasie, because I hadn't seen her for two days. I nearly died of joy! I must ask you, whenever you talk about me, to insist on how good my daughters are to me. They would heap presents on me if I didn't forbid them. I say: 'You keep your money!

What use do you think it is to me? I need nothing.' After all, my dear sir, what am I? An old bag of bones, whose soul is wherever my daughters are. When you've met Madame de Nucingen you'll be able to tell me which of them you like the better," added the old man after a moment's silence, watching Eugène as he got ready to go for a walk in the Tuileries until it should be time to call on Madame de Beauséant.

That walk was fatal for Eugène. A number of women noticed him. How young and handsome he was, and how well dressed! Once aware of being the object of an almost admiring attention, he thought no further of his plundered aunt and sisters, or of his noble qualms of conscience. He had seen passing over his head the demon it is so easy to mistake for an angel, the bright-winged Satan who scatters rubies and shoots his golden arrows at palaces, who clothes women in purple, and invests thrones with an idiot brightness, however humble their origins; he had heard the god of that crackling vanity whose false glitter we take for a symbol of power. Vautrin's remarks, cynical as they were, had lodged in his heart, much as the ignoble profile of an old clothes-woman is engraved in the memory of a young girl to whom she has prophesied "oceans of love and money."

He strolled about idly till five o'clock, when he called at Madame de Beauséant's. There he received one of those terrible blows against which the heart of youth is defenseless. Until now, he had found the viscountess full of the polished kindliness, the flowing graciousness, that come only from an aristocratic upbringing but are imperfect unless they come also from the heart.

When he entered, Madame de Beauséant said curtly, with an impatient gesture: "Monsieur de Rastignac, I can't possibly see you, at any rate just now. I'm very busy. . . ."

To an observer, and Eugène had quickly become one, her words, her look, and tone of voice were a historical summary of the character and habits of her caste. He recognized the iron hand in the velvet glove, the egoism and selfishness under the breeding, the wood under the polish, the WE, THE KING that extends from the plumes of the throne to the crest of the smallest gentleman. Eugène had been too ready to trust in this woman's nobility. Like all unfortunates, he had put his hand in good faith to the delightful pact binding benefactor and petitioner, whose first article declares complete equality between two noble minds. The kindness that unites two people is a divine passion as rare and little understood as love itself. Both are the overflow of the good heart.

Eugène, however, was bent on getting to the Duchesse de Carigliano's ball, and he swallowed the rebuff.

"Madame," he faltered, "if it weren't important, I wouldn't have come pestering you. If you'll be kind enough to see me later, I will wait. . . ."

"Very well, come and dine with me," she said, a little ashamed at her own harshness. For this woman was in fact as kind as she was highborn.

Though touched by this abrupt change, Eugène said to himself as he left: "Crawl; put up with anything. . . . What must the rest be like, if the best of women can suddenly wipe out a promise of friendship and cast you off like an old shoe? Is it a case of every man for himself, then? It's true her house isn't a shop, and I'm wrong to be dependent on her. But as Vautrin says, you have to be like a cannon ball. . . ."

However, his bitter reflections were soon dispelled in the pleasurable anticipation of dining with the viscountess. And so, almost by fatality, the smallest incidents in his life were conspiring to force him into the career in which, according to the terrible sphinx of Maison Vauquer, he would have, as on a battlefield, to kill to avoid being killed, to cheat to avoid being cheated; where he would have to leave his conscience behind at the entrance gate, put on a mask, sport unpityingly with others and, like the men of Sparta, win the crown by stealing fortune undetected.

When he returned, he found the viscountess restored to her former gracious kindness of manner. They went into the dining room, where the viscount was already waiting. The splendor and pleasures of the table were, as everyone knows, brought to a high perfection under the Restoration; and Monsieur de Beauséant, like many jaded people, had few pleasures left in life save good food and drink. He was an epicure of the school of Louis XVIII and the Duc d'Escars; and his table offered the double luxury of what you ate and what you ate it from. Eugène's gaze had never beheld such a spectacle. He was dining for the first time in a house where social grandeur was hereditary. It was becoming customary to do away with the suppers that under the Empire had always ended a ball; where the military had always needed sustenance for the combats that in those days awaited them out of doors as well as in. So far Eugène had attended only a ball.

The self-possession that was so greatly to distinguish him later in life, and that he was already beginning to acquire, enabled him not to gape in amazement. But the sight of the highly chased silver, the innumerable other details of the sumptuous table, the silent movements of the servants as they waited on him, made it difficult for a man of lively imagination not to prefer this life of perpetual elegance to the life of privation he had that morning determined to embrace. His thoughts wandered back to his lodgings, and he felt such profound horror that he vowed to leave in the new year, not only to live in a decent house, but also to escape from Vautrin, whose great hand he could feel on his shoulder.

When we consider the myriad forms that corruption, out-spoken or silent, takes in Paris, a man of common sense may well wonder what aberration causes the State to put up schools and collect young people in them; and how pretty women can remain respected there; and how the money set out there by the moneychangers doesn't fly magically away from their wooden bowls. And when we further consider how little crime or even delinquency there is among young people, what respect we must feel for those suffering Tantaluses, continually—and almost always victoriously—wrestling with themselves! Adequately treated, the poor student's struggles with Paris could provide one of the most dramatic themes in modern civilization.

Madame de Beauséant kept glancing at Eugène in the vain hope of making him talk; but he would say nothing in the presence of the viscount.

"Are you taking me to the Italiens tonight?" she asked her husband at last.

"Nothing, as you know, would give me greater pleasure," he said, with a mocking gallantry that was lost on Eugène, "but I have to go and see someone at the Variétés."

"His mistress," she said to herself.

"Isn't Ajuda coming for you this evening?" he asked.

"No," she replied distantly.

"Well, if you absolutely can't go alone, let Monsieur de Rastignac take you."

The viscountess looked at Eugène with a smile.

"That would be very compromising for you," she said.

"Chateaubriand says: 'A Frenchman loves danger, because in it he finds a path to glory,' " said Eugène with a bow.

A few minutes later he was at Madame de Beauséant's side, in a fast brougham, speeding toward the fashionable theater. As they took their places in one of the boxes facing the stage, he seemed to have entered fairyland. He saw that all the opera glasses in the house were trained on himself and the viscountess, who looked ravishing. Enchantment was succeeding enchantment.

"You wanted to ask me something," said Madame de Beauséant. "Ah, look! There's Madame de Nucingen three boxes along from ours. Her sister and Monsieur de Trailles are on the other side."

As she spoke, she looked toward the box where Mademoiselle de Rochefide must have been; and not seeing Ajuda there, her face became radiant.

Eugène had been observing Madame de Nucingen. "She's charming," he said.

"But she has white eyelashes."

"Yes, but how slim and pretty her figure is!"

"And those great big hands."

"And lovely eyes!"

"And that long, long face of hers."

"But long faces are very distinguished."

"It's nice for her that something is, then. Look how she keeps fidgeting with her opera glasses. The Goriot comes out in her every time she moves," said the viscountess, greatly to Eugène's astonishment.

As she surveyed the theater with her glasses, Madame de Beauséant did not in fact appear to be noticing Madame de Nucingen, though not a single one of the latter's gestures escaped her. The whole audience looked exquisitely beautiful. Delphine de Nucingen was not a little flattered at the exclusive attention of the young, the handsome, the elegant cousin of Madame de Beauséant; he had eyes for no one else.

"You'll cause a scandal if you keep staring at her like that, Monsieur de Rastignac. You'll never get anywhere if you throw yourself at people's heads in that way."

"My dear cousin," said Eugène, "you have already looked after me most kindly. If you wish to complete your task I ask only one more kindness; it will cost you very little and will be of great help to me. Here I am: caught."

"Already?"

"Yes."

"And by that woman?"

"Why, do you think my attentions would be accepted anywhere else?" he asked, with a penetrating glance at his cousin. "Madame la Duchesse de Carigliano is a great friend of Madame la Duchesse de Berry," he went on, after a pause. "You are bound to see her; will you be kind enough to introduce me, and take me to her ball on Monday? I shall meet Madame de Nucingen there and hurl myself into my first skirmish."

"Gladly," she said. "If you really feel drawn to her so quickly, your love affairs look very promising. There's Monsieur de Marsay in Princess Galation's box. Madame de Nucingen is on the rack, she's heartbroken. There's no better moment to tackle a woman—especially a banker's wife. Those ladies from the Chaussée d'Antin all love revenge."

"What would you do in the same position?"

"I would suffer in silence."

At this moment the Marquis d'Ajuda appeared in Madame de Beauséant's box.

"I'm neglecting duty in order to come and see you," he said. "And I mention that, so that it may not be a sacrifice."

From the sudden radiance of the viscountess's face Eugène recognized the difference between genuine love and the grimaces of Parisian coquetry. He looked admiringly at his cousin, was silent, and with a sigh yielded his place to Monsieur d'Ajuda. "How sublime and noble a creature must be, to love as she does," he thought. "And this man is willing to betray her for a doll. How can anyone bear to betray her?" He felt a boyish rage in his heart. He wanted to throw himself at Madame de Beauséant's feet; he longed for a magic power so that he might bear her away pressed to his heart, as an eagle bears off to its aerie a young suckling kid from the plain.

He felt humiliated to be in this great art gallery with no picture, no mistress, of his own. "The mark of power," he thought, "is to have a mistress and an almost royal rank." And he looked across at Madame de Nucingen as an affronted man looks at his opponent. The viscountess turned round to him and signaled her gratitude for his tact with a flicker of her eyelashes.

"Do you know Madame de Nucingen well enough to introduce Monsieur de Rastignac to her?" she asked Ajuda, at the end of the first act.

"She'll be enchanted to meet him," said the marquis.

The handsome Portuguese stood up, took Eugène's arm, and in a second he found himself bowing to Madame de Nucingen.

"Madame la Baronne," said the marquis, "may I have the honor of presenting Monsieur Eugène de Rastignac, a cousin of Madame de Beauséant's? You've made so striking an impression on him that I wanted to complete his happiness by bringing him a little nearer his idol."

His bantering tone mitigated the slight crudity of the implication. Madame de Nucingen smiled, and pointed to the seat her husband had just vacated.

"I don't dare to suggest you should stay here with me, monsieur," she said. "People fortunate enough to be in Madame de Beauséant's company usually stay there."

The marquis withdrew.

"I have the feeling, madame," said Eugène, "that if I really want to please my cousin, I shall stay with you. Just before Monsieur d'Ajuda arrived we were talking about you and saying how very distinguished you looked."

"Are you really going to stay with me?" asked the baroness. "Then I'm sure we shall become friends. Madame de Restaud made me look forward very much to meeting you."

"Then, in that case she's completely insincere; she won't have me in the house."

"What!"

"Madame, I will be honest and tell you the reason. But I must ask all your indulgence when I tell you the secret. I live in the same house as your father. I was unaware that Madame de Restaud was his daughter. I was rash enough to mention him—in complete innocence—and your sister and her husband were annoyed. My cousin and the Duchesse de Langeais laughed like anything when I told them about it; but they did both say they thought such disloyalty on a daughter's part was extremely ill-bred. And then Madame de Beauséant began to compare your sister with you, and she spoke so warmly about you, and said how kind you were to my neighbor, Monsieur Goriot. And indeed how could you fail to love him? He adores you so passionately I'm jealous already. We talked for two hours about you this morning. Then, still full of what he'd said to me, I remarked to my cousin at dinner this evening that you couldn't possibly be as fair as you were kind. It was no doubt to show she approved of the warmth of my admiration that Madame de Beauséant brought me here; with her usual kindness, she said I would see you."

"So I'm indebted to you already?" said the banker's wife. "We shall be old friends in no time!"

"I am sure that friendship with you would be no commonplace experience, madame," said Eugène; "but it is not your friend I wish to be."

Women are always delighted with these stereotyped banalities, intended for the use of beginners; and only in cold print do they look pathetic. A young man's gesture or tone or glance can give them incalculable point. Madame de Nucingen was finding Eugène charming. Then, like all women, having no reply to his ardent questions, she replied to something else instead.

"Yes, it's wrong of my sister to treat poor Father as she does. He's been an angel to us. It was only because Monsieur de Nucingen absolutely forbade me to see him except in the mornings that I gave way on that point. I've been unhappy about it ever since. How I wept! These violent arguments coming on top of the brutalities of our marriage are one of the things that have made my life so terribly unhappy. I know people think I must be the happiest woman in Paris; in fact I'm quite the saddest. You'll think I'm crazy, talking to you like this. But you know my father, so I can't look on you as a stranger."

"You can never have met anyone," said Eugène, "more keenly anxious to devote himself to you. What are all women looking for? Happiness," he said in a voice that went to the heart. "Well, if a woman's idea of happiness means being loved, adored, having a friend she can confide all her longings and fancies and joys and sorrows to, whom she can bare her soul to, in all its sweet faults and lovely qualities, without fearing to be betrayed; then believe me, that keen, ever-devoted heart can be found only in a young man, still full of illusions, who would die at a single sign from you, who knows and wants to know nothing of the world, because for him you have become the world. I know you'll laugh at my simplicity. I come from the wilds, I'm completely

raw, I've ever known only good, simple souls; and I
counted on not falling in love. I happened to meet my
cousin, who has shown me a great deal of her heart. She
has made me guess the thousand treasures a passion
must contain; I'm like Cherubino, every woman's lover,
till I find one I can really devote myself to. When I came
in and saw you, I felt myself borne toward you as by a
tide. I'd thought so much about you! But I'd never
dreamed you were as beautiful as you are in reality.
Madame de Beauséant ordered me not to stare so hard
at you. She can't realize how enchanting it is to see your
pretty red lips, your white skin, and your gentle eyes. I
know I am talking foolishly, but let me. . . ."

Nothing delights women more than to hear such soft
words uttered. The most devout of them will listen, even
though they mustn't reply. After this beginning, Eugène
continued his rosary in a flirtatiously intimate tone; and
Madame de Nucingen encouraged him with smiles. From
time to time she looked over to Marsay, who was still
in Princess Galation's box. Eugène stayed with her till
her husband came back to take her home.

"Madame," said Eugène, "I shall have the pleasure of
calling on you before the Duchesse de Carigliano's ball."

"Zince Matame infites you," said the baron, a thickset
Alsatian whose round face hinted at a dangerous cunning, "you are zure of a goot vellcome."

"Things are going along nicely. She didn't seem particularly shocked when I said: 'Will you love me?' Well,
the horse is saddled, all I have to do is get on and break
him in," thought Eugène, as he went to bid good-bye to
Madame de Beauséant, who had risen and was preparing
to depart with Ajuda. The poor student did not know
that Madame de Nucingen was in despair, and was daily
expecting from Marsay one of those final letters that tear
the soul. Completely happy at his illusory success, he
accompanied the viscountess to the peristyle, where people stood waiting for their carriages.

"Your cousin doesn't look like the same man,"
laughed the Portuguese after Eugène had left them.
"He's going to break the bank! He's as slippery as an

eel. I fancy he'll go a long way. You alone could have picked out for him a woman who's just on the point of needing consolation."

"But we have yet to find out," said Madame de Beauséant, "if she's still in love with the man who's leaving her."

2

Eugène walked back from the opera to the Rue Neuve-Sainte-Geneviève with the most charming plans forming in his mind. He had observed how attentively Madame de Restaud had watched him, both in the viscountess's box, and in her sister's; and he surmised that the countess's door would no longer be closed to him. So he would soon have four important footholds in the heart of Parisian society; for he felt sure the marshal's wife would take to him. Without exactly deciding how, he foresaw that in the complex interplay of interests in this mechanical world, he would somehow have to hook himself on to part of the machinery.

"If Madame de Nucingen takes me up, I'll teach her how to manage her husband. . . . The husband is in the gold market. . . . He could help me to a fortune at one stroke. . . ." It was not put as crudely as this, and he was not yet sufficiently expert to sum up a situation and calculate its possibilities. So far, his ideas were like feathery clouds floating on the horizon; and though they hadn't the harshness of Vautrin's, if they had been tested in the crucible of conscience they wouldn't have revealed anything very pure. By a series of compromises of this nature, men reach that point of moral laxity that is the boast of our age. More rarely than ever before do we come upon those upright men of fine will who refuse to stoop to evil and who regard the slightest deviation from the straight path as a crime—such magnificent images of probity as have inspired two masterpieces, Molière's

Alceste, and, more recently, Sir Walter Scott's Jeanie Deans and her father. Perhaps a work of opposite intention, painting the devious ways by which an ambitious man of the world gets the better of his conscience as he tries to skirt round evil, so as to achieve his aim while preserving appearances, might be no less fine and no less dramatic.

By the time he reached the door of his lodgings, Eugène was in love with Madame de Nucingen. He had found her graceful and delicate as a swallow; the intoxicating sweetness of her eyes, the soft silken tissue of her skin, under which he had almost seen the blood coming and going, the bewitching tones of her voice, her golden hair, he could remember it all; and perhaps his walk, stimulating his blood, helped on the captivation. He knocked loudly at Goriot's door.

"My friend, I've seen Madame de Nucingen."

"Where?"

"At the Opéra."

"Was she enjoying herself? Do come in." The old man, who had risen in his nightshirt, opened the door and hastily got back into bed.

"Tell me all about her," he demanded.

This was the first time Eugène had been in Goriot's room, and he could not repress a start of amazement at the contrast between the father's squalid hovel and the daughter's finery he had just been admiring. The window was uncurtained; the wallpaper had peeled from the walls in places because of the damp, and hung in coils, revealing patches of smoke-yellowed plaster. The old man lay on a ramshackle bed, covered only by a blanket and a padded eiderdown made from the better remnants of Madame Vauquer's old dresses. The floor was damp, too, and covered with dust. Opposite the window stood an old bulging rosewood chest of drawers with brass handles in the shape of vine stems with flowers or leaves. An old wooden-topped washstand, with a water jug in a basin, and shaving things; shoes in a corner. The small table at the head of the bed had lost both its marble top and its door. Beside the fireplace (there was no trace of a fire) stood the square walnut table whose crossbar Goriot had used in wrecking his silver porringer. A battered writing desk with the old man's hat on it, a straw-bottomed armchair, and a couple of upright chairs completed the miserable furnishings of the room. The canopy over the bed, attached to the ceiling by a rag, consisted of a faded piece of some cheap red and white checked material. The poorest errand boy living in a garret could not have been worse off than Goriot at Madame Vauquer's. The chilling comfortlessness of the room wrung the heart; it might have been the most dismal cell in a prison. Fortunately Goriot did not see the expression on the young man's face. Eugène set down his candle on the table by the bed. The old man, pulling the bedclothes over him, turned on his side.

"Well, who do you like better: Madame de Restaud, or Madame de Nucingen?"

"I prefer Madame Delphine," said Eugène, "because she's fonder of you."

He had spoken warmly, and the old man reached out an arm from the bed and pressed Eugène's hand.

"Thank you, thank you," he said, deeply touched. "Why, what did she say about me?"

Eugène repeated the baroness's words, elaborating them a little. Goriot listened as if he were hearing the word of God.

"The dear girl! Yes, yes, she's very fond of me. But you mustn't believe what she said about Anastasie. They're sisters, and jealous of each other, of course; it's just another sign of how devoted they are. Madame de Restaud loves me too. I know she does. A father knows his children as God knows us: he can see into their hearts and know what's really there. They're both equally loving. Ah, if I'd only had good sons-in-law, how happy I might have been! No happiness on earth is ever perfect, of course. But if I could have lived with my girls . . . just to hear their voices, and know they were there, to see them come and go, like when they were at home with me . . . my heart would have leaped with joy! Were their clothes nice?"

"Yes," said Eugène. "But, Monsieur Goriot, when you have daughters living in such luxury, how can you bear to stay in a hovel like this?"

"Good heavens," Goriot replied, with apparent unconcern, "why should I want anything better? I can't quite explain these things to you, I barely know how to put two words together. It's all here," he said, striking his heart. "*My* life is in my two daughters. So long as they enjoy themselves and are happy and smartly dressed, and can have carpets to walk on, what does it matter what rags I wear, or the sort of place I sleep in? I'm not cold so long as they're warm; and I'm never dull provided they can laugh. I'm distressed only when they're distressed. When *you* become a father one day, and hear your children prattling away, and can say to yourself: 'They sprang from *me*!'—when you realize the little creatures are part of your very own flesh and blood . . . the flower of your being . . . yes, yes, that's what I mean: you feel their very flesh is part of yours; when they walk, they seem to move inside you! If I see them looking sad, my blood runs cold. You'll realize one day that your children's happiness means more to you than your own. I can't explain it to you; it's like a movement inside you that spreads gladness all through you.

"It means I have three lives! Shall I tell you something strange? Well, when I became a father, I understood God. He's all of Him everywhere, for the whole of creation came from Him. I feel like God about my daughters. Only I love my daughters more than God loved the world, because the world isn't as beautiful as God, and my daughters are more beautiful than I am. They are so much part of my inmost soul that I was able to guess you'd see them tonight. . . . Oh, God, if only there was a man who could make my little Delphine as happy as a woman is when she's really loved, I'd clean his boots and run his errands for him. I knew from her maid that this little Marsay was a rotten dog. I've felt like wringing his neck. Fancy not loving a jewel of a woman like that! She has the voice of a nightingale. She's shaped like a lovely statue. What was she thinking of, marrying that fat Alsatian blockhead? They both ought to have married handsome, nice young men. But anyway, they did as they pleased. . . ."

Goriot was sublime. Never before had Eugène seen him irradiated by the fires of his paternal passion. This power that feelings have of pervading a man's outward appearance is worth noticing. However gross a man may be, the minute he expresses a strong and genuine affection, some inner secretion alters his features, animates his gestures, and colors his voice. The stupidest man will often, under the stress of passion, achieve heights of eloquence, in thought if not in language, and seem to move in some luminous sphere. Goriot's voice and gesture had at this moment the power of communication that characterizes the great actor. Are not our finer feelings the poems of the human will?

"Well," said Eugène, "you probably won't be sorry to hear that she's certainly breaking with Marsay. The young buck's left her for Princess Galation. But tonight . . . I fell in love with Madame Delphine myself."

"Nonsense!" said Goriot.

"It's quite true. And she didn't dislike me. We talked love for a whole hour, and I'm to go and call on her the day after tomorrow, Saturday."

"Oh, how I would love you, my dear sir, if she found she liked you. You're a good man, you would never torture her. In any case, if you betrayed her, I'd cut your throat. But a woman doesn't have two loves in her life. Ah, good God, what nonsense I'm talking, Monsieur Eugène. It must be cold in here for you. . . . So you've actually heard her speak. What message did she give you for me?"

"None," said Eugène to himself. Aloud he said: "She said she sent you a true daughter's kiss."

"Good night, dear friend. Sleep well, and have happy dreams. Mine are certain after what you say. May God look after you in all you attempt. You've been like a good angel to me tonight. You bring a breath of my daughter with you."

"Poor man," thought Eugène, as he got into his bed,

"he would melt a heart of stone. His daughter gave no more thought to him than she did to the Grand Turk."

After this conversation, Goriot saw in his neighbor an unhoped-for confidant, a friend. There had been established between them the only relationship that could have tied the old man to anyone else. Passions never err in their calculations. Goriot saw himself as a little closer to his daughter Delphine, he saw that she might make him more welcome if she grew fond of Eugène. He had also confided to Eugène one of his griefs. Madame de Nucingen, whose happiness he prayed for a thousand times a day, had never known the blessings of love. Eugène was certainly, as he himself put it, one of the nicest young men he had ever met, and he seemed to anticipate that Eugène would give her all the delights she had hitherto missed. And so the old man's friendship for his neighbor grew steadily. Otherwise we would probably never have known the outcome of this story.

He sat beside Eugène at breakfast next morning, and the affection with which he looked at him, the remarks he made to him, the change in his expression, ordinarily that of a plaster mask, surprised their fellow boarders. Vautrin, who was seeing Eugène for the first time since their discussion, seemed to be trying to read his mind. As he recalled the man's proposal, Eugène, who before dropping off to sleep the night before had surveyed the vast scene that now opened in front of his eyes, inevitably thought of Mademoiselle Taillefer's dowry. He could not help looking across at her in the way even the most virtuous young man looks at a wealthy heiress. By chance their eyes met. The poor girl naturally found Eugène charming in his new clothes. The glance they exchanged was significant enough for Eugène to be certain that he had become for her the object of those confused longings that rise in every girl and attach themselves to the first attractive man in sight. A voice was crying at him: "Eight hundred thousand francs!" But suddenly his thoughts reverted to the evening before, and he decided that his assumed passion for Madame de Nucingen was the best antidote to these wicked, involuntary thoughts.

"It was Rossini's *Barber of Seville* last night at the Italian Opera. I've never heard such enchanting music," he said. "My goodness, how wonderful it would be to have one's own box there."

Old Goriot leaped at this remark as a dog leaps at his master's slightest movement.

"You men live in clover the whole time," said Madame Vauquer. "You have only to ask, to have."

"How did you get back?" asked Vautrin.

"I walked," replied Eugène.

"I wouldn't like half-pleasures, myself," observed the tempter. "I'd want to go there in my own carriage, have my own box, and come back in comfort. All or nothing, that's my motto."

"And a very good one," said Madame Vauquer.

"Perhaps you'll be going to see Madame de Nucingen today," Eugène murmured to Goriot. "She'll receive you with open arms; she'll want to know a hundred and one details about me. I've been told she would do anything in the world to be received by my cousin, the Vicomtesse de Beauséant. Don't forget to tell her I'm too fond of her not to try to achieve her desire for her."

He left immediately after breakfast for the law school. He wished to spend as little time as possible in the loathsome Maison Vauquer. He strolled about most of the day, prey to the feverishness known to all young men whose hopes are running too high. He was reflecting on Vautrin's commentary on social life, when he ran into his friend Bianchon in the Luxembourg Gardens.

"Why are you looking so serious?" asked the medical student, taking his arm. They began to stroll up and down in front of the palace.

"I'm tormented by wicked impulses."

"What sort? You can cure impulses, anyway."

"How?"

"By giving in to them."

"You laugh only because you don't know what I'm talking about. Have you ever read Rousseau?"

"Yes."

"Do you remember that passage where he asks the

reader what he would do if he could get rich by killing
an old mandarin in China without moving from Paris,
just by willing it?"

"Yes."

"Well?"

"Pooh! I've got through thirty-two mandarins
already."

"Don't joke about it. Come, if it were proved to you
that you could do it—just by a nod of the head, would
you?"

"Is he a very old mandarin? . . . Well, anyway, young
or old, paralytic or healthy, of course I . . . well, damn
it, no, I wouldn't."

"You're a fine, noble boy, Bianchon. But suppose you
were so much in love with a woman you'd sell your soul
for her; and suppose she needed money, lots of money,
for her clothes, and her carriage, and everything
else . . . ?"

"But you deprive me of my reason, and then ask me
to use it!"

"Well, anyway, Bianchon, I'm mad. Kindly cure me.
I have two sisters, lovely, innocent angels, and I want
them to be happy. Where can I get two hundred thousand francs for the dowries they'll be needing five years
from now? There are, you see, situations in life when
you must play for high stakes, and not use up your luck
in winning pennies."

"What you're asking is what everyone has to ask at
the beginning of a career; and you want to cut the Gor-
dian knot with a sword. To do that, you must either be
Alexander the Great or else face prison. I'm happy with
the minor existence I shall make for myself in the country, where I shall dully follow in my father's practice. A
man's affections can be satisfied in the smallest circle
just as fully as in a gigantic one. Napoleon himself
couldn't eat two dinners, and couldn't cope with any
more mistresses than a medical student at the Capu-
cines'. Our happiness, my dear boy, always lies between
the soles of our feet and the occiput; and whether it costs
a million francs a year or only a couple of thousand, the

intrinsic gratification is just the same inside us. So I vote you should spare the Chinaman's life."

"Thanks, you've done me good, Bianchon! We'll always be friends."

"Now listen, I want to tell you something too," said Bianchon. "Just as I came out of Cuvier's lecture at the Jardin des Plantes, I saw Michonneau and old Poiret. They were sitting on a bench and they were talking to a man I saw during the riots last year around the Chamber of Deputies. Well, he looked to me exactly like a police detective, disguised as a respectable retired shopkeeper. . . . So let's just keep an eye on that couple: I'll tell you why later. . . . So long, I've got to go and answer the four o'clock roll call."

3

Back at his lodgings, Eugène found Goriot waiting for him.

"Look!" said the old man. "There's a letter from her. Ah, what pretty handwriting!"

Eugène unsealed the letter, and read:

Monsieur: My father tells me you are fond of Italian music. I would be very happy if you would do me the honor of accepting a place in my box on Saturday. Fodor and Pellegrini are singing, so I am sure you will not refuse me. Monsieur de Nucingen joins me in hoping you will come and dine with us informally beforehand. He will be very happy if you accept, as this will relieve him of the conjugal duty of accompanying me himself. Don't bother to answer this, just come.

With my kindest regards,
D. de N.

"Let me see it," said Goriot as soon as Eugène had finished reading. "You'll go, won't you?" he asked, as he sniffed at the paper. "How nice it smells! Her fingers have gone over it, that's why!"

Eugène was thinking: "A woman doesn't throw herself at a man's head like this. She just wants to make use of me to bring Marsay back. People do this sort of thing only out of spite."

"Well?" said Goriot, "what are you thinking about?"

Eugène was unaware of the feverish anxiety that possessed women of a certain class at that time. No one had told him that a banker's wife would go to any lengths to get through a door into the Faubourg Saint-Germain, the ladies of which—the "Royal Circle," as they were sometimes called—were coming to be regarded as the highest order of womankind; and among them Madame de Beauséant, her friend the Duchesse de Langeais, and the Duchesse de Maufrigneuse were in the first rank. Of the frantic efforts made by women of the Chaussée d'Antin to enter this firmament where the constellations of their sex twinkled, Eugène knew nothing. But his mistrust of Delphine's motives served him well. It cooled his ardor a little, and gave him the melancholy power of imposing conditions instead of submitting to them.

"Yes," he said, "I'll go."

And so it was curiosity that took him to Madame de Nucingen's. If she had slighted him, perhaps passion might have taken him there instead. Even so, it was not without a trace of impatience that he looked forward to the next day, and the time of setting out. A young man may well find quite as many enchantments in a first intrigue as in a first true love. The certainty of success brings with it countless delights a man will not admit to; and the whole attraction of some women lies in these.

Desire can arise equally from difficulty and from ease in these matters. One or other of them is certainly responsible for rousing or maintaining all of men's passions; they divide the empire of love between them. And this division is, in its turn, perhaps, a consequence of the existence of the two great temperaments which, whatever people say, dominate society. If the melancholy man needs the fillip of coquetry, the sanguine man perhaps retreats if the struggle goes on too long. In other words, the elegy is essentially lymphatic, the dithyramb full of bile.

As he dressed, Eugène indulged himself in all those little pleasures young men never dare confess to for fear of being laughed at, but which nonetheless gratify their vanity. As he brushed his hair, he could imagine a pretty woman's gaze lingering over his dark curls. He pulled as

many childish faces in the mirror as a girl dressing for a
ball. He looked complacently at his slim figure, as he
smoothed down his coat. "Certainly," he said to himself,
"you might find worse." Then he went downstairs. The
regular boarders were all at table. He grinned cheerfully
at the satirical hurrah that greeted his dashing appearance. The astonishment caused by any attention to dress
is one of the regular characteristics of boardinghouses.
If you put on a new suit everyone has to have his say
about it.

"Clk! Clk! Clk!" cried Bianchon, clicking his tongue
like someone urging on a horse.

"He's dressed like a lord!" said Madame Vauquer.

"Is the gentleman going courting?" inquired Mademoiselle Michonneau.

"Cock-a-doodle-doo!" cried the painter.

"My compliments to your lady wife," said the museum clerk.

"Has the gentleman a lady wife?" asked Poiret.

"A lady wife with compartments! Goes on the water,
guarantees a good complexion, prices ranging from
twenty-five to forty francs!" cried Vautrin, imitating the
rapid, voluble patter of a barker. "Latest squared designs, washable, good-wearing, part cotton, part thread,
part wool, cures the toothache and other complaints approved by the Royal Academy of Medicine! Excellent
for children also; even better for headache, overeating,
and other troubles of the throat, eyes, and ears! Now,
how much am I offered for this miracle, gents? Two
cents? No! Nothing doing! It's a remainder from the
furnishings made for the Great Mogul, sought after by
all the crown-deads of Europe, including the Grrrrand
Duke of Baden! Step right in! First door on the left.
Music, please! B'rroomm! La, la, la, *trinnng*! La, la, la
boom-*boom*! Mister Clarinet, I heard a wrong note
just then!" he growled. "I'll rap you one across the
knuckles!"

"Oh, dear, *isn't* he a sweet man?" said Madame Vauquer, turning to Madame Couture. "I could listen to
him forever!"

During the laughter and joking that greeted this comic outburst, Eugène caught a surreptitious glance from Mademoiselle Taillefer, who leaned over to whisper something in Madame Couture's ear.

"Your cab's here," said Sylvie.

"Where's he dining?" asked Bianchon.

"At the Baronne de Nucingen's."

"Monsieur Goriot's daughter," said Eugène.

At this name, everyone turned to look at Goriot, who was contemplating Eugène almost with envy.

Eugène's destination, in the Rue Saint-Lazare, was one of those flimsy villas with thin pillars and shallow porticoes, which are what Paris considers pretty: a typical banker's house, crammed with expensive luxuries, bits of stucco, and marble mosaic stair landings. He found Madame de Nucingen in a little drawing room with Italian paintings on the wall. The decorations might have been those of a café.

The baroness was downcast. Her efforts to conceal the fact were all the more intriguing to Eugène because they were quite obviously sincere. He had been expecting to delight a woman by his presence, and he found her in despair. This disappointment piqued his vanity.

"I know I have no claims on your confidence, madame," he said, after teasing her about her preoccupation, "but if I am in the way, I hope I can count on you to tell me so frankly."

"No, do stay," she said. "I shall be all alone if you go away. Nucingen's dining out, and I don't want to be alone. I want to be amused."

"But what is the matter?"

"You'd be the very last person I'd tell!" she exclaimed.

"I want to know. You must mean I have something to do with the mystery."

"Perhaps you have . . . ! No, no," she added quickly, "it's just one of those family quarrels one ought to bury in one's heart. Wasn't I telling you the other night? I'm far from happy. Chains of gold are the heaviest of all."

When a woman tells a young man she is unhappy, and the young man is intelligent, well dressed, and has fifteen hundred francs pocket money, he is bound to think as Eugène was thinking at this moment; and he becomes a little superior.

"What more can you want?" he asked. "You are beautiful, young, beloved, and rich."

"Don't let's talk about me," she said with an ominous shake of the head. "We'll dine together, just the two of us, and then we'll go and hear the most delicious music. How do you think I look?" She rose and displayed her white cashmere dress with its elaborate and exquisite Persian embroidery.

"You're enchanting," said Eugène. "I wish you were all mine."

"I'd be a very sorry possession for you," she said with a bitter smile. "I know everything looks very happy here, but I'm in the depths of despair. I can't sleep for worry! I shall be so ugly!"

"Ah, that's impossible," said Eugène. "But I'm curious to know exactly what these troubles are that a devoted love like mine wouldn't remove?"

"Oh, if I told you, you'd just run away," she said. "Your love for me is only one of those fashionable compliments men are expected to make. If you really loved me, you'd be horribly distressed. I mustn't say any more, truly. *Please*," she went on, "let's talk about something else. Come and see my own rooms."

"No, let's stay here," said Eugène, sitting down on a sofa by the fire, close to her, and boldly taking her hand in his.

She did not withdraw it, and even pressed his own, with one of those sharply convulsive movements that betray intense emotion.

"Listen," said Eugène. "If you're in trouble, you must tell me. I can prove I love you for yourself alone. Either you tell me why you're unhappy, so that I can put a stop to it—even if it means killing six men to do so—or else I go away and never come back."

"Very well, then!" she cried, striking her forehead in despair. "I'll put you to the proof this very instant. Yes," she muttered. "It's the only way."

She rang the bell.

"Is the master's carriage ready?" she asked the footman.

"Yes, madame."

"I will take it. Get mine out for him, and my horses. Don't serve dinner till seven.

"Come on, then," she said, turning to Eugène, and a moment later he was sitting by her side in Monsieur de Nucingen's brougham. He had a feeling that all this was a dream.

"To the Palais-Royal," she told the coachman, "near the Théâtre-Français."

On the way she seemed agitated and refused to answer the innumerable questions Eugène asked. He did not know what to make of this blank, intense, obstinate silence.

"In another minute she'll have slipped away from me," he thought.

The carriage stopped. The baroness looked at Eugène in a way that silenced his wild flow of words. "Do you really love me?" she said.

"Yes," he replied, concealing the anxiety that suddenly gripped him.

"You won't think badly of me, whatever I ask you to do?"

"No."

"Are you prepared to obey me?"

"Blindly."

"Have you ever gambled?" she asked in a trembling voice.

"Never."

"Ah, I can breathe again. You're bound to be lucky. Here's my purse," she said. "Take it, take it! There's a hundred francs in it: every penny this happy woman possesses. Go into one of the gambling houses, I don't know where they are, but I know there are some at the

Palais-Royal. Throw the hundred francs in one go at the game they call roulette; and either lose the lot, or bring me back six thousand francs. I will tell you about my troubles when you come back."

"I wish to God I had the slightest idea of what it is I have to do, but I'll do what you say," he said. And he felt happy as he thought: "She's compromising herself with me; she won't be able to refuse me anything."

Eugène took the pretty purse, asked an old clothes man the way to the nearest gambling place, and hurried to the house numbered nine. He went up, left his hat, and asked for the roulette table. To the astonishment of the regular clients, the attendant led him to a long table. Everyone stared at Eugène, as he asked, without embarrassment, where to place his stake.

"If you put one louis on a single one of these thirty-six numbers and it comes up, you will get thirty-six louis," a respectable, white-haired old man told him.

Eugène threw down the hundred francs on the number of his own age, twenty-one. A cry of amazement went up, before he realized what was happening. He had won without knowing it.

"Pick up your money," said the old gentleman. "You won't win twice on that system."

Eugène took the rake the old gentleman handed him, and drew in the thirty-six hundred francs and, still without any understanding of the game, placed them on the red. The audience watched him enviously as they saw that he intended to go on playing. The wheel went round, he won again, and the banker threw him another thirty-six hundred francs.

"You have won seven thousand two hundred francs," the old gentleman whispered to him. "If you'll take my tip you'll stop now; the red has turned up eight times running. If you're feeling charitable, you will acknowledge the bit of advice I gave you by relieving the poverty of a former prefect under Napoleon, reduced to dire need."

The bewildered Eugène allowed the white-haired gentleman to take ten louis from him, and went downstairs with his seven thousand francs, still understanding nothing of the game but staggered by his good luck.

"Well then! And now where will you take me?" he said, as he showed the seven thousand francs to Madame de Nucingen when the carriage door had shut behind him.

Delphine gave him a frantic hug and a warm but unimpassioned kiss. "You've saved my life!" she cried. Tears of joy streamed down her cheeks. "Now I'll tell you everything, my friend. You *will* be my friend, won't you? You think I'm rich, wealthy, you think I want for nothing, don't you? That's how I seem? Well, let me tell you that Monsieur de Nucingen never gives me a penny: he pays for the housekeeping, the carriages, my box at the theater; he won't give me a proper dress allowance. He deliberately plunges me into a secret poverty no one knows of. I'm too proud to beg from him. And I'd be the most despicable creature on earth if I accepted money from him on his own terms. I suppose you wonder how someone like me, with seven hundred thousand francs, can have let myself be robbed. It was pride; it was indignation. We're so young and simple when we get married. The words I'd have had to use to ask for money from my husband would have burned my lips. I would never utter them. I spent all my savings, and the money my poor father managed to give me. Then I ran into debt.

"My marriage has been the most appalling disillusionment. I can't bear to speak about it. I'll tell you only that I'd throw myself out of the window if Nucingen didn't allow me to live in a separate apartment. When I was forced to tell him about my debts—the debts any young woman incurs for jewelry, little trinkets (with my poor father we'd been used to having everything we asked for)—I suffered agonies. But at last I did pluck up courage, and told him. Hadn't I a fortune of my own? Nucingen lost his temper; he said I was ruining him! I wished I was dead and buried. As he'd taken my dowry, he paid up; but he stipulated that in future my personal

expenses should come out of an allowance. I accepted
for the sake of peace and quiet.

"Since then, I've had to live up to the standards of
someone you know about. . . ." she went on. "He has
been unfaithful to me, but it would ill become me to
deny the nobility of his character. But now he's left me—
shabbily. No one ought ever to desert a woman after
throwing her a heap of gold in her distress! He ought to
love her forever! You are young, only twenty-one, and
kind and upright and fine. You'll ask me how a woman
can take money from a man. Oh, God, isn't it natural
to share everything with the one we owe all our happiness to? When one has given everything, how can one
quibble about a mere portion of it? Money is important
only when feeling has ceased. Isn't one bound for life?
How can you foresee separation when you think someone loves you? When a man swears eternal love—how
can there be any separate concerns in that case?

"You can't know what I've suffered today. Nucingen
positively refused to give me six thousand francs; but he
gives his mistress—a girl from the Opéra—as much
every month. I could have killed myself! The wildest
ideas kept going through my brain. There have been
times when I've envied my own maid: a servant has a
better life than mine. To have asked my poor father
would have been madness. Anastasie and I have bled
him white already. He would have sold himself for six
thousand francs. It would only have meant distressing
him pointlessly. You've saved me from disgrace. I owed
you this explanation, monsieur—I've been preposter-
ously silly with you. When you left me just now, as soon
as you were out of sight, I almost got out and ran
away . . . but where could I go?

"And that's the life of half the women in Paris—a
great parade of luxury, and cruel worries underneath it.
I know poor women even more unfortunate than I am.
Some of them have to ask the tradesmen to send in
faked bills for them. Some of them are forced to steal
from their husbands. Some men think you can get a two-
thousand-franc shawl for five hundred; some think a

cashmere shawl costing five hundred must have cost two thousand. Some poor women who want a dress will get it by pilfering, or starving their children. At least I haven't sunk as low as that.

"But I won't go through such agony again. And if some women sell themselves to their husbands in order to manage them, I at least am free! I could make Nucingen cover me with gold; but I'd rather weep on the heart of a man I can respect. Ah! tonight Monsieur de Marsay won't have the right to look on me as a woman he's paid." She buried her face in her hands so that Eugène should not see her tears. But he drew her hands apart and looked at her. She was wonderful at this moment. "Mixing money up with love—it's horrible, isn't it?" she said. "You'll never love me now."

This intermingling of the finer feelings that make women so great with the faults that present-day society forces them to acquire, completely baffled Eugène. He talked gently and comfortingly to her, and wondered that such a beautiful woman could be so innocently imprudent in her cry of grief.

"You won't hold all this against me?" she begged. "Promise me you won't!"

"Ah, madame! How could I?" he said.

She took his hand and placed it against her heart. The gesture was full of gratitude and gentleness. "Thanks to you, I'm free and happy again. I was living with a hand of iron gripping me. Now I want to live simply, and never spend anything. I hope you're going to like me as I shall be from now on? You keep this," she said, taking only six of the bank notes. "Properly speaking, I owe you three thousand francs, because I considered we were going halves." Eugène struggled like an assaulted virgin. But when she said, "I shall regard you as an enemy if you won't be my accomplice," he took the money.

"It'll be a reserve for future emergencies," he said.

"That was what I was afraid you'd say," she exclaimed. She had gone pale. "If you want me to mean anything to you, promise me you'll never go into a gambling house again. Oh, God, if I thought I'd led you astray, it would kill me!"

They were back at her house. The contrast between her poverty and the opulence surrounding her stunned Eugène, and the sinister words of Vautrin seemed to murmur in his ears.

"Sit there," said the baroness, pointing to a sofa by the fire. "I have to write a very difficult letter. I want your advice."

"Don't write at all," said Eugène. "Put the money in an envelope, write the address on it, and send your maid with it."

"What a love of a man you are!" she said. "Ah, what it is to have been properly brought up! That's pure Beauséant," she added with a smile.

"She's enchanting," thought Eugène, who felt more and more in love with her. He looked round the room. It suggested the voluptuous taste of a well-to-do harlot.

"Do you like it?" she asked, as she rang for her maid. "Thérèse, take this yourself to Monsieur de Marsay, and deliver it to him personally. If he isn't in, bring it back to me." Thérèse went out, with a mischievous glance in Eugène's direction. Dinner was served. Eugène gave Madame de Nucingen his arm, and she led him into a pretty dining room, where once again he found the lavishness of table that had charmed him at his cousin's.

"Whenever the Italians are singing, you must come and dine, and we'll go on there afterward," she said.

"I should grow very used to this pleasant life, if it could last," he said. "But I'm only a poor student, and I still have my way to make."

"You will," she said, laughing. "You'll see: everything will all come right. . . . I never thought I'd feel so happy again."

It is a woman's nature to prove the impossible by the possible, and to demolish facts by intuitions. When the baroness and Eugène entered her box at the Bouffons, she looked so radiantly happy that she provoked those inevitable murmurs against which women are defenseless

and which often cause the most idle invention to be
taken for truth. Once a man knows Paris, he believes
nothing of what is said there, and says nothing of what
is done. Eugène held the baroness's hand, and both of
them indicated by varying squeezes the degree of pleasure the music was giving them. It was an intoxicating
evening for both of them. They left together, and Madame de Nucingen insisted on driving Eugène back as
far as the Pont-Neuf, struggling the whole way to avoid
a single kiss—though she had lavished them on him
warmly enough at the Palais-Royal. Eugène complained
of this inconsistency.

"Ah, but that," she said, "was gratitude for unex-
pected devotion; now it would be a promise."

"And you don't want to promise anything, you ungrateful woman!" he said angrily. With one of those gestures of impatience that ravish a man in love, she gave
him her hand to kiss, and he took it with a sulkiness
that charmed her.

"Till Monday, at the ball," she said.

As he walked the rest of the way home, under a fine
clear moon, Eugène fell into serious reflection. He was
at once happy and disgruntled—happy at an adventure
that in the end would probably give him one of the prettiest and smartest women in Paris, the prize he desired;
disgruntled because his first plans for making a fortune
had collapsed. It was now that he realized the full seri-
ousness of his vague cogitations two nights before. Un-
success always underlines the extent of our ambitions.
The more Eugène enjoyed the life of Paris, the less
pleased he was at the thought of remaining obscure and
penniless. He crumpled the thousand-franc note in his
pocket and thought up a thousand plausible reasons for
keeping it for himself. At last he reached the Rue
Neuve-Sainte-Geneviève, and as he mounted the stairs,
he saw a light burning. Goriot had left his door ajar and
his candle still burning, so that the student should not
forget to "tell him about his daughter," as he had put
it. Eugène kept nothing back.

"But they think I'm ruined!" cried Goriot in an outburst of jealous dismay. "I still have thirteen hundred francs a year! Why didn't the poor child come to me? I'd have sold my investments and we could have drawn on the capital, and I could have bought myself an annuity with the rest. My dear good neighbor, why didn't you come to me and tell me about her troubles? How could you bring yourself to risk her poor little hundred francs at the gambling tables? It's heartbreaking. You see what sons-in-law are like! Oh, if I could get my hands on them, I'd wring their necks. Good God! Crying! She *cried,* you said?"

"With her head on my waistcoat."

"Oh, give it to me," said Goriot. "It's actually had my dear little Delphine's tears on it; and she never used to cry when she was a little girl! I'll buy you another one, don't wear it again, leave it with me. . . . I shall go and see Derville the lawyer tomorrow! The marriage contract gives her control over her own property. I'll insist on her fortune being invested. I know the law, I'm an old wolf. I'll soon show my teeth again!"

"Look, father, here's a thousand francs she wanted to give me from our winnings. Keep them for her, in the waistcoat."

Goriot looked at Eugène, reached out a hand to his; and a tear fell on it.

"You will succeed in life," the old man said. "God is just, you know that? I know what integrity is, and I can assure you there are very few men like you. And you want to be my dear child too? Go now, and sleep. You can sleep: you're not a father yet. . . . She wept. I learn *that,* after sitting placidly eating here, like a fool, while she was suffering. And I'd sell Father, Son, and Holy Ghost to spare either of them a single tear!"

"Upon my word," thought Eugène, as he climbed into bed, "I've a good mind to be an honest man for the rest of my life. There's pleasure to be had from doing what conscience tells you."

Perhaps only men who believe in God do good by stealth; and Eugène did believe in God.

PART FOUR

TROMPE-LA-MORT

1

At the appointed time two nights later, Eugène called for Madame de Beauséant, and escorted her to the Duchesse de Carigliano's ball. His cousin presented him to the marshal's wife, who gave him a gracious welcome. Madame de Nucingen was already there, dressed with the deliberate aim of appealing to all eyes, knowing that thereby she would seem even more attractive to Eugène. With an impatience she thought she concealed, she waited for him to look in her direction. For a man capable of understanding a woman's feelings, this can be a very agreeable moment. And what man has not, in his day, taken pleasure in making others wait for him to speak, in teasingly withholding his admiration, in extracting an implicit confession of love from the anxiety he is causing, in prolonging the apprehension he knows he can dispel with a single smile?

It was on this evening that Eugène suddenly realized the full significance of his status in society as the acknowledged cousin of Madame de Beauséant. That he had already conquered the Baronne de Nucingen was generally taken for granted. This lifted him into such high prominence that every other young man there looked at him in envy. Intercepting some of their glances, he felt for the first time the pleasures of smugness. As he moved from room to room, threading his way through the crush, he heard people commending his good fortune. All the women were prophesying a great future for him. Delphine, fearful of losing him, promised that tonight she would not deny him the kiss she had so firmly refused two nights before.

During the course of the ball, Eugène received a number of invitations to other houses. He was introduced by his cousin to a number of women, all of a certain distinction, all with houses alleged to be charming. He realized that he was launched into the highest, most exclusive society in Paris. So that the evening held for him all the enchantment of a brilliant debut, and he was to remember it in his old age as a girl remembers the ball where she had her first successes.

At breakfast next morning, he recounted his triumphs to Goriot in the presence of the other boarders. Vautrin's face was suddenly lit by a diabolical smile.

"And do you imagine," the remorseless logician demanded, "that a young man-about-town can go on living in the Maison Vauquer, in the Rue Neuve-Sainte-Geneviève? As a boardinghouse, it is, admittedly, the height of respectability in every way; but it's almost everything except fashionable. It's sumptuous, as we know. It's very lavish in the way it treats us all; it's proud to be the temporary manorial home of a Rastignac; but when all's said and done, it *is* in the Rue Neuve-Sainte-Geneviève, and it does cut out luxury, because it is, purely and simply, a home-from-homorama.

"My young friend," Vautrin went on, in mock-paternal tones, "if you're to cut a dash in Paris, you'll need a tilbury and three horses for the morning, and a brougham for the evening; and that means nine thousand francs simply to get about. You'd be unworthy of your high destiny if you spent less than three thousand francs a year at your tailor's, six hundred at the haberdasher's, three hundred at your bootmaker's, and another three hundred at your hatter's. You must allow another thousand a year for your laundry. A smart young man must be particular about his linen: isn't that the first thing people examine? Love and religion both require fine cloths on the altar. That's fourteen hundred francs so far. I needn't mention what gambling, betting, and giving presents will run you in for. You can't possibly get along without at least two thousand for pocket money. I've lived that life, I know what it costs. Add to these bare necessities six thousand francs for the dog biscuits you eat, and a thousand for your kennel. Why, my child, it'll mean you'll have to have twenty-five thousand a year coming in, or down in the gutter you go, and we shall all laugh at you, and there'll be no future, no career, no mistresses! Oh, and I forgot your valet and groom. Or is Christophe going to deliver your love letters? And will you be writing them on the paper you use now? It would be social suicide. Take the word of an experienced old man," he concluded, with a *rinforzando* of his deep bass voice, "either go and live in a chaste little garret, and wed yourself to your studies . . . or find some other way."

And Vautrin winked, with a sidelong glance at Mademoiselle Taillefer, as if to reemphasize the seductive arguments he had already laid before Eugène in the hope of corrupting him.

The next weeks were for Eugène a period of reckless dissipation. He dined alone with Madame de Nucingen almost every evening, and escorted her into society. He came home at three or four in the morning, got up and dressed himself at midday, and whenever the weather was fine, went walking with Delphine in the Bois. The squandering of his time he disregarded; he was busy absorbing the seductive lessons of luxury, like the calyx of the female date palm greedily breathing in the fertilizing pollen. He gambled heavily, losing and winning large sums of money. In almost no time he had adopted all the expensive habits of the fashionable young man-about-town. Out of his first winnings he had sent fifteen hundred francs to his mother and sisters, accompanying the repayment with handsome presents.

Although he had declared his intention of moving out of the Maison Vauquer, he was still there at the end of January, powerless to leave. Almost all young men are subject to a law, apparently inexplicable but actually inherent in youth itself and in the near-frenzy with which young men hurl themselves at pleasure. Rich or poor, they never have any money for the prosaic necessities of life, though they can always find enough to gratify the desires of the moment. Lavish with whatever can be had on credit, they are like misers over anything that has to be paid for in cash. They seem to avenge themselves for all they lack by squandering the little they have. In fact, to put it briefly: a student is always more careful with his hat than with his suit. For a tailor's immense profits make him essentially a creditor, while a hatter's modest gains make him one of the most intractable people with whom a young man has to deal. If you see a young man in a theater box, displaying a stunning waistcoat for the benefit of some pretty girl with an opera glass, you may be fairly certain he has no socks; his hosier is another weevil at his purse.

Such was Eugène's position. The erratic ebb and flow of his exchequer took no account of normal requirements. It could cope with the demands of vanity, but not with Madame Vauquer. In order to leave the low, stinking lodgings that so often dashed his pride, would he not have to pay his landlady a month's rent, and buy furniture for his gentleman's apartment? And this was always impossible. If he needed money for gambling, he could always go to that somber, discreet friend of youth, the pawnbroker, and pledge the expensive gold watches and chains he had bought with previous winnings; but his invention and boldness deserted him when he needed money for food and lodging or the things necessary for his conquest of society. Inspiration failed him likewise when he was confronted by debts for needs now satisfied. Like most people who have known this life of insecurity, he always waited till the last moment before settling claims that the respectable middle classes regard as sacred. He was like Mirabeau, who never paid his baker's bill until it was presented in the threatening form of a solicitor's letter. . . .

And now Eugène had no money left, and was in debt. He had begun to see that it would be impossible to continue in his present mode of life without a settled income. But though he groaned under the torments of his precarious situation, he knew he could not now renounce this life of luxury; he was determined to continue in it, whatever the upshot. His hope of making a fortune quickly had proved illusory, and real obstacles were increasing. Now that he was initiated into the domestic secrets of the Nucingens, he realized that to turn love into an instrument of success he would have to swallow any feeling of shame and abandon the noble ideals that do much to absolve the faults of youth. This life, outwardly so magnificent but inwardly ravaged by the worms of guilt, its fleeting pleasures dearly paid for in nagging remorse, was the life he had embraced. He wallowed in it, making for himself, like La Bruyère's Absentminded Man, a bed in a muddy ditch; still, like the Absentminded Man, he had so far soiled only his clothes.

"So we've killed that mandarin?" Bianchon said to him one night at the end of dinner.

"Not yet," said Eugène, "but he's at his last gasp."

Bianchon took this for a joke; but it was not. It was the first time in several weeks that Eugène had dined in the boardinghouse, and he had been lost in thought throughout the meal. Instead of leaving after dessert, he stayed behind in the dining room, sitting beside Mademoiselle Taillefer, and throwing an expressive glance at her from time to time. Some of the boarders were still at table, eating nuts; others wandered up and down the room, chatting. As on most evenings, everyone left when they felt like it, according to the degree of interest they felt in the conversation, or the varying effects the recent meal was having upon their digestion. In winter, rarely did the dining room empty completely before eight o'clock, at which point the four women were left alone and could make up for the silence their sex had imposed on them while the men were there.

Vautrin had noticed Eugène's preoccupied air, and though he had at first seemed in a hurry to depart, had stayed behind in the dining room in a place where Eugène could not see him. Eugène thought he had left. Then, when the last of the men went out, Vautrin slyly took up a position in the drawing room. He had gathered what was going on in Eugène's mind, and was expecting some decisive move.

Eugène was in fact in a state of perplexity known to many young men. Whether from love or sheer wantonness, Delphine had, with all the feminine artfulness characteristic of Parisian women, been dragging him through all the agonies of a genuine passion. She had compromised herself in the public eye, in order to attach Madame de Beauséant's cousin to herself; but she was still hesitating before according him the rights everyone by now assumed he had already been granted. For a whole month she had so teased Eugène's senses that she had begun to attack his heart. In the early stages of their relationship, Eugène had assumed he was the master, but she had reversed the position with a skill that stirred in Eugène all the feelings, good and bad, that inhabit the two or three men who coexist inside every young Parisian. Was this a design on her part? No: women are always true, even in the midst of their greatest falsities, because they are always influenced by some natural feeling.

Perhaps Delphine, who had allowed the young man so much early power over her and had shown him so much affection, was obeying a sense of dignity that was making her retract her concessions, or at least suspend them. It is so natural to a woman of Paris, even in the grip of passion, to pause before her fall, to test the heart of the man she is about to entrust with her future! Delphine's hopes had already been betrayed once, and her devotion to a young egotist had just been slighted. She had good reason for caution. Perhaps she had discerned in Eugène's manner—his rapid success had made him conceited—a certain disrespect caused by the oddness of their situation. She no doubt wished to impress so young a man, and to feel important in his eyes after feeling small for so long in those of the man who had betrayed her. It was precisely because he knew she had belonged to Marsay that she was reluctant for Eugène to think her an easy conquest. Moreover, after submit-

ting to the degrading will of a monstrous young rake,
she now found it a great sweetness to wander in the
flowery regions of love, to linger over all its aspects, to
listen again and again to its stirrings, and to be caressed
again and again by its chaste breezes. True love was
paying for false. This unhappy state of affairs will unhap-
pily persist so long as men fail to realize how many
flowers are blasted in a young woman's heart at the first
stroke of betrayal.

Whatever her reasons, Delphine was playing with Rastignac, and enjoying doing so, probably because she
knew she was loved and was capable of putting an end
to her lover's miseries at her own right, royal, feminine
moment. Self-respect made Eugène unwilling to let his
first battle end in defeat, and he continued his pursuit
like a hunter absolutely determined to shoot a partridge
on the opening day of his first season. His anxieties, his
wounded self-esteem, his despairs, real or imaginary,
were binding him ever more closely to her. The whole
of Paris assumed that Delphine was his, and he was in
fact no nearer to her than on the day he had first seen
her. He did not yet know that a woman's hesitation is
sometimes more of a blessing than her eventual acquies-
cence; and he would fall into bouts of black rage. The
season of love when a woman still delays was allowing
Eugène to taste its first fruits. And however fresh, sharp,
and delicious on the tongue they might be, he was beginning to find them expensive. Sometimes, feeling penniless and futureless, his thoughts would revert to Vautrin's
suggestion of the possibility of fortune in a marriage to
Mademoiselle Taillefer. At this particular moment his
poverty was speaking so loud that he yielded almost involuntarily to the wiles of the terrible sphinx whose
glance so often fascinated him.

Poiret and Mademoiselle Michonneau had just gone
upstairs. Under the impression that he was alone except
for Madame Vauquer and Madame Couture, who was
dozing near the stove over a pair of woolen mittens she
was knitting, Eugène looked so tenderly at Victorine
that she lowered her eyes.

"Are you worried about something, Monsieur Eugène?" she asked after a time.

"What man isn't worried?" said Eugène. "If young men like me were ever sure they were loved, with a devotion that repaid us for some of the sacrifices we always have to make, perhaps we might never be worried."

Victorine's only answer was a look; there could be no mistake about its meaning.

"You, mademoiselle, you think you are quite certain about your affections today. But could you swear they would never change?"

A smile flitted over the poor girl's mouth. It was like a ray of sunlight from her soul, making her face so radiant that Eugène was startled at the intense feeling he had provoked.

"Suppose," he said, "suppose tomorrow you suddenly became rich and happy, suppose an immense fortune fell on you out of the blue, would you still love a young man whom you'd happened to care for when you were poor?"

She nodded prettily.

"A very unhappy young man?"

Another nod.

"What are you two tattling about over there?" demanded Madame Vauquer.

"Don't worry," said Eugène. "We understand each other."

"What! An engagement has been announced between the Chevalier de Rastignac and Mademoiselle Victorine Taillefer, has it?" came the booming voice of Vautrin, who suddenly appeared at the dining-room door.

"Oh, you did make me jump!" exclaimed Madame Couture and Madame Vauquer simultaneously.

"I might choose worse," laughed Eugène, though Vautrin's voice had given him the most painful shock he had ever known.

"Now, no unseemly joking, gentlemen," said Madame Couture. "Victorine, let us go upstairs."

Madame Vauquer followed her two boarders out. She

would be able to economize on fire and candles by passing the evening with them. Eugène was alone and face to face with Vautrin.

"I was sure you'd come round to it," Vautrin said, with his customary unshakable composure. "But, you know, I have my feelings just like any other man! Don't make up your mind just now, you're very much out of sorts today. You're in debt. And when you decide to come to me, I want it to be deliberately, not because you're in trouble or despair. Perhaps a few thousand francs might help you? If so, here they are."

The tempter took his wallet from his pocket, extracted three bank notes, and fluttered them before Eugène's eyes. Eugène was in a difficult predicament: he owed two thousand francs in gambling debts to the Marquis d'Ajuda and the Comte de Trailles. He had no money to pay them with, and dared not go to spend the evening at Madame de Restaud's, where he was expected. It was to be one of those informal gatherings, where little cakes and tea are served, but where, even so, it is possible to lose six thousand francs at whist.

Eugène had difficulty in suppressing a convulsive tremor. He said: "Sir, after what you've told me about yourself, you must realize that it's impossible for me to be under any obligation to you."

"Good! I'd have been upset if you'd said anything else," said Vautrin. "You're a fine fastidious young man, as proud as a lion, as gentle as a girl. You'd make a good catch for the devil. I prefer young men like you. A few more meditations on the state of society, and you'll see it as it really is. If an intelligent man will only play his way through a few little scenes of virtue, he can do whatever on earth he chooses afterward, with howls of applause from the fools in the pit. Another day or two, and you'll be ours. Ah! If only you'd let me teach you, I could make you achieve anything in the world. Everything you could possibly desire would be instantly granted, whatever it was: honor, fortune, women. The whole of civilization would turn to milk and honey for you. You'd be our spoiled child, our little Benjamin;

we'd wear ourselves down to skin and bone for you. All obstacles in your path would be razed to the ground. You still hesitate: does that mean you think I'm a criminal? Well, a man who had just as much integrity as you think you still have, Monsieur de Turenne, wasn't above dealing with criminals occasionally, without ever thinking he'd lowered himself.

"You don't want to feel under any obligation to me, eh? Don't let that stop you! Here, take these things," he said, handing the notes to Eugène. Then he took out a stamped paper. "Just write across this: 'Received the sum of three thousand five hundred francs, repayable in one year.' And date it! The interest is stiff enough to quiet even your conscience; you can say I'm a Jew, and you won't have any need to feel grateful. I can let you despise me today, because I know you'll be fond of me later on. You'll find immense depths in me, deep vortexes of feeling. Fools call such things vices. But you'll never find me base or ungrateful. You see, I'm not a pawn or a bishop; I'm a castle, dear child."

"But *what are you*?" cried Eugène. "You were born to torture me!"

"Not at all, I'm a good man ready to dirty my hands to spare you from the mire for the rest of your life. Why this devotion, you wonder? Well, one of these days I'll whisper it softly in your ear. I surprised you when I first explained to you the tricks of the social order, the way the machine works; but you'll soon get over your first fright, as a conscript does on the battlefield. And you'll get used to the idea of men being ready to die like soldiers in the service of people who've consecrated themselves kings. Times have greatly changed. In the old days, you could say to a *bravo*: 'Here's a hundred crowns, go and kill So-and-So for me.' And you could sup in peace after putting a man out of the way for one rude word. Today, I propose to give you a great fortune for a mere nod which doesn't disgrace you in any way; and you hesitate. It's a soft age we live in."

Eugène signed the draft, and was given the bank notes.

"Well, well! Now let's talk seriously," said Vautrin. "In a few months from now I want to leave for America, to go and plant my tobacco. I'll send you some cigars. If I make my fortune, I'll help you. If I have no children (and it's unlikely I ever shall have, I'm not very keen on perpetuating my stock in this world) I'll leave you my fortune. Is that being a man's friend? But there it is: I'm fond of you. I have a passion for devoting myself to other men. I've done it before. You see, my child, I live on a higher plane than other men. I regard actions as means, and I look only at the end. What does a man matter to me? *That!*" he said flicking his thumbnail against his teeth. "A man is all or nothing. He's less than nothing if he's like, say, Poiret. You can squash him like a bug: he's flat and he stinks. But when a man looks like you, he's a god. He's something more than a machine covered with skin, he's a stage for fine feelings to stride about on. And feelings are the only things I live for. A feeling: isn't it the whole world in a single thought? Look at old Goriot: his two daughters are his whole universe—they're his guiding thread through the whole creation. Well! I've plumbed life to its depths, and for me there's only one real feeling, the friendship of one man for another. Pierre and Jaffeir: that's my sort of passion. I know *Venice Preserved* by heart. How many men have you met who, if a friend says to them, 'Let's go and bury a corpse!' have the guts to go and do it, without blabbing, or preaching a sermon? *I've* done it, however. I wouldn't talk like this to everyone. But you're a man of intelligence, I can say anything to you, and you can understand. You won't be floundering about for long in the bogs these tadpoles around us live in. Well, it's settled then. You'll get married. We'll both press our points. Mine's steel, and it never gives way! Ha-ha-ha!"

Vautrin went out, not wishing to hear a refusal from the young man. He wanted to put Eugène at his ease. He seemed to know all about the little protests, the struggles men put up to reassure themselves and justify their own wrongdoing in their own eyes.

"He may do as he likes," thought Eugène. "I shall never marry Mademoiselle Taillefer!"

The thought of a compact with this man gave him an inward fever. Vautrin horrified him, but somehow seemed to grow greater in his eyes by the very cynicism of his views, and his bold, inclusive contempt for the world. Eugène dressed, ordered a cab, and went to Madame de Restaud's. For some days past, Anastasie had been doubly attentive to the young man; for it seemed as if his every step was a further progress into the heart of society, and his power was one day to be momentous. He paid his debts to Monsieur de Trailles and Monsieur d'Ajuda, played whist into the small hours, and won back all he had lost. Superstitious, like most men who have yet to make their way and who are more or less fatalistic about it, he tried to regard his good luck as a reward from heaven for his perseverance in the path of virtue.

The following morning he hastened to ask Vautrin if he still had his promissory note. On Vautrin's affirmative reply, he gave him back his three thousand francs with a natural air of satisfaction.

"All is going well," said Vautrin.

"But I'm not your accomplice," said Eugène.

"I know, I know," Vautrin interrupted. "You're still behaving like a child. You dawdle too long over the knickknacks round the shop door."

2

A few days later, Poiret and Mademoiselle Michonneau were sitting on a bench in the sun, in one of the deserted walks of the Jardin des Plantes, deep in conversation with the gentleman whose appearance had rightly aroused suspicions some time before in the mind of Bianchon.

"Mademoiselle," Monsieur Gondureau was saying, "I cannot see why you should hesitate. His Excellency the Minister for Police—"

"Ah!" cried Poiret, *"His Excellency the Minister!"*

"Yes," said Monsieur Gondureau, "His Excellency is looking into the matter personally."

It may surprise the reader that Poiret, an ex-clerk, a man of simple virtues and even simpler mind, should be willing to go on listening to this impostor once he had let fall the word "police," and disclosed the features of a detective from the Rue de Jérusalem behind his gentlemanly mask. Nothing, however, could have been more natural. The reader will better understand the particular species to which Poiret belonged in the great family of nitwits, if we draw on some hitherto unpublished observations, made by certain researchers, on the habits and distribution of the departmental fauna known as the *pennifera*. In the government budget estimates, these creatures are huddled away between the first parallel of latitude (that departmental Greenland where only salaries of twelve thousand francs are to be found) and the more temperate zone on the third parallel, where slightly warmer salaries of three to six thousand are discovered, and the *bonus* is acclimatized and known to flower, despite difficulties of cultivation.

Now the salient characteristic of this subordinate tribe is its involuntary, automatic, instinctive respect for the Grand Lama at the head of each ministry, who is known to the clerk by an illegible signature and the designation of HIS EXCELLENCY THE MINISTER: four words as potent in their effect as the name of "Bondo Cani" in *The Caliph of Baghdad*. In the eyes of this depressed class, the words represent a sacred, unassailable power. Like the Pope to the Catholic believer, His Excellency is, in the clerk's eyes, administratively infallible. The radiance he sheds illumines his every deed and word, and any word uttered in his name. His robe of office covers everything and legalizes every action he commands. His title, the mere word "Excellency," vouches for the purity of his intentions and the sanctity of his desires, and is a passport for ideas otherwise inadmissible.

Things that the wretched creatures under him would never do on their own, they rush to carry out the minute the word "Excellency" is spoken. Government offices have their form of passive obedience just as the army has: a system that stifles a man's conscience, obliterates his humanity, and ultimately makes him no more than a cog or screw in the government machine. Monsieur Gondureau, apparently an accurate judge of men, had been quick to recognize in Poiret one of these bureaucratic simpletons, and was therefore able to produce the shibboleth "His Excellency" as a *deus ex machina* and dazzle Poiret at the very moment of uncovering his own batteries. He regarded Poiret as a male version of Mademoiselle Michonneau, just as he regarded Michonneau as a female Poiret.

"Ah, well . . . of course, if His Excellency is *personally* . . . I mean, if His Excellency the Minister is personally . . . well, I mean, of course that's different, if His Excellency," observed Poiret.

Monsieur Gondureau turned to Mademoiselle Michonneau. "You hear what this gentleman says. And gather you trust his judgment. Well! His Excellency is absolutely certain that the man who calls himself Vautrin, now staying at the Maison Vauquer, is an escaped convict from Toulon Prison, where he goes by the name of Cheat-Death: *Trompe-la-Mort*."

"He's very lucky if he really deserves the name!" exclaimed Poiret.

"Yes," said the detective. "He's been given the nickname because he's been lucky enough not to lose his life in any of the extremely daring operations he's carried out. He's a dangerous man, I can tell you! And an exceptionally gifted one. His last sentence alone was enough to give him an immense reputation among his associates. . . ."

"Ah, he's a man of reputation, too?" inquired Poiret.

"In his way. He agreed to take the blame for someone else's crime, a forgery committed by a very handsome young man he was greatly attached to, a young Italian who gambled a great deal, and who has since gone into the army and done very well there."

"But if His Excellency the Minister of Police is sure that Monsieur Vautrin is Trompe-la-Mort, why does he need any help from me?" asked Mademoiselle Michonneau.

"Yes, yes," said Poiret, "if the Minister, as you so kindly mentioned, is really certain—"

"Certain is not quite the word; he only suspects. I'll explain. Jacques Collin, alias Trompe-la-Mort, is highly trusted by all the three great prisons. He's their agent and banker. He makes a lot of money out of these transactions—which naturally call for a man of mark."

"You observe the pun in that, mademoiselle?" said Poiret. "The gentleman calls him a man of mark, because he's been *marked*!"

"The so-called Vautrin," the detective went on, "looks after the money these convicts have, and invests it or saves it for them. He keeps it available for any of them that escape; or for their children when they make wills; or, if they ask him to, for their mistresses."

"Mistresses! You mean wives, surely?" said Poiret.

"No, sir. As a rule, convicts have only illicit relations, and we call the women concubines."

"You mean they all live in a state of concubinage!"

"What else?"

"Well!" said Poiret. "His Excellency certainly mustn't tolerate such abominations. Since you have the honor of His Excellency's confidence, and seem to be a public-spirited man, you must enlighten him about these people's immoral behavior. They give a very bad example to the rest of society."

"But the government doesn't exactly offer them as a model—"

"Quite so, but I really do think—"

"Do let the gentleman get on, my dear," said Mademoiselle Michonneau.

"You understand, mademoiselle," Gondureau went on, "that Collin's illegal treasury is thought to be very large, and the government is naturally very anxious to lay hands on it. Very substantial sums are involved, because Trompe-la-Mort not only looks after his comrades' funds but also those of the Ten Thousand Society—"

"Ten thousand thieves!" cried the terrified Poiret.

"No, the Ten Thousand Society is an association of major thieves—men who work only on a large scale, and refuse to meddle in anything that brings in less than ten thousand francs. This society includes all the most notable men we ever bring to the assizes. They know the law, and they never do anything that may involve the death penalty if they're caught. Collin is their confidential adviser. With his immense resources, he's managed to build up a private police force with agents everywhere; and he has surrounded it with impenetrable secrecy. We've had spies all around him for twelve whole months, and we still can't make out what his game is. His money and his talents are always at the service of crime and vice, and the whole thing keeps an army of blackguards in a perpetual state of war against society. If we can lay hands on Trompe-la-Mort, and get hold of his bank, we can cut the evil at its root. The hunt for him has become a matter of official high policy, and it will honor anyone who contributes to its success. You yourself, Monsieur Poiret, might be found a job in the administration again. You might become, say, a secretary to a police superintendent, and still be allowed to draw your retirement pension."

"But why doesn't Trompe-la-Mort run off with the money?" asked Mademoiselle Michonneau.

"Because wherever he went," said the detective, "he'd be followed by someone with orders to kill him, if he robbed the prison. And in any case you can't run off with a bank in the way you can with a respectable girl. Besides, Collin's not the sort of fellow to play a trick like that. He'd think it was dishonorable."

"Sir," said Poiret, "you are quite right. It *would* be dishonorable."

"All this still doesn't explain why you don't simply come and get him yourselves," said Mademoiselle Michonneau.

"Well, mademoiselle, I'll tell you. . . . But," he went on in an undertone, "do stop your gentleman from interrupting, or we'll never finish. If people have got to listen to this old boy, he ought to pay them. When Trompe-la-Mort came here, he set himself up as a good, solid, respectable Paris tradesman. He took lodgings in a modest boardinghouse. You see, he's smart; we shan't catch him napping. And 'Monsieur Vautrin' is a respected man, carrying on a respectable business."

"Oh, naturally," murmured Poiret.

"Now, if there were a mistake, and someone really called Monsieur Vautrin were arrested, the Minister would have the whole business world of Paris, and public opinion as well, turning on him. The Prefect of Police is in a shaky position. He has his enemies. If there were a mistake, all the Liberals would be squalling and bawling at us, and the men who are after his job would get him kicked out. We have to go about this business as we did in the Coignard case, with the sham Count of Saint Helena. If there'd been a real Count of Saint Helena, we'd have been in the soup. We have to have proof."

"Yes, but what you need is a pretty woman," said Mademoiselle Michonneau brightly.

"Trompe-la-Mort would never let a woman get near him," said the detective. "I'll tell you a secret: he doesn't like women."

"Then I don't see how I can help you to prove his identity . . . even supposing I agreed to do it for the two thousand francs you mentioned."

"Nothing easier," said Gondureau. "I'll give you a phial with a prepared liquid inside that will bring on a stroke—not a serious one in any way, but it'll look like a fit. It's a drug you can put in wine or coffee, either will do. You'll immediately lay your man on a bed, and undress him to make sure he isn't dying. The minute you're alone with him, you give him a hard slap on the shoulder, and you'll see the branded letters reappear."

"Why, that's nothing," said Poiret.

"Well, do you agree?" Gondureau asked the old maid.

"But, my dear sir," she replied, "suppose there aren't any letters, do I still get the two thousand francs?"

"No."

"What would my expenses be in that case?"

"Five hundred francs."

"What, do all that for such a little? It's just as heavy on the conscience, and I have to keep my conscience quiet, after all."

"I can assure you," said Poiret, "that mademoiselle has a very large conscience, quite apart from being so nice and clever."

"Well," said Mademoiselle Michonneau, "give me three thousand francs, if he's Trompe-la-Mort, and nothing if he's respectable."

"It's a deal," said Gondureau, "but only on condition it's done tomorrow."

"That's too soon. I have to consult my confessor."

"Shrewd article," said the detective, rising. "Till tomorrow, then. If you want me in a hurry, come to the Petite Rue Sainte-Anne, at the end of the Cour de la Sainte-Chapelle. There's only one door under the arch. Ask for Monsieur Gondureau."

The end of this conversation was heard by Bianchon,

on his way home from Cuvier's lecture. He was much struck by the unusual expression "Trompe-la-Mort"; and by the way the well-known police chief had said, "It's a deal."

"Why not get it over with at once?" asked Poiret, as they walked back. "It would buy you an annuity of three hundred francs."

"Yes, why not?" she said. "But I must think it over first. Suppose Monsieur Vautrin *is* this Trompe-la-Mort. It might be better to fix something up with him. Though if I asked him for money it would warn him, and he's the sort who'd clear out without paying up. That'd be an awful letdown."

"But even if he was warned," said Poiret, "didn't the gentleman tell us he was being watched? But *you'd* lose everything that way."

"In any case," brooded Mademoiselle Michonneau, "I don't like the man. Whenever he speaks to me, it's only to say something nasty."

"Much better to do what the gentleman asked," said Poiret. "He seemed a decent sort of man, quite apart from being so nicely dressed. And he did say it would be acting according to the law and ridding society of a criminal, however noble he may be. Once a thief always a thief. Why, suppose he took it into his head to murder us all? Good God, we'd be guilty of the murders, quite apart from being the first victims. . . ."

Mademoiselle Michonneau's problem prevented her from listening to the sentences that fell from Poiret's lips like drops of water from a tap not quite turned off. Whenever he embarked on a series of reflections, and Mademoiselle Michonneau omitted to stop him, he went on talking like a wound-up machine. After broaching some initial subject, he would be led by a succession of parentheses to talk of completely different matters, without concluding any of them. By the time they reached the Maison Vauquer he had drifted on through a maze of connecting passages and references, and was now relating his testimony in the case of Ragoulleau and Madame Morin, in which he had appeared as a witness for the defense.

As they went in, Mademoiselle Michonneau observed Eugène and Mademoiselle Taillefer engaged in so intimate and engrossing a conversation that neither of them looked up as the two old boarders passed through the dining room.

"It was bound to come to that," said Mademoiselle Michonneau. "They've been making sheep's eyes at each other for the past week."

"Yes," said Poiret, "that was why they found her guilty."

"Who?"

"Madame Morin."

"I was talking about Mademoiselle Victorine," said Mademoiselle Michonneau, absently wandering into Poiret's room. "Who's Madame Morin?"

"Why, whatever's Mademoiselle Victorine guilty of?" asked Poiret.

"She's guilty of falling in love with Monsieur Eugène de Rastignac; and she doesn't realize what it'll lead to, poor simple child. . . ."

That morning Madame de Nucingen had reduced Eugène to despair. In his mind he had surrendered completely to Vautrin; he refused to consider either the motives for the friendship this extraordinary man professed for him, or the outcome of such an alliance. Only a miracle could now drag him back from the abyss toward which he had, in the past hour, taken the first step by exchanging tender vows with Victorine. To the girl herself his voice was like that of an angel. The heavens had opened, the Maison Vauquer seemed to glitter with the fantastic colors of a palace on a stage. She was in love. Her love was returned, or so at least she believed. And so would any woman have believed who had seen and heard Eugène during this stolen hour away from the watchful eyes of the household. Struggling against his conscience, knowing he was doing wrong and determined to do so, telling himself he would atone for this venial sin by making a woman happy, Eugène had grown handsomer in his despair, and the fiery torment in his heart shone in his face.

Luckily for him, the miracle did take place: Vautrin came cheerfully in, and instantly read the minds of the young couple he had brought together by the operations of his satanic genius, but whose joy the sound of his deep, mocking voice now disturbed:

> "My Fanchette is delightful
> In her sweet simplicity. . . ."

Victorine fled, the happiness in her heart as great now as its former sadness. Poor girl! A pressure of the hand, Eugène's hair brushing against her cheek, a word murmured so close to her ear that she had felt the warmth of his mouth, a trembling arm around her waist, a light kiss on her neck: these were her betrothal rites, and the threat that Sylvie might at any moment enter the resplendent dining room gave them a passion, a life, an enchantment beyond the fairest vows exchanged in the whole literature of passion. These little liberties, as our grandparents so prettily called them, seemed like criminal acts to the devout girl who went once a fortnight to confession! She had squandered in the past hour more of her soul's treasure than she would spend, later in life, when she was rich and happy, in giving herself completely.

"It's all agreed," said Vautrin. "Our two young bucks are at each other's throats. It was all very civilized. A difference of opinion. Our pigeon insulted my falcon. It's to be tomorrow in the fortress at Clignancourt. At eight-thirty, Mademoiselle Taillefer will become heir to her father's love and fortune, while she sits here calmly eating bread and milk. Seems odd, doesn't it? Little Taillefer's very clever with his sword, and as sure of himself as a man with a fistful of trumps. But he'll be finished off with a thrust I invented myself—a little trick of bringing the sword upward and piercing the forehead.

I'll show you how it's done, sometime; it's frightfully handy."

Eugène listened in stupefaction. He could say nothing. At this moment Goriot, Bianchon, and some of the others came in.

"That's how I wanted you to be," said Vautrin. "You know just what you're doing. Good, my little eagle! You'll be a ruler of men; you're strong, firm, tough. I respect you." He moved to take Eugène's hand, but the young man quickly withdrew it, and sank into a chair, his face white. He seemed to see before him a pool of blood.

"Ah! We still cling to a few grubby swaddling clothes of virtue, don't we?" whispered Vautrin. "Never mind. Papa Taillefer is worth three million. The dowry will wash you white as a wedding dress—even in your own eyes."

Eugène's mind was made up. He would go and warn both the Taillefers that evening. As soon as Vautrin had left him, Goriot came over to him and whispered: "You're sad, my boy! But I've some news that will cheer you up. Come with me!" He lit his candle at one of the lamps. Eugène followed him, filled with curiosity.

"Let's go in your room," said the old man. He had already asked Sylvie for Eugène's key. "This morning you thought she'd stopped loving you, didn't you?" he went on. "She sent you away and that made you angry and miserable. Silly boy! She was expecting me! Do you understand? We had to go and put the finishing touches to a dear little apartment we've taken for you. You're to move in, in three days' time! Don't give me away. She wants it to be a surprise; but I didn't want to keep it a secret from you any longer. You'll be in the Rue d'Artois, just round the corner from the Rue Saint-Lazare. You'll be like a prince there. The furniture we've bought for you is just like a young bride's! We've been doing lots of things for you in the last month without saying a word about them! My lawyer's been at work; Delphine will have her thirty-six thousand francs a year, the interest on her dowry; and I shall insist on her eight hundred thousand francs being invested in good sound land."

Eugène was silent as he walked up and down his dismal, untidy room, his arms across his chest. Goriot seized a moment when his back was turned, and placed on the mantelpiece a red morocco box bearing the Rastignac arms stamped in gold.

"My dear boy," the poor old man was saying, "I've put my heart and soul into all this. But you must understand that I'm being very selfish as well. I have an interest in your move too. . . . You won't refuse me, will you, if I ask you something?"

"What is it?"

"There's a servant's room belonging to your apartment, two floors above. I can come and live there, can't I? I'm getting old, and I'm too far away from my girls. I won't be in your way. I'll just be there, that's all. You'll tell me about her every night. You won't mind that, will you? When you come home, and I'm in bed, I shall hear you, and think: 'He's just been seeing my little Delphine. He's taken her to the ball, she's happy because of him.' And if I were ill, it would be a great comfort to hear you coming and going and moving about. There'd be so much of my girl in you! And I shall have only a few steps to get from there to the Champs-Elysées, where they go every day. I'll be able to see them every time. As it is, I sometimes get there too late. . . . And then perhaps she'll come and stay with you! I shall hear her, I shall see her, pattering about in her soft morning coat, as pretty as a kitten. During this last month, she's grown to be just like she used to be: a girl again, happy and bright. Her soul is convalescing; and she owes it all to you. Oh, I'll do anything in the world for you! She said just now as we walked back: 'Papa, I'm so happy.' When they call me 'Father,' so formally, it makes me shiver with cold, but when they call me 'Papa,' I seem to see them as little girls again. I seem more their father, and they don't seem to belong to anyone else." He wiped the tears from his eyes as he spoke.

"It was such a long time since I'd heard that word,

so long since she'd taken my arm. Yes, yes, it must be
ten years, at least, since I last walked out with one of
my daughters. It's lovely to feel her dress near you, to
walk in step with her, to feel her warmth! This morning
I went everywhere with Delphine. I went into shops
with her. And then I took her home. Oh, do let me
live near you! Sometimes you'll need someone to do
things for you, and I shall be there. . . . Oh, if only
that great Alsatian blockhead would die, if his gout
had the sense to go to his stomach, wouldn't my daughter be happy? You'd be my son-in-law, you'd be her
husband openly. . . . She's so unhappy at missing all
the pleasures of the world that I can forgive her anything. God must surely be on the side of a father who
loves his children.

"She loves you too much," he said, raising his head a
moment later. "As we went along, she talked about you.
'Isn't he good, Father? He has a good heart! Does he
ever talk about me?' Why, she must have said enough
about you to fill a book while we were walking from the
Rue d'Artois to the Passage des Panoramas! She poured
her whole heart into mine. For a whole blessed morning
I stopped being old, I didn't seem to weigh an ounce. I
told her you'd given me the thousand-franc note. Ah,
the dear girl, she was moved to tears. . . . What's that
you have on your mantelpiece?" he said, at last. He was
dying with impatience as he saw Eugène standing there
without moving.

Eugène looked at his neighbor in astonishment. The
duel that Vautrin had announced would take place on
the following day was in such violent contrast with this
realization of his dearest hopes, that he felt all the sensations of a nightmare. He turned to the mantelpiece and
saw the little square box, opened it, and found inside a
piece of paper, folded over a Bréguet watch. On the
paper was written:

I want you to think of me all the time, *because* . . .
                                                    Delphine

The last word doubtless referred to something that had passed between them. Eugène was touched by it. His family arms were enameled on the gold lining of the box. This long-desired trinket, the chain, the key, the molding, the whole design, answered his every wish. Goriot was beaming. He had no doubt promised to report to his daughter the smallest details of the surprise her present would cause Eugène; for he shared in these youthful emotions and seemed by no means the least happy of the three of them. He already loved Eugène, both on his daughter's account and on his own.

"You must go and see her this evening, she's expecting you. The fat Alsatian lump is having supper with his dancer. Ha ha ha, he did look a fool when my lawyer told him off! I thought he pretended he always worshiped my daughter? Let him touch her, and I'll kill him. The thought of my Delphine . . ." He broke off, and sighed. "It would drive me to crime. But it wouldn't be murder, he's just a calf's head on a pig's body. You will let me live with you, won't you?"

"Of course, dear Monsieur Goriot, you know how fond I am of you."

"I can see it. *You* aren't ashamed of me. Let me give you a hug." He pressed the young man to him. "Promise me you'll make her happy! You'll go this evening, won't you?"

"Oh, yes! I have to go out in any case. I have some urgent business."

"Can I help in any way?"

"Why, yes, you can! While I'm at Delphine's, will you go to Monsieur Taillefer's—the father's—and ask him if I can see him for an hour some time this evening, on a matter of great importance?"

"Is it true then, young man," demanded Goriot, his expression changing, "that you're courting his daughter? By God! You don't know what a blow from Goriot's fist can be like, and that's what it'll come to, if you're deceiving us! But it's impossible!"

"I swear to you I love only one woman on earth," said Eugène. "I only knew it a moment ago."

"I'm happy!" breathed Goriot.

"But Taillefer's son is fighting a duel tomorrow," Eugène went on, "and I've heard that he will certainly be killed."

"But what's that to you?" asked Goriot.

"But he must be told to stop his son from going!" cried Eugène. At this moment he was interrupted by the voice of Vautrin, singing outside the door:

> *"Oh, Richard, oh, my king!*
> *The whole world leaves you now. . . .*
> *Broom! Brroom! Brroom! Brroom!*
> *I've traveled the whole world over,*
> *Tra-la-la-la-la. . . ."*

"Gentlemen!" Christophe was heard calling. "The soup's on! Everybody's at table."

"Let's have a bottle of my claret!" Vautrin called back.

"It's a pretty watch, isn't it?" said Goriot. "Ah, she has such good taste!"

Vautrin, Goriot, and Eugène went down together and, being late, found themselves sitting side by side at the meal. Eugène maintained the greatest coldness toward Vautrin during dinner, although the man, so charming in Madame Vauquer's eyes, had never been so gay and witty. His jests sparkled, and his gaiety communicated itself to the others. His assurance and self-possession filled Eugène with dismay.

"What's the matter with you today?" asked Madame Vauquer. "You're as merry as a cricket."

"I'm always merry when I've done good business," said Vautrin.

"Business?" said Eugène.

"Yes, indeed. I've delivered a parcel of merchandise that will bring me in a very good commission. Mademoiselle Michonneau," he said, noticing the old maid's eyes on him, "is there something about my face that displeases you? Out with it! I'll get it changed specially for you. . . . You and I won't come to blows over that, will we, Poiret?" he said, with a wink at the old clerk.

"Damn it," said the young painter to Vautrin, "you ought to sit for a statue of Hercules Jesting."

"By God, I will! If Mademoiselle Michonneau will sit as the Graveyard Venus," replied Vautrin.

"What about Poiret?" Bianchon demanded.

"Oh, Poiret will sit as Poiret, he'll be the god of gardens," said Vautrin. "The name derives from *poire*. . . ."

"A sleepy pear!" said Bianchon. "You'll go between the pear and the cheese then. . . ."

"What a lot of nonsense you all talk," said Madame Vauquer. "You'd do better to give us a drop of your claret. I can see a bottle poking its nose out down there! It'll cheer us all up, quite apart from being so good for the tummy."

"Gentlemen," said Vautrin, "our lady chairman calls us to order. Madame Couture and Mademoiselle Victorine will not protest at your frivolity; but do respect the innocence of Monsieur Goriot. I offer you a small bottleorama of claret, rendered doubly distinguished by the name of Lafite—no political allusion, I need hardly add! Come on, Chung-Foo!" he said, looking at Christophe, who did not move. "Here, Christophe! Didn't you hear your name called? Chung-Foo, bring the liquids."

"Here, sir," said Christophe, offering him the bottle.

Vautrin filled a glass each for Eugène and Goriot, and slowly poured a few drops into his own glass, which he sipped while his two neighbors were drinking. Suddenly he pulled a face.

"Damnation! Hell, it tastes of the cork! You have that for yourself, Christophe, and go and get us some more. On the right, you know where they are. There are sixteen of us, so bring eight bottles."

"Well, since you're throwing your money about," said the painter, "I'll stand us a hundred chestnuts."

"Oh! Oh!"

"Wuff! Wuff!"

"Prrrrrrr!"

The varied shouts that went up were like the explosions at a fireworks display.

"Now, come on, Mamma Vauquer, you stand us a couple of bottles of champagne!" called Vautrin.

"What's that? Why don't you ask for the whole house while you're about it? Two bottles of champagne! Twelve francs! You must think I make a profit! But if Monsieur Eugène will pay for the champagne, I will provide some currant wine."

"Her currant wine works on you like a dose of salts," muttered Bianchon.

"Shut up, Bianchon!" cried Eugène. "The minute anyone mentions that, I—yes, yes, get the champagne, I'll pay for it," he added.

"Sylvie," said Madame Vauquer, "put out the biscuits and the little cakes."

"Your little cakes are too grown up, they've got whiskers," said Vautrin. "But shell out the biscuits by all means."

All at once the claret was circulating, and the gaiety of the party redoubled. Wild laughter mingled with sudden farmyard imitations. The museum clerk suddenly let out a Paris street cry resembling the yowling of an amorous tomcat, and immediately eight voices were bawling:

"Knives to grind!"

"Birdseed for the little birdies!"

"Biscuits, ladies, biscuits!"

"China to mend!"

"Oysters . . . ? Who wants oysters?"

"Beat your carpet, beat your missis!"

"Old clothes, old laces, old hats to sell!"

"Cherry ripe!"

Bianchon was awarded first prize for the nasal drawl in which he cried: "Um-ber-ellers! Um-ber-ellers!"

The noise increased to head-splitting volume, a babel of jokes and riddles, an opera with Vautrin conducting the orchestra. But he kept an eye on Eugène and Goriot, who seemed drunk already. Slumped in their chairs, they contemplated the unwonted disorder with solemn expressions. They drank little; they were both preoccupied

with what they had to do later in the evening. Nevertheless they felt incapable of getting to their feet. Vautrin,
who was following their changing expressions out of the
corner of his eye, seized the moment when Eugène's
eyelids began to droop to lean over him and murmur:
"My little lad, we aren't clever enough to fight against
our Papa Vautrin; and he's too fond of you to let you
do anything silly. When I've made up my mind to do
something, God alone can bar my way. Ha ha, we
wanted to go and warn Papa Taillefer. What a schoolboy
howler! The oven's hot, the flour's ground, the bread's
on the griddle! Tomorrow when we bite it, the crumbs'll
leap over our heads. . . . And we'd like to stop the bread
being baked? No, no, it'll all be baked! If we feel a wee
bit guilty, digestion will cure that. While we're all
asleep, Colonel Count Franceschini will open Michel
Taillefer's estate up for you with the point of his sword.
Victorine will inherit from her brother a sweet fifteen
thousand francs a year. I've already made inquiries, and
I know her mother left her more than three hundred
thousand. . . ."

Eugène heard the words and was unable to reply to
them. His tongue seemed stuck to the roof of his mouth;
he felt an irresistible drowsiness overcoming him; and
the table and the shapes of the revelers appeared
through a luminous mist. Soon the noise died down, the
boarders went out one by one until only Madame Vauquer, Madame Couture, Victorine, Vautrin, and Goriot
remained. He observed, as in a dream, Madame Vauquer resourcefully trotting about, making new full bottles of wine out of what was left in the old ones.

"How wild they are, how young they are," she said.

And this was the last thing Eugène remembered.

"There's nobody like Monsieur Vautrin for starting
this sort of a lark," said Sylvie. "Look at old Christophe,
snoring like a top."

"So long, Mamma," said Vautrin. "I'm going to the
Gaiety to see Monsieur Marty in *The Wild Mountain*, a
fine play based on *The Solitary*. If you'd like it, I'll take
you, and these ladies as well."

"No, thank you," said Madame Couture.

"What's that, my dear?" cried Madame Vauquer. "You won't go and see a play taken from *The Solitary*— a book by Atala de Chateaubriand? Why, we used to love reading it; it was so nice, we used to cry our eyes out like Mary Magdalen, about poor Elodie, down there by the artlechokes, last summer. It's a very moral book too, it would be very good for your young lady."

"We're not allowed to go to theaters," said Victorine.

"Look, they're out for the night, those two," said Vautrin, giving the heads of Goriot and Eugène a light, playful push.

He settled the young man's head against the chair so that he might sleep more comfortably, kissed him warmly on the forehead, singing:

> *"Sleep my pretty ones, sleep.*
> *Eternal watch I will keep. . . ."*

"I'm afraid he's ill," said Victorine.

"Stay and look after him, then," said Vautrin. He added in a whisper: "It's your duty as a devoted wife. And you'll certainly be his little wife, I prophesy that. The young man worships you. Yes," he said aloud. *"They were honored throughout the land, lived happily after, and had many children.* That's how all love stories finish. Come on, Mamma," he went on, giving Madame Vauquer a squeeze, "go and put your hat on, and your nice flowered dress, and the countess's scarf. I'll go and get a cab for you, my very self." And he went out, singing:

> *"Oh, sun, oh sun, oh beaming sun.*
> *Ripening pumpkins, one by one . . ."*

"My goodness me, Madame Couture," said Madame Vauquer, "I could live with that man in a garret and not complain once. Look at *him*!" She pointed to Goriot. "That old miser's never taken me out anywhere. Gracious, he'll fall on the floor! It's disgusting. A man of his age! He must have taken leave of his senses. Not that you can lose what you haven't got, I suppose. Sylvie, get him up to his room."

Sylvie, grasping the old man by the arm, forced him to walk upstairs and threw him like a parcel onto the bed, fully clad.

"Poor young man," said Madame Couture, brushing back Eugène's hair, which had fallen over his eyes. "He's like a girl, he doesn't know what drinking means. . . ."

"I can truthfully declare," stated Madame Vauquer, "that in all the thirty-one years I've run this boarding-house, I've had hundreds of young men go through my hands, as you might say, but never a one as pleasant and select as Monsieur Eugène. Looks very handsome when he's asleep, doesn't he? Lay his head on your shoulder, Madame Couture. Oops! He's going to fall on top of Mademoiselle Victorine! Ah, no, there's a God looks after children. He nearly banged his head on the chair. The two of them would make a pretty pair, wouldn't they?"

"Hush, my dear," said Madame Couture, "you mustn't say such things."

"Nonsense!" said Madame Vauquer. "He can't hear. Come and help me dress, Sylvie. I shall put my large corset on."

"Your large corset after all that dinner!" exclaimed Sylvie. "Then you must get someone else to squeeze you into it, I don't want the responsibility if it kills you. You must be careful; it might cost you your life."

"I don't care! I must be worthy of Monsieur Vautrin."

"You must be very fond of your heirs!"

"Sylvie! Stop arguing!" said the widow, and she left the room.

"At her age, too," murmured Sylvie with a wink at Victorine, as she followed her mistress out.

Madame Couture and Victorine were left alone in the dining room. Christophe's snores resounded through the silent house, in contrast with the peaceful, childlike slumber of Eugène, who still lay with his head on Victo-

rine's shoulder. There was something proud and mater-
nally protective in the expression on her face. She was
happy at the opportunity for one of those acts of goodness in which all women's hearts overflow; and she
could, without sin, feel the young man's heart against
her own. Among a thousand confused feelings in her
soul was a wild thrill of pleasure at the innocent warmth
of him close to her.

"My poor dear girl," said Madame Couture, pressing
her hand. She looked at the girl's pale, pathetic face,
surrounded as it now seemed by a halo of happiness.
She looked like one of the primitive paintings of the
Middle Ages, in which the painter omits all details of
the scene and concentrates the magic of his calm proud
brush on the face whose ivory pallor seems suffused with
a golden light from heaven.

"But he didn't drink more than two glasses," she said,
running her fingers through Eugène's hair.

"Yes, but if he'd been a bad young man, he'd have
carried his wine like the others. The fact that he's drunk
does him credit."

The sound of a cab was heard in the street.

"Mamma," said Victorine, "here's Monsieur Vautrin.
Look after Monsieur Eugène. I wouldn't like that man
to catch me like this. He says things that make you feel
horrid, and when he looks at a woman, it's as if someone
were taking her clothes off."

"No, you're quite wrong," said Madame Couture.
"Monsieur Vautrin is a fine man. He reminds me a little of
the late Monsieur Couture. He's rough, but kind."

Vautrin came softly into the room and looked at the
picture formed by the two children in the gentle lamplight.

"Well, well," he said crossing his arms, "this is a scene
that would have inspired Bernardin de Saint-Pierre, the
noble author of *Paul et Virginie*. Youth is very beautiful,
Madame Couture. Sleep on, poor child," he said, looking
at Eugène. "Good befalls us while we sleep, sometimes.
What I find so appealing, so touching, about this young
man," he said to Madame Couture, "is the knowledge

that the beauty of his soul is in keeping with the beauty of his face. Don't you think he looks like a cherub, resting on an angel's shoulder? He deserves to be loved. . . . If I were a woman, I'd like to die—no, that's foolish, I'd like to *live* for him! When I see the two of them together like that, madame," he said, dropping his voice to a whisper, "I can't help feeling God must have made them for each other. The ways of Providence are inscrutable, searching us body and soul. Seeing you together, my children, united in innocence and in all your human impulses, I'm sure it's impossible the future should ever part you. God is just. And I'm sure I've seen the prosperity line on your hand, Mademoiselle Victorine. Show me. I know my palmistry, I've often told fortunes. Don't be afraid. Oh! What's this I see? I swear on my honor that before long you'll be one of the richest heiresses in Paris. You will crown the happiness of the man who loves you. Your father will call you to him. You will marry a handsome, titled, adoring young man."

The heavy tread of the skittish widow was heard on the stairs. This put a stop to Vautrin's prophecies.

"Here comes Mamma Vauquerrr, fair as a starrr; and strung up like a bunch of carrots. Aren't we suffocating ourselves a wee bit?" he asked, placing a hand on the top of her corset. "A bit of a crush in the vestibule, here, Mamma! If we start crying, there'll be an explosion. Never mind, I'll be there to collect the bits—just like an antiquary."

"Now, there's the language of true French gallantry," murmured Madame Vauquer in an aside to Madame Couture.

Vautrin turned to Eugène and Victorine. "Good-bye, children," he said, placing a hand on either head, "you have my blessing. And take my word for it, mademoiselle, a good man's blessing is worth having. It should bring happiness; it is heard by God."

"Good-bye, dear friend," said Madame Vauquer to her boarder. "You don't think," she said, dropping her voice, "that Monsieur Vautrin has designs on me, I suppose?"

"Tut-tut!"

The two women were left alone. Victorine sighed and looked down at her hands. "Ah," she said, "if only good Monsieur Vautrin were telling the truth."

"Well, it needs only one thing," said the old lady, "and that's for your monstrous brother to fall off his horse."

"Ah, no!"

"Well, I suppose it's a sin to wish even our enemies harm," the widow added. "I'll do penance for it. Though I can't help saying it: I'd gladly take flowers to his grave. The heartless creature! He hasn't the courage to speak up for his own mother; and he hangs on to all she left you just by a swindle. My cousin was a rich woman. Unfortunately for you, it's never been asked how much she brought with her when she got married."

"I could never be happy if it had cost someone's life," said Victorine. "If I could be made happy only by my brother's death, I'd rather stay here forever."

"Ah, my God! (As good Monsieur Vautrin keeps saying—what a religious man he is; I'm glad he's not an unbeliever, like the rest of them—they have more respect för the devil than they have for God.) Who can tell what ways Providence may be pleased to lead us by?" sighed Madame Couture.

Assisted by Sylvie, the two women managed to get Eugène up to his room. They laid him on the bed, and the cook loosened his clothes to make him more comfortable. Before they left him, while her guardian's back was turned for a moment, Victorine dropped a kiss on Eugène's brow, with all the bliss implicit in such a sinful act. She looked round the room and gathered into one single thought this day's countless joys, contemplating it searchingly, as though it were a picture. She fell asleep the happiest creature in Paris.

It was that evening's festivities, under cover of which Vautrin had made Eugène and Goriot drink opiated wine, that sealed Vautrin's fate. First, Bianchon, half-drunk, completely forgot to question Mademoiselle Mi-

chonneau about Trompe-la-Mort. Had he uttered this
name, he would certainly have put Vautrin on his guard—
or Jacques Collin, to give the famous convict his real
name. Secondly, the nickname "Graveyard Venus" had
decided Mademoiselle Michonneau to give Collin up, at
the very moment when, trusting to the convict's generosity, she had been debating whether it might not be more
profitable to warn him, and so help him to escape during
the night.

She had just gone out with Poiret to see the famous
chief of the Sûreté in the Petite Rue Sainte-Anne. She
still believed she was dealing with a high-ranking clerk
named Gondureau. The chief received her courteously.
Then, after a discussion about details, she asked for the
potion she was to use in verifying the "mark." From the
satisfied expression on the great man's face as he took
the phial from a drawer in his desk, Mademoiselle Michonneau guessed that there was something more important in this capture than the arrest of a mere convict.
Racking her brains, she began to suspect that the police
had been given information by traitors in the prison, and
were hoping to get there in time to lay hands on some
rich haul of treasure. When she mentioned these conjectures, the old fox smiled and tried to divert her suspicions.

"You're mistaken," he said. "Collin is the most dangerous *sorbonne* we've ever known among thieves.
That's all it comes to. The rascals know it. He's their
banner, their mainstay, their Bonaparte, shall I say? This
fellow will never leave his *tronche* on the Place de
Grève."

She looked blank, and Gondureau explained the two
slang words he had used. *Sorbonne* and *tronche* are two
racy expressions from the lingo of thieves, who as a class
were the first to find it necessary to distinguish two separate aspects of the human head. . . . *Sorbonne* is the
head of a living man, his judgment, his thought. *Tronche*
is a contemptuous word, devised to express how little a
head matters once it is cut off.

"Collin is playing with us," he went on. "When we

have men as tough as steel, like this one, to deal with,
we have the option of killing them if they put up the
slightest resistance to arrest. We count on some assault
to let us kill Collin tomorrow morning. In that way we
avoid a trial, and the expense of keeping and feeding
him in jail; and it rids society of a nuisance. The proceed-
ings, the summoning of the witnesses and their expenses,
the execution, and all the legal paraphernalia we have
to go through to get rid of these scoundrels, costs even
more than your three thousand francs. And we save time
too. A bayonet in Trompe-la-Mort's belly will prevent a
hundred other crimes, and we shall avoid the corruption
of fifty good-for-nothings who'll be much better off staying sensibly in the penitentiary. That's how police work
should be done. Any real philanthropist would tell you
that's the best way to keep down crime."

"It's a service to one's country too," said Poiret.

"Quite so," commented the chief. "You're talking
sense tonight for a change. Yes, to be sure, we're serving
the country. And people are very unjust to us about it.
We do a good deal of service to society unbeknown. In
any case an intelligent man has to learn to rise above
prejudice; and a good Christian has to accept the insults
you always get for doing good if you don't entirely con-
form to conventional ideas. Paris is Paris, that's what it
comes to. That word explains my life. My best respects,
mademoiselle. I shall be with my men at the Jardin-du-
Roi tomorrow. Send Christophe to ask for me at the
Rue de Buffon, in the house where I am living. My best
respects, Monsieur Poiret. If anything of yours ever gets
stolen, just call on me to get it back for you. I am at
your service."

"There!" said Poiret to Mademoiselle Michonneau on
the way back. "And there are fools about who fall over
if you so much as mention the word 'police.' This gentleman is very nice. And what he asks you to do is as easy
as kiss your hand."

3

The following day was to be among the most extraordinary in the whole history of the Maison Vauquer. The most notable event in its peaceful existence hitherto had been the meteoric passage of the bogus Comtesse de l'Ambermesnil. But that was to pale beside the adventures of this great day, which was to figure in Madame Vauquer's discourse ever after.

To begin with, Goriot and Eugène slept till eleven. Madame Vauquer, who had returned from the Gaiety at midnight, stayed in bed till half past ten. Christophe, who had finished the wine provided by Vautrin, slept late, and the service in the house was delayed. Poiret and Mademoiselle Michonneau were not distressed at the lateness of breakfast. As for Victorine and Madame Couture, they slept all morning. Vautrin went out before eight and came back just as breakfast was being served. No one therefore complained that it was already a quarter past eleven when Sylvie and Christophe knocked at everyone's door, calling out that breakfast was getting cold.

While the two servants were out of the room, Mademoiselle Michonneau, who was down first, poured the potion into Vautrin's personal silver goblet, in which the cream for his coffee was being kept warm on the stove, along with all the other cups. She had relied on this detail for the success of her plan.

It was not without some difficulty that the seven boarders were finally assembled. Just as Eugène, who was last of all, came down, stretching and yawning, a messenger handed him a letter from Delphine. It ran as follows:

> I have no false vanity, and I'm not angry with you, my dear; but I waited up for you till two o'clock this morning. Waiting for the person one loves! Anyone who has known this torture doesn't inflict it on anyone else. I can see now that this is the first time you've been in love. Whatever has happened? I am terribly worried. If I hadn't been afraid to reveal the secrets of my heart to everybody, I'd have come to see what had happened to you, happy or unhappy. But to come out at such an hour, either on foot or in the carriage, would surely have been fatal. I felt all the unhappiness of being a woman. Do reassure me, do explain why you didn't come, after what my father told you. Are you ill? Why do you live so far away? Just one word, I beg you. You will come soon, *please*? If you're busy, one word will be enough. Just say: "I'm coming" or "I'm ill." But if you'd been ill, my father would have come and told me. What *can* have happened. . . ?

"Yes, what's happened?" cried Eugène, rushing into the dining room, crumpling up the letter without finishing it. "What time is it?"

"Half past eleven," said Vautrin, sugaring his coffee.

The escaped convict cast on Eugène the coldly fascinating look that some pre-eminently magnetic men are gifted with—a look capable, it is said, of quelling raving lunatics in an asylum. Eugène trembled in every limb. The noise of a cab was heard from the street, and a frightened-looking servant in the livery of Monsieur Taillefer's household rushed in. Madame Couture recognized him at once.

"Mademoiselle," he cried, "your father is asking for you. A terrible thing has happened. Monsieur Frédéric has been in a duel. He's been cut in the forehead, the doctors don't think they can save him; you'll only just have time to say good-bye to him. He's no longer conscious."

"Poor young man!" exclaimed Vautrin. "Why do people with thirty thousand francs a year have to pick quarrels? Certainly the young don't know how to behave."

"Sir!" shouted Eugène.

"Well, what, big baby boy?" asked Vautrin, placidly finishing his coffee, an operation Mademoiselle Michonneau was following too attentively to show any emotion at the astounding event that had stunned everyone else. "Isn't there a duel every morning in Paris?"

"I shall come with you, Victorine," said Madame Couture.

And the two women rushed out without shawl or hat. On her way out Victorine, her eyes full of tears, looked at Eugène as though to say: "I never thought our happiness could cause me to weep!"

"Well, you must be a prophet, Monsieur Vautrin," said Madame Vauquer.

"I'm everything," said Jacques Collin.

"How very strange it all is!" went on Madame Vauquer, proceeding to string together a series of platitudes on the event: "In the midst of life we are in death. Often the young are called before the old. We women are lucky we don't have anything to do with duels. Though we have other ills that men are free from. We bear children, and mother-trouble lasts forever. . . . What a windfall for Victorine! Her father will be obliged to adopt her."

"There you are," said Vautrin with a glance at Eugène. "Yesterday she hadn't a penny, today she's worth millions."

"Ah yes," cried Madame Vauquer, "you *have* struck it lucky there, Monsieur Eugène."

At this remark, Goriot looked at the young man, and saw the crumpled letter in his hand.

"You never finished it! What does this mean? Are you just like the others?" he asked.

"Madame," said Eugène, turning to Madame Vauquer, and speaking in tones of horror and disgust that surprised the others, "I shall never marry Mademoiselle Victorine."

Old Goriot seized the student's hand and pressed it. At that moment he could have kissed it.

"Oho!" said Vautrin. "The Italians have a good expression: *col tempo.*"

"I was told to wait for an answer," Delphine's messenger said to Eugène.

"Say I'll come."

The man departed. Eugène was in a state of such anger that he was incapable of caution. "What can I do," he said aloud, though addressing himself. "There's no proof!"

Vautrin smiled. At this moment the drug had reached his stomach and was beginning to take effect. However, the convict was so strong that he could still stand up, look at Eugène, and say to him in a hollow voice: "Young man, good befalls us while we sleep."

And he fell like a log to the floor.

"So there is a divine justice!" said Eugène.

"Why, whatever's the matter with poor Monsieur Vautrin?"

"He's having a fit!" cried Mademoiselle Michonneau.

"Quick, Sylvie, run and get the doctor, girl!" cried Madame Vauquer. "Oh, Monsieur Rastignac, go and get Monsieur Bianchon at once. Perhaps Sylvie will find that Monsieur Grimprel, our doctor, has gone out."

Eugène, glad of an excuse to escape from this frightful den, slipped quickly away.

"Christophe, quick, run round to the druggist and see if he has anything for fits."

Christophe hurried out.

"Monsieur Goriot, help us get him up to his room."

They lifted Vautrin, struggled upstairs with him, and laid him on his bed.

"I'm no use to you here. And I have to go and see my daughter," said Goriot.

"Selfish old thing!" exclaimed Madame Vauquer. "Go. . . . I hope *you* die like a dog."

"Go and see if you've any ether," Mademoiselle Michonneau ordered Madame Vauquer. She and Poiret had loosened Vautrin's clothing. Madame Vauquer went down to her room, leaving Mademoiselle Michonneau in possession of the field.

"Quick, take his shirt off and turn him over! Do try and do something useful, if it's only sparing me the sight of his nakedness," she said to Poiret. "Don't stand there like a sheep."

Vautrin was turned over, and Mademoiselle Michonneau gave the sick man a sharp slap on the shoulder; and the two fatal letters showed white in the middle of the red patch.

"My word, you *have* earned your three thousand franc reward quickly!" cried Poiret, holding Vautrin up while Mademoiselle Michonneau restored his shirt. "Ouff, he's heavy," he said, laying him down again.

"Be quiet. I wonder if there's a strongbox?" she said sharply. Her glance seemed to pierce the walls, so avidly did her eyes dart over even the smallest piece of furniture in the room. "I wonder if we could make some excuse for opening that desk?" she said.

"That might be wrong," observed Poiret.

"No. Money that's been stolen from all over the place doesn't belong to anybody. But there's no time," she added. "I can hear Madame Vauquer coming."

"Here's the ether," said Madame Vauquer. "Heavens, what a day of excitement! Why, that's not a fit he's having; he's as white as a chicken."

"A chicken?" inquired Poiret.

"His heart's regular," said the widow, placing a hand on it.

"Regular?" asked the astonished Poiret.

"He's all right."

"D'you think so?" asked Poiret.

"Why, he just looks as if he was asleep. Sylvie's gone for the doctor. Look! He's sniffing the ether. It's just a spasm! His pulse is all right. He's as strong as a horse. Just look at all that hair on his chest; he'll live to a hundred! His wig hasn't even come off. . . . Why, look, it's stuck on! And he's got false hair! It must be because his own hair's red. They say redheads are all good or all bad. He's one of the good ones, isn't he, though?"

"Good for hanging," said Poiret.

"Hanging around a pretty woman, oh *yes!*" amended Mademoiselle Michonneau hastily. "Run along, Monsieur Poiret. It's a woman's job to look after you men when you're ill. In any case, for all the good you are here, you might as well go out for a walk," she added. "Madame Vauquer and I will look after dear Monsieur Vautrin."

Poiret departed, placid and unmurmuring, like a dog his master has just aimed a kick at.

Eugène had gone out. He felt as though he were suffocating. He wanted fresh air; he had to walk. The crime he had hoped to prevent the night before had been committed at the appointed time. What had happened? What was he to do? He trembled at the thought of being an accomplice. He was still appalled at Vautrin's coolness.

"If only he might die without speaking again," he thought; and he wandered up and down the Luxembourg gardens with the feeling that a pack of hounds was barking at his heels.

"Hi!" Bianchon greeted him. "Have you seen the *Pilote*?"

The *Pilote* was a radical daily newspaper edited by Monsieur Tissot. It provided country readers, some time after the morning papers, with an edition where they found the latest news, twenty-four hours before their own newspapers appeared.

"There's an amazing story in it," said Bianchon. "Young Taillefer fought a duel last night with Count Franceschini of the Old Guard, and got two inches of steel in his forehead. And little Victorine is going to be one of the richest girls in Paris! Well, if only one knew these things beforehand . . . ! What a game of chance death is! Is it true Victorine has taken a fancy to you?"

"Be quiet, Bianchon, I shall never marry her. I'm in

love with an enchanting woman; she loves me, and I'm . . ."

"You say that as if you were having to flog yourself into not being unfaithful to her. Just show me any woman who's worth giving up the Taillefer fortune for."

"Are all the devils in hell after me?" cried Eugène.

"What's the matter with you? Are you mad? Give me your hand," said Bianchon. "Let me take your pulse. You're feverish."

"You must go to Mother Vauquer's," said Eugène. "That blackguard Vautrin has gone off in a dead faint."

"Ah!" said Bianchon. "That confirms something suspicious I want to try and verify." And he hurried away.

Eugène's long walk was a solemn one. It was as if he were walking round and round his own conscience. He wavered, he questioned, he hesitated, but at last his integrity emerged from this bitter, terrible colloquy as strong as a bar of unyielding steel. He recalled Goriot's confidences of the previous night, remembered the apartment chosen for him near Delphine, in the Rue d'Artois. He took out the letter again, reread it, kissed it.

"A love like that is my sheet anchor," he thought. "This poor old man has been tortured. He never talks about his sufferings, but who can't see them? Well! I shall look after him as if he were my own father. I'll find a thousand ways to please him. If she loves me, she'll often come and pass the day with me, near him. The great Comtesse de Restaud is a disgraceful woman, she'd turn her father into a lackey. . . .

"Dear Delphine, she's kinder to the old boy. She deserves to be loved. . . . And tonight, I shall be happy!" He took out the watch and admired it. "I've succeeded in everything! Provided people love one another forever, they're allowed to help one another. I can accept this. Besides, I know I shall get on, and I shall be able to return things a hundredfold. There's nothing criminal in our relationship, nothing that even the strictest person could frown at. How many decent people contract such unions! The only degrading thing is telling lies; and we shall be deceiving no one. Lying is cowardice, surely. Everything was over long ago between her and her husband. Anyway, I shall tell the Alsatian myself that he must give her up to me, since he can't make her happy himself."

Eugène's struggle lasted a long time. Although his youthful virtue was to win the day, nevertheless at about half past four, as night was closing in, an overpowering curiosity drew him back to the Maison Vauquer, although he vowed to himself to leave it forever. He wanted to know if Vautrin was dead.

After giving him an emetic, Bianchon had sent the matter thrown up by Vautrin to be chemically analyzed at the hospital. Observing Mademoiselle Michonneau's efforts to get the vomit thrown away, his suspicions grew. Moreover, Vautrin had recovered so quickly that Bianchon began to suspect some plot against their gay companion of the boardinghouse. When Eugène arrived, Vautrin was standing by the stove in the dining room. The day boarders, attracted earlier than usual by the news of the Taillefer duel and curious to hear the details of it, and of the effect it would have on the future of Victorine, were already assembled—except for Goriot— and were discussing the event. As Eugène came in, his eyes met those of the imperturbable Vautrin, who gave him such a disturbingly searching look that he shivered.

"Well, dear boy!" he said, "death won't get her hands on me for a long time yet, it seems. The ladies tell me I've just recovered triumphantly from a stroke that would have killed an ox."

"A bull, even!" exclaimed Madame Vauquer.

"Are you sorry to see me still alive?" Vautrin whispered to Eugène, whose thoughts he seemed to divine. "I must be a damned strong man, mustn't I?"

"Why, good heavens, that reminds me!" said Bianchon suddenly. "I heard Mademoiselle Michonneau talking the day before yesterday about a gentleman called 'Trompe-la-Mort:' that'd be a jolly good name for you."

The words struck Vautrin like a thunderbolt. He went pale, and staggered back. His magnetic glance fell like a beam of bright sunlight on Mademoiselle Michonneau, and her legs gave way beneath her. She collapsed into a chair. Poiret hastily moved between her and Vautrin, realizing that she was in danger. A ferocious purpose had appeared in the convict's face, as the benevolent mask that concealed his true character was cast aside. Still in the dark as to what was happening, the boarders looked on in astonishment. Suddenly, from the street outside came the sound of men's voices, and the clatter of soldiers' rifles on the pavement. Collin had automatically looked around at the walls and the windows for a way of escape, when four men appeared at the drawing-room door. The first was Gondureau; the three others were his officers. A murmur of astonishment greeted them that almost drowned the words solemnly pronounced by one of them: "In the name of the king and the law!"

Silence fell, and the boarders drew aside to allow the three officers to pass. Each man was grasping a loaded pistol in his side pocket. Two gendarmes who had followed them stood in the doorway of the drawing room; two more appeared at the door leading to the stairs. The rifles of a group of soldiers rattled on the pebbled path along the house front. There was thus no hope of flight for Trompe-la-Mort, toward whom all eyes had irresistibly turned. Gondureau marched up to him and gave him a sharp rap on the head which caused his wig to fall off; and Collin's head was revealed in all its horror. The short red-brick hair gave his face a frightful appearance of cunning strength, matching his huge chest and shoulders. His whole bearing seemed to glow with a fire from hell.

Vautrin was at last revealed complete: his past, his present, his future, his ruthless doctrines, his religion of hedonism, the regality conferred on him by his cynical thoughts and deeds and his devil-may-care strength of character. The blood mounted to his cheeks, and his eyes gleamed like a wildcat's. He sprang back with savage energy and let out a roar that drew shrieks of terror from the boarders. At this tigerish movement, and with the general clamor as their excuse, the officers drew their pistols. Collin recognized his danger the moment he saw the glitter of the steel, and suddenly gave proof of superhuman self-control. A terrifying, majestic sight! His rage suddenly dissolved. It was like the phenomenon produced when a vast caldron of steaming vapor, powerful enough to split a mountain, is dissolved in the twinkling of an eye at the touch of a drop of cold water. The drop of water that cooled Collin's wrath was a lightning thought. He broke into a smile, and looked down at his wig.

"You're not in your politest mood today," he said to Gondureau. And he held out his hands to the gendarmes, nodding to them to come closer. "Gentlemen," he said, "put the handcuffs or bracelets on me. I call on all present to witness that I offer no resistance." A murmur of admiration at the quick ebb and flow of fire and lava in this human volcano went through the room.

"That's one for you, you old housebreaker," continued Collin, smiling at Gondureau.

"Come on, undress," said Gondureau contemptuously.

"Why?" asked Collin. "There are ladies present. I deny nothing, and I give myself up."

He paused, and surveyed the company like an orator about to say something surprising.

"Take this down, Papa Lachapelle," he said, to a little white-haired old man who had taken from a portfolio the warrant for arrest, and had sat down at the end of the table. "I admit to being Jacques Collin, known as Cheat-Death, under sentence of twenty years in irons; and I've just proved that I haven't stolen my nickname. If I'd so much as lifted my hand," he said to the boarders, "these three stoolpigeons would have spattered my juice all over Mamma Vauquer's floorboards. These bastards are very adept at ambushes."

"Oh, my goodness, Sylvie, I do feel poorly," said Madame Vauquer suddenly. "And to think I was at the Gaiety with him only last night!"

"Come, be philosophical about it, Mamma," said Collin. "Does it do you any harm to have been in my box at the Gaiety last night? Are you any better than I am? I've less shame stamped on my back than you have in your heart. You're nothing more, any of you, than the flabby limbs of a gangrened society. The very best among you couldn't hold out against me." His eyes fixed on Eugène, and he smiled gently at him—a strange contrast to the cruelty in his face. "Our bargain still holds good, my angel, provided of course you accept! Remember?" And he sang:

> *"My Fanchette is delightful,*
> *In her sweet simplicity. . . .*

"Don't be embarrassed," he said. "I know how to collect my debts. No one would dare try and bitch *me*!"

The prison, with its manners and language, its swift twists from the facetious to the horrible, its appalling grandeur, its familiarity, its depravity, was suddenly demonstrated in this aside, and by this one man. But Collin was no longer a man; he was the epitome of a whole degenerate race, at once savage and calculating, brutal and docile. In a single moment he became a poem from hell, in which all human feelings were painted save one, that of repentance. His expression was that of a fallen archangel bent on eternal war. Eugène lowered his gaze, acknowledging this criminal kinship as an expiation of his own wicked thoughts.

"Who betrayed me?" asked Collin, sweeping the assembly with a terrifying glance. He paused at Mademoiselle Michonneau: "It was you, you old squealer, you gave me that fake stroke, you prying old bag! Why, a couple of words from me, and you'd find your throat cut before the week was out . . . ! But I forgive you. I'm a Christian—and besides it wasn't you who sold me. But who was it? . . . Ah!" he shouted to the detectives upstairs, who could be heard opening his cupboards and collecting his belongings. "Rummaging about up there, are you? The birds left the nest yesterday. And you'll never find where they've gone. I keep my ledgers here," he said, striking his forehead. "Now I know who sold me. It must have been that blackguard, Fil-de-Soie. That right, Father Copper?" he said to Gondureau. "It wouldn't do to keep our bank notes up there, obviously. No, there's nothing left, stoolie boys! As for Fil-de-Soie, he'll be in his grave before a fortnight's out, even if you put the whole police force around him. . . .

"And what did you give Michonnette here? A few thousand francs? You'd have got far more from me, you poor rotting Ninon, you poor ragged Pompadour, you poor old graveyard Venus. If you'd warned me, you'd have had six thousand francs. . . . Didn't think of that, did you, you old huckster? Otherwise, you'd have come to me instead. Yes, I'd have given you that to save myself a journey I'm going to find very annoying, quite apart from the money it'll cost me," he said, as they fastened the handcuffs on him. "These chaps will enjoy spinning my case out just to try and wear me down. If they sent me straight back to Toulon, I'd soon be back on my old job, in spite of our little boobies from the Quai des Orfèvres. Why, down there, they'd turn themselves half inside out to try and get their General Trompe-la-Mort out of the place. Have any of the rest of you ten thousand brothers ready to do anything on earth for you?" he demanded proudly. "There's goodness here," he said, striking his breast. "I've never betrayed anybody! D'you see, you old bag? Look at them," he said, turning to the old maid. "They may be frightened when they look at me, but the very sight of you turns their stomachs. Take your blood money."

He paused, and surveyed the boarders one by one. "Are you all loony, I wonder? Have you never seen a convict before? A convict of Collin's stamp—and you see him before you—is far less despicable than other men; and he protests against the ungodly sham of the social contract, as dear Jean-Jacques calls it—whose pupil I am proud to declare myself. In short, I stand alone against the government with all its law courts and policemen and budgets; and I can beat the lot of them."

"My God," said the painter, "he'd be a great subject for a painting."

"Tell me, little Lord Butcher's Boy," Collin went on, turning to Gondureau, "be a nice guy, and tell me if it was Fil-de-Soie who traded me in? I wouldn't like him to pay for someone else, it wouldn't be fair; would it, now, old Widow's Bully?" (The Widow is the grim, poetic name given by convicts to the guillotine.)

At this point, the officers who had been examining and listing his possessions came downstairs and spoke in undertones to the leader of the expedition. The warrant had been drawn up.

"Gentlemen," said Collin, addressing the boarders, "they're taking me away. You have all been very kind to me during my stay here, and I shall always remember that. I must now say good-bye to you. I hope you'll allow me to send you some figs from Provence." He moved toward the door, then turned back and looked at Rastignac. "Good-bye, Eugène," he said in a sad, gentle voice, which contrasted strangely with the harshness of his earlier discourse. "If you should be in difficulties, I've left a devoted friend behind for you." In spite of the handcuffs, he put himself in the on-guard position, and shouted like a fencing-master, "One! Two!" and lunged. "In any emergency, just turn in that direction; man and money are both ready for you."

These last words were spoken in deliberately burlesque tones so that their meaning might be lost on all save Eugène and himself.

After the gendarmes, soldiers, and policemen had left, Sylvie, who was rubbing her mistress's temples with vinegar, looked round at the astonished boarders. "Well," she said, "he was a good man all the same."

This observation broke the spell that had been cast on everybody by the flood of varied emotions the scene had aroused. First the boarders looked at one another; then they all looked at Mademoiselle Michonneau, huddled by the stove, gaunt, shriveled, and bloodless as a mummy, her eyes lowered as if she were afraid her eyeshade was not strong enough to hide her expression. This face, which they had all so long disliked, was now suddenly explained to them. A low dull murmur, so perfectly uniform that it showed their unanimous disgust, went through the room. Mademoiselle Michonneau heard it, and did not move. Bianchon was the first to speak. In a low voice he said to his neighbor:

"I'm leaving here, if that whore is to go on dining with us."

Instantly, everyone except Poiret murmured approval. Bianchon, fortified by the general support, went over to the old boarder and said:

"As you're so intimate with Mademoiselle Michonneau, will you speak to her, and explain to her that she must leave at once?"

"At once?" said Poiret, aghast.

Then he went up to Michonneau and spoke a few words in her ear.

"But I've paid my quarter's rent! I'm going to get my money's worth just like everybody else," she said, with a viperish glance at the boarders.

"Don't worry about that. We'll all club together to pay you that back," said Eugène.

"The gentleman sides with Collin," she said, with a searching, poisonous look. "It isn't hard to guess why."

At these words, Eugène jumped up as though he meant to leap on the old maid and strangle her. He had understood the low meaning in her look, and a hideous light flooded his mind.

"Leave her alone!" the others called out.

He folded his arms, and did not speak.

"Let's finish with Mademoiselle Judas," said the painter, turning to Madame Vauquer. "Madame, if you don't turn Michonneau out, we shall all leave your old dump, and tell everyone that the only people you have here are spies and convicts. But if you do as we say, we'll keep quiet about what's happened, which after all might happen in the best of circles, so long as the government refuses to brand criminals on the forehead and forbid them to dress up as respectable citizens of Paris and go on in the silly way they all do."

This speech miraculously restored Madame Vauquer

to health. She sat up, crossed her arms, and opened her eyes very wide. There were no tears in them now.

"But, my dear sir, do you want to ruin my house for me? Now that Monsieur Vautrin—oh, my goodness, I can't stop calling him by his respectable name! Well, anyway, *his* room's empty. You don't want me to have two more on my hands at this time of year, when everybody's settled, do you?"

"Gentlemen, let's get our hats," said Bianchon, "and go and have dinner at Flicoteaux's, in the Place Sorbonne."

It took Madame Vauquer only a second to calculate the more profitable side to take. She wheeled round on Mademoiselle Michonneau.

"Now, you don't want to be the ruin of my establishment for me, do you, my dear sweet friend? You see what these gentlemen are reducing me to. Go and stay up in your room for this evening."

"No! No!" cried the lodgers. "She's got to go at once."

"But the poor young lady hasn't eaten yet," said Poiret pathetically.

"She can go and eat somewhere else," said several voices.

"Kick out the squealer!"

"Kick both the squealers out!"

"Gentlemen," said Poiret, suddenly rising to those heights of courage that love inspires in the male sheep, "please respect a person of the weaker sex!"

"Squealers don't have any sex," said the painter.

"A fine sexorama she must—"

"Chuck her in the streetorama!"

"Gentlemen, this is indecent! When people are told to leave, they have a right to be told politely. We have paid, and we shall stay," said Poiret, putting his cap on, and sitting down beside Mademoiselle Michonneau, with whom Madame Vauquer was now pleading.

"Naughty!" said the painter mockingly, "naughty boy, go 'way!"

"Well, if you're not going, then the rest of us are," said Bianchon.

And the boarders began to move in a mass toward the drawing room.

"But, mademoiselle, how *can* you?" cried Madame Vauquer. "I'm ruined! You can't stay here, they'll start getting violent if you do."

Mademoiselle Michonneau got up.

"She's going! She isn't! She's going! She isn't!" This antiphonal chant, and the increasing hostility of the remarks made about her, compelled Mademoiselle Michonneau to leave, after a number of stipulations made in an undertone to her landlady.

"I'm going to Madame Buneaud's," she said threateningly.

"Go wherever you wish, mademoiselle," said Madame Vauquer, who saw a cruel insult in this choice, for Madame Buneaud was a rival landlady whom she detested. "Go to Buneaud's: the wine there would make a goat sick, and they buy their meat at the scrap counter. . . ."

The lodgers, in deep silence, ranged themselves in two rows. Poiret looked so amorously at Mademoiselle Michonneau, and was so innocently undecided whether to follow her or to stay behind, that the boarders, delighted at Mademoiselle Michonneau's departure, looked at one another and began to laugh.

"Xi, xi, xi, Poiret," shouted the painter. "Ooops-a-daisy!"

The museum clerk began to sing the opening of the well-known song:

> "Setting out for Syria,
>   Dunois, so young and fair. . . ."

"Go on after her; you're dying to," said Bianchon. *"Trahit sua quemque voluptas."*

"Every man has his special girl (Virgil, freely translated)," said a schoolmaster.

Mademoiselle Michonneau had looked at Poiret, and moved to take his arm; he could not resist this appeal, and he allowed the old maid to lean on him. There were bursts of applause and laughter. "Bravo, Poiret! Good old Poiret! Poiret-Apollo! Poiret-Mars! Bold, brave Poiret!"

At this moment a messenger appeared with a letter for Madame Vauquer. She read it, and collapsed over the back of a chair.

"The only thing left to do now is to set fire to the house," she moaned. "Thunderbolts are falling on it. Young Monsieur Taillefer died at three o'clock. It's a judgment on me for wishing those ladies good at the expense of that poor young man. Madame Couture and Victorine have sent for their things; her father is letting Madame Couture stay with her as his daughter's companion. Four rooms empty! Five guests gone!" She sat down, and seemed on the verge of tears. "Disaster has come upon me," she groaned.

Suddenly a carriage was heard drawing up outside.

"More trouble!" said Sylvie.

Goriot appeared. His face was so bright and shining with joy that he appeared to have been reborn.

"Goriot in a cab," murmured some of the lodgers. "It must be the end of the world!"

The old man went straight up to Eugène, who was standing lost in thought in a corner of the room. He took him by the arm. "Come along," he said happily.

"Don't you know what's happened, then?" said Eugène. "Vautrin is a convict; they've just arrested him. And young Taillefer is dead."

"But what's that to do with us?" asked Goriot. "I'm to dine with my daughter at your new home, don't you understand? She's waiting for you! Do come!" With a vigorous tug at Eugène's arm, he compelled him to move. It was as though he were abducting a mistress.

"Let's eat!" cried the painter.

Immediately everyone sat down at table.

"Oh, drat it all," said Sylvie. "Everything's going wrong today, my mutton stew's all stuck to the pot. You'll have to eat it burnt, that's all!"

At the sight of only ten people at table instead of

the usual eighteen, Madame Vauquer was reduced to
speechless despondency; but everyone tried to console
and cheer her. The boarders began to talk about Vautrin
and the other events of the day, but soon the conversation, in its customary rambling fashion, moved on to dueling, penitentiaries, justice, laws to be amended, jails.
Soon Jacques Collin, and Victorine and her brother,
were left far behind. The ten of them made quite enough
noise for twenty; indeed, there seemed more people
present than on normal occasions. That was the only
difference between tonight's dinner and that of the night
before. The habitual indifference of this small self-
centered world, that tomorrow would find in the daily
round of Paris some fresh prey to devour, reasserted
itself, and even Madame Vauquer allowed herself to be
lulled into hope, encouraged by comforting words from
Sylvie.

Right until evening this day was destined to be a phan-
tasmagoria for Eugène. Despite a strong character and
a sound brain, he could no longer think clearly. He sat
in the cab beside Goriot, whose conversation revealed a
rare happiness and sounded in Eugène's ears, after the
emotional storms of the day, like the words we hear
in dreams.

"It was settled this morning. We're all three dining
together—together! Think of it! It's four years since I
dined with Delphine, my little Delphine! I'm going to
have her with me for a whole evening. We've been at
your apartment since morning. I've been working in my
shirt sleeves, like a laborer. I helped to carry the furniture in. Ah! You can't imagine how kind she is at meals,
she'll look after me: 'Look Papa, have some of this, it's
good.' And then I can't eat! Oh, it's so long since I was
as happy with her as we're going to be tonight."

"The whole world seems to have turned upside down
today," said Eugène.

"Upside down?" said Goriot. "The world has never
been so good. All the faces in the street are happy. Everyone's shaking hands and embracing; they look as

happy as if they were *all* going to dine with their daughters, and all smacking their lips at the thought of the
splendid little dinner she ordered, just before I left, from
the chef at the Café des Anglais. But in any case, when
she's there, chicory tastes as sweet as honey."

"I feel I'm coming back to life again," said Eugène.

"But do hurry along, cabby!" shouted Goriot, opening
the glass before him. "Drive faster, and I'll give you five
francs extra if you get where I told you to in ten minutes." At this promise the cabman began to race across
Paris with the speed of lightning.

"This cabby doesn't know how to move," said Goriot.

"But where are you taking me?" asked Eugène.

The carriage drew up in the Rue d'Artois. The old
man got out first, and threw the cabman ten francs, with
the extravagance of a newly widowed man who, in the
first paroxysm of delight, stops at nothing.

"Let's go up," he said to Eugène, leading him across
a courtyard and up to the door of an apartment on the
fourth floor at the back of a pleasant new house. There
was no need for Goriot to ring the bell. Delphine's maid,
Thérèse, was there to open the door to them. Eugène
found himself in a delightful bachelor's apartment, with
an anteroom, a small drawing room, a bedroom, and a
study overlooking a garden. In the little drawing room,
as pretty and charming in its furnishings and decoration
as could be found anywhere, he saw, in the candlelight,
Delphine. She rose from a sofa near the fire, placed her
hand-screen on the mantelpiece, and said in a voice
charged with warmth: "So we had to send for you, Monsieur Know-Nothing!"

Thérèse went out. Eugène took Delphine in his arms,
held her close, and wept with joy. This final contrast
between what he saw before him now and what he had
just left behind, at the end of a day when so many exas-
perations had wearied his heart and head, suddenly overwhelmed him, and he sank in helpless exhaustion onto
the sofa.

"I knew how much he loved you," whispered Goriot.
Eugène was lying on the sofa, unable to speak a word

or to understand as yet how this last magic stroke of the wand had come about.

"But do come and look around," said Delphine, taking his hand and leading him into a room where the carpets, furniture, and minor details seemed to be a smaller replica of her own room.

"There's no bed," said Eugène.

"No, sir," she said, with a blush, pressing his hand.

He looked at her, and young as he was he saw how much genuine modesty there is in the heart of a woman in love.

"You are one of those creatures who are worthy of eternal love," he whispered. "And the more sincere and real love is, the more it needs to be veiled and mysterious. I know I dare say that, because we understand each other. Don't let's share our secret with anyone."

"Oh, so I shall be 'anyone'?" asked Goriot plaintively.

"You know quite well that *you* are us. . . ."

"That's what I hoped you'd say. You won't pay any attention to me, will you? I'll come and go like a guardian angel who is everywhere, and you know he's there without seeing him. Ah! Delphinette, Ninette, Dedel, wasn't I right when I said: 'There's a pretty apartment in the Rue d'Artois, let's furnish it for him'? You didn't want to! Ah, it's I who've begotten your happiness, just as I once begot your life. Fathers have to be always giving, if they're to be happy. Always giving: that's what being a father means."

"But what do you mean?" said Eugène.

"Yes, she didn't want to. She was afraid people would gossip; as if that mattered, so long as she was happy! But this is something every woman dreams of doing. . . ." By now, Goriot was talking to himself, for Delphine had drawn Eugène into the study whence the sound of a kiss could be heard, however lightly it might have been given.

This room too was in keeping with the elegance of the whole place. Nothing was lacking anywhere.

"Have we guessed everything you wished for?" she

asked, as they came back into the sitting room for dinner.

"Only too well, alas," he said. "The perfect luxury of it all is just like a happy dream come true; all the romance of youth and elegance. I *feel* them so much that I'm sure I deserve to have them. But I can't accept them from you, and I'm still too poor to—"

"So you're raising objections already!" she said, with a touch of mocking authority. She pouted in the pretty way women do, when they wish to laugh away some scruple.

Eugène had questioned himself very seriously that day; and the arrest of Vautrin, which had shown him the depths he had almost fallen into, had so strongly reinforced his better feelings and his sense of decency that he could not yield to this beguiling refutation of his noble ideas. A profound sadness had come over him.

"Do you mean you refuse?" exclaimed Delphine. "Do you know what that means? You doubt the future, and you don't dare commit yourself. So you're afraid you may betray my love for you? If you love me, and I . . . love you, why fuss about such trivial obligations? If you knew what pleasure I've had in fitting out this little place you wouldn't hesitate for a minute, and you'd ask me to forgive you. I had money that was yours, and I put it to good use, that's all. You think you're being very grown-up, and you're just being childish. You ask for far more than this. . . . Oh, yes!" she said, at a passionate look from Eugène, "and you make a fuss about trifles. If you don't really love me, of course don't accept! My fate is in your hands. Answer! Father, talk some sense into him," she said after a pause, turning to Goriot. "Does he think I'm less squeamish than he is about our reputations?"

Goriot was contemplating this pretty quarrel with the fixed smile of an opium addict.

"You child!" she went on, taking Eugène's hand. "Your life is only just beginning. You come up against an obstacle that many people never overcome; a woman's hand is there to help you over it, and you run away! But you'll succeed, you'll have a dazzling career, success is written on your handsome forehead. Surely you can pay me back, *then*, anything I lend you today? Didn't the ladies of old present their knights with armor and swords and helmets and coats of mail and horses, so that they could go and fight in their name in the tournaments? Well, Eugène, what I'm giving you is the armor of the present day, the tools necessary to anyone who intends to be something. The garret where you're living now must be very pretty, if it's anything like Papa's room! Well, aren't we going to dine? Do you want to make me sad? Do answer me!" She seized his hand as she spoke. "Good heavens, Father, make him decide, or I'll go away and never see him again!"

"I'll make him decide," said Goriot, emerging from his trance. "My dear Monsieur Eugène, you're going to borrow from the moneylenders, aren't you?"

"I shall have to," he said.

"Well, it's settled then," said the old man, pulling out a grubby, worn, leather wallet. "I've turned moneylender, I've paid all the bills, here they are. You don't owe a penny for anything here. It isn't a large sum, five thousand francs at the most. I shall lend it to you! You won't refuse me, I'm not a woman. You'll make me an acknowledgment on a scrap of paper, and pay me back later on."

Tears stood in Eugène's and Delphine's eyes as they looked at each other in surprise. Eugène held out his hand to the old man.

"Well, why not? Aren't you both my children?" asked Goriot.

"But, my poor Father," asked Delphine, "how did you do it?"

"Ah, that!" he replied. "When I persuaded you to set him up near you, and saw you buying all those things—as though he was a young bride—I thought to myself: 'She'll be in trouble!' The lawyer says the suit against your husband for the restoration of your fortune will take over six months. Good. I went and realized the

capital that gives me my thirteen hundred and fifty
francs a year. I spent fifteen thousand francs on an annuity of twelve hundred a year, which is well secured, and
with the rest of the capital I paid your tradespeople. I
have a room upstairs at a hundred and fifty francs a
year. I can live like a prince on two francs a day, with
money to spare. I never wear things out; I hardly ever
need new clothes. For two weeks now I've been chuck-
ling to myself and thinking: 'Won't they be happy!' Well:
aren't you?"

"Oh! Papa! Papa!" she cried, bounding toward him.
He took her on his lap. She covered him with kisses,
her golden hair brushing against his cheeks, her tears
dropping on the old, bright, beaming face. "Dear Father,
you *are* a father! No, there can't be another father like
you on earth! Eugène loved you before; what will he
feel like now?"

"Oh, children," said Goriot, who for the last ten years
had not felt his daughter's heart beat against his own,
"oh, Delphinette, do you want to make me die of joy?
My poor heart's breaking. . . . There, all's square, Monsieur Eugène." And the old man held his daughter in
an embrace so savage and frantic that she said:

"Oh! you're hurting me!"

"Hurting you!" he said, turning pale. He looked at
her. There was more than human grief on his face. To
paint as it should be painted the face of this Christ
among fathers, we would need to search among the images created by the princes of the palette to depict the
agony suffered on the world's behalf by the Saviour of
mankind. Goriot bent and imprinted a gentle kiss on the
girdle his fingers had pressed too tightly. "No, no, I
haven't hurt you. No," he said with a questioning smile.
"It was you who hurt me when you cried out." Very
cautiously, he kissed her ear, whispering as he did so:
"It did cost more than that. But we must cajole him a
little, otherwise he'll be offended."

Eugène, overwhelmed by the man's inexhaustible devotion, looked at him with the simple wonderment that,
in the young, constitutes faith.

"I will make myself worthy of it!" he exclaimed.

"Ah, Eugène, what a nice thing to say." And Delphine kissed him on the brow.

"He turned down Mademoiselle Taillefer and her millions for you," said Goriot. "Yes, that girl loved you, Monsieur Eugène. And now her brother's dead, she'll be as rich as Croesus."

"Oh, why speak of that?" cried Eugène.

"Eugène," whispered Delphine, "now I shall be a tiny bit sad tonight. Ah, but I shall love you deeply . . . and always."

"This is the best day I've known since you and Nasie got married," said Goriot. "God can make me suffer as much as He chooses, so long as it isn't on your behalf; and I'll still be able to say: 'For one moment this February I was happier than some men are in a whole lifetime.' Look at me, Fifine. . . . She's very beautiful, isn't she? Tell me, how many women have you met with such a pretty color, and a little dimple like that? Not many, have you? Well, it was *I* who created this darling woman. And if she finds you make her happy, she'll be a thousand times more beautiful. If you want my share of heaven, dear neighbor," he said, "I make you a present of it—I'll be happy to go to hell. Let's eat! Let's eat!" He no longer knew what he was saying. "The world is ours!"

"Poor Father!"

"If only you knew, my child," he said, going to her and taking her head in his hands, and kissing the plaits of her hair, "how cheaply you can buy happiness for me! Just come and see me once in a while. I shall be upstairs, you'll only have a few steps to take. Say you will. Promise."

"Yes, dear Father."

"Say it again."

"Yes, my dear Father."

"Hush! I could listen to you saying it a thousand times. Let's have dinner."

The evening passed in childish play, Goriot behaving no less absurdly than the other two. He lay on the floor and kissed his daughter's feet; gazed for long moments into her eyes; rubbed his head against her dress. The tenderest young lover could not have been more ridiculous.

"You see?" Delphine murmured to Eugène. "When my father's with us, he wants all our attention. It'll be a great nuisance sometimes."

Eugène, who had felt twinges of jealousy several times during the evening, could hardly reproach her for this remark, however much ingratitude was concentrated in it.

"When will the place be ready?" he asked, looking around the room. "Do we have to leave each other tonight?"

"Yes, but tomorrow you'll come and dine with me," she said slyly. "It's the Italian Opéra tomorrow night."

"I shall be in the pit," said Goriot.

It was midnight. Delphine's carriage was waiting. Goriot and Eugène returned to the Maison Vauquer, talking with such mounting enthusiasm that the two men seemed to be oddly competing with each other in expressing the strength of their love. Eugène could not disguise from himself the fact that Goriot's passion, untainted by self-interest, eclipsed his own by its endurance and intensity. To the father, the goddess was forever pure and beautiful and his worship drew strength from the long past as well as from the future.

They found Madame Vauquer sitting by her stove, alone save for Sylvie and Christophe. The old landlady looked like Marius surveying the ruins of Carthage. She was waiting up for the two lodgers she had left, and bemoaning her fate to Sylvie. Lord Byron has put some extremely fine words of lament into the mouth of the poet Tasso; but they are as nothing compared with the profound truths that were dropping from the lips of Madame Vauquer at this moment.

"You'll have only three cups of coffee to make tomorrow morning, Sylvie. My house, deserted! Wouldn't it break anyone's heart? What is life to me without my boarders? Nothing at all. My house, stripped of its men!

They were like furniture to me. You can't live without furniture, can you? What have I done that Heaven should visit all these disasters on me? I've got enough beans and potatoes in the place for twenty. Police in my house! We'll have to live on potatoes! I shall have to get rid of Christophe!"

Christophe, who was asleep, immediately awoke, and asked:

"Madame?"

"Poor lad! He's as faithful as a watchdog," said Sylvie.

"The slack time of the year, everybody already fixed up! Where shall I find boarders? It will drive me out of my mind! And that old witch Michonneau, taking Poiret away with her! What's she done to the man, to get him to follow her about everywhere like a little dog?"

"Ah well," said Sylvie, shaking her head, "these old maids, you never know what they're up to."

"Fancy turning poor Monsieur Vautrin into a convict!" went on Madame Vauquer. "Oh, Sylvie, I can't help it, I still don't believe it. A cheerful man like that who always had brandy in his coffee, at fifteen francs a month, and always paid on the dot."

"And so openhanded," said Christophe.

"There must be some mistake," said Sylvie.

"No, he admitted it himself," said Madame Vauquer. "And to think it all happened in my house, in a neighborhood where never even a cat goes by. I feel I'm in a dream, I must be. I know we've seen Louis the Sixteenth have his accident, we've seen the Emperor fall, and come back, and fall again; it's all perfectly natural, I know. But you don't expect ups and downs like that in a boardinghouse! You can get along without a king, but people always have to eat. And when an honest woman, a de Conflans by birth, offers dinners like mine, with everything you could ask for, why, unless the end of the world's coming, I . . . but it *is* the end of the world!"

"And to think that Mademoiselle Michonneau, who brought all this on you, is going to get three thousand francs a year!" exclaimed Sylvie.

"Don't speak of it, she's just a criminal!" said Madame Vauquer. "And she's gone to Buneaud's into the bargain! But she'd do anything, she must have done terrible things in her time, killing, stealing, everything you can think of! *She* ought to go to jail instead of that poor dear man. . . ."

At this moment Eugène and Goriot rang the bell.

"Ah, here are my two faithful ones," said the widow, with a sigh.

But the two faithful ones, who had only a hazy recollection of the disasters that had overtaken the boarding-house, announced without ceremony that they were both going to live in the Chaussée d'Antin.

"Ah, Sylvie," said the widow, "that was my last trump card. . . . You've given me my deathblow, gentlemen. It's gone to my stomach. It feels like an iron bar. This day has put ten years on me. I shall go mad, I swear it! What's to be done with all those beans? Well, if I'm to be here all by myself, you'll have to leave tomorrow, Christophe! Good-bye, gentlemen, good night."

"What's the matter with her now, Sylvie?" asked Eugène.

"Why, everyone's left, because of what happened today. It's affected her head. Listen, I can hear her crying. She'll be better after a good cry. It's the first time I've ever known her to do that, all the years I've been here."

By the next day, Madame Vauquer had, as she put it, "rallied herself together." If she seemed afflicted, as was natural in a woman who has lost all her boarders and whose life has been turned upside down, she still had her wits about her. Her grief was plain and real to her; it was deep grief, the grief caused by injured interests, and the breaking of habit. Indeed, a lover throwing a last look around the place inhabited by his mistress could not have looked sadder than Madame Vauquer contemplating the empty places at her table. Eugène comforted her by telling her that Bianchon, whose period as an intern was coming to an end in a few days, would doubtless come and take his place; and that the museum clerk had often expressed the wish to have Madame Couture's room; and that within a few days she would have replaced the whole of them.

"May God hear your wish, my dear sir! But misfortune has come on the place. Before ten days are out, there'll be death here too, you mark my words," she said with a lugubrious glance around the dining room. "Whom will it come for?"

"I'm glad we're getting out," said Eugène quietly to Goriot.

Suddenly Sylvie ran into the room, a look of terror on her face.

"Madame!" she cried. "I haven't seen Pussy for three whole days!"

"Oh! Oh, dear, if my cat's dead . . . if *he's* run away from us, I—"

The poor woman did not finish. She placed her hands together and collapsed against the back of her chair, overwhelmed by this terrible portent.

PART FIVE

THE TWO
DAUGHTERS

1

At noon, when the postman usually reached the Panthéon area, Eugène was handed a letter in an elegant envelope, sealed with the Beauséant arms. It contained an invitation for Monsieur and Madame de Nucingen to the great ball announced a month earlier, to be given in the viscountess's house. Enclosed with the invitation was a little note for Eugène:

> I thought, monsieur, you might enjoy delivering this expression of my respect for Madame de Nucingen yourself. I send you the invitation you asked me for, and shall be enchanted to make the acquaintance of Madame de Restaud's sister. So do bring the pretty person to see me; and please do not let her monopolize all your affection. You owe me a great deal in return for mine toward you.
>
> Claire de Beauséant

"It's quite clear," thought Eugène, reading the note a second time, "that she doesn't want anything to do with the Baron de Nucingen." He went round to Delphine's at once, happy to have procured a pleasure for her, and confident of being rewarded for it. She was in her bath. He waited in the boudoir, consumed by the natural impatience of an ardent young man to take possession of his mistress. He felt as if he had been hankering after her for a couple of years.

These emotions do not occur twice in any young man's

life. There is no later rival to the first woman a man becomes attached to—the first woman, that is to say, who is really a woman, the first one who appears to him surrounded by all the magnificence Parisian society insists on. Love in Paris is like no other sort of love. Paris is a kingdom where no one, man or woman, is deceived by the brave show of commonplaces with which everyone, in the interests of propriety, disguises a so-called disinterested affection. A woman is expected to satisfy not only the heart and the senses; she knows she has further and greater obligations to fulfill toward the immense vanity of Parisian life. Love in that city is essentially spectacular, brazen, elaborate, hypocritical, and extravagant. All the ladies of Louis XIV's court envied Mademoiselle de la Vallière the outburst of passion that made the great prince forget that his cuffs had cost a thousand crowns apiece as he tore them into strips to assist the entry into the world of their bastard son. So what may one expect of the rest of mankind? Be young, and rich, and titled; be even better, if you can. For the more incense you can bring to burn before your idol, the more she will favor you—provided, of course, that you have an idol. Love is a religion, and its rituals cost more than those of other religions. It goes by quickly and, like a street urchin, it likes to mark its passage by a trail of devastation. Real feeling is a luxury to be indulged only in a garret; without such wealth what would become of love in such a place?

If there are exceptions to the draconian laws of the Parisian code, they are to be found in solitude, in men who ignore society completely and pass their lives near some clear, hidden, but ever-running brook; who are faithful to their green shades and content to listen to the language of the Infinite written all about them, which they rediscover in their own selves. Such men can wait patiently for their heavenly wings and commiserate the earth-bound. But Eugène, like most young men who have had a foretaste of splendor, wanted to dash fully armed into the lists of society. He had absorbed its fever; he felt he had the strength to dominate, but how, or to what end, he could not have said. In the absence of a pure and sacred love, the thirst for power may become a fine thing in itself: all that a man needs is to discard self-interest and to live for the glory of his country. Eugène, however, had not yet reached the point where a man can look at the whole of a life and judge it. He was not yet even completely free of the fresh, sweet notions that twine like leaves around a country-bred childhood. He had continually hesitated to cross the Paris Rubicon. Under all his burning curiosity there was still an inner vision of the happy life a real gentleman leads in his country house.

But the evening before, when he had seen himself in his own apartment, his last scruples had vanished. Now that the material advantages of wealth had been added to the moral ones of breeding, which he had long enjoyed, he had shed his provincial's skin and slipped quietly into a position from which a fine career might be descried. As he sat comfortably waiting for Delphine in her boudoir, which was becoming in a sense his also, he felt so different from the Rastignac of a year ago that he began to wonder, as he regarded himself through a mental quizzing-glass, if he even looked the same.

He started as Thérèse came in and said: "Madame is in her room."

Delphine was lying, fresh and relaxed, on her sofa by the fire. Waves of muslin billowed around her. It was impossible not to think of those beautiful Indian plants in which the fruit nestles inside the flower.

"Well, here we are," she said tenderly.

"Guess what I've brought you," said Eugène, sitting beside her and kissing her hand.

Tears of joy started to her eyes as she read the invitation. Throwing her arms around his neck, she drew him to her in a rapture of gratified vanity.

"And I owe this happiness to you . . . darling." The last word was whispered in his ear. "Thérèse is in my bathroom, we must be careful," she explained. "Ah, yes! I can certainly call it a happiness. And since *you've* given it to me, it's something more than a triumph for my vanity, isn't it? No one has ever been willing to introduce me to this society. I expect you're thinking I'm petty and shallow and frivolous, like any other Parisian woman; but do remember that I'm willing to give you everything, and if I'm now more anxious than ever to be received in the Faubourg Saint-Germain, it's because you're there."

"Don't you get the impression," asked Eugène, "that Madame de Beauséant rather hints that she doesn't want to see the Baron de Nucingen at her ball?"

"Of course," said Delphine, handing the letter back. "These women have a genius for rudeness. Never mind, I shall go. My sister's bound to be there, I know she's ordered the most marvelous dress. Eugène," she went on, dropping her voice, "she's really going there in order to disarm some terrible rumors. You've not heard? Nucingen came and told me this morning that it was being openly talked about at his club. Oh, God, the things the honor of a wife and children may depend on! Poor Anastasie, I almost felt they were attacking and wounding me at the same time! It's rumored that Monsieur de Trailles had signed drafts for a hundred thousand francs; they'd almost all fallen due, and he was going to be sued. They say that in despair, Anastasie sold all her diamonds to a Jew—those lovely diamonds you may have seen her wearing. They came from Monsieur de Restaud's mother. People have been talking of nothing else for the last two days. So I can understand why she's having a brocade dress made. She wants to make everyone stare at her at Madame de Beauséant's, by appearing in all her glory, wearing the diamonds. But I don't want to be outshone by her. She's always been trying to snub me, she's never been nice to me, although I've done so much for her and always found money for her when she hadn't any . . . But let's stop talking about other people! Today, I just want to be happy."

Eugène was still with her at one in the morning. As she lavished a lover's farewell on him—the kind of farewell so full of future joys—she said in melancholy tones: "I'm so frightened, so superstitious—call my fears whatever you will—but I keep fearing I may have to pay for my happiness by some dreadful catastrophe."

"Child," said Eugène.

"Ah, so *I'm* the child tonight?" she said with a laugh.

Eugène returned to the Maison Vauquer, confident that he would be leaving it the next day; and on his way he gave himself over to those pleasant dreams all young men have while the taste of happiness still lingers on their lips.

"Well?" Goriot called, as Eugène passed his door.

"Well!" Eugène replied. "I'll tell you everything tomorrow."

"Yes, everything, won't you?" said the old man. "Go to bed. Tomorrow we shall begin our happy life."

The next day, Goriot and Eugène were waiting for a porter in order to leave the boardinghouse when, at about midday, the sound of a carriage was heard in the Rue Neuve-Sainte-Geneviève. It drew up outside the Maison Vauquer. Delphine got out and asked if her father was still in the house. Sylvie replied that he was, and Delphine ran quickly upstairs. Eugène was still in his room, but this his neighbor did not know. At breakfast he had asked Goriot to bring his things after him, saying that they would see each other at four o'clock in the Rue d'Artois. But while the old man was out looking for porters, Eugène, who had dashed to the law school to answer the roll call, had come back, unseen by anyone, to settle his account with Madame Vauquer. He was unwilling to leave this task to Goriot, who in his enthusiasm would no doubt have paid for both of them. The landlady was out, and Eugène had gone up to his room to see that he had not forgotten anything; he congratulated himself on having done so, for he found in the drawer of his table the IOU made out to Vautrin, which he had casually thrown there on the day he had discharged it. There was no fire in the grate, and he was about to tear the bill into little pieces, when he heard Delphine's voice. He remained silent in order to hear what she was saying, assuming that she could have no secrets from him. But the first words he heard were so interesting that he found himself listening intently.

"Oh, Father," she said, "I hope to God your thought of asking for an account of my fortune has come in time for me not to be ruined! Can I talk here?"

"Yes, the house is empty," said Goriot.

There was something strange in his tone that made her ask: "What's the matter, Father?"

"You've just given me such a stunning blow," said the old man. "God forgive you, my child, but if you knew how much I love you, you'd never spring things on me like that, especially if they're not really desperate. What can have happened so important that you have to come round here? In a few minutes we'd have been at the Rue d'Artois."

"But Father, how can one be expected to behave in a moment of disaster? I feel I'm going mad! Your lawyer has just found out for us a little earlier what was bound to come out eventually. We shall need all your business experience now. When Monsieur Derville saw that Nucingen was quibbling over every point, he threatened him with a lawsuit and said he could get a summons from the president of the tribunal immediately. Nucingen came and asked me this morning if I was trying to ruin both of us. I said I knew nothing about that, and that I owned a fortune and it ought to be at my own disposal, and everything connected with the whole dispute was in the hands of my lawyer. I said I was completely ignorant in such matters and incapable of understanding them—isn't that what you told me to say?"

"Certainly," said Goriot.

"Well," Delphine continued, "he then told me how his affairs stand. He's thrown the whole of his capital and mine into some new speculations for which he's had to lay out vast sums of money. If I compelled him to give me back my fortune, he said he would have to go bankrupt. Whereas if I waited for twelve months, he gave me his word of honor to pay me twice or three times the sum by investing in building land for me and arranging that I should have sole control of the entire

funds. Dear Father, he was quite sincere about it; he
frightened me. He asked me to forgive his behavior, he
gave me liberty to do exactly whatever I wanted, on
condition I let him manage everything himself, but under
my name. As a proof of good faith, he promised to send
for Monsieur Derville whenever I wanted, to make sure
that all the title deeds in my name were properly drawn
up. In fact, he's put himself completely in my power,
tied hand and foot. He asks for complete control of the
household expenses for two more years and begs me not
to spend any more on myself than my allowance. He
proved that all he could do was just keep up appearances. He's given up his ballet girl, and said he was going
to be forced to exercise the strictest economy (though
not openly, of course) in order to push the speculations
through to the end without shaking his credit. I was rude
to him, and said I didn't believe anything he told me.
That was so as to make sure he told me everything. In
the end he showed me his books, and burst into tears.
I've never seen a man in such a state. He was out of
his mind, threatening to kill himself, raving. I felt sorry
for him."

"And you believe such fairy tales?" demanded Goriot.
"He's just a humbug, that's all! I've met Germans in
business before. They're almost all of them full of good
faith, very open with you; but when they decide to be
cunning and deceitful under their frankness and friendli-
ness, they're worse than anybody else. Your husband's
deceiving you. He knows he's hard pressed and he's
shamming dead. He's hoping to control even more with
your name than he can with his own. He's taking advan-
tage of what has happened to try and cover his own
risks. He's cunning, and he's treacherous—a thorough
bad lot.

"No, no, when I go to my grave, I'm not going to
leave my daughters stripped bare. I still know my way
about these matters. He says he's sunk his capital in new
speculations—well then, his interests are represented by
securities, and agreements, and contracts! Let him produce them, and settle up with you. *We'll* decide which

are the best investments, and run the risks ourselves, and have the title deeds in our name: *Delphine Goriot, separate in her estate from her husband, the Baron de Nucingen.* Does he think we're imbeciles? Does he think I could bear it for a single day, to think of leaving you penniless and starving? I couldn't bear it for an hour, let alone a day! The very thought of it would kill me!

"I worked for forty years of my life, I carried sacks on my back, I toiled and sweated; I went short the whole of my life, for you, my angels, and you made every burden seem like nothing. And am I now expected to watch my whole life's work go up in smoke? It would make me die of sheer rage! By all that's holy in heaven and earth, we'll drag all this out into the daylight, we'll go through his books, his bank accounts, his investments. I won't sleep or eat or rest until I have the proof that your fortune is there, intact. Thank God your estate is separate; you'll have Monsieur Derville to look after you, and he's honest, thank God. You shall keep your little million, and your fifty thousand francs a year till the end of your life, or, by God, the whole of Paris shall hear about it. Yes, I'll appeal to the government, if the courts try and cheat us. To know you were happy and free from money troubles was enough to comfort me in sickness and grief. Money is life itself. Wealth can buy everything.

"Does this fat Alsatian lump think he can blackmail us? Delphine, don't give the great brute one quarter of a penny! He's chained you up, and made your life a misery. If he needs your help, then we'll take a stick and keep him in order . . . Oh, God, my head's on fire, it's like a fire burning inside my skull. . . . My Delphine, in want! You, my Fifine, you! Where are my gloves? Come on, let's go at once, I want to see everything, the books, the business, the bank accounts, the correspondence, right away. I shan't rest till I see with my own eyes that your fortune is still safe."

"But, Father dear, do go carefully about this. If there's the slightest suggestion of revenge, or if he sees you're set against him, I shall be lost. He knows you, and he found it quite natural that, at your suggestion, I should be concerned about my fortune. But the money's in his hands, I swear it; and he intends to keep it. He's quite capable of making off with the whole capital and leaving us stranded! He knows perfectly well I wouldn't dishonor my own name by prosecuting him. He's strong and weak at the same time. I've looked into everything thoroughly. If we press him too far, I'm ruined."

"But is he a common swindler, then?"

"Yes! Yes, Father, he is!" she said, throwing herself into a chair and bursting into tears. "I didn't want to admit it. I wanted to spare you the misery of having married me to such a man. He's all of a piece: his private habits and conscience, body and soul. I hate him and despise him. I can never respect him after all he said to me. He's wicked. A man capable of the commercial undertakings he described to me can have no decent feeling at all. And it's because I've seen right into the depths of his soul that I'm so afraid. He—*he*, my husband—bluntly offered me my freedom—and you know what he means by that—on condition that I agreed, in any emergency, to be an instrument in his hands and let him use my name."

"But there are laws, aren't there? There's a Place de Grève for that sort of son-in-law!" cried Goriot "And I'd guillotine him myself, if there were no one else to do it."

"No, Father, the law can't touch him. Listen to what he said—I'll spare you the roundabout way in which he put it. '*Either* everything is lost, and you won't have a penny, you'll be ruined—because I can't find any other partner except you; *or*, you let me go through with my speculations to the end.' Is that clear? He still depends on me. My honesty as a woman is his guarantee. He knows I'll let him keep his money, and be satisfied with my own. I either acquiesce in a dishonest, fraudulent association, or I'm ruined. He buys my conscience, and pays for it by not interfering between me and Eugène. 'I condone your misdeeds,' he said. 'Allow me to commit crimes by ruining poor people.' Isn't that what it really

comes to? And do you know what he means by speculation? He buys wasteland under his own name, and then
sets up 'straw men' to build houses on it. These men
carry out all the arrangements with the actual builders,
and get them to accept deferred payment. Then for a
small sum they sell the leases to my husband. He thus
becomes the owner of the houses, and the other men
get out of their obligations to the builders by going
bankrupt. The name of the house of Nucingen will have
been enough to dazzle the poor builders. . . . I understood all that. I also understood that in order to prove,
if he should have to, that he has paid out enormous
sums of money, he has sent vast securities to Amster-
dam, London, Naples, and Vienna. However should we
retrieve those?"

Eugène heard a dull heavy sound. Goriot had dropped
to his knees on the floor.

"O God, what have I done? My daughter in the hands
of this villain! He'll take everything he wants from her.
Forgive me, Delphine!" he cried.

"Well, yes, if I'm in trouble, perhaps it is a little bit
your fault," said Delphine. "We know so little when we
get married. How should girls know about business, and
society, and men, and the things men do? Our fathers
ought to think for us. Oh, Father dear, I'm not blaming
you for anything, forgive me for saying that. This is all
my own fault, completely. No, don't cry, Father," she
said, kissing his forehead.

"Don't you cry either, my little Delphine. Let me kiss
your tears away. There! I must shake my wits up, and
find some way of untangling all this."

"No, leave it to me. I'll be able to manage him. He
loves me, and I shall use my influence over him and get
him to invest some of my capital in property for myself
immediately. I may be able to get him to buy back Nucingen, in Alsace, in my name. He's fond of the place.
Just come round tomorrow and simply look into his
books and business dealings. Derville knows nothing at
all about commercial matters. . . . Oh, no, I forgot: don't
come tomorrow. I don't want to get upset. There's Ma-

dame de Beauséant's ball the day after, I want to take care of myself so as to look nice and relaxed there, and do honor to my dear Eugène! Shall we go and see his room?"

At this moment a carriage stopped in the Rue Neuve-Sainte-Geneviève, and the voice of Madame de Restaud was heard below asking Sylvie: "Is my father in?" This gave a lucky escape to Eugène, who was about to throw himself on his bed and pretend to be asleep.

"Ah, Father, have you heard about Anastasie?" said Delphine, as she heard her sister's voice. "It seems there's something very strange going on at her place too."

"What!" said Goriot. "No, that would be too much. My poor head wouldn't stand another trouble like this."

"Good morning, Father," said the countess as she came in. "Ah! You're here too, Delphine!" She seemed embarrassed at finding her sister there.

"Good morning, Nasie," said Delphine. "Do you find that so extraordinary? *I* see my father every day."

"Since when?"

"If you ever came here, you'd know."

"Don't nag at me, Delphine," said the countess piteously. "I'm so unhappy. I'm lost, Father! Really ruined, this time!"

"What is it, Nasie?" cried Goriot. "Tell us everything, my child. She's gone white! Delphine, do help her! Be kind to her! I'll love you even more for it!"

"My poor Nasie," said Delphine, making her sister sit down, "tell us. We're the only two people in the world who will always love you enough to forgive you anything. After all, family affection is the surest." She gave her some smelling salts to inhale, and the countess revived.

"This will kill me," said Goriot. "Come closer, both of you," he said, poking his peat fire. "I'm cold. What has happened, Nasie? Tell me quickly, I shall die—"

"Well," said the poor woman, "my husband's found out everything. Father, you remember that bill of Max-me's some time ago? Well, that wasn't the first one. I paid a large number of them before that. About the beginning of January, he seemed very depressed. He never said anything about it; but it's so easy to see what's on the mind of someone you love, the slightest thing is enough. Besides, one has premonitions. And he'd been more kind and affectionate than I ever remembered, and I was so very happy! Poor Maxime! He was mentally saying good-bye to me, he told me later. He was going to blow his brains out. I pestered him and begged him and went down on my knees to him. At last he told me he owed a hundred thousand francs! Oh, Father! A hundred thousand francs! I almost went out of my mind. You didn't have it, you'd given me everything—"

"No," said Goriot, "I couldn't have found it, short of going out and stealing it. But I'd have done it, Nasie! I will do it!"

He spoke so mournfully, in the full agony of his helplessness before this situation, that the two sisters fell silent for a moment. What selfishness could have remained unmoved by that cry of despair and the depths of bitterness it revealed beneath?

"I found it myself, by disposing of what didn't belong to me, Father," said the countess, bursting into tears.

Delphine was moved, and laying her head against her sister's, also wept. "So it's all true then?" she asked.

Anastasie hung her head. Delphine threw her arms round her, kissed her tenderly, and held her against her heart. "I shall always love you, Nasie, and never judge you," she said.

"My angels," said Goriot, weakly, "why does it take misfortune to bring you together?"

"To try to save Maxime's life, indeed to save everything I live for," the countess went on, encouraged by this evidence of warm and palpitating affection, "I went to that usurer you've heard about—that devil from hell, Gobseck. Nothing moves him. I took the family diamonds Monsieur de Restaud is so proud of, his and mine, all of them; and I sold them. Sold them! Do you

realize? It saved Maxime. But it will kill me. Restaud
has found out everything."

"Who betrayed you? I'll kill him!" cried Goriot.

"Yesterday he sent for me to come to his room. I
went. 'Anastasie,' he said to me, in a—oh, his voice was
enough, I guessed at once—'where are your diamonds?'
'In my room,' I said. 'No,' he said, looking at me. 'There
they are, on my dressing table.' And he showed me the
jewel case, which had been covered by his handkerchief.
'Do you know where they've come from?' he asked. I
fell on my knees. . . . I wept, I asked him what death
did he want me to die."

"You said that!" exclaimed Goriot. "God in Heaven!
Anyone who lays a finger on either of you while I'm
alive can be sure I'll burn him inch by inch! I'll tear
him limb from limb, like . . ." The words died away in
his throat.

"But, oh, Delphine, he asked me something harder
than dying. Heaven keep any woman from hearing what
I've had to hear!"

"I will murder that man," said Goriot quietly. "But
he's only got one life, and he owes me two. Well, go
on," he urged, looking at Anastasie.

"Well," said the countess after a moment's silence,
"he looked at me and said: 'Anastasie, I'll bury all this
in silence, we shall stay together, we have children. I
won't challenge Monsieur de Trailles, I might miss him,
and if I got rid of him in any other way I might come
up against the law. To kill him in your arms would mean
disgracing the children. But if you don't want to see your
children perish, nor their father, nor me, I must impose
two conditions. Answer me: Have I a child of my own?'
I said yes. 'Which?' he asked. 'Ernest, our elder son,' I
said. 'Good,' he said. 'Now, swear to obey me henceforth
on one single point.' I swore. 'You will sign away your
property to me, whenever I ask you to do so.' "

"Don't sign!" cried Goriot. "Never sign such a thing.
Ha-ha! Monsieur de Restaud, you don't know what it is
to make a woman happy. She goes and looks for happi-

ness where it really is; and you punish her for your own silly impotence . . . ! But *I'm* here! He won't push me out of the way! Nasie, don't worry. He's fond of his son and heir, is he? Good, good. . . . I'll kidnap that son of his! Great God, he's my own grandson, I've got a right to see the little monkey, haven't I? I'll hide him in my village; I'll look after him, don't be afraid. I'll force that monster to come to terms. I'm ready for him! I'll say: 'If you want your son, give my daughter back her fortune, and let her go her own way.' "

"Oh, Father!"

"Yes, your father. . . . I'm a true father. This swaggering imbecile isn't going to ill-treat a daughter of mine. God! I don't know what it is in my veins, but I feel like a bloodthirsty tiger, I could eat those two men! Oh, my children, is this what your life has come to? It's death to me. What will become of you when I'm not here any more? Fathers ought to live as long as their children. Oh, God, how badly planned your world is! You too had a Son, if what they tell us is true. You should keep us from suffering through our children. . . . Oh, my dear angels, is it only when you're in trouble that I'm ever to have a sight of you? All I ever know of you is your tears. . . . Yes, I know you love me. Bring, bring your sorrows here! My heart is big enough to hold them all! Yes, you can tear it to pieces, each fragment will still be a father's heart! I wish I could suffer your troubles for you. Ah, when you were both little, how happy you were. . . ."

"That was the only happy time we've ever known," said Delphine. "Oh, Nasie, where are the days when we used to slide down the sacks in the big loft?"

"Father dear, I haven't told you everything," whispered Anastasie. Goriot started. "The diamonds didn't fetch a hundred thousand francs. An action is pending against Maxime. We have only twelve hundred more francs to pay. He's promised to be good, and not gamble any more. My love's the only thing I have left in the world, and I've paid so dearly for it I shall die if I lose it now. I've sacrificed fortune, and reputation, and peace of mind. Oh, do at least do something so that he can be free, and respected, and stay in society, where he'll be able to make his way. He owes me more than happiness now, there are the children. They'll be penniless otherwise. Everything will be lost if he's put in the debtors prison."

"I haven't the money, Nasie. There's nothing left, nothing, nothing at all! It's the end of the world. The world's falling about us, I know it is. . . . Go away, run away in time! Ah! I still have my silver buckles and half a dozen spoons and forks, the first I ever had. Apart from that I've nothing but my life annuity of twelve hundred francs. . . ."

"But what have you done with your securities?"

"I sold them; I kept only just a little scrap of income for my own needs. I had to have twelve thousand francs to furnish some rooms for Delphine."

"In your own house, Delphine?" asked Madame de Restaud.

"Oh, what difference does it make where they are?" said Goriot. "The twelve thousand francs have been spent."

"I can guess," said the countess. "For Monsieur de Rastignac. Oh, my poor Delphine, don't. . . . Look where it's brought me."

"My dear, Monsieur de Rastignac is not the sort of young man who would ruin his mistress."

"Thank you, Delphine. In a crisis like this, I expected better of you; but you've never loved me."

"She does love you, Nasie," cried Goriot. "She was saying so only a moment ago. We were talking about you, and she was insisting that you were beautiful, and she was only pretty."

"*Her* beauty's like a block of ice!" said Anastasie.

"Whatever it is," said Delphine, reddening, "how have you behaved toward me? You've dropped me; you've made people shut their doors against me wherever I've wanted to go! You've always seized the slightest opportunity of humiliating me. And have I ever come here, like you, squeezing poor Father's money out of him, a thousand francs at a time? That's why he's in the state he's in now; and it's all *your* doing. I've been to see my father whenever I could, I've never turned him out of the house, and I've never come fawning on him when I needed his help. I didn't even know he spent those twelve thousand francs on my behalf. I have a sense of what's right, even if you haven't. And if Father's given me presents, it isn't because I've come begging for them."

"You were better off than I was. Monsieur de Marsay was rich, as you know only too well. You've always been as mean as dirt. Good-bye, I have no sister, nor—"

"Be quiet, Nasie!" cried Goriot.

"Only a sister like you would dare go on saying what no one believes any longer! You're a monster!" said Delphine.

"Children, children, if you say any more, I'll kill myself, here in front of you!"

"Well, Nasie, I forgive you," said Delphine. "I know you're unhappy. But I'm a better woman than you are. To speak to me like that when I was prepared to do anything in the world to help you—even going to my husband's room, which I wouldn't either for myself, or— but it's just like everything else you've done to me in these last nine years."

"Children, children, put your arms round each other," said their father, taking Anastasie by the arm. "You are two angels."

"No, let me go!" she said, shaking him off. "She has less pity for me than my husband has. You'd think she was a model of all the virtues!"

"I'd rather people thought I owed money to Monsieur de Marsay than admit Monsieur de Trailles had cost me over two hundred thousand francs," retorted Delphine.

"Delphine!" cried Anastasie, taking a step toward her.

"I'm telling the truth! You're capable only of slander," Delphine said icily.

"Delphine, you are a—"

Goriot darted forward, pulled the countess back, and stopped her words with his hand across her mouth.

"Good heavens, Father," she exclaimed in disgust, "what have you been handling this morning?"

"I'm sorry," said her unfortunate father, wiping his hands on his trousers. "But I didn't know you'd be coming. I'm moving my things." But he was glad at having diverted his daughter's anger toward himself. "Ah!" he said as he sat down again, "you've broken my heart between you. This is killing me. My head feels as if there's a fire inside it. Do be kind to each other. Or you'll kill me. Delphine, Nasie, listen: you're both right and you're both wrong. Look, Dedel," he went on, turning his tearful eyes on Delphine, "she must have twelve thousand francs. Let's see if we can find them. Don't look at one another like that." He dropped on his knees at Delphine's feet. "Beg her pardon, just to please me," he whispered. "She's unhappier than you are, can't you see?"

"My poor, dear Nasie," said Delphine, alarmed at the wild, unnatural expression of grief on her father's face, "I was being naughty, kiss me. . . ."

"Ah! that's balm to my heart," said Goriot. "But where are we going to find twelve thousand francs? Sometimes, men are allowed to take other men's places in the army. Perhaps, if I—"

"Father!" cried the two girls, throwing their arms around him. "No, no!"

"God will reward you for the thought; we could never do so in a whole lifetime, could we, Nasie?" said Delphine.

"In any case, Father dear," said Anastasie, "it would be only a drop in the ocean."

"But is a man's lifeblood worth nothing, then?" cried Goriot in despair. "I'll sell my soul to any man who'll save you, Nasie! I'll do murder for him! I'll be like Vautrin, and go to jail! I—" He broke off as though thunderstruck. "There's nothing left!" he said, tearing his hair. "If only I knew where I could steal it . . . but it's difficult to think of anywhere to rob. It takes time to rob a bank, and you need help. I must die, I'm not fit for anything else. Let me die. I'm not a father any more. She asks for help, she's in need, and I'm so contemptible I have nothing to give her! You could buy life annuities for yourself, you old villain, while you still had daughters! Didn't you love them? You deserve to die like a dog. You're worse than a dog, a dog wouldn't behave like that! Oh! My head! It's bursting!"

He would have dashed his head against the wall, had the girls not clung to him to prevent him. "Papa! Don't go on like this!"

Goriot was sobbing. Eugène, who had been listening in horror, took up the bill Vautrin had signed. The stamp on it was sufficient to cover a larger sum. He altered the figure, and made it into a regular bill of exchange for twelve thousand francs payable to Goriot. Then he went next door.

"Here is the whole sum, madame," he said, handing the paper to Anastasie. "I was asleep next door, and your conversation woke me up; and so I was able to find out how much I was in Monsieur Goriot's debt. Here is a bill for the amount; you will be able to negotiate it. I will discharge it punctually."

Anastasie stood still, the paper in her hand.

"Delphine," she said, white-faced, and trembling with anger, fury, and rage. "I forgave you everything, as God is my witness. But *this*! This gentleman was in there the whole time, and you knew it! You were mean enough to revenge yourself by letting me betray my secrets, my life, my children, my disgrace, my reputation! You're nothing to me any more, I hate you. I will do you all the harm I can, I—" But her anger dried her throat, and she broke off.

"But he's my son, our child, your own brother, your savior!" cried Goriot. "Kiss him, Nasie! Look, I'll kiss him myself!" He clutched Eugène to him in a frenzied embrace. "Oh, my child! I'll be more than a father to you, I wish I could be a whole family. I wish I were God, to throw the universe at your feet. But do kiss him, Nasie! He isn't a man, he's an angel, an angel from heaven."

"Let her alone, Father, she's out of her mind," said Delphine.

"Am I indeed?" demanded Anastasie. "And what about you?"

"Children, I shall die if this goes on," howled the old man. Suddenly he dropped on the bed as though struck by a bullet. "They're killing me," he muttered.

The countess looked at Eugène, who stood there unable to move, overwhelmed by the violence of the scene. "Sir," she said, and her eyes, voice, and look were all a question. She did not look at her father. Delphine had rapidly unbuttoned his waistcoat.

"Madame, I will pay, and I will hold my tongue," he said, without waiting for her question.

"You have killed poor Father, Nasie!" said Delphine. She pointed to the motionless figure on the bed. Her sister ran from the room.

"I forgive her for everything," said Goriot, opening his eyes. "It's a terrible situation for her; it would drive any woman to distraction. Comfort Nasie, and be kind to her. Promise your poor dying father that," he begged Delphine, pressing her hand.

"But what is the matter?" she asked in terror.

"Nothing, nothing," her father answered. "It will pass. There's something pressing on my temples, a migraine. . . . Poor Nasie, what a terrible future. . . ."

The countess returned as he spoke, and threw herself at his feet. "Forgive me!" she cried.

"Don't!" said Goriot. "That only makes me worse."

"Sir," said Anastasie, turning to Eugène, her eyes brimming with tears, "my misery made me unjust. Will you really be a brother to me?" she asked, holding out her hand.

"Nasie," said Delphine, putting her arms around her sister, "let's forget everything."

"No," said Anastasie, "*I* shall remember!"

"What angels you are," said Goriot. "This tears the curtains from my eyes. The sound of you gives me new life. Kiss each other again. Nasie, will this bill of exchange really save you?"

"I hope so. Look, Papa, will you put your name to it?"

"How stupid of me to forget that! But I felt so unwell.

Don't be cross with me, Nasie. Send word and let me
know when you're out of trouble. No, I'll come
myself. . . . But oh, no, I can't, I mustn't see your husband, I might kill him on the spot. As for signing away
your property, I'll be there. Run along, my child, and
see that Maxime behaves in the future."

Eugène was looking on in astonishment.

"Poor Anastasie has always been quick-tempered,"
said Delphine. "But she has a good heart."

"She came back for the endorsement," whispered
Eugène.

"Do you think so?"

"I'd like not to. Don't trust her," he said, looking
upward as if to confide in God the thoughts he did not
dare put into words.

"Yes, she's always been a bit of a hypocrite, and my
poor father is always taken in by her."

Eugène turned to the old man. "How are you feeling
now, dear Monsieur Goriot?"

"I'd like to sleep," was the reply.

Eugène helped the old man into bed. Still holding
Delphine's hand in his, he fell asleep.

"Till this evening, at the Opéra, then," she said to
Eugène. "You can tell me how he is then. And tomorrow, sir, you will leave here. Let me see your room. . . .
Oh, how awful!" she exclaimed as she went in. "You
were even worse off than Father. Eugène, you've been
a good boy. I'd love you even more, if that were
possible. . . . But, my dear child, if you want to make
your way, you mustn't go throwing twelve thousand
francs out of the window like that. Monsieur de Trailles
is a gambler. My sister refuses to see that. He would
have gone and found his twelve thousand francs where
he has lost and won wads of money before now."

The sound of a groan drew them back to Goriot's
room; he appeared to be asleep, but as the two lovers
came nearer they heard the words: "They aren't happy!"
Whether he was asleep or awake, the tone of these
words affected his daughter's heart so strongly that she
went up to the wretched bed on which her father was

lying, and kissed his brow. He opened his eyes, and said, "That's Delphine!"

"And how are you now?" she asked.

"All right," he said. "Don't worry, I'm going out. Run along, my children. Enjoy yourselves."

Eugène took Delphine home. Anxious about the state in which he had left Goriot, he refused to dine with her, and went back to the Maison Vauquer. Goriot was out of bed, already downstairs, about to sit down to dinner. Bianchon had placed himself where he could observe the old man's face. When he saw him take up his bread and sniff it to judge the flour it was made from, the medical student noticed that the action had been performed without any real consciousness, and he made an ominous sign.

"Come and sit by me, Mr. Resident Physician," said Eugène.

Bianchon came over all the more readily since he would be nearer the old man.

"What's wrong with him?" said Rastignac.

"Unless I'm mistaken, it's all up with him. Something extraordinary must have happened inside; he looks as if he might have a serious apoplexy at any moment. The lower part of his face is normal enough, but the features of the upper part are involuntarily drawn up toward the forehead. Can you see? Then his eyes are in that peculiar state which indicates that the serous fluid has begun to enter the brain. Wouldn't you say they looked as if they were full of a fine dust? I shall know more tomorrow morning."

"Would there be any cure for it?"

"Nothing. His death might perhaps be delayed if one could stimulate some sort of reaction toward the extremities, toward the legs. But if the symptoms haven't disappeared by tomorrow night, the poor man's done for. Have you any idea what can have brought it on? He must have had some violent shock that's caused a collapse of the brain."

"Yes," said Eugène, and thought of the two sisters fighting ceaselessly over their father's heart. "At least," he said to himself, "Delphine loves her father."

2

At the Opéra that evening he was careful not to alarm her.

"Don't worry," she said as soon as he began to speak. "My father's a strong man. Only we upset him a little this morning. You do realize how important all this is? Our whole fortunes are at stake. This sort of thing would have killed me a short time ago; but your love makes me indifferent now. I have only one fear. Only one disaster could possibly happen to me now, and that would be to lose the love that has brought me back to life. Outside that, nothing in the world matters to me. If I'm anxious to have money, it's because I can make you happier. I'm afraid I'm a better lover than I am a daughter. Why? I don't know. You are my whole life. My father gave me a heart, but you made it beat. I don't care if the whole world condemns me, provided you acquit me; and you haven't any right to think ill of me, it's only the strength of my attachment that drives me to my crimes. Am I an unnatural daughter, do you think? I'm not; it's impossible not to love a father as good as ours. Could I have prevented him from seeing the natural consequences of our appalling marriages? Why didn't he stop them? Surely it was his duty to think for us? I know, of course, that he's suffering as much as we are, now. But what could we do about it? Comfort him? Nothing we could do would comfort him. He used to be just as much distressed by our submissiveness as if we had blamed him and complained the whole time. In some situations in life, there's no avoiding bitterness."

Eugène said nothing. He was filled with love by this artless expression of true feeling. Parisian women may be false, blind with vanity, selfish, flirtatious, cold; but when they are really in love they sacrifice more than other women to the object of their love. They divest themselves of all their pettiness, and emerge sublime. Eugène was also struck by the insight with which a woman can sum up the most natural emotions, when a privileged affection enables her to see them with detachment.

Delphine was troubled by his silence.

"What are you thinking about?" she asked.

"I'm still thinking about what you just said. Up till now I thought I loved you more than you loved me."

She smiled, and hardened herself against the pleasure she felt lest their conversation should go beyond propriety. She had never before heard the intense expression of a young, sincere love. A few words more, and she would have been lost. She thought it safer to change the subject.

"Eugène," she said, "I suppose you've not heard what's going on? The whole of Paris will be at the Beauséants' tomorrow. The Rochefides and the Marquis d'Ajuda have agreed to keep things quiet; but tomorrow the king will sign their marriage contract, and your poor cousin still doesn't know. She won't be able to put off her reception, and the marquis won't be there. No one can talk about anything else."

"And the world laughs at an outrage, and revels in it! Don't you realize this will kill Madame de Beauséant?"

"No," Delphine smiled, "you don't know what those women are made of. Anyway, all Paris will be at her house, and so shall I! And of course I owe that pleasure to you."

"But isn't it just one of those rumors that are always flying about Paris?" said Eugène.

"We shall know the truth tomorrow."

Eugène did not return to the Maison Vauquer that night. He could not tear himself away from the delights of his new rooms. The night before, he had been compelled to leave Delphine at one o'clock; tonight it was she who left him—at two. He slept very late the next morning and waited in for Delphine, who came to breakfast with him at midday. With a young man's gluttony for happiness, he had almost forgotten Goriot. Getting used to all these new and elegant possessions was itself like one long feast. And Delphine's presence added a further glory to everything. However, Goriot did cross the two lovers' minds round about four o'clock, as they remembered his happiness at the thought of coming to live here. Eugène remarked that it would be necessary to bring him there at once, if he were going to be ill. He left Delphine, and hurried back to Madame Vauquer's. Neither Goriot nor Bianchon was at dinner.

"Ah!" said the painter. "Old Goriot's collapsed. Bianchon is up there with him. The old boy saw one of his daughters—the Comtesse de Restaurama. . . . Then he insisted on going out, and that made him worse. Society is about to lose one of its most distinguished ornaments."

Eugène leaped toward the stairs.

"Hey! Monsieur Eugène!"

"Monsieur Eugène! Madame's calling you!" shouted Sylvie.

"Monsieur," said the old woman, "Monsieur Goriot and you were to have left on February the fifteenth. That was three days ago; it's the eighteenth today. I ought by rights to have a month's pay from you and him, but if you'll be security for old Goriot, that'll satisfy me."

"Why? Can't you trust him?"

"Trust him? What if the old thing goes out of his mind, and dies? I wouldn't get a penny piece out of his daughters, and his clothes wouldn't fetch ten francs, the whole lot of them. He took his last bits of silver out with him this morning, I don't know why. He was dressed up like a young man. God forgive me, but I'd have sworn he had makeup on. He looked years younger."

"I'll answer for everything," said Eugène, cold with horror, and fearing disaster.

He went up to Goriot's room. The old man was in bed, Bianchon bending over him.

"Good evening, Father," said Eugène.

Goriot smiled gently and, looking at him through glazed eyes, asked: "How is she?"

"Very well. And you?"

"Not bad."

"Don't tire him," said Bianchon. He drew Eugène into a corner of the room.

"Well?" said Eugène.

"Only a miracle can save him now. The serous congestion has begun. He has mustard plasters on; fortunately he can feel them, they're working."

"Can he be moved?"

"Impossible. He must be left here, and avoid all physical movement or emotional disturbance. . . ."

"My good Bianchon," said Eugène, "we'll look after him together."

"I've already called in the head physician from my hospital."

"Well?"

"He'll give his opinion tomorrow evening. He promised to come in after he's finished work tomorrow. Unfortunately, the stupid old boy did a very dangerous thing this morning, and he won't say why. He's as stubborn as a mule. When I talk to him he pretends not to hear, and sleeps so as not to answer. Or if his eyes are open, he starts groaning. He went out early on foot to some place in the town, no one knows where. He took everything of value he had with him, and did some blasted piece of business which has completely overtaxed his strength! One of his daughters came around."

"The countess?" asked Eugène. "A tall, dark, bright-eyed girl with pretty feet, and a good figure?"

"Yes."

"Leave me alone with him for a minute," said Eugène. "I'll get it out of him. He won't mind telling me."

"I'll go and eat in the meantime. Only do try and not upset him; there's still a faint hope."

"Don't worry."

"They'll enjoy themselves tomorrow," said Goriot, as soon as he and Eugène were alone. "They're going to a great ball."

"What did you do this morning, Papa, to make you so ill you can't get up this evening?"

"Nothing."

"Did Anastasie call?" asked Eugène.

"Yes," replied Goriot.

"Well? Don't keep anything from me. What else did she come to ask you for?"

"Ah! she was so unhappy!" said Goriot, gathering his strength to speak. "You see, my boy, since that business over the diamonds, Nasie hasn't had a penny. And she had already ordered a brocade dress for this ball. She'll look a jewel in it. Her dressmaker, a disgraceful woman, wouldn't allow her credit, and her maid had paid a thousand francs on account for her. Poor Nasie—to have to come to that! It made my heart bleed! But the maid, who knew Restaud didn't trust Nasie any more, was frightened of losing her money and persuaded the dressmaker not to deliver the gown unless the thousand francs were repaid. The ball is tomorrow, the dress is ready, Nasie was at her wits' end.

"She wanted to borrow my forks and spoons and pawn them. Her husband wants her to go to the ball, to show everyone in Paris the diamonds they all say she sold. Could she say to that monster: 'I owe a thousand francs, will you please pay it?' No, I could understand her feelings. Her sister Delphine will be there, looking marvelous. Anastasie can't look inferior to her younger sister. She was crying her eyes out, my poor daughter! I was so ashamed at not having the twelve thousand for her yesterday that I'd have given the rest of my wretched life to make up for it. Don't you understand? I could have borne anything, but having no money like this has broken my heart. Well, I didn't hem and haw about it, I spruced myself up somehow, and went out and got six hundred francs for my bits of silver and my buckles; then I sold the first year's income from my annuity to Papa Gobseck for a lump sum of four hundred. Never mind, I can live on bread. It was enough for me when I was young, it can be enough again. And at least Nasie will enjoy her evening; she'll look dazzling.

"I have the thousand-franc note here under my pillow. It warms my heart to have something lying there right under my cheek that is going to give pleasure to poor Nasie! She can turn that wicked maid of hers out of doors! Did you ever hear of servants not trusting their masters? I shall be well again by tomorrow, Nasie's coming at ten o'clock. I don't want them to think I'm sick, otherwise they won't go to the ball, they'll want to stay and look after me. Nasie will come and put her arms around me tomorrow as if I were her own little child; that will cure me. And after all, I'd otherwise be spending a thousand francs on medicine, wouldn't I? I'd rather give it to my Nasie, who can cure everything! I shall at least be a comfort to her in her misery. That will atone for the wrong I did in buying the annuity. . . . She's in the depths, and I'm no longer strong enough to pull her out.

"I'm going back into business. I'm going to Odessa to buy up grain. Wheat there costs only a third of what we pay for it here. I know there are laws against the import of raw grain, but the clever men who made the laws never thought of prohibiting grain products. Ha-ha-ha! I thought of it this morning, all by myself! There's good money to be made out of starch!"

"He's mad," thought Eugène, as he watched the old man. "Come," he said, "you must rest, you mustn't talk. . . ."

Eugène went down for dinner as soon as Bianchon came back. The two of them took turns looking after the sick man during the night, Bianchon reading his medical textbooks, Eugène writing home to his mother and sis-

ters. Next morning, Goriot's symptoms were, according
to Bianchon, hopeful; but he would need continual care,
which only the two students could provide. It would be
impossible to describe their attentions in detail in the
modest phraseology of our own day. The leeches applied
to the old man's emaciated body were accompanied by
poultices and footbaths; other medical necessities demanded all the strength and devotion the two young
men could summon.

Madame de Restaud did not call; she sent a messenger
around for her money.

"I thought she'd have come herself. But it's just as
well; she'd only have been upset," said her father, apparently pleased at the fact.

At seven in the evening Thérèse brought a letter
from Delphine:

> What are you doing, my dear? I feel neglected almost
> before I'm loved! We've opened our hearts to each
> other, and knowing the infinite subtleties of love, I
> know you have too fine a nature ever to be unfaithful.
> As you said when we listened to the prayer in *Mosè*:
> 'Some people hear it as just one note, for others it's
> the infinite in music!' Do remember I expect you this
> evening for Madame de Beauséant's ball. Monsieur
> d'Ajuda's marriage contract was definitely signed at
> court this morning, and the poor viscountess didn't
> hear till two this afternoon. The whole of Paris is
> going to be there, like people crowding to the Place
> de Grève for an execution. Isn't it horrible, they're
> simply going to see if she'll be able to hide her grief,
> and die nobly? I'd certainly never go, my dear, if I'd
> ever been to her house before; but this is bound to
> be the last reception she'll ever give, and all my efforts
> would have been wasted. My position is very different
> from other people's. And besides, I'm going for your
> sake, too. If you're not here in two hours' time, it will
> be a betrayal I'm not sure I shall forgive.

Eugène took up his pen, and replied:

I'm waiting for a doctor, to find out if there is any hope for your father. He is dying. I will bring you the verdict, and I greatly fear it may be a sentence of death. You will decide then if you can still go to the ball. All my love.

The doctor came at half past eight, and though his opinion was not encouraging, he did not consider that death was imminent. There would be improvements and relapses, he said; on these the life and reason of the old man would depend.

"He'd be better off if he died right away," he said as he left.

Leaving Goriot in Bianchon's care, Eugène set out to take the sad news to Delphine—news which to a person like himself, still affected by family ties, seemed to forbid all enjoyment.

"Tell her she's to enjoy herself all the same!" Goriot called after him. He had appeared to be dozing, but struggled up into a sitting position as Eugène left.

The young man appeared before Delphine sunk in grief. He found her with her hair dressed, and her shoes on, with only her ball dress to put on. Yet the final details, like the finishing touches a painter puts to his picture, required more time than the whole groundwork of the canvas.

"Why, you're not dressed!" she cried.

"But, madame, your father—"

"My father again," she interrupted impatiently. "Please don't try to teach me my duty to my father. I've known my father a very long time. Not another word, Eugène. I won't listen to you till you've got dressed. Thérèse has laid everything out for you, in your room. My carriage is ready, take that; and hurry back. We'll talk about Father on our way to the ball. We must start out early. If we're caught in the line of carriages, we shall be lucky if we get there by eleven."

"Delphine!"

"Go on! Not another word," she said, running into her boudoir for a necklace.

"Do go, Monsieur Eugène, you'll make madame cross," said Thérèse, giving the young man a slight push. He was appalled by this elegant parricide.

He went away to dress, sad and disheartened. Society seemed to be nothing but an ocean of mud; any man who ventured a foot into it would be plunged in it up to the neck. "How shabby its crimes are!" he said to himself. "Vautrin is greater than this."

He had seen the three attitudes of men toward the world: obedience, struggle, and revolt; the family, society, and Vautrin. He dared not choose among them. Obedience was dull, revolt impossible, struggle uncertain. His thoughts went back to his family. He remembered the pure emotions of their quiet life, the days he had passed among those who loved him. Those dear creatures found a full, continuous, unclouded happiness in obeying the simple laws of the domestic hearth. But despite these exemplary thoughts, Eugène did not feel brave enough to go and preach the doctrine of simple faith to Delphine and command virtue from her in the name of love. His education, begun so recently, had borne fruit already; already he was selfishly in love. He had enough insight into Delphine's character to know that she would be quite capable, if necessary, of marching over her father's body in order to go to the ball; and he had neither the boldness to find fault with her, nor the temerity to offend her, nor the strength to leave her. "She would never forgive me for placing her in the wrong over this," he told himself.

Then he began to question the opinions of the doctors, and tried to persuade himself that Goriot was not so dangerously ill as he had thought. Soon he was piling up heartless arguments to justify Delphine. She didn't realize the state her father was in. The old man himself would send her back to the ball if she went to see him. The implacable laws of society often condemn as a crime something that may, in fact, be simply due to the innumerable complexities of family life occasioned by differences in character, or conflicting interests and problems.

Eugène was anxious to delude himself; he was ready to sacrifice his own conscience for the sake of his mistress.

Within the last two days his whole life had altered. A woman had introduced confusion there, had eclipsed his family, and appropriated all of him for herself. Eugène and Delphine had met at a time calculated to make them take the liveliest delight in each other's company. A love for which they were both long prepared, had increased by what normally kills love: its gratification. Now that he had possessed her, Eugène realized that before then he had only desired her; he had begun to love her only now that she was his. Love is perhaps simply gratitude for pleasure. Infamous or sublime, whichever she was, he worshiped her for the delight he had received from her; and Delphine loved him as Tantalus would have loved an angel come to satisfy his hunger, or quench the thirst in his parched throat.

"Well, how is my father?" she asked when he returned, dressed for the ball.

"Extremely ill," he answered. "If you wish to give me a proof of your love, we will hurry over to see him."

"So we will," she said, "but after the ball. Dear Eugène, do be nice, and not lecture me. Come."

They set out. Eugène sat in silence for part of the way.

"What's the matter now?" she asked.

"I keep hearing your father's death rattle," he said with a flash of anger. And he began, with the heated eloquence of youth, to describe Anastasie's brutal act of vanity, the mortal crisis brought on by Goriot's final act of devotion, and the cost of Anastasie's brocade dress. Delphine was weeping.

"I'm going to look terrible," she thought; and her tears ceased. "I shall go and nurse Father," she said. "I won't move from his bedside."

"Ah! That's how I wanted you to be!" cried Eugène.

The lamps of five hundred carriages lit up the approaches to the Beauséant mansion. On either side of the brightly lit entrance was a mounted gendarme. Everyone in the fashionable world had flocked so eagerly to see this great lady in the hour of her downfall that the reception rooms on the ground floor of the great house were already packed by the time Delphine and Eugène appeared. Never since the day when the whole royal court rushed to call on Mademoiselle de Montpensier, after Louis XIV had torn her lover from her, had a disastrous love affair created so much stir. But tonight Madame de Beauséant, the youngest daughter of the quasi-royal house of Burgundy, was to rise above her grief and dominate to the very end a world whose vanities she had tolerated only that they might underline the triumph of her love.

The drawing rooms were bright with the smiles and dresses of the most beautiful women in Paris. The most distinguished men from court, ambassadors, ministers, famous men from every walk of life, bedecked with crosses, stars, and colored ribbons, were crowding around the viscountess. The orchestra boomed out its music under the gilded ceilings of a palace that was now a desert to its queen. Madame de Beauséant stood at the door of the first drawing room to receive her so-called friends. She was dressed in white, and her simply braided hair was without ornament; she appeared calm, and showed no sign of sorrow, or pride, or artificial gaiety. No one could read her thoughts. You might have taken her for a marble Niobe. Her smile to her intimate friends was occasionally a mocking one; but to everyone she seemed so like her normal self, and showed so well what she had looked like in the glowing heyday of her happiness, that the most insensitive of her guests admired her, as young Roman women applauded the gladiator who could smile at the moment of death. Society seemed to have arrayed itself in order to bid good-bye to one of its sovereigns.

"I was afraid you weren't coming," she said to Eugène.

He took the remark for a reproof, and said in a troubled voice: "Madame, I came intending to be the last to leave."

"Thank you," she said, taking his hand. "You are

probably the only person I can trust. My friend, love only a woman whom you can love forever. Don't ever forsake any woman."

She took his arm and drew him to a sofa in the room where some of the guests were playing cards.

"I want you to go to the marquis," she said. "My footman Jacques will go with you, and give you a note for him. I am asking him to return my letters. He will give you all of them, or so I like to think. If he does, go upstairs to my room with them. Someone will come and tell me."

She rose to greet the Duchesse de Langeais, her best friend, who was coming toward them. Eugène went, and asked for the Marquis d'Ajuda at the Rochefides', where he would probably be spending the evening. The marquis appeared and took Eugène to his own house, where he handed a box to the young man, saying: "They are all there." He appeared to wish to say something to Eugène, perhaps to ask him about the progress of the ball, or about the viscountess; or perhaps to admit that he was already regretting the marriage, as he was soon after to do. But there was a sudden flash of pride in his eyes, and with melancholy courage he kept his nobler feelings to himself. "Don't say anything to her about me, my dear Eugène." He pressed Eugène's hand sadly and affectionately, and nodded good-bye. Eugène returned to Madame de Beauséant's and was admitted to the viscountess's room, where he saw the signs of her impending departure. He sat down in front of the fire, looked at the cedarwood casket, and sank into deep dejection. In his eyes, Madame de Beauséant had the magnificence of one of the goddesses in the *Iliad*.

"Ah! my friend!" she said as she came in. She laid a hand on his shoulder, and as she raised her eyes he saw that she was in tears. Suddenly, with a shaking hand, she took the box, placed it on the fire, and watched it burn.

"They're dancing! They all came very punctually; while death will come late. Sh! My dear," she said, placing a finger on Eugène's mouth as he was about to speak. "I shall never see Paris or the world of fashion again. At five tomorrow morning I am leaving, to bury myself in the depths of Normandy. Ever since three this afternoon I've been busy making preparations, signing documents, seeing to business matters; I couldn't send anyone to the—" She broke off. "I felt sure he would be at—" She broke off once more, overcome by grief. At these moments everything is agony, and there are words it is impossible to utter.

"So," she went on, "I counted on you for this last service this evening. I would like to give you a token of my friendship. I shall often think of you. You seem to me good and noble, young and frank, in a world where such qualities are very rare. I hope you will sometimes think of me too. . . . Ah, yes," she said, glancing around the room, "here is the box I used to keep my gloves in. Every time I took them out, before going to a ball or a theater, I felt I was beautiful, because I was happy, and I never touched it without leaving some pleasant thought with it. There's a great deal of me in it, a whole Madame de Beauséant who no longer exists. Do please accept it. I will see that it's brought to you at the Rue d'Artois. Madame de Nucingen looks very charming this evening. Love her well. If we never see each other again, my friend, you may be sure I shall pray for you, who have been so good to me. . . .

"Let's go down. I don't want to let them think I'm crying. I have eternity before me, I shall be alone in it, and no one will ask me there the reason for my tears. One last look around this room." She stopped. She stood there for a moment. Then, after shielding her eyes with her hand for a moment, she wiped them, bathed them in cold water, and took Eugène's arm. "Let us go!" she said.

Eugène had never in his life been so painfully moved as he was by this suffering so nobly borne. Returning to the ball, they made the tour of the rooms together—a last graceful act of courtesy on the part of this gracious woman. He soon noticed the two sisters, Madame de Restaud and Madame de Nucingen. The countess was magnificent under her display of diamonds. Fiery indeed they must have felt to her; she was wearing them for the last time. However resolute her pride and love might be, she attempted to avoid her husband's eye. This sight was not of a kind to make Eugène's thoughts less sad. He could still see, beyond the two sisters' diamonds, the mean bed on which Goriot was lying.

The viscountess, misinterpreting his melancholy air, let go of his arm. "Go! I don't want to deprive you of a pleasure," she said.

Eugène was quickly claimed by Delphine, who was delighted at the effect she was creating and eager to lay at her lover's feet the compliments she was receiving from this world into which she hoped to be adopted.

"How do you think Nasie looks?" she asked him.

"She's even turned her father's death into money," he replied.

About four in the morning, the crowd in the reception rooms began to thin out. Shortly afterwards, the music stopped. The Duchesse de Langeais and Eugène were left alone in the great ballroom. Madame de Beauséant, expecting to find Eugène alone there, came back after bidding good-bye to her husband, who had retired to bed saying once more: "It's a mistake, my dear, to go and shut yourself away at your age. Do stay with us."

Seeing the duchess, Madame de Beauséant could not repress an exclamation.

"I know what you are thinking, Clara," said Madame de Langeais. "You are leaving us forever; but I can't let you go without hearing what I have to say, or with misunderstanding between us." She took her friend's arm and led her into the adjoining room; and there, looking at her with tears in her eyes, she took her in her arms and kissed her on both cheeks.

"I don't want to part from you in coldness, my dear, it would be too much guilt to bear. You can count on me as if I were your own self. You have been a great woman this evening; but I'm still worthy of you, and I want to prove it. I have behaved badly toward you, and I haven't always been kind. Forgive me, my dear; I take back everything that may have wounded you. If I could,

I would unsay my words. The same grief has united our souls, and I don't know which of us may be the more unhappy. Monsieur de Montriveau wasn't here this evening; you realize what that means . . . ? Anyone who saw you during the ball tonight, Clara, will never forget you. Myself, I'm going to make one last effort. If I fail, I shall go into a convent. And, where are you going?"

"To Normandy, to Courcelles—to love and pray there till it pleases God to take me from this world."

Then she remembered that Eugène was still waiting, and called in a shaking voice: "Do come in here, Monsieur de Rastignac."

The young man knelt and kissed his cousin's hand.

"Good-bye, Antoinette," she said to her friend. "Be happy. . . . As for you, you *are* happy," she said to Eugène. "You are young, you can still believe in something. I say good-bye to this world, knowing I've had, as a few privileged people have on their deathbeds, sincere and devoted feelings around me."

Eugène came away about five that morning, after seeing Madame de Beauséant into her traveling carriage. Her last farewell to him was a tearful one, which proved that the most exalted personages are not exempt from the laws of the heart, and do not lead lives free from misery, as some wooers of the people would have it. Eugène came back on foot to the Maison Vauquer. The weather was damp and cold. His education was all but complete.

"We're not going to save poor old Goriot," Bianchon told him, as he entered his neighbor's room.

"My friend," Eugène said, as he looked at the sleeping man, "always stick to the modest career you've decided on. I am in hell, and I have to stay there. Whatever evil you are told about society, you can be sure it's true. It would take more than a Juvenal to describe the horror under the gold and the jewels."

PART SIX

DEATH OF A FATHER

1

Next day, Eugène was awakened at two in the afternoon by Bianchon. He was obliged to go out and asked Eugène to look after Goriot, whose condition had become much worse during the morning.

"The fellow hasn't a couple of days to live, perhaps not even six hours," the medical student said. "But we still mustn't stop trying to fight the illness. The care he needs is going to be expensive. We can nurse him well enough, but I haven't a penny. I've been through his pockets and his chest of drawers; there's nothing at all there. I questioned him while he was conscious for a moment, and he said he hadn't a penny left. What have you got?"

"I've got twenty francs," said Eugène, "but I'll go and gamble with them and win some more."

"What if you lose?"

"I shall ask his sons-in-law and his daughters for some money."

"And what if they don't give you any?" asked Bianchon. "The most urgent thing at the moment isn't finding money; but the old man must be covered from his feet halfway up his thighs with a boiling mustard plaster. If he shouts, there'll be some hope. You know how it's done. And Christophe will help you, in any case. I'll call at the pharmacist's and say I'll be responsible for all the stuff we shall need from there. It's a pity the poor man wasn't fit to be taken to our hospital, he would have been better off there. Come and let me install you. And don't leave him till I come back."

The two young men went into the room where the old man lay. Eugène was shocked by the change in the twisted, white, utterly exhausted features.

"Well, Father?" he said, bending over the squalid bed.

Goriot turned his dulled eyes to Eugène, and looked at him attentively without recognizing him. The sight was more than the young man could bear. Tears came to his eyes.

"Bianchon, oughtn't we to have curtains at the windows?"

"No. Atmospheric conditions don't affect him any more. It would be too much to hope for that he should feel heat or cold. Still, we must have some fire to heat drinks on, and for a lot of other things. I'll send up a few bundles of sticks till we can get some wood. I burned up all yours yesterday and during the night, and all the old man's peat, too. It was damp, the walls were streaming. I could hardly keep the room dry. Christophe swept it, it was like a pigsty. I burnt some juniper, the place stank so."

"My God!" said Rastignac. "And think of his daughters!"

"Listen, if he asks for a drink, give him some of this," said Bianchon, showing Rastignac a large white jug. "If you hear him groan, and his stomach is hard and hot, then ask Christophe to help you to give him . . . well, you know all about that. If by any chance he becomes very excited, if he talks a good deal, even if he's slightly delirious, leave him alone. It won't be a bad sign. But send Christophe right over to the hospital. Either our doctor or my fellow-student, or I, will come round and give him cauteries.

"While you were asleep this morning, we had a big consultation with a pupil of Dr. Gall's, and a senior physician from the Hôtel-Dieu, and our own. These gentlemen thought they recognized peculiar symptoms, and we're going to follow the course of the disease to try to get light on several very important scientific details. One of them claims that if the serum presses more on one organ than on another, it causes a specific emotional reaction. So listen to him carefully, if he should talk, and take particular note of what subjects he talks about—whether they seem to involve his memory, or perception, or judgment; whether it's material matters or feelings he worries about; if he makes plans, or if he reverts to the past. In short, be able to give us an exact report. Possibly the invasion may affect the whole brain at once—in which case he will die in the imbecile state he's in now. Everything is unpredictable in this kind of disease! If the bomb goes off here," said Bianchon pointing to the back of the patient's head, "the most unusual things can happen. The brain recovers certain of its faculties, and death takes place more slowly. The liquid may drain away from the brain, and follow channels we can ascertain only afterward, by an autopsy. At the Hospital for Incurables there's an old imbecile in whose case the discharge has gone down the spinal cord. He's in horrible pain, but he's still alive."

"Did they enjoy themselves?" said Goriot, suddenly recognizing Eugène.

"He can't think of anything but his daughters," said Bianchon. "He must have said over a hundred times last night: 'They're dancing! She's got her dress!' He kept calling their names. Hell, it made me cry, the way he kept moaning: 'Delphine! My little Delphine! Nasie!' I can tell you, it would have made anybody break down."

"Delphine," said the old man, "she's there, isn't she? I was sure she was." He was making a desperate effort to see the walls and the door.

"I'm just going down to tell Sylvie to get the mustard plasters ready," said Bianchon. "This is the moment for them."

Eugène was left alone with the old man. He sat at the foot of the bed, staring at the terrifying, painful spectacle.

"Madame de Beauséant is running away, this man is dying," he thought. "Finer spirits can't stay long in this world. And how indeed can deep feeling reconcile itself with a society so shabby and petty and superficial?"

Images of last night's ball came back into his mind and contrasted sharply with the sight of the deathbed.

Bianchon suddenly reappeared: "Look, Eugène, I've just seen our hospital chief; I ran all the way back. If he shows any signs of consciousness—if he talks at all—place a long mustard plaster under him so that he is covered with mustard from his neck to the small of his back. Then send for us."

"My dear Bianchon," said Eugène.

"Oh, it's very interesting from the scientific point of view," said Bianchon, with a neophyte's enthusiasm.

"So I suppose," said Eugène, "I'll be the only one looking after this poor old man from simple affection?"

"You wouldn't say that if you'd seen me this morning," said Bianchon, unoffended by the remark. "Doctors already in practice see only the illness; I can still see the sick man, my dear boy."

He departed, leaving Eugène alone with the old man, terrified lest there should be a crisis—and soon there was.

"Ah, it's you, my dear child," said Goriot, recognizing Eugène once more.

"Are you feeling better?" Eugène asked, taking his hand.

"Yes, my head felt as if it were being screwed in a vise, but it's getting free again. Have you seen my daughters? They'll be here soon. They'll rush here the minute they know I'm ill. They took such care of me when we lived in the Rue de la Jussienne! Oh, God, I do wish my room were fit for them to come to. There was a young man here who burned up all my peat."

"I can hear Christophe coming upstairs," said Eugène. "He's bringing up some wood that young man has sent you."

"Good, but how can I pay for it? I haven't a penny left, my boy. I've given everything away; everything. I'm living on charity. But at any rate the brocade dress was pretty, wasn't it? (Aah . . . ! This does hurt!) Thank you, Christophe. God will reward you, my boy; I haven't a thing."

"I'll pay you, don't worry; and Sylvie too," Eugène whispered to the man.

"My daughters did tell you they were coming, didn't they, Christophe? Go and see them again; I'll give you five francs. Tell them I don't feel well, that I'd like to kiss them and see them just once more before I die. Tell them that, but be careful not to frighten them too much."

Christophe departed at a nod from Eugène.

"They'll soon be here," said Goriot. "I know them. How my good Delphine will suffer if I die. . . . Nasie, too. I don't want to die; they'll cry if I do. And if I die, I shall never see them again, dear Eugène. It'll be very dull for me, where I'm going. For a father, hell means being away from his children. And I've had my apprenticeship in that ever since they married. Heaven, for me, meant the Rue de la Jussienne. Do you think if I go to heaven, I shall be able to come back to earth as a spirit to be near them? I've heard such things said. Are they true? I can almost see them now, just as they were in the Rue de la Jussienne. . . . They'd come downstairs in the morning. 'Good morning, Papa,' they used to say. I used to take them on my knee, and tease them, and play with them. They'd stroke my face. We had breakfast together every morning; we had supper together. I was a real father then; I delighted in my children. When we lived in the Rue de la Jussienne, they didn't have to use their brains, they knew nothing about the world; they just loved me. Oh, God, why didn't they stay young forever . . . ?

"I'm in such pain! My head's splitting. . . . Oh, forgive me, my children, I'm in horrible pain. . . . And this must be real pain, you've hardened me so well to ordinary suffering. God, if I could only have their hands in mine, I wouldn't feel any pain at all! Do you think they'll come? Christophe's so stupid. I ought to have gone myself. *He'll* be seeing them. But you were at the ball last night. Tell me how they were. They knew nothing about my being ill, did they? They would never have danced, if so, poor little things. Ah, I don't want to go on being ill; they still need me too much. Their fortunes are in danger. And what husbands they're tied to! Make me well! Make me well! I'm in such pain! Aaaah! I must get better, you see, they need money and I know where to go and make some. I shall go and make *pasta* in Odessa. I'm clever, I shall make millions. . . . But this pain's more than I can bear!"

Goriot was silent for a moment. He seemed to be summoning all his strength to bear the pain.

"If only they were here, I wouldn't complain," he said. "I'd have nothing to complain of."

There was a slight respite that lasted for some time. Christophe returned. Eugène, thinking Goriot asleep, allowed the man to report on his errand aloud.

"Sir," he said, "I went to the countess's first but they wouldn't let me speak to her. They said she was very busy with her husband. I insisted, and Monsieur de Restaud came out to speak to me himself. He said: 'Monsieur Goriot's dying, is he? It's the best thing he could do. I need Madame de Restaud here on important business, she'll come when it's all over.' The gentleman seemed very angry. I was on my way out, when the countess came into the anteroom through a door I hadn't seen, and she said to me: 'Christophe, tell my father I have to discuss things with my husband. I can't leave him at the moment; it's a matter of life or death for my children. But as soon as it's over, I'll come. . . .' As for the baroness, I never even saw her or spoke to her. Her maid told me, 'Madame didn't get back from the ball till a quarter past five, she's asleep. If I wake her up before midday, she'll scold me. I'll tell her her father's worse when she rings for me. Bad news can always wait.' It was no use begging her. I asked to speak to the baron, but he'd gone out."

"Neither of his daughters would come!" cried Eugène. "I'll write to both of them."

"Neither of them," echoed the old man, sitting up. "They are busy, they're asleep, they won't come. I knew it. You have to be dying to know what children are.

"Ah, my friend, never marry, never have children! You give them life, and they give you death. You help them into the world, and they drive you out of it. No, they won't come! I've known that for the last ten years. I sometimes thought it, but I never dared believe it."

Tears stood in the inflamed lower lids of his eyes, but did not fall.

"Ah! if I were rich, if I'd kept my money and never given it to them, they'd be here now, licking my cheeks with their kisses! I'd be living in a mansion, in splendid rooms, with servants, and a fire in the grate; and they'd all be in tears, with their husbands and children. I'd have had all that. But I have nothing. Money buys you everything, even daughters. Ah! Where is my money? If I had money to leave, they'd be nursing me and looking after me. I'd see them, and hear them. Ah, my dear boy, my only child, I prefer my loneliness and poverty. At least, when a poor man is loved, he knows the love is genuine. . . . No, I wish I were rich, then I could see them.

"My God, who would have thought it? They both have hearts of stone. I loved them too much; that's why they couldn't love *me*! A father should always hold on to his money. He ought to put the rein on his daughters like vicious horses. And I went down on my knees to them, the wretched girls! This is a fitting end to the way they've treated me for the last ten years. If you knew the fuss they made over me when they were first married! (Oh, this pain is torture!) I had just given them nearly eight hundred thousand francs apiece. They couldn't be hard with me then, nor could their husbands. I was greeted with 'dear Father this,' 'dear Father that.' There was always a place for me at their table then. Yes, I dined with their husbands, and they treated me with respect. They thought I still had something. Why did they think so? I'd never told them about my affairs. But a man who gives his daughters eight hundred thousand francs each is someone worth being attentive to; and they *were* attentive. But it was only for my money. The world isn't a beautiful place, I've seen that for myself! The girls took me in their carriages to the theater; I could stay on for their parties if I wanted to. Yes, they called themselves my daughters; they acknowledged me as a father!

"But I've never lost my shrewdness, nothing escaped me. All this had an aim. It was that that cut me to the heart! I saw through the whole sham of it; but there was no remedy. I wasn't at my ease at their dinner tables, as I am downstairs in this place. I never knew what to say to people. And fashionable people would whisper to my sons-in-law: 'Who's that gentleman?'—'Oh, it's our father, the one with the money, he's very rich,' they'd say. 'Oh, really!' the others would say, and they'd stare at me with the respect you have to show to the 'one with the money.' But if I did annoy them a little sometimes, I paid for my faults. And who's perfect, after all? (Oh, my head! It's like one great wound!) I'm suffering now what every man has to go through in order to die, Monsieur Eugène, but it's nothing to the pain I felt when Anastasie let me know by one single look that I'd said something out of place, and humiliated her. That look seemed to tear me wide open. I wanted to learn how to behave, but the only thing I did learn was that there was no longer a place for me on this earth!

"Next day I went to Delphine's for comfort, and there again I did something that made *her* angry with me too. I felt I was going mad. A whole week went by, and I still didn't know what to do. I didn't dare go and see them for fear they'd reproach me! Turned out of my own daughters' homes! O God! if Thou knowest the misery, the torment I've had to bear, and hast counted the dagger blows they gave me in those days that aged me, changed me, killed me, and turned my hair white, why dost Thou make me suffer today? I've surely atoned for the sin of loving them too well. And they've avenged themselves well on my affection, they've tortured me like executioners.

"Ah, how foolish fathers are! I loved them so much that I went back to them again, like a gambler going back to the gambling tables. My daughters were *my* vice; they were my mistresses. It was like that! They might both need something, some jewel or other. Their maids would tell me, and I'd send it to them so as to be sure of a welcome from them! But even then, they'd always have their little lectures to give me about the way I behaved in society. Ah, they couldn't even wait till the next day to tell me! They were beginning to be ashamed of me; that's what comes of giving children an education. At my age it was too late to go back to school again, I was too old to learn. (Oh, I'm in such horrible pain! Where are the doctors? If only they would break my head open I wouldn't be in such pain!)

"My daughters! Anastasie! Delphine! I want to see them! Send the police for them; bring them by force! I have justice on my side, everything on my side, nature, the law! *I protest!* The country will perish if fathers are trodden underfoot. Of course it will. Society, the whole world, turns on fatherhood. Everything will collapse if children don't love their fathers. Ah, just to see them and hear them! Never mind what they say, so long as I can hear their voices, that will soothe my pain. Delphine especially. But tell them when they come not to look at me coldly, as they always do. Ah, my friend, Monsieur Eugène, you don't know what it's like to see a golden smile turn into dull lead. Ever since the day when their eyes stopped shining on me, it's been winter to me here. I have had nothing but grief upon grief to feed on; and I have fed on it. I've lived to be humiliated and insulted. I loved them so much that I swallowed all the outrages. I had to. That was the price I had to pay for the little shamefaced joy they allowed me. A father, hiding in order to see his daughters. . . . I've given them my life. Today they won't give me one hour. I'm thirsty, and hungry, and my heart is burning, and they won't come even to soothe my last hours. For I know they are my last, I can tell they are. . . . And don't they know what it means to trample on a father's corpse?

"There is a God in Heaven! He avenges us fathers in spite of ourselves. Oh, they'll come! Come, my darlings, come and kiss me once more, a last kiss, the last sacrament for your father, and I'll pray to God for you, and

tell Him you've been good daughters. I'll plead for you.
After all, you are innocent. They *are* innocent, my
friend, tell everyone that, so that they shan't be upset
by anyone because of me. It is all my fault; it was I who
taught them to trample me underfoot. That was what I
liked. And it's no one's business, human justice doesn't
come into it, nor divine either. God would be unjust if
He condemned them because of me.

"I didn't know how to behave properly, I was foolish
enough to renounce my rights. I would have degraded
myself for them! How could things have turned out otherwise? The finest nature, the best soul on earth, would
have succumbed to the corruption of such weakness on
a father's part. I am a wretch; I am justly punished. I
alone was the cause of all they did. I spoiled them myself, and today they crave for pleasures as they used to
crave for sweets. I allowed them to gratify every girlish
fancy. At fifteen they had their own carriage! Nothing
was denied them. I alone am to blame, but only because
I loved them. Their voices opened my heart.

"I can hear them, they're coming! Oh, yes, they'll
come! The law requires that people should come and
see their fathers die, the law is on my side. It will only
cost them one drive. I will pay for it. Write and tell them
I have millions to leave them! On my honor! I will go
and make Italian *pasta* at Odessa. I know how to. My
scheme will bring in millions. No one has thought of it
before; it won't spoil in transit like grain and flour. Aha!
Starch, you see? There'll be millions in it. It's not a lie,
tell them—millions. And even if they come only out of
greed, I'd rather be deceived! I shall see them then! I
want my daughters! It was I who made them, they belong to me!" he cried, clambering into a sitting posture.
Every feature of his old white head and face seemed
to Eugène to express the most violent threats he was
capable of.

"Come, come," said Eugène, "lie down again, dear
Monsieur Goriot. I'll write to them. As soon as Bianchon comes back I'll go myself, if they don't come."

"If they don't come!" repeated the old man, sobbing.

"But I shall be dead! Dead in an outburst of rage, rage! Rage is getting the better of me! I can see my whole life. I've been fooled! They don't love me, they've never loved me, it's quite plain. If they haven't come by now, they won't ever come. The longer they delay, the less willing they'll be to give me this last joy. I know them. They've never once guessed my pain, my grief, my yearning for them; and they'll never guess the meaning of my death either. They don't even know the secret of my love for them. Yes, I can see it all now. I was always willing to give them the very heart out of my body— and that's taken away the value of everything I ever did. If they'd asked me for the eyes in my head, I'd have said, 'Pluck them out!' I'm too foolish. They think all fathers are like theirs. We ought always to insist on being respected. Their children will be my revenge. But it's in their own interest to come here! Warn them they're endangering their own moment of death. They're committing every crime in one. Go, go and tell them that it's a father's murder if they don't come! They've done enough, without adding that. Cry to them like me: 'Nasie . . . Delphine . . . come to your father, who's been so good to you, and now he's in pain!'

"Nothing; no one. Am I to die like a dog then? This is my reward: desertion. They are vile and criminal! I abominate them and curse them. I'll come from the grave at night and curse them again. After all, friend, am I wrong? They're behaving very badly, aren't they? What am I saying? Didn't you tell me Delphine was here? Yes, she's the better of the two. You're my son, Eugène: love her, be a father to her. The other one's so very unhappy. And their fortune! Oh, God, I'm dying. . . . I'm suffering just a little too much. Cut my head off, and leave me only my heart."

"Christophe, go and find Bianchon!" shouted Eugène down the stairs. He was terrified by the character of the old man's wailing and screaming. "And get me a cab.

"I will go and see your daughters, dear Monsieur Goriot, and make them come to you."

"Use force, use force! Ask for the police, the troops,

anything, anything!" said Goriot, with the last look at Eugène that was to show any spark of reason. "Tell the government, tell the public prosecutor to force them to come, I insist on it!"

"But you've cursed them."

"Who said so?" demanded the old man, aghast. "You know I love and worship them! I shall be well again if I can see them. . . . Go, my good neighbor, my dear child, go; *you* are good. I would like to thank you, but I have nothing left to give you but the blessing of a dying man. Ah, if I could just see Delphine, to tell her to discharge my debt to you! If the other one can't come, at least bring Delphine. Tell her you won't love her anymore if she won't come—she loves you so much, she's bound to come. . . . Give me something to drink, I'm burning inside . . . Put something on my head. My daughters' hands would save me, I am sure of it. . . . Oh, my God, who will repair their fortunes once I'm gone? I want to go to Odessa for their sakes, to make *pasta* there."

"Drink this," said Eugène. Supporting the dying man with his left arm, he held a cup of medicinal tea to his lips with the other.

"I'm sure you love your father and mother," said the old man, clutching Eugène's hand in his failing grasp. "Do you realize that I'm going to die without seeing my daughters again? Always thirsting, and never drinking! That's the way I've lived these last ten years. My sons-in-law have killed my daughters. Yes, I've had no daughters since the day they married. Oh, fathers! Tell parliaments everywhere to make a law about marriage! Yes, and if you love your daughters, never let them marry. A son-in-law is a criminal who spoils and sullies everything in a girl. No more marrying! That's what robs us of our daughters and leaves us without them when we're dying. Make a law about dying fathers. . . . Oh, this is terrifying! It's my sons-in-law that prevent them from coming. Kill them! Death to Restaud, death to the Alsatian, they are my murderers! Death or my daughters . . . ! But,

ah, it's all over, I'm dying without them! Nasie! Fifine!
Do come, do come! Your daddy's leaving you. . . ."

"Dear good Monsieur Goriot, do keep calm, try to lie
quietly, don't worry, don't even think."

"Not to see them . . . it's the final blow!"

"You are going to see them."

"Is it true?" cried the distracted old man. "Oh, to see
them! I'm going to see them, and hear their voices! I
shall die happy. Yes indeed! I don't ask to live any
longer, life means nothing, only more and more pain.
But to see them, and touch their dresses, only just their
dresses, it's not much to ask; just to feel something belonging to them! Let me touch their hair . . . hair. . . ."

His head fell back on the pillow as though he had
been struck by a club. His hands rambled over the cover-
let as if in search of his daughters' hair.

"I give them my blessing," he said with difficulty,
"my blessing."

Suddenly he crumpled up. At this moment Bianchon
came in.

"I've just seen Christophe," he said. "He's getting you
a cab." Then he looked at the dying man, and forced
his eyelids open. The two students saw that his eyes were
dull and expressionless. "He won't come to again," said
Bianchon. "At least, I don't think he will." He took the
old man's pulse and laid a hand against his heart.

"The machine is still going. But in his state, it's a pity.
He'd be better off dead."

"My God, yes," said Eugène.

"What's the matter with you? You're as pale as
death yourself."

"My friend, I've just heard such cries and groans!
There *is* a God! Oh, yes, there's a God, and He's made
a better world for us, or else this one has no meaning.
If it hadn't been so tragic, I should have burst into tears;
my heart feels horribly oppressed."

"Look, we're going to need a lot of things. Where's
the money coming from?"

Eugène took out his watch.

"Here: go and pawn this at once. I don't want to stop on the way, I'm frightened of losing a single minute, and I'm waiting for Christophe. I haven't a penny, and I shall have to pay the cabman when I get back here."

Eugène rushed downstairs, and set off for Madame de Restaud's in the Rue du Helder. On the way, his imagination, struck by the horrible scene he had just witnessed, added fuel to his indignation. He was shown into the anteroom. When he asked for Madame de Restaud, he was told by the footman that she could not be seen.

"But I've come on behalf of her father, who is dying."

"We have the strictest orders from Monsieur le Comte, sir."

"If Monsieur de Restaud is in, please tell him the state his father-in-law is in, and inform him that I must speak to him immediately."

Eugène was kept waiting a long time.

"He may be dying at this very moment," he thought.

The footman led him into the smaller drawing room, where Monsieur de Restaud was standing before the fireless hearth. He did not ask Eugène to sit down.

"Monsieur le Comte," said Eugène, "your father-in-law is dying at this very moment in a disgraceful hovel, without a penny to buy firewood. He is at the very point of death, and is asking to see his daughter."

"Sir," replied the count frigidly, "you must have observed already that I have very little love for Monsieur Goriot. He has behaved very discreditably in connection with Madame de Restaud, he has been the sorrow of my life, and I regard him as the enemy of my peace of mind. It is a matter of complete indifference to me whether he lives or dies. Those are my feelings in the matter. Society may disapprove of them, but I have more important things to occupy my mind than the opinions of fools and outsiders. As for Madame de Restaud, she is in no condition to go out. In any case, I do not wish her to leave the house. Tell her father that as soon as she has fulfilled her duties to my child and myself, she shall go and see him. If she loves her father, she can be free to do so in a matter of moments—"

"Monsieur le Comte, it is not my place to criticize your conduct; you are your wife's master. But may I count on your word? If so, please promise me only to tell her that her father has not twenty-four hours to live, and has already cursed her for not being at his bedside!"

"You shall tell her that yourself," said the count, surprised by the indignation in Eugène's voice.

He led Eugène into the countess's drawing room. He found her bathed in tears and sunk into an armchair like a woman who wished only that she were dead. He felt sorry for her. Before she looked at Eugène, she cast a terrified glance at her husband that revealed how completely prostrate and crushed she was by his mental and physical tyranny. The count nodded, and this seemed to embolden her to speak.

"I overheard all you said, sir. Will you tell my father that if he knew the state I am in, he would forgive me." She turned to her husband and said: "I did not expect such torture as this, it is more than I can bear; but I shall hold out to the very end. I am a mother. . . . Tell my father," she cried, desperately turning again to Eugène, "that he has nothing to reproach me for, however things may look."

Eugène, guessing the terrible ordeal the woman was passing through, bowed to them both, and withdrew in bewilderment. The count's manner had convinced him that his effort was useless, and he saw that Anastasie was no longer free. He hurried around to the Nucingens'. Delphine was in bed.

"I'm so ill, my dear friend," she said. "I caught cold as I left the ball. I'm afraid I may have pneumonia. I'm waiting for the doctor—"

"Even if you're at death's door," Eugène interrupted her, "you must be got somehow to see your father. He's calling for you! If you could hear even the faintest of his cries, you couldn't feel ill any longer."

"Eugène, my father is probably not so ill as you say; but I couldn't bear you to think me guilty of the slightest wrong, and I'll do what you ask, though I know he'd die of grief if I developed a fatal illness as a result of going

out. But I will come, as soon as the doctor has been. . . .
Ah! Why aren't you wearing your watch?" she asked,
noticing that only the chain was there. Eugène blushed.

"Eugène! Eugène! If you've already sold it, or lost
it . . . oh, that would be terrible!"

Eugène bent over Delphine's bed, and whispered:
"Do you want to know? Well then, I'll tell you! Your
father hasn't enough left to buy the shroud they'll wrap
him in this evening. Your watch is at the pawnshop. I
had nothing else left."

Delphine leaped at once from her bed, ran to her
desk, took her purse, and handed it to Eugène. She rang
the bell, crying: "I'm coming, I'm coming, Eugène! Let
me get dressed. Why, I'd be a monster, if—! You go on
ahead; I shall be there before you! Thérèse!" she called
to her maid. "Tell Monsieur de Nucingen to come up
and see me at once."

Eugène, happy that he could tell the dying man that
one of his daughters was coming, was almost cheerful
by the time he got back to the Rue Neuve-Sainte-
Geneviève. He fumbled in Delphine's purse in order
to pay the cabman at once; and found that this rich,
elegant young woman's purse contained exactly seventy francs.

Upstairs, he found Goriot in Bianchon's arms, receiving
treatment from the hospital surgeon. Another doctor
looked on. Cauteries were being applied to the old man's
back—the last, desperate, useless resource of science.

"Can you feel them?" the doctor was asking.

Goriot had caught sight of Eugène, and asked:
"They're coming, aren't they?"

"He may pull through," said the surgeon. "He can
still speak."

"Yes," said Eugène, "Delphine's on her way here."

"He's been shouting for his daughters," said Bianchon, "like a man at the stake shouting for water."

"That's enough," the doctor said to the surgeon.
"There's nothing more we can do; we shan't save him."

Bianchon and the surgeon laid the dying man flat on
his back, on the filthy mattress.

"But even so, we must get his linen changed," said the doctor. "Even if there's no hope, we must have some respect for human nature. I'll be coming back, Bianchon. If he complains again, apply opium to the diaphragm."

The surgeon and the doctor left together.

"Pull yourself together, Eugène," said Bianchon, as soon as they were alone. "We must put a clean shirt on him, and change the bedclothes. Go and tell Sylvie to bring some sheets up, and to come and help us."

Eugène went downstairs and found Madame Vauquer helping Sylvie to set the table. At his first words, the widow came up to him, with the acid-drop smile of a cautious shopkeeper who wants to lose neither her money nor the customer.

"My dear Monsieur Eugène," she said, "you know just as well as I do that old Goriot hasn't a penny left. To put out fresh sheets for a man who'll be popping off any minute is just throwing them away, especially as one of them is bound to have to be used for the shroud. And you're already in my debt a hundred and forty-four francs; and with forty, say, for the sheets, and the other oddments like the candle—Sylvie'll get that for you— it'll come to at least two hundred all told, and a poor widow like me can't afford to lose all that. Gracious, do be fair, Monsieur Eugène. I've lost quite enough already here these last five days, since my troubles began. I'd have given thirty francs if the old man had gone when you said he was going. It's affecting my boarders. For two pins I'd have him put in the workhouse. I mean, put yourself in my place. My establishment must come first: it's my life."

Eugène ran back upstairs to Goriot's room.

"Bianchon, where's the money for the watch?"

"There, on the table. There's three hundred and sixty francs left. I paid everything we owed with it. The pawn ticket's under the money."

"Here, Madame Vauquer," said Eugène, with disgust, when he was downstairs again. "Let me pay our bills. Monsieur Goriot won't be with you much longer, and I—"

"Yes, he'll be going out feet first, poor old thing," she said, as she counted the two hundred francs with melancholy gaiety.

"Hurry up," said Eugène.

"Sylvie! Get some bedclothes, and go and help the gentlemen upstairs. . . . You won't forget Sylvie, will you?" she whispered to Eugène. "She's been up two whole nights."

As soon as Eugène's back was turned, the old woman darted into the kitchen. "Give them the top-to-bottoms from number seven," she whispered. "Heaven knows they're good enough for a corpse."

Eugène was already halfway upstairs, and did not hear her.

"Come," said Bianchon. "Let's get his shirt on. Hold him up straight."

Eugène stood at the head of the bed and held the dying man while Bianchon took off his shirt. Goriot made a movement as if to keep something on his chest, and uttered plaintive, inarticulate cries like an animal trying to express great pain.

"Oh, yes," said Bianchon. "He wants that little chain with the hair and the medallion. We took them off a moment ago, when we gave him the cauteries. Let the poor man have the locket back; it's on the mantelpiece."

Eugène went for it. The chain was inwoven with a tress of ash-blond hair, doubtless that of Madame Goriot. On one side of the locket he read: *Anastasie*, on the other: *Delphine*. A symbol of Goriot's heart that had always lain on his heart. The curls of hair inside were both so fine that they must have been cut off when the girls were babies. As soon as he felt the locket touch his chest, Goriot uttered a prolonged sigh of satisfaction, appalling to hear. It was one of the last echoes from his consciousness, which seemed to be retreating to that unknown center from which all our sympathies rise and to which they finally withdraw. An expression of morbid delight spread over his contorted features. The two students, shaken by the terrible sight of a feeling so powerful that it had outlasted thought itself, were so moved that a few hot tears fell on the dying man's body. He uttered a sharp cry of pleasure:

"Nasie! Fifine!" he cried.

"He's still alive," said Bianchon.

"What good is that to him?" asked Sylvie.

"It enables him to suffer," said Eugène.

Bianchon knelt down and passed his arms under Goriot's thighs and motioned to his friend to help him. Eugène slipped his arms under Goriot's back. Sylvie stood waiting to take off the sheets as soon as the old man was lifted free, and to replace them with the fresh ones she had brought. Deceived, no doubt, by the young men's tears, Goriot expended his fatal strength in reaching out his hands. On either side they encountered the head of one of the young men; he clutched them violently by the hair, and was heard to murmur feebly: "My angels. . . ." Two words, two murmurs, given breath by the soul that fled as he spoke.

"Poor dear man," said Sylvie, touched by this exclamation.

It had expressed a supreme tenderness, aroused for the last time by the most grotesque and involuntary lie of all. The father's last sigh must have been a sigh of bliss. It was the summing-up of his whole life. He had deceived himself to the end.

Goriot was reverently lowered onto his sordid bed. From this moment on, although his features bore the painful imprint of a mechanical struggle between life and death, the cerebral consciousness that makes a man aware of pleasure or pain no longer existed. The ultimate destruction was only a matter of time.

"He'll be like that for some hours; you won't be able to tell when he dies. There won't even be a death rattle. The brain must be completely overrun."

At this moment a breathless young woman was heard coming up the stairs.

"She's too late," said Eugène.

It was not Delphine, but Thérèse, her maid.

"Monsieur Eugène," she said, "there's been a terrible scene between monsieur and madame over the money

the poor lady asked for her father. She fainted, they sent
for the doctor, and he had to bleed her. She shouted:
'My father's dying, I want to see papa!' It would have
broken your heart."

"Hush, Thérèse, even if she came now, her presence
would be useless. Monsieur Goriot is no longer conscious."

"Oh, the poor good man, is he as bad as that?"
cried Thésèse.

"You don't need me any more, I must go and get the
dinner; it's half-past four," said Sylvie. At the top of the
stairs she almost collided with Madame de Restaud.

The appearance of the countess was grave and terrible. She looked toward the deathbed, poorly lit by a
single candle, and burst into tears at the sight of her
father's masklike face, flickering still with the last glim-
mers of life. Bianchon tactfully withdrew.

"I couldn't get away in time," said the countess to
Eugène.

He nodded sadly in acknowledgment. Anastasie took
her father's hand and kissed it.

"Oh, Father, forgive me! You said my voice would
call you back from the grave. Come back to life for a
moment, and bless your penitent child. Oh, Father,
please hear me! This is horrible. No one on earth except
you will ever bless me from now on. Everybody hates
me; you are the only one who loves me. Even my own
children will hate me. Take me with you, I'll love you
and look after you. . . . He can't hear me, I'm out of
my mind!" She fell on her knees and gazed frantically
at the human wreck before her.

"My misery is complete," she said at last, looking up
at Eugène. "Monsieur de Trailles has gone, leaving enormous debts behind him; and I knew he was deceiving
me. My husband will never forgive me, and I have given
him control of my fortune. I've lost every illusion I ever
had. Alas, for whom have I betrayed the only heart who
ever loved me?" She pointed to her father. "I've slighted
him, and repulsed him, I've done him a thousand
wrongs. Oh, I've been a disgraceful creature!"

"He knew it," said Eugène.

At this moment Goriot opened his eyes; but this was merely the effect of a convulsion. The countess's startled movement of hope was no less terrifying than the dying man's eyes.

"Can he hear me?" she asked. "No," she murmured, sitting down by the side of the bed.

Since Madame de Restaud had indicated her wish to watch over her father, Eugène went downstairs in search of a little food. The boarders were already assembled.

"Well!" said the painter. "It looks as though we're going to have a little corpsorama up there?"

"Charles," said Eugène, "I think you might find some less depressing subject to be funny about."

"So we mustn't laugh any more!" said Charles. "What harm does it do? Bianchon says the old man's no longer conscious."

"In that case," said the museum clerk, "he'll be dying as he lived."

"My father's dead!" shrieked the countess suddenly. At this terrible cry, Sylvie, Eugène, and Bianchon ran upstairs and found Madame de Restaud in a faint. They revived her and led her to the waiting cab. Eugène put her into Thérèse's care, with instructions to take her to Madame de Nucingen's.

"Yes, he's dead," said Bianchon, coming downstairs.

"Now then, gentlemen, dinner's ready," said Madame Vauquer. "The soup's getting cold."

The two students sat down side by side. "What do we do now?" Eugène asked Bianchon.

"Well, I've closed his eyes and laid him out in the usual way. When the local doctor has certified his death—which we have to go and register—we can sew him in his shroud, and bury him. What else do you want done for him?"

"He won't ever sniff at his bread like that again," said one of the boarders, imitating the old man's grimace.

"Good God, gentlemen, can't we leave old Goriot alone?" said the tutor. "We don't want to eat any more of him; we've talked of nothing else for the last hour. One privilege we have in the good city of Paris is that we can

be born, live, and die here, without anybody ever noticing.
We must make the most of the advantages of civilization.
Sixty people have died today. Do you want us to weep
over every death in Paris? If Goriot's dead, all the better
for him! If you're so devoted to him, go and sit with his
body, and leave the rest of us to eat in peace."

"Oh yes," said Madame Vauquer, "it's better for him
he's dead! The poor man seems to have had a lot of
unpleasantness to put up with while he was alive."

This was the only funeral oration over a man who had
for Eugène symbolized fatherhood itself.

The fifteen diners were soon chatting in their usual
way. Eugène and Bianchon ate enough to sustain them
after their long watch. But the sound of forks and
spoons, the laughter and the talk, the varied expressions
on the gluttonous, impassive faces of the boarders, their
lack of concern, froze the young men with horror. They
went out to find a priest to watch and pray that night at
the dead man's side. Such last rites as could be adminis-
tered to the old man had to be accommodated to the little
money they had left. About nine o'clock that evening
the body was placed on a piece of burlap, a candle on
either side, and a priest came and sat beside it in the
bare bedroom. Before going to bed, Eugène asked the
priest for details about the cost of the funeral service,
and wrote to the Baron de Nucingen and the Comte de
Restaud, begging them to send their representatives to
arrange for the burial expenses. He sent Christophe with
these messages, and then went to bed and fell asleep,
utterly exhausted. The next morning, Bianchon and Eugène were obliged to go and give notice of the death
themselves; it was certified about midday.

Two hours passed, and neither of the sons-in-law had
sent money. No one had come on their behalf, and Eugène
had already been obliged to pay the priest's fee. Sylvie had
demanded ten francs for laying out the old man's body
and sewing it into the shroud; and Eugène and Bianchon
calculated that if the dead man's relations were unwilling
to do anything at all, they would scarcely have enough for
the remaining expenses. So the medical student undertook

to place the old man in a pauper's coffin himself. This he ordered to be brought from the hospital, where he had managed to get it at a reduced price.

"Let's show those scoundrels up," he said to Eugène. "Go and buy a five-year lease on a plot of ground at Père-Lachaise, and order a third-class service at the church and the undertaker's. If the sons-in-law and daughters refuse to reimburse you, let's have engraved on the tombstone: 'Here lies Monsieur Goriot, father of the Comtesse de Restaud and the Baronne de Nucingen, interred at the expense of two students.' "

Eugène did not do as his friend suggested until after he had made fruitless calls on the Restauds and the Nucingens. He got no farther than their doors. At both houses the servants had been given strict orders.

"Monsieur and Madame," they said, "are not receiving; their father has died, and they are in deep mourning."

By now Eugène was sufficiently versed in the ways of Paris to know that it was pointless to insist. He felt a strange pang at the heart when he realized that he was not to be allowed to see Delphine.

"Do sell some small ornament," he wrote to her, in the porter's lodge, "and let your father be taken decently to his last resting place."

He sealed the note, and asked the porter to give it to Thérèse to take to her mistress. But the porter handed it to the baron, who threw it in the fire.

After completing his various errands, Eugène went back to the boardinghouse at about three o'clock. Tears came to his eyes as he saw, outside the gate, a coffin, barely covered by a black cloth, standing on two chairs in the empty street. In a silver-plated copper bowl of holy water lay a cheap sprinkler, which no one had so far bothered to use. The gateway had not even been draped in black. It was to be a pauper's funeral: without ceremony, or mourners, or friends, or family.

Bianchon, who was on duty at the hospital, had sent Eugène a note saying what he had arranged with the church. A mass, he said, was beyond their means; they would have to make do with vespers, which cost less.

He had sent Christophe with a message to the undertaker's. As he finished reading Bianchon's scribbled words, Eugène noticed that Madame Vauquer had in her hand the gold-rimmed medallion that contained the locks of the two girls' hair.

"How dare you take that?" he demanded.

"But, good gracious, it's gold! Does it have to be buried with him?" asked Sylvie.

"Certainly it does," said Eugène indignantly. "Let him at least have one small thing to represent his daughters at his funeral."

When the hearse arrived Eugène had the coffin lifted onto it; then he unnailed it and reverently placed on the old man's chest the memento of the days when Delphine and Anastasie had been young, fresh, and innocent, and "didn't have to use their brains," as Goriot had cried out while he lay dying.

Eugène and Christophe, alone except for two hired mourners, accompanied the hearse that took Goriot to the nearby church of Saint-Etienne-du-Mont. The coffin was carried into a little, low, dark chapel: Eugène looked around in vain for Goriot's daughters or their husbands. He was alone with Christophe, who felt in duty bound to perform these last offices for a man who had put him in the way of so many large tips. As they waited for the two priests, the choirboy, and the verger, Eugène wrung Christophe's hand, unable to speak.

"Yes, Monsieur Eugène," said Christophe, "he was a good, honest man. He never raised his voice, he never harmed nobody, and he never did no wrong."

The two priests, the choirboy, and the verger appeared, and provided all that can be expected for seventy francs in an age when the church cannot afford to pray for nothing. They chanted a psalm, and the *Libera,* and the *De Profundis.* The service lasted twenty minutes. There was only one funeral coach. This was for one of the priests and the choirboy, who agreed to let Eugène and Christophe go with them.

"There are no others coming," said the priest, "so we

may as well drive fast, and not waste time. It's half past five already."

Just as the coffin was being placed in the hearse, two carriages drove up. One of them bore the arms of the Comte de Restaud, the other those of the Baron de Nucingen. Both were empty. They followed the procession to the cemetery of Père-Lachaise. At six o'clock Goriot's body was lowered into its grave, around which were grouped his daughters' coachmen who, at the end of the brief prayer that the student had bought for the old man, disappeared with the priest and choirboy.

As soon as the two gravediggers had thrown a few spadefuls of earth on the coffin, they stood up and one of them turned to Eugène and asked for their tip. Eugène fumbled in his pockets but could find nothing, and was obliged to borrow a few coppers from Christophe. The incident, slight as it was, plunged Eugène into a mood of deep sadness. The light was failing, damp twilight fretting the nerves. He looked at the grave, and buried in it the last tears of his youth. They were tears wrung from him by the sacred emotions of a pure heart; they would rise from the earth on which they fell, and reach to heaven. He crossed his arms over his chest, and stared at the clouds. Seeing him thus, Christophe slipped away.

Eugène, now alone, walked a few steps to the topmost part of the graveyard. He saw Paris, spread windingly along the two banks of the Seine. Lights were beginning to twinkle. His gaze fixed itself almost avidly on the space between the column in the Place Vendôme and the cupola of Les Invalides. There lived the world into which he had wished to penetrate. He fastened on the murmurous hive a look that seemed already to be sucking the honey from it, and uttered these words:

"Now I'm ready for you!"

And, as the first move in the challenge he was flinging at society, he went back to dine with Madame de Nucingen.

AFTERWORD

With good reason, Balzac is usually not taken seriously as a writer before the year 1829 when, at the age of thirty, he published a story of love and adventure called *Le Dernier Chouan*. Any full account of his life before that date would have to recall his years of undistinguished schooling in Touraine, his arrival in Paris to study law, his years as a notary's clerk, his numerous love affairs, and his immense commercial failures as printer, publisher, and type manufacturer. By 1829, he also had ten years of apprenticeship as a novelist behind him. Of these early days he is reported to have said: "I wrote seven novels simply for practice: one to learn about dialogue, one to learn about description, one for grouping characters, one for composition."

It was quite characteristic of Balzac to think that one and one and one and one make seven. For though in the manipulating of large numbers of francs he has no equal among novelists, he was often poor at small numbers of anything else; and in this translation of *Le Père Goriot* I have taken the liberty of correcting two or three kindred slips. More striking, however, is the disarming practicality of the rest of the statement. From adolescence onward Balzac was determined to be a writer, and he had no intention of being an inefficient, unprolific, obscure, overaesthetic one. He also intended to make money by his pen: partly in order to pay off his very large debts, since only by occasionally paying these could he be allowed to incur yet larger ones; and his whole

287

life shows clearly that the state of being in debt had some profound psychological value for him.

A large quantity of the prehistoric Balzac has been disinterred and republished and studied, and scholars intrepid enough to read it have not unnaturally been prone to reward themselves by discovering, in these tales of pirates and adventurers and magicians, embryonic versions of all the motives and preoccupations of the later Balzac. And doubtless they are right. It is not an assertion one would wish seriously to test for oneself. What is of interest in this early work, sometimes written in collaboration with other hack writers, is that Balzac would sign it only with pseudonyms. But in 1829, with *Le Dernier Chouan,* he clearly thought he had made a new and important beginning as a serious writer, and he graced the book with his name, Honoré Balzac. The "de" was a later emendation, as simple, bold, and unjustifiable as any he ever made.

He had twenty-one more years before him. In the five that elapsed before he began *Le Père Goriot,* he had produced as much as many novelists produce in a long lifetime. He had an extraordinarily varied experience to call on, and he deliberately and painstakingly extended this experience by systematic observation, and by concentrated pursuit of anything that seemed to promise significant eccentricity. He had, I think, no particular views about what a novel ought to be; but he had very decided ones about what his own were meant to be like. They were to represent, without flinching, "human feelings, social crises, the whole pell-mell of civilization." He sometimes claimed that he had "invented" nothing, but such statements mean very little. In the accepted sense of the word, invention was the breath of life to him. To any listener who happened to be at hand he was able to narrate long and detailed stories, unfalteringly and with great powers of persuasion. At the end he would say, in response to the obvious, surprised question: "No, of course it didn't; it's pure Balzac."

His work habits are well known: the white priest's

robe, pint after pint of strong black coffee, long sessions of anything up to eighteen hours. He would write the complete first draft of a story, and have it set up in proof sheets with wide margins. While waiting for these he would begin another story. When the first proofs arrived, he would proceed to double the length of the original by marginal additions, and then, as further proofs came in, he would begin to "revise." He was not one of those writers to whom revision means much in the way of cutting and pruning: to Balzac it meant further expansion. An incentive to expand was provided by the fact that he was paid according to length; a further incentive, perhaps, was that the great expense of repeated printers' proofs would keep him safely in debt. It is small wonder that he often seems to be saying the same thing one and a half times, or even twice; or that emendation has occasionally clouded the meaning of passages originally fairly simple. And for Balzac, mere publication was but a stage in a book's life: he emended from edition to edition, rarely improving matters, sometimes making them worse.

Le Père Goriot is the climax of the first period of Balzac's serious work, and a turning point in his own view of his destiny as a writer. There is in particular one scene in it which, quite apart from its own virtues, has for the student of Balzac a uniquely thrilling import. For the manuscript of the book survives, and from it we can see that at the beginning of the scene Balzac will have had only a vague idea of what his future *Comédie Humaine* was to be, to him and to his readers; and that halfway through the scene, the idea, for him, becomes suddenly precise. We detect this precise moment from a single one of those emendations I have been talking about. The scene itself is Eugène's afternoon call on his cousin, Madame de Beauséant. The Duchesse de Langeais has also called. In Balzac's manuscript, up to this point—that is to say, in Balzac's mind also—the young, not very interesting hero has always been called Eugène de Massiac. Suddenly, halfway through writing this name, Balzac crosses it out and substitutes another one. It has since become a household word: *Rastignac*. And that is the true beginning of *The Human Comedy*.

But let us try to be exact about it. Between *Le Dernier Chouan* of 1829 and *Le Père Goriot*, begun in September 1834, Balzac had written a score of novels and stories. He had at some time begun to see that they might be a good deal more than an ordinary procession of novels and tales, and that numbers of them seemed to group themselves together: scenes of country life, scenes of life in Paris, philosophical tales. . . . At a later point he realized that all of his work, future and past, must cohere into a large planetary system. He was very pleased with himself over this discovery, and is recorded as saying to his sister Laure: "Congratulate me: I'm on the way to becoming a genius." (The remark is attributed to 1833. Had the idea that he was a genius never occurred to him before?) But he had not, it appears, seen how the unification of his work was to be brought about. Nor does it appear that he had seen it by the time he began *Goriot*, which was originally intended to be a short story on the single, simple theme of an old man ruined by two selfish daughters.

Proust has written with understanding of the moment of intoxication Balzac must have felt "when, casting over his works the eye at once of a stranger and of a father . . . he suddenly decided, as he shed a retrospective illumination upon them, that they would be better brought together in a cycle in which *the same characters would reappear*. . . ." (The italics are not, of course, Proust's.) It is in *Goriot* that this happens for the first time, suddenly, thoroughly, and enthusiastically. I have suggested that we must try to be exact about the matter, because rather than one sudden moment, as Proust suggests, I feel that there was a brief series of them, crowned by the moment when Massiac's name was changed to Rastignac. For, after all, the idea of linking various works together by having certain characters common to more than one book is hinted at by the introduction of Madame de Beauséant and the Duchesse de

Langeais. They had already been heroines of previous tales by Balzac; and now he was presenting them as they had been at a time *before* the episodes in those tales. Then, suddenly indeed, the infection spreads to the man in the room with them: the fairly nondescript, innocent Massiac becomes Rastignac . . . the Rastignac of whom Balzac has already given us cynical "later" glimpses in *La Peau de Chagrin*. There, Rastignac had been shown as an experienced and ruthless man of the world, giving sophisticated ill counsel to a young man. And now, "suddenly," in *Le Père Goriot*, Rastignac reappears, a young man himself, himself receiving sophisticated ill counsel from an older person. Balzac had gone only a little way by reviving Madame de Beauséant and Madame de Langeais; for after all, their fate had already been sealed and most of their possible interest exhausted in the earlier stories in which they had appeared. But Rastignac has not been exhausted by his later appearance as a minor figure in *La Peau de Chagrin*: Balzac divines that here is a character of infinite possibility: he will be able to keep him going forever, if necessary. And he does. Altogether, Rastignac appears as a major or minor character in twenty-two novels in the Balzac canon. And, as we know, Balzac died before his task was near completion.

Proust stresses that the success of Balzac's scheme, the "unity" of it, depends on the fact that it was "ulterior": by which Proust means that the scheme is a judgment and an interpretation of work already done, as well as a plan for what is to come. "Otherwise," says Proust, "it would have crumbled into dust like all the other systematizations of mediocre writers who with the elaborate assistance of titles and subtitles give themselves the appearance of having pursued a single and transcendent design." One half-wonders what writers Proust was referring to. Certainly some of them were not yet writing.

It is sometimes possible to feel that *La Comédie Humaine*, with its scheme of "reappearing characters," is not an unmixed blessing if only because so many of the characters reappear without much further reason than to hook each book on to as many others as possible. Large-scale characters like Rastignac and Vautrin are perennially intriguing, and they develop from book to book. But some secondary characters (Delphine, in *Père Goriot*, is an example) do not grow by their reappearance; or not very much. There are times when Balzac becomes a bit like a kindly and duty-ridden hostess who, looking through her address book and wondering whom she has neglected lately, spots the names of Madame A and the Comte de B, and decides that it is about time they were invited in for another drink. This, very literally, is what sometimes happens in the *Comédie Humaine*. When it does, we are conscious of being encouraged in a hobby rather than asked to participate in an artistic experience. And there are many cases where Balzac rechristens characters in earlier, pre-*Goriot* novels, in order to bring them into the address book.

But by and large, the great scheme works. And *Goriot*, which was Balzac's real entree into *La Comédie Humaine*, is the novel that may best serve the reader as his entrée, too. It may be expected that the book suffers a little as "art" from the fact that three novels are crowded into one—or rather that one novel (the story of Goriot) has been expanded to accommodate the beginnings of two other sets of novels (Rastignac's climb to success, and the Vautrin cycle). And Balzac certainly sets out to pique us into curiosity about what will happen to Rastignac and Vautrin.

How much of the book must have been the original *Goriot* story that Balzac himself had expected to finish in a week? (The book finally took four months, a long time for Balzac to spend on a not especially long novel.) Certainly the Vautrin intrigue, and most of Rastignac's affair with Delphine, can be detached from the rest: or so at first it seems, until one attempts to do this; then one discovers with what immense craft Vautrin has been made to penetrate the whole story, and how much has been made of the recurrent to and fro among the squalid Maison Vauquer and the flashy homes of Goriot's daughters and the elegant serenity of the home of the Beauséants.

Le Père Goriot can rightly be regarded as one of the greatest of Balzac's novels. The intense, potent theme at its center, Goriot's obsessed fatherhood (this is the "point" of its French title, not reproducible in English) will strike at the heart of most readers as a more frequent occurrence than we like to think; and the same may be said of Goriot's spoiled daughters. From this painful center the book spreads widely out into the "pell-mell of civilization." Its characters, of both background and foreground, are vividly distinct and memorable. It is part of Balzac's personal vision that his characters are shown with one layer of normal defense and disguise removed: common obsessions that in normal life would be found to be, as it were, subcutaneous, are brought by Balzac to the top and regarded as the surface of life. It is his form of dramatic poetry, and if a reader cannot accept this, then Balzac is not for him.

The three main characters in the book, Goriot, Rastignac, and Vautrin, whatever "objective" models Balzac may have used for them, all have their remoter starting points in some potential or actual element in Balzac himself; and this—perhaps unconsciously—contributes to holding the three disparate themes together. Goriot is the type of father in whom paternal passion approaches psychosis; and at the time of writing Balzac himself had recently become an enthralled father. Rastignac is the eternally ambitious young man from the provinces who stops at very little to achieve his ambitions, and yet is meant to retain a good deal of our sympathy: there are plain elements of his creator here. Vautrin, the Napoleon of crime, the rebel denigrator of society, is also interesting as the first homosexual in fiction, the man who finds it necessary to have young men to devote himself to and to dominate—handsome idealizations of his own missed youth. The resemblance to Balzac here has not escaped attention. He was sometimes even addressed as "Cher Vautrin" in his lifetime. Naturally there is much more than his own selves, real or suppressed, in these characters, but what there is of him probably gives them that extra quantity of him that makes them great and permanent creations. One could elaborate such observations indefinitely without adding much to what has been said elsewhere. The book is in no sense a difficult one, and can stand alone without interpretation or commentary.

Though, as I have hinted, Balzac's revisions often malformed his text, I have felt it best to translate his own final version. Almost all French editions of the book follow the practice (much disliked by Balzac) of suppressing all chapter divisions and presenting paragraph after paragraph without break. This was originally done in the interest of saving space. The recently published Garnier edition (1960) aerates the text a little by dividing it into four titled sections. But Balzac wanted six, and provided them with titles. I have followed his own intention: I think this is the first version of *Goriot* to do so, and I think that the excellent final shape of the book is thereby emphasized. I have further divided some sections into chapters where it seemed logical and helpful to do so.

—HENRY REED

SELECTED BIBLIOGRAPHY

Works by Honoré de Balzac

Physiologie du Mariage (Physiology of Marriage)
Le Dernier Chouan, 1829
"Une Passion dans le Désert" (A Passion in the Desert), 1830
"L'Élixir de longue vie" (The Elixir of Life), 1830
La Peau de Chagrin (The Fatal Skin), 1831
Les Proscrits (The Exiles), 1831
"Le Chef-d'oeuvre inconnu" (The Unknown Masterpiece), 1831
Le Colonel Chabert, 1832
Louis Lambert, 1832–35
Le Médecin de Campagne (The Country Doctor), 1833
Ferragus, 1833
L'Illustre Gaudissart (The Illustrious Gaudissart), 1833
Eugénie Grandet, 1833
La Recherche de l'Absolu (The Quest of the Absolute), 1834
Séraphita, 1835
Le Lys dans la Vallée (The Lily of the Valley), 1835
Le Contrat de Mariage (A Marriage Settlement), 1835
"L'Enfant Maudit" (A Father's Curse), 1836
La Vieille Fille (The Old Maid), 1837
L'Histoire de la Grandeur et de la Décadence de César Birotteau (The Rise and Fall of César Birotteau), 1837
Gambara, 1837

Les Illusions Perdues (Lost Illusions), 1837–43
La Maison Nucingen (The Firm of Nucingen), 1838
Une Fille d'Eve (A Daughter of Eve), 1839
Le Cabinet des Antiques (The Gallery of Antiquities), 1839
Le Curé de Village (The Village Rector), 1839
Beatrix, 1839–44
Ursule Mirouet, 1841
Une Ténébreuse Affaire (The Gondreville Mystery), 1841
Un Début dans la Vie (A Start in Life), 1842
La Muse du Département (The Muse of the Department), 1843
Honorine, 1843
Modeste Mignon, 1844
Les Paysans (The Peasantry), 1845
Les Comédiens sans le Savoir (The Unconscious Humorists), 1846
La Cousine Bette (Cousin Bette), 1846
Le Cousin Pons (Cousin Pons), 1847
La Dernière Incarnation de Vautrin (Vautrin's Last Avatar), 1847

Selected Biography and Criticism

Bell, David F. *Real Time: Accelerating Real Time from Balzac to Zola.* Champaign: University of Illinois Press, 2004.

Bellos, David. *Honoré de Balzac: Old Goriot.* Cambridge: Cambridge University Press, 1987.

Brooks, Peter. *The Melodramatic Imagination.* New Haven, CT: Yale University Press, 1976.

Butler, Ronnie. *Balzac and the French Revolution.* Lanham, MD: Rowman & Littlefield, 1983.

Dargan, Joan. *Balzac and the Drama of Perspective.* Lexington, KY: French Forum Publishers, 1985.

Farrant, Tim. *Balzac's Shorter Fictions: Genesis and Genre*. New York: Oxford University Press, 2002.

James, Henry. *The Question of Our Speech; The Lessons of Balzac: Two Lectures*. Boston and New York: Houghton Mifflin, 1905.

Kanes, Martin. *Critical Essays on Honoré de Balzac*. London: Macmillan, 1990.

——. *Balzac's Comedy of Words*. Princeton, NJ: Princeton University Press, 1975.

Levin, Harry. "Balzac." In his *The Gates of Horn: A Study of Five French Realists*. New York: Oxford University Press, 1963.

Lucey, Michael. *Misfit of the Family: Balzac and Social Forms of Sexuality*. Durham, NC: Duke University Press, 2003.

Maurois, Andre. *Prometheus: The Life of Balzac*. Trans. Norman Denny. New York: Harper & Row, 1965.

Pritchett, V. S. *Balzac*. New York: Knopf, 1973.

Robb, Graham. *Balzac: A Biography*. New York: W. W. Norton, 1995.

Stowe, William W. *Balzac, James, and the Realistic Novel*. Princeton, NJ: Princeton University Press, 1986.

Taine, Hyppolite. *Balzac: A Critical Study*. Trans. Lorenzo O'Rourke. New York: Haskell House, 1973.

Tilby, Michael, ed. *Balzac*. London: Addison-Wesley, 1995.

Zweig, Stefan. *Balzac*. Trans. William and Dorothy Rose. New York: Viking, 1946.

AVAILABLE FROM

ALEXANDRE DUMAS, PÈRE

THE COUNT OF MONTE CRISTO
This quintessential tale of revenge has thrilled readers since its
first publication. Filled with adventure, romance, and suspense,
Dumas' writing captures the imagination and ennobles the
human spirit.

THE THREE MUSKETEERS
D'Artagnan, a young worthy, wishes to join the roguish band of
adventurers known as the King's Musketeers. This is the tale of
their struggle to restore the authority of the Monarchy and
wrestle power from the corrupt and evil Cardinal Richelieu in
17th-century France.

THE MAN IN THE IRON MASK
The final chapter in the adventures of the Three Musketeers.
Bribing his way into the Bastille, Aramis discovers a secret that
could topple the King of France. Thus forced into conflict with
his fellow Musketeers, he may have no choice but to betray his
vow of "All for one, and one for all!"

READ THE TOP 20
SIGNET CLASSICS

1984 BY GEORGE ORWELL

ANIMAL FARM BY GEORGE ORWELL

LES MISÉRABLES BY VICTOR HUGO

ROMEO AND JULIET BY WILLIAM SHAKESPEARE

THE INFERNO BY DANTE

FRANKENSTEIN BY MARY SHELLEY

BEOWULF TRANSLATED BY BURTON RAFFEL

THE STORY OF MY LIFE BY HELEN KELLER

NARRATIVE OF THE LIFE OF FREDERICK DOUGLASS
   BY FREDERICK DOUGLASS

HAMLET BY WILLIAM SHAKESPEARE

TESS OF THE D'URBERVILLES BY THOMAS HARDY

THE FEDERALIST PAPERS BY ALEXANDER HAMILTON

THE ODYSSEY BY HOMER

OLIVER TWIST BY CHARLES DICKENS

NECTAR IN A SIEVE BY KAMALA MARKANDAYA

WHY WE CAN'T WAIT BY DR. MARTIN LUTHER KING, JR.

MACBETH BY WILLIAM SHAKESPEARE

ONE DAY IN THE LIFE OF IVAN DENISOVICH
   BY ALEXANDER SOLZHENITSYN

A TALE OF TWO CITIES BY CHARLES DICKENS

THE HOUND OF THE BASKERVILLES
   BY SIR ARTHUR CONAN DOYLE

"Do you know what it took to get you to come to the Caribbean?" he said. *"Worse than negotiating a store lease agreement. It was quite a challenge, I must say."*

Her smile widened. "Yet another one that you've met and conquered."

"Was that a compliment? Or a dig? Somewhat hard to tell."

She shrugged, watched as a gaggle of dancing teenagers pranced by them. "Merely a statement."

He took another sip of the coconut drink. "Pity. I was hoping for the former."

"Fishing for compliments, are you?"

"My ego is a fragile thing." He held his hand to his chest with mock melodrama.

That laugh again; he could easily get used to it. "Something tells me you come by compliments quite often," she said.

He took a moment to respond, deciding to throw caution to the wind. "Some compliments mean more than others, given the source."